The Gamov Incident

Sam Lutton

Copyright © 2015 by Samuel J. Lutton

ISBN: 978-1-59113-921-8

All rights reserved. No part of this publication may be reproduced, stored in a retrieval system, or transmitted in any form or by any means, electronic, mechanical, recording or otherwise, without the prior written permission of the author.

Published by BookLocker.com, Inc., Bradenton, Florida, U.S.A.

Printed on acid-free paper.

Although based on an actual shootdown incident, this book is a work of fiction. The characters and events are either fictitious or are used fictitiously. Any similarity to real persons, living or dead, is coincidental and not intended by the author.

Booklocker.com, Inc.
2015

First Edition (Revised)

For Nada, the love of my life; and for our children and grandchildren;

    Family is *everything*

And for Colonel Richard Arlen Wagner, USAF, 1934-1978;

    Requiescat in Pace

And for the United States Air Force;

> *I have eaten your bread and salt,*
> *I have drunk your water and wine*
> *The deaths ye died I have watched beside,*
> *And the lives that ye led were mine.*

                            - Rudyard Kipling

ACKNOWLEDGEMENT

On July 29, 1953, Soviet MiG fighter planes shot down a U.S. Air Force RB-50 electronic reconnaissance aircraft over the Sea of Japan. Of the seventeen aircrew members, one survived, one died in the crash, and two bodies washed ashore. The fate of the remaining thirteen airmen has not been resolved. On January 26, May 25, and October 9, 1954 the American Ambassador at Moscow delivered protests to the Soviet Foreign Ministry regarding the incident. The note in Chapter 12, modified to accommodate the fictional narrative, closely follows the wording and tone of the October communication.

There are numerous reports of American servicemen held captive in the Soviet Far East. One source is *The Gulag Study*, Joint Commission Support Directorate, U.S.-Russia Joint Commission on POW/MIAs, dated 20 November 2001. Anne Applebaum's *Gulag: A History* also provided valuable background information and terminology.

Finally, Paul Lashmar's *Spy Flights of the Cold War* along with Curtis Peebles's *Shadow Flights* refreshed and augmented the author's recollections of a time long past.

It was man who ended the Cold War… It wasn't weaponry, or technology, or armies or campaigns. It was just man. Not even Western man either, as it happened, but our sworn enemy in the East, who went into the streets, faced the bullets and the batons and said: we've had enough.

                        -John le Carre

One generation plants the trees, another gets the shade.

                        -Russian Proverb

Prologue

Grand Ballroom
Washington Hilton Hotel
November 1969

If one could ignore the pretension and phony-baloney camaraderie, the glittering ambiance of the National Debutante Cotillion and Thanksgiving Ball might have pleased Anne Seymour. Unfortunately, what troubled her was less obvious. In Anne's mind, the annual coming out event was not only a snobby rite of passage for privileged young women such as herself, but also an upscale version of *Let's Make a Deal*.

The elegant charade began when a select group of young men escorted Washington's most socially desirable females to a reserved table occupied by the debutante's family. Parents and relatives would closely observe those brief ceremonial couplings, their watchful eyes alert to every detail. While fondly expressed interest was natural and expected, Anne had little doubt regarding their unspoken but clearly understood motives.

The Thanksgiving Ball was a seminal occasion, an exclusive gathering where liberals and conservatives—the former reeking of Chanel and Canoe, the latter of Arpege and Old Spice—temporarily suppressed irreconcilable political and social opinions to pursue a common interest. As the evening progressed, discerning parents would discretely test the air, sniffing out potential mates for their respective progeny, a practice guaranteed to produce another generation of wealthy, marginally literate dullards.

Anne and her peers formed a single rank, one debutante standing behind the other, as did their male escorts opposite, the first person in each row facing the other, both awaiting their turn for formal introduction. Like her colleagues, Anne wore a specially designed wedding-white satiny gown and matching long gloves. A pink nosegay added a colorful touch to her ensemble—a pastel hue matched by at least a dozen other debs. Bowing to her mother's wishes, she had also learned the proper way to curtsey: left knee tucked behind the right, torso descending vertically, head erect, eyes forward, hands at her side—a courtly maneuver dutifully mastered by every young lady making her social debut.

Yet, despite reluctant conformity to social custom, Anne possessed an unshakable awareness of her individuality; a conviction that her life was destined for something other than bland existence among privileged peers. Understandably, this particular event challenged Anne's perception of her own self-worth. Waiting her turn at introduction, she felt less like a uniquely gifted young lady and more akin to a mass-produced game show prize destined for some giddy contestant.

She concealed those uncharitable thoughts behind a pleasantly neutral facial expression, a demeanor perfected during her first two years at Bryn Mawr, a female-only liberal arts college huddled in woodsy suburbs eleven miles west of Philadelphia. With focused effort, Anne re-committed herself to making the best of what promised to be an exquisitely dreadful evening. As she edged closer to the brightly illuminated center of attention, Anne surveyed the males opposite and began counting noses.

Anne was now sixth in a line of nineteen and twenty-year-old debutantes facing a matching array of young men. Following introductions to each other, deb and escort would then walk arm in arm to her assigned table, gliding across the huge ballroom floor in full view of two thousand guests.

Although loath to admit it, her immediate concern—anxiety, really—was pairing up with an escort who lacked sufficient height, someone like that conceited runt Skip Worthen. For Anne, who stood five feet eight inches tall without spike heels, that grim possibility was more likely than not.

As she inched forward, a ghastly scene took shape in her mind. There she was, towering over Skippy the Penguin as they crossed the endlessly wide ballroom floor: she, striding and gracefully tall—he, clinging to her arm, stubby legs churning like a distressed puppy in tow. The image, captured forever on film and in the society pages of the *Washington Post*, made her stomach flutter. She could imagine nothing more humiliating.

Luckily, the sixth escort in the facing line did indeed meet her height requirement, and then some. He was also a commissioned Army officer—not one of the hundred-plus third and fourth year cadets from one of the military academies, but instead a man who looked several years older. He was obviously part of the specially invited contingent of socially unattached junior officers assigned to posts in and around the Capitol.

As was customary for such occasions, this officer wore mess dress complete with miniature versions of the medals he had earned: colorful attire that stood out from the tuxedoed sameness of the more numerous civilian males. Unlike Anne however, the gentleman in question was not searching for the opposite sex corresponding to his place in line. Rather, his studious gaze explored the massive ballroom, pausing now and then on a particular spot as though evaluating a weak point that might provide opportunity for a quick escape.

When they drew closer, their eyes finally met. He nodded slightly and offered a token smile, the stoic expression of one who recognizes but cannot avoid a distressing obligation. Anne also detected something else—a subtle undertone—and the surprising discovery left her a trifle miffed. Despite her cynicism regarding this ostentatious event, she had nevertheless taken great care with her appearance, tastefully enhancing her natural good looks. However, his escort duties notwithstanding, this rather distinguished looking young officer showed absolutely no interest in her. None whatsoever.

A much older gentleman, the proctor or head chaperone—she couldn't remember his name or exact title—glanced at a list, leaned closer to the microphone, and solemnly voiced the ritual phrases.

"Miss Anne Teasdale Seymour, allow me to introduce Captain William Cody Ballantine. Captain Ballantine, Miss Seymour."

"A pleasure Miss Seymour," the officer said, bowing slightly as she curtseyed.

"Oh, my. Can this really be happenstance?" she asked, taking his offered arm.

His eyes narrowed slightly. "Please don't say it."

"Say what?" she replied, affecting cool innocence as they began the long, easy stroll to her table.

"Whatever 'Buffalo Bill Cody' remark you were about to share. I've already heard most of them."

"A fascinating notion, Captain Ballantine, but also presumptuous. My thought had nothing to do with Western folklore."

In fact, a snide comment about his given names was precisely what she had in mind. It would serve him right for being so conspicuously bored.

"Is that so? Then I stand corrected. What *were* you going to say, Miss Seymour?"

Still piqued over his polite inattention, she uttered the first words that popped into her mind. "I was going to ask where you purchased all those pretty little medals dangling from your lapel."

His lips formed a tight smile, but his eyes lacked humor. "They're standard issue, Miss Seymour," he replied calmly. "They come packaged as a set. Almost every Post Exchange has them nowadays."

As they approached her table in silence, ambling across the parquet floor amidst flashes from myriad cameras, Anne suddenly felt ashamed of herself. At Bryn Mawr, she had participated in several anti-war demonstrations, spirited gatherings on Merion Green, her presence there not evidence of support, but more from curiosity and a desire to participate in a popular campus event. Eventually, perhaps sensing the artificial enthusiasm displayed by many in attendance, she had lost interest in those well-choreographed productions.

Unlike many of her contemporaries, Anne did not share their neurotic eagerness to embrace the latest popular cause, a wearisome malady common among affluent students. If truly pressed about American involvement in Southeast Asia, she could admit to nothing more than uncomfortable ambivalence, hardly a defensible position in a nation stridently polarized by the Vietnam War. Her despicable conduct toward this decorated soldier had little to do with her politics or his profession, but rather from a bruised ego. After working so diligently to cultivate an aloof disregard for this gala extravaganza, she resented Captain Ballantine for being equally bored and therefore oblivious to how nice she looked. Vanity, it seemed, had once again triumphed over good manners.

Just before reaching her table, Anne stopped abruptly, surprising them both.

"Captain Ballantine, please accept my apology. I know better, and so do you. Why did you let my witless remark go unchallenged?"

He hesitated for a moment, his slate blue eyes evaluating her, much as they had measured the ballroom's dimensions. It was not an uncomfortable feeling. Finally, he shrugged. "*Ut Romae, mimic Romanorum.*"

The familiar phrase, uttered in Latin, was not what Anne expected. She replied, "But we are not in Rome, and therefore should not necessarily do as the Romans."

"I don't see much difference, Miss Seymour. Do you?"

"In other words, those who disparage soldiers rather than the politicians who sent them off to fight an unpopular war are incurably ignorant so why bother. Is that what you believe?"

He maneuvered her forward again, gently. "You should not concern yourself with the beliefs of others, Miss Seymour. Instead, it might be better to focus on what *you* believe, and then live your life accordingly."

"Ah, words of wisdom from a Warrior/Sage. I am truly flattered."

"And I am truly sorry our little journey has come to an end."

He smiled and held a chair while she smoothed the long dress with a sweep of her hand and then sat. Anne was about to thank him but he was already moving away, striding toward the general direction of the bar where escorts, now free of their temporary charges, gathered in tight clusters, tuxedos and military dress uniforms crisply segregated as though by mutual consent. As he blended into the crowd, she was reasonably certain Captain Ballantine would not ask her to dance.

"That was a very impressive entrance, my dear," said her mother, *sotto voce*. "You were fortunate to match up with a tall, nice looking military man, especially one with so many decorations. What were you two talking about?"

Anne turned and faced her mother. "Oh…nothing, really."

"No matter. I can hardly wait to see the photographs."

"You lucked out again," her fifteen-year-old sister added with a smirk. "I was hoping you'd get Skippy the Penguin. That would have made an even better picture."

Anne smiled as her mother made shushing noises.

Yes, she was indeed lucky—and bright enough to appreciate such a capricious gift.

Anne, as did her compulsive do-gooder friends and acquaintances, secretly harbored a measure of guilt regarding her good fortune. Obviously, neither she nor they had yet *earned* the wealth and social status they enjoyed, a niggling reality that no doubt sharpened their tedious addiction to high-toned causes. Yet, despite her inclusion among them, Anne did not share their passion for such matters. Instead, she had somehow acquired a deeply personal set of moral and social values, a sense of right and wrong only she understood. Her apology to Captain Ballantine was a reflection of one such principle, and her need to repudiate a thoughtless discourtesy was a powerful impulse she could not ignore.

She expelled a long, wistful breath of air.

Being born into society's upper echelon offered far more advantages than did life at the opposite end, a fact she readily acknowledged. Privilege however, sometimes came with a price. This evening's levy was easy to calculate: She and the potentially interesting Captain Ballantine were clearly travelling separate paths.

Despite her deplorable behavior toward him, Anne had felt an odd connection, a sense of companionship she wished to experience again.

However, nothing more would happen between them. After tonight, they would never meet again—would not have an opportunity to discover what might have been. The reality of unexplored possibilities replaced some of what she felt—resigned acceptance, mostly—with a touch of melancholy. The road not taken would always be a tantalizing mystery, an unseen vista forever denied.

On the other hand, having no further contact with Captain Ballantine was probably best, what with the war and all. Soldiers, especially those decorated for service in Vietnam, were not very popular these days.

Was that being lucky, too?

Anne was not so sure about that.

Chapter 1

Vladivostok
Russian Federation
September 1992

Cody Ballantine pushed open the heavy glass door to Number 32 Pushkinskaya—a featureless redbrick building perched on the bayside slope of a long-neglected city—and strode into America's newest consulate. The temperature inside the lobby was slightly warmer than the frost-tinged air outside—an early morning chill foreshadowing the relentless approach of Siberian winter.

The Duty Officer, a fair-complexioned, thick-shouldered man in his early thirties, stood behind a waist-high reception desk anchored a few yards beyond the marble-tiled main entrance. "Good Morning, Boss," the DO said as Cody approached.

"Hello, Paul. Anything interesting happen overnight?"

The DO's expression soured, as though he had bitten into a wormy peach. "You mean here, or someplace pleasant and exciting?"

"Are you suggesting Vladivostok is drab and boring?"

Studied innocence replaced the dour expression. "Drab? Boring? Of course not. It has everything a brooding recluse could possibly want. Howard Hughes would love it."

"Howard Hughes is dead," Cody observed.

"Well, there you go."

Cody stepped into an elevator and pressed the numeral '3'.

Although he would never express it outwardly, Cody shared the DO's gloomy point of view. Except for the *Vory v Zakone*—organized criminals who operated a thriving black market—the largest city in the Russian Far East would never challenge Europe's grander capitals for intrigue, architectural elegance, or political duplicity. Among Cody's associates in the CIA, Vladivostok and the phrase 'small potatoes' were synonymous. His recent banishment to a desolate outpost in a far corner of Russia offered one last chance to revive his moribund career—or perhaps end it. As far as Cody was concerned it did not matter which of the two occurred, a bothersome fact he would likewise keep to himself.

The elevator doors slid open and Cody turned left down a wide corridor. He paused in a small reception area expecting to find his assistant, but Phyllis was nowhere in sight. Coffee dribbled from the machine into a Pyrex pot, filling the air with freshly roasted Arabica.

He unlocked his office door and stepped inside. The telephone Message Waiting light blinked impatiently, filling the dimly lighted room with an intermittent ruby glow. He flicked on the overhead lights and hung his overcoat in the closet. Then he visited the coffee maker, filled a porcelain mug and added a dribble of fresh cream.

Armed with morning brew, Cody settled himself behind the desk and took a careful sip. It was, as usual, perfect. He set the mug on a coaster, picked up the telephone, keyed his access code, and then listened to the message.

"Hi, Cody. Al Jensen here. It seems the Company has finally recognized true talent and posted your sorry ass to Siberia, metaphorically and actually." The Moscow station chief's good-natured chuckle echoed from the handset. *"All kidding aside, most of us have screwed up at one time or another. It's the unfortunate consequence of what we do for a living. You are not the first guy to stub his toe in the Balkans and you won't be the last. There's something spooky about that part of Europe—pun intended. Anyway, give me a call if you want to chat about the New Russia, or anything*

else for that matter. You might also want to think about King Solomon's advice. Meanwhile, keep your dobber up."

The recorder stopped and the red light blinked out. He replaced the handset and sipped more coffee.

Cody's precipitous fall from grace four months ago still provided grist for the Agency's gossip mill. Most field agents, including Al Jensen, truly sympathized. However, as one might expect, the majority of Langley's stay-at-home careerists quietly welcomed the potential elimination of a professional rival. Their bogus commiserations reinforced Cody's belief that deception and hypocrisy were easily acquired human traits, especially in an organization that valued expertise in those unsavory but often-necessary practices.

He felt himself slipping into a cynical mood, a mental state that occurred with greater frequency these days, a sure sign he might be losing his edge. Cody found this troubling. Wallowing in self-pity was a pathetic exercise, a loathsome practice he abhorred. Winning and losing were normal outcomes of his profession. As the saying went: *Some days you eat the bear; some days the bear eats you.* In Bosnia, the proverbial bear had feasted on Fricassee of Cody Ballantine.

Al Jensen's reference to the Aramaic inscription etched inside King Solomon's golden ring was a reminder that victories and defeats were transitory—and often illusory. The biblical king's words, advice first brought to Cody's attention by the same Al Jensen, initially a mentor and now one of his few friends, emerged from memory: *This too shall pass.*

Well, maybe it would, and maybe it wouldn't.

He pushed those thoughts aside, checked his Breitling chronograph and subtracted seven time zones. It was two A.M. in the Russian capitol, a six thousand mile westward journey along the Trans-Siberian Railway. He made a mental note to return Al's call later in the day.

The intercom buzzed and he lifted the handset. "Good morning, Phyllis."

"How did you sneak by me, Cody? I left my desk for ten seconds."

"Oh, you know. Stealth, guile and some other stuff I'm not supposed to talk about."

"Yeah, right. Why do I bother to ask? Anyway, Paul is on line one."

"Thanks, Phyllis."

Had the Duty Officer remembered something? Cody pushed a lighted plastic button. "What's up, Paul?"

"Sorry to interrupt your morning coffee, but there's a gentleman in our lobby, a stranger who's not on the Authorized Visitor list. He insists on speaking with the Consul General."

"And you called *me* because…" Cody let the question dangle.

"Mr. Zane said you should handle this."

Unlike the banished CIA officer, Consul General Whittier Hancock Zane considered his Vladivostok posting the crowning achievement to a long career in America's Foreign Service. One's perspective, Cody mused, was indeed a matter of one's personal situation.

"I see," he replied. "And why did Mr. Zane say that?"

"First, he was on his way to a meeting. Second, he said the situation appeared to be something you ought to handle."

"Really? What exactly does our gentleman visitor want?"

"He won't say. Not to me, that is."

Cody felt his internal warning light switching to a higher intensity, a psychologically wary status a notch or two below maximum. "Who is this guy, Paul? Does he have proper identification?"

"Yes, he does. His papers ID him as Andrei Danilov, a Russian citizen."

Cody sensed hesitation—a reluctance to volunteer extraneous information—and wondered whether the DO was another hapless exile, perhaps condemned to vile durance for excessive chattiness.

"What else did he tell you, Paul?"

"The gentleman claims to be an American citizen, one who arrived here under unusual circumstances."

Cody's grip tightened on the handset, then relaxed. "And what do you suppose that means?"

"I have no idea. Mr. Danilov is unwilling to convey anything additional at this time."

Cody did not respond immediately. Memories of his recent Balkan assignment and the terrible calamity arising from bad judgment and misplaced loyalty came to mind. He toyed with the coffee mug while he considered possibilities.

An American citizen with Russian ID? ...in Siberia? How could that be?

Because Vladivostok served as home to the Russian Navy's Pacific Fleet, the Soviets had closed the aging port city to all non-residents and foreigners for more than thirty years.

In light of the Soviet Union's collapse, that particular Cold War restriction no longer applied. The once-formidable USSR was dead, a victim of self-inflicted economic and social wounds. The city's reopening signaled a major shift in the political atmosphere.

Could this 'gentleman' be a deep cover agent seeking refuge? Cody doubted it. Other than covert operatives already in place, he had no information regarding additional clandestine assets in this part of the world. On the other hand, a nasty little scheme perpetrated by the discredited but still mischievous KGB wasn't out of the question either.

After a moment he said, "I'm coming down, Paul. Please escort Mr. Danilov to the visitor's conference room and keep an eye on him."

"Will do."

He broke the connection and buzzed Phyllis. She picked up immediately.

"Is Colonel Butler in his office?" Cody asked.

"Yes, I believe so."

"Please have him meet me near the first floor elevator."

"You mean right now?"

"Sooner, if possible."

"I'll track him down."

Five minutes later, Cody approached the conference room accompanied by the military attaché, an Air Force lieutenant colonel. Like Cody, Butler wore a worsted wool Navy blue suit, a button-down collared white shirt, and regimental striped tie. Although similar, their neckties did not match exactly. Cody found that happenstance mildly comforting.

The DO, similarly attired, stood beside the door. "Mr. Danilov is waiting inside," he confirmed. "Other than a thick document stashed inside a briefcase, the gentleman is clean."

"Thanks, Paul," Cody replied. With enormous effort, he restrained himself from making a derisive 'Three Musketeers' remark. Instead, he silently vowed to retire his Navy blue suit. Or perhaps burn it.

The Duty Officer headed back toward his station in the lobby.

Cody stepped into the oak-paneled conference room trailed by the attaché. Andrei Danilov stood facing the picture window, his posture erect, arms folded across his chest. Beyond the window, Golden Horn Bay glittered in weak autumn sunlight.

A heavy gray overcoat and matching fur cap lay across one chair. Nearby, a fat leather briefcase squatted beside the conference room table. Danilov turned, dropped his arms and smiled politely. Cody studied his unexpected guest.

If one ignored the mediocre Russian-made suit and shoes, Danilov did indeed project a gentleman's demeanor. Neat and clean-shaven, his clear brown eyes reflected guarded intelligence, like those of a chess master facing a highly rated opponent. The suit and shoes, although pressed and shined, contrasted with the imported cotton shirt and patterned silk tie, evidence Danilov shopped restricted access stores or had black market connections; perhaps both. Overall, his appearance and manner were those of an alert, moderately prosperous senior citizen.

"Good Morning, Mr. Danilov. I am Cody Ballantine, the Consul General's personal envoy. And this," he nodded toward the Air Force officer, "is Mr. Butler, my associate." Not exactly the complete truth, he reflected—maybe not even close, but good enough for the time being. "Mr. Zane is engaged in another matter and regrets his absence. Rather than have you wait, he asked me to represent him."

Danilov nodded, apparently satisfied with the explanation. "Then I bid you good morning, gentlemen." His smooth, resonant voice lacked the thick, easily identified Slavic accent. "And thank you for seeing me without an appointment."

The courteous reply notwithstanding, the old man followed Cody's example and did not extend his hand in greeting. That was noteworthy. Offering to shake hands when his American host did not might seem obsequious, thus placing the Russian at a psychological disadvantage. It was an interesting facet to Danilov's frame of mind.

"Not at all," Cody replied. "How might we be of service?"

"Before we get into that," the Russian began, "if you don't mind, may I confirm your identities, please?"

"Is that supposed to be a joke?" Colonel Butler said. The attaché's voice carried a slight edge.

Danilov's apologetic tone seemed genuine. "I understand your indignation sir, and please forgive my bad manners, but allow a cautious old man this small courtesy."

Butler looked at Cody and raised an eyebrow.

The question was unexpected but Cody maintained his composure. "Mr. Danilov," he said. "May I first see your papers?"

"Certainly." Danilov produced a small booklet from an inside jacket pocket.

Cody scanned the passport-sized document. The photograph revealed a much younger Andrei Ivanovich Danilov. His hair, still thick, was much grayer now. Cyrillic text on the opposite page contained personal information. Assuming his papers were authentic, Danilov was sixty-three years old.

"I see you live in Ussurijsk," Cody said.

"Yes, I have an apartment on Blyukher Prospekt, easy walking distance to my employer."

"Which is?"

"The Primorski Agricultural Institute."

"Do you teach there?"

Danilov shook his head. "I work as a linguist for the Institute's Department of Agronomy. I translate agricultural textbooks, journals and research papers from English to Russian."

That might explain the man's excellent pronunciation and vocabulary. "Do you enjoy your work?" Cody asked.

"I find it interesting and challenging."

Cody returned the identification. "How so?"

"For the most part, scientists and researchers rarely seek to inform the general population of their findings. Instead, they write to impress each other. The harder they try, the less coherent they become. I often restructure their prose to better explain what they actually mean."

Cody suppressed a smile. His visitor possessed intelligence *and* a wry sense of humor, character traits common among many Russians. "I see. Well, you've traveled a long way this morning, haven't you?"

"Indeed. One hundred and ten kilometers along the Trans-Siberian Railway is a great distance. Vladivostok, as the train conductors say, is the end of the line. Perhaps that phrase may prove accurate for other things as well."

The Russian's words seemed carefully chosen, the inflections deliberately applied. Was he alluding to a hidden past or an uncertain future? Cody's earlier belief, that Danilov was *not* an American deep cover agent, began to waver.

Colonel Butler, obviously impatient with nuance and philosophical small talk, pressed the issue. "How might we assist you, Mr. Danilov?"

"First, your credentials please."

"Of course." Cody offered his ID. After a slight hesitation, Butler followed suit.

Danilov tilted the laminated plastic cards against the fluorescent lighting, his eyes lingering on the diplomatic identification. "Thank you, gentlemen. I appreciate your indulgence." He returned the cards.

Despite his long-cultivated professional deportment, Cody found it difficult to conceal his growing interest. Danilov seemed to exude *substance*, a hard-to-define quality Cody immediately recognized. Not exactly an aura, he supposed, but something similar. The word 'gravitas' came to mind, and experience taught him that such men warranted careful scrutiny. He said, "At the risk of repeating ourselves, what can we do for you, sir?"

Danilov responded with a slight downturn of his lips. Quiet resignation flickered across the Russian's face followed by a look of determined reluctance. It seemed as though the old man had no choice but to commit an irrevocable act. Finally he said, "Mr. Ballantine, please be advised that my name is not Andrei Danilov. I am, in fact, a native born American citizen."

"So the Duty Officer told me." Cody nodded toward the leather briefcase resting on the floor. "I presume you have convincing evidence that you wish to present?"

"I do, but it is not in my valise."

"I see. Then what are you offering as proof?"

"Only the truth."

"Candor is a wise approach, especially when accompanied by reliable documentation."

"Mr. Ballantine, such documents exist, I assure you, but they are not in my possession."

"Oh? Then where are they?"

"In the United States, presumably hidden away and moldering in some dusty archive."

Cody noted Danilov's word choice: *archive*, a repository for older, perhaps historically relevant documents, rather than *file*, a term generally used to delineate records that are more current. Was that another subtle reference to his past?

"We can look into that," Cody said, "and we shall, once you provide us with some basic information."

"I understand."

"You told the Duty Officer you arrived here under unusual circumstances. What, exactly, does that mean?"

Danilov's resigned expression gave way to firm resolve, as though he had struggled with difficult questions before reaching a decision. Now, apparently committed, he seemed to grow taller, an unexpected transformation Cody found mildly disconcerting.

"I was—am—Captain Andrew George Thompson, United States Air Force, serial number 45935A." His eyes strayed for a moment to Butler, who did not respond. Danilov continued: "On August 3, 1954, Russian MiG fighter planes intercepted, fired upon, and destroyed my electronic surveillance aircraft, a four-engine RB-50 manned by fourteen crewmen. The attack occurred in international airspace, approximately fifteen miles south of Cape Gamov, over the Sea of Japan. That incident happened thirty-eight years ago last month."

He paused and his face clouded for a moment as though bewildered. Then his voice softened to a disbelieving murmur. "Thirty-eight *years*? How is that possible?"

In the brief silence that followed, Cody sensed that Danilov's mind was somewhere else, perhaps visiting a bizarre universe where the past folded itself into the present; where one's future became knowable and terrifying and unchangeable—a madhouse of asynchronous realities from which there was no respite or escape.

The old man's eyes refocused and he fixed Cody with a granite stare. "Sometimes, what life demands of us is difficult to accept, yet what I say is true. It now appears history and circumstances have given me an opportunity to return home and perhaps correct the official record."

From the corner of his eye, Cody saw Butler's lips compress into a thin line. The next questions were obvious. Cody spoke to his guest: "Your aircraft had a crew of fourteen? Are there others like you?"

"Perhaps, but I cannot be certain. Including the gentleman out front, you three are the only Americans I have spoken with since my capture."

Cody, unsure how to proceed, stalled for time. "I see. Well, as you might imagine, I have no knowledge of that specific event, Mr. Danilov."

A true statement, Cody admitted, but he also knew that incidents between Russian and American aircraft had been a common

The Gamov Incident

occurrence during the Cold War. Colonel Butler, who might have more knowledge about such events, remained silent, thus allowing the CIA officer to lead the discussion, a courtesy Cody appreciated. What he did *not* want, at least at this moment, was the attaché to confirm or corroborate any of what Danilov claimed.

"I am Drew Thompson," Danilov insisted. Then a half-sheepish expression creased his face. "I have not spoken that name in a long time. Nevertheless, it *is* mine."

"With all due respect sir," Cody said, resuming his original line of inquiry, "we require a bit more than your word. Do you have any kind of reliable evidence to substantiate your claim?"

Danilov extended both hands, palms up. "I have these. Take my fingerprints. I presume the consulate has such facilities. Send them to Washington. Check them against archival records. You may also take x-rays. I lost two molars and acquired several more fillings—stainless steel of course—but dental records, along with fingerprints, will verify my identity beyond doubt. Do you agree?"

Cody's mind raced. What in hell was going on here? Danilov looked healthy and affluent, the antithesis of the bedraggled Russian citizen. How could an American military officer survive and prosper for nearly *four decades* in Russian captivity? Had he compromised himself? Were there others like him? Finally, and perhaps more interesting, what was he carrying in that damned briefcase—*valise*? Cody's thoughts leaped beyond the present.

If Danilov was indeed a captured, uncompromised American airman and his ordeal became known—as it surely would—then public outrage would be difficult to contain. No amount of *glasnost*, the improved atmosphere between the United States and grudgingly democratic Russia, could diminish America's compassion for soldiers who suffered captivity while serving their country. Likewise, there were the families of those servicemen who remained unaccounted for—relatives who stubbornly held out hope for missing husbands, fathers, sons, and brothers.

Although Cody felt growing anticipation, bitter experience and long hours of training tempered his enthusiasm. He thought about all those courses and seminars in behavior analysis—ideas rooted in the teachings and philosophy of one Jack Paraday: a late, sorely lamented CIA interrogator and lecturer.

"Every human being is capable of lying," Paraday once told a small audience of Agency operatives, one of whom happened to be Cody. "Whether president or pope, every man, woman, and child will, under the right set of circumstances, tell an outright lie; or, at best, conceal unpleasant facts or embarrassing information. In this unusual business we have chosen for a career, the natural-born ability to willfully mislead our fellow creatures is the one thing you can absolutely rely on."

Paraday's instruction focused on body language, eye movement, facial gestures, and a host of other techniques. However, schooling in those same methods had occurred on the other side. In short, everyone in CIA and KGB became expert at telling and concealing lies. To Cody, it seemed like a zero sum game.

However, Jack Paraday—a man of extraordinary ability—had also possessed an infallible gift. The aging cold warrior could somehow determine precisely when an individual lied. His often-proved talent was one of those rare, sometimes scary abilities that appear randomly among human beings every now and then. Some believed Paraday was a true psychic, a genius perhaps; others thought him a savant, or maybe a borderline psychopath. Differing opinions notwithstanding, one might fool a polygraph or another skilled interrogator, but one could never slip a lie past old man Paraday.

Cody, not similarly gifted, fully understood his shortcoming.

Yet, despite that caution, his curiosity nagged like an unsatisfied itch; he wanted to begin his questioning immediately, to hear Danilov's story and probe for weaknesses. That approach was not possible, not yet, not without first briefing the Consul General and certainly not before informing his boss in Washington. Already treading on thin ice, Cody suppressed his natural instinct to push forward; instead, he chose what seemed like the next logical step.

He said, "Yes, what you suggest is a good place to start. Taking your fingerprints will not be a problem and we even have a portable x-ray machine in the dispensary. I'm sure someone even knows how it works. First things first however: Are you requesting asylum and safe-housing inside the consulate?"

The old man shook his head. "Not at this time. Much has changed here. The communist apparatus is dysfunctional. The Interior Ministry, what is left of it, no longer follows me or monitors my activities. Like most Federation citizens nowadays, I come and go as funds allow, not as the MVD dictates. Until my true identity is confirmed however, I should continue my life as before."

Danilov's logic made sense. After decades of living inside the Soviet state, prematurely committing himself to a course of action was probably unwise. Assuming, of course, the man was indeed who he claimed to be.

"Are you on holiday today?" Cody asked.

"No, I work four days each week. This is my scheduled day off." He lifted one shoulder, a tiny gesture. "The perquisites of old age. I am not due back at the Institute until Monday morning."

"I see," Cody said. "However, as you may already know, the verification process could be lengthy. Today is Friday. We will send your photograph and fingerprints, along with the Consul General's report, to Moscow via the afternoon courier. They will forward the originals to Washington, probably by Monday. The findings should arrive here the latter part of next week, or possibly not until the week after."

The heavy hitters in Washington would no doubt offer guidance regarding next steps; recommendations Cody intended to follow without deviation. Still, the process would take time.

"Mr. Danilov, if necessary may I contact you at the Institute?"

"I would prefer you did not."

Although the firm response was not surprising, Cody's professional curiosity remained piqued. He desperately wanted to probe for personal information: hometown, schools attended, and details regarding the shootdown. Equally important, he also wanted to explore the possibility of other survivors. Still, questions asked prematurely—or due to ignorance—could add credence to Danilov's claim. That approach might also conflict with specific directions from higher authority. Take this slow, Cody reminded himself, one step at a time.

"I appreciate your caution, sir, but it's clear we should meet again. Can you return here next Friday at the same time?"

"Yes, I can. But if our meetings continue, I suggest we do so in other places, discreetly, or somehow conceal my arrival and departure from the consulate."

It was a good suggestion, a cautionary procedure Cody had already considered. "I will make the necessary arrangements before you leave." He turned to Butler who had remained silent but attentive.

"Robert, let's handle this like a standard visa request: take photographs, fingerprints and gather the usual personal information. Make it look routine. I don't want to arouse undue interest among consular staff. I'll brief the Consul General as soon as he's free."

"I understand."

"Is there anything else?" Cody asked. He nodded toward the briefcase and wondered about the 'thick document' inside. "Perhaps something you'd like to leave with us for safekeeping?"

"Not at this time. But maybe later."

Cody resisted the impulse to ask: Why then, Mr. Danilov, did you bring your *valise* with you today? Instead, he smiled and offered his hand. "In that case, this has been an unexpected pleasure. I look forward to our next meeting and formal confirmation of your identity."

Danilov's handshake was firm, dry and definitely European. "As do I," he said. "Once again, thank you for seeing me without an appointment."

"Under the circumstances, we could hardly do less," Cody replied. "In the meantime, you've given us much to think about and even more to do."

Danilov reached for his overcoat, cap and briefcase.

"I understand, Mr. Ballantine. And I will not hinder your efforts." He looked at Butler and smiled. "Shall we begin?"

Chapter 2

Returning from a morning meeting with his administrative staff, Consul General Whittier Zane paused outside his office. Like almost everyone else in the consulate, his secretary—a young woman who looked to be in her late twenties—was new to her post. "Angela, has Mr. Ballantine called?"

"Yes, Mr. Zane. He'd like to speak with you at your earliest convenience."

"Ask him to come up now, please."

"Yes, sir."

The air inside Zane's elegantly furnished office still carried faint residues of fresh paint, an aura that seemed to emphasize the newness of the consulate. He ignored the lingering odor and wondered what the CIA resident had learned about their unexpected morning visitor.

During his long and moderately successful diplomatic career, Zane had come to terms with the Central Intelligence Agency's unofficial but widely known presence in America's foreign consulates and embassies. Intelligence gathering was important—a critical function, indeed—but the enigmatic organization also pursued other activities. Their clandestine successes would probably remain secret for decades. On the other hand, failures in Cuba, the Middle East and elsewhere were widely publicized, as were speculations about their alleged role in less noble pursuits.

Zane chose not to dwell upon the Agency's unsavory dealings. And rightly so. The CIA wasn't the only government agency with skeletons hovering inside dark closets. Zane had personal knowledge of several State Department fiascos, debacles better left unacknowledged. However, similar culpability did not necessarily correspond to comparable ethos.

Like most State Department professionals, Zane believed CIA types were culturally deficient. Although deeply committed to furthering American interests, the spy agency exuded a tainted arrogance, a rather depressing quality somewhat like that of a great vintage Bordeaux slightly past its prime. Nevertheless, their often-shadowy presence was a reality he accepted. This he did, albeit reluctantly, as one might acknowledge and accommodate the company of a somewhat disreputable blood relative.

A few minutes later, Ballantine—a tall, athletic-looking man in his mid-forties—stood in the doorway.

"You've heard about our unexpected guest?" Ballantine asked, without preamble.

For reasons unknown to Zane, the CIA officer's voice brought to mind sonorous Gregorian chants, a deep resonance more suited to a 13th century Frankish cathedral than a modern American consulate. The tone matched perfectly with Zane's preconceived notion of CIA operational types, especially Ballantine, whom Zane saw as a dedicated but morally tattered character: a flawed warrior-monk plucked whole from a crumbling Templar abbey.

"Yes, I have," Zane replied. He waved the CIA resident inside, motioned toward a chair and waited until Ballantine seated himself. The Consul General likewise got to the point immediately. "If we had deep cover agents in this part of Russia, I presume you would have knowledge of their existence."

"Probably so, but there are always exceptions. If Danilov *is* one of ours, then nobody bothered to let me in on it."

"I see. Well then, tell me about our guest."

Zane spent the next few minutes listening to the resident describe his meeting with Andrei Danilov. As expected, Ballantine limited his narrative to facts, apparently unwilling to reveal personal feelings for the time being, or so it seemed.

Ballantine concluded by saying, "At this moment the gentleman is with Colonel Butler, pretending to apply for a visa. That will take about an hour. I'm not sure what excuse the attaché will invent to obtain dental x-rays."

"I'm sure Colonel Butler will think of something appropriate."

"I expect so. He seems like a resourceful type."

"We shall find out soon enough."

Cody changed the subject. "When do you intend to notify the Ambassador?"

Zane glanced at his Rolex. "Later today. I imagine he's still asleep. I'll write my report first and contact Moscow this afternoon. Meanwhile, I suggest you monitor Mr. Danilov's activities. Perhaps check into his background."

"I've already started the process."

"I thought as much." He paused before continuing. "How trustworthy are your local informants?"

"Mr. Zane, the consulate opened four days ago." Ballantine wrinkled his nose and sniffed the air. "The paint is still fresh."

"True, but you and your people have been in town for months. Presumably you've developed prospects?"

"Yes, I have. But we're still evaluating their backgrounds and potential usefulness."

"Do you have other, more personal contacts?"

Ballantine hesitated before speaking. "There are several retired military officers whom I tend to trust, one in particular. Of course, none will divulge Russia's national secrets, even if they knew any. Still, they enjoy reminiscing about the Cold War. Like most soldiers, they are proud of their service. Until recently however, personal military experiences were considered State property."

"How often do you meet with those fellows?"

"Every now and then for drinks, sometimes dinner. It's very informal. They do not believe the official story about me being your cultural advisor. Instead, they think I'm either CIA or an unacknowledged member of the military attaché. I encourage the latter at every opportunity."

"I see."

Although he wasn't positive, Zane believed Cody Ballantine had served as a military officer, perhaps in the Army, before joining the Agency. The resident's eyes reflected too much unpleasant knowledge prematurely acquired. His Russian contacts probably noticed that characteristic as well, and the world-weary demeanor would tend to reinforce Ballantine's fictitious military guise.

Another thought occurred to Zane. "By chance, have any of your more trustworthy friends been invited to the consulate's opening reception tomorrow evening?"

"I believe Cultural Minister Trushin is on the guest list."

Zane cocked an eyebrow. "I thought you said your best contacts were retired military officers."

"Trushin was an Air Force senior colonel. After completing thirty years of service, he retired, became a politician, and acquired a bit of wealth."

Zane chose to ignore the unspoken implication. "Well, if it's appropriate and the opportunity presents itself, you should speak with him. Any information, especially from Minister Trushin's point of view, regarding American reconnaissance flights over the Russian Far East would be helpful. He was, after all, a senior colonel in the Soviet Air Force."

"Isn't that risky?"

"Are you suggesting such inquiries might generate suspicion?"

"It's possible."

Zane drummed his fingers on the desk. "I understand your caution, but the Cold War seems a natural topic of discussion between former adversaries. Handled properly, the risk should be minimal."

"How far should I go?"

Zane considered the question for a moment. "You mentioned sharing war stories. I'm sure you can think of several. Start there. However, do not initiate discussions about American overflights. Figure a way to allow that topic to occur naturally."

Ballantine nodded but said nothing.

"Back to Mr. Danilov. I presume we will be seeing him again?"

"Yes. I asked and he agreed to return next Friday morning. By then, Washington should have provided enough information so we can begin debriefing him, which I assume they will authorize. If so, then I would like you and Colonel Butler to participate. Will that be possible?"

"Of course. I'm as curious about Mr. Danilov as you are. I'll keep the entire day open, just in case things get interesting."

"I appreciate that, Mr. Zane."

"Well then, do you have anything else?"

"Not at this time."

"Thank you, Cody. I'm looking forward to meeting Mr. Danilov."

***

Later that day, following a long discussion with a colleague in Moscow, Zane cradled the secure telephone on his credenza, turned to his desk and opened a personal journal.

From habit, Zane recorded the date, time, and general nature of his conversation with the Ambassador's deputy, adding a few personal comments to the brief entry. The current volume of his journal was sixth in a series begun when he first joined the Foreign Service more than thirty years ago. The notes would refresh his memory should he ever decide to write his memoirs, which seemed unlikely. Instead, his journals would probably end up collecting dust in the library at Princeton, his alma mater.

A moment after completing the latest entry, Colonel Butler appeared in the doorway carrying a large unsealed manila envelope.

"Come in, Robert. Have you taken care of our visitor?" Zane returned his leather bound journal to the middle desk drawer.

"Yes, sir. He left about two hours ago." Butler placed the envelope on Zane's desk. "This is ready for the courier. Inside are photographs, fingerprints—the whole works. All it needs is your cover letter."

"Angela is typing it now. Please sit down."

Butler slouched in an armchair. "And now we wait."

"An unglamorous necessity, I fear. In the meantime, what is your assessment of Mr. Danilov?"

"I'm not sure. It's a fantastic scenario—one that's entirely possible—but I took Ballantine's cue and did not ask personal questions, only those necessary to complete the visa application."

"And the dental x-rays? Did you manage those?"

"No, I didn't. There were too many people in the dispensary."

"Oh? Should I be concerned?"

"No. It wasn't a contagion, just a morning gab fest over coffee."

"I see."

"A complete set of fingerprints should be enough," Butler suggested.

"I'm sure that will suffice. Did you learn anything new?"

The attaché shifted his weight. "Not really. Mr. Danilov did not volunteer any information other than what I requested. For a man professing to be an American military officer, a brother in arms so to speak, his behavior struck me as unusual."

"He is understandably cautious. Can you blame him?"

"I suppose not."

"Where does he reside when in town?"

"The Amursky Zaliv. He wanted a place close to the railway station."

"That's a fairly new hotel, isn't it?"

"It opened about four years ago."

"Expensive?"

"Not for Russians. Federation citizens get a huge discount."

Zane paused for a moment, then he said, "You are a rated flying officer, are you not?"

Butler nodded. "Both single and multi-engine."

"Presumably, you and your fellow pilots shared experiences. Did you by chance recall any unusual stories regarding Cold War reconnaissance flights?"

"A few. I remember Francis Gary Powers and the U-2 affair."

"How could you possibly remember the Powers incident? That was in 1960. You were what, three years old when that happened?"

"Four, actually. I learned about Powers and the U-2 at the Academy. The poly-sci professor made it sound like a big deal."

"Believe me Robert, it was all that and a great deal more. In actual fact the incident was nothing short of an utter catastrophe. Premier Khrushchev turned the U-2 shootdown into a diplomatic circus with the entire U.N. as audience—a public embarrassment President Eisenhower never forgot. In any event, Powers flew northwesterly from his base in Pakistan, toward Norway, in the opposite direction. What about flights over the Russian Far East?"

"I take it you mean our flights over places like Cape Gamov, Sakhalin Island and the Kamchatka Peninsula?"

"Exactly."

Butler rubbed his chin, as though checking his shave. "That was long before my time, but I've heard a few rumors. It seems we overflew most of the Soviet Union during the Cold War. We also lost some people and airplanes in the process, but few seem to know much else. Either that or they aren't talking about it. Should I make inquiries?"

"Yes, but be discreet. We must keep Danilov's claim utterly confidential, at least for now. Learn what you can about our aerial reconnaissance efforts during that era, including bases and missions. Focus on operations specific to this part of the world. I've already made diplomatic inquiries. Moscow promised to query Washington and send me what they have."

"Meanwhile, more waiting."

"Perhaps, but I suspect not all of us will be content to sit and wait."

Butler smiled. "Buffalo Bill the Spook?"

"I'm told he prefers Cody or, if you insist on formality, Mr. Ballantine."

"What do you suppose he's up to?"

Whittier Zane had been wondering the same thing.

Chapter 3

Cody stepped inside the Kaffe Ldinka, a popular coffeehouse on Aleutskaya Street. The small shop stood adjacent to the Arsenev Museum, a massive structure dedicated to preserving the indigenous cultures of Siberia's Primorski region. In his bogus role as cultural attaché, Cody had visited the museum twice, once out of curiosity and once to attend an informal lecture followed by tea and the usual academic chitchat.

He approached an isolated table occupied by a rather plain featured, middle-aged man dressed in the fashion preferred by many male inhabitants of the city: a turtleneck sweater—maroon today—worn under a short leather coat, and dark trousers. Studiously ordinary, Cody's field agent would seldom rate a second glance.

"Good morning, Freddie," he said, taking the chair opposite.

Freddie Benner looked up from his newspaper. "Is it really, or are you merely trying to raise my lagging spirits?"

A young waiter appeared and Cody ordered cappuccino. When he was out of earshot Cody said, "That depends."

Freddie smiled and waited.

Cody said, "Have your travels ever taken you to Ussurijsk? It's located about a hundred kilometers north of here, on the main railroad line."

"No, they haven't."

"I'm surprised to hear that."

"There is nothing in Ussurijsk to warrant a visit. But I'm getting the uncomfortable feeling that situation is about to change."

"Your intuition is exceeded only by your pleasant demeanor."

Freddie re-folded his newspaper and set it aside. He sipped coffee and then asked, "Why am I going to Ussurijsk?"

"We had an interesting visitor this morning," Cody began. He then related what he knew about Andrei Danilov, omitting the alleged shootdown incident and the old man's claim to American citizenship. "I'd like you to conduct a low key surveillance—home, workplace, friends—you know the drill. But keep under the local radar," he cautioned. "In fact, I would prefer you not make any personal inquiries whatsoever. I don't want anyone alerted to our interest in Mr. Danilov."

The waiter delivered cappuccino in a tiny cup. Cody thanked him, took the equally tiny spoon and stirred the dark liquid.

"In other words," Freddie said after the waiter had left, "a quick little Sneak and Peek."

Cody nodded.

"What's my cover?"

"You mean the cover to cover your current cover?"

Freddie smiled. "Your command of the English language is awe inspiring. Have you ever considered tutoring?"

"No, but perhaps I should."

"It would be something to fall back on during hard times."

"Do you think I need a backup career plan?"

"Haven't you heard? The Cold War is over. We may *all* need a backup career plan."

According to his Agency file, Frederic Benner had lived quietly in East Germany for nearly four years. As instructed, he never made contact with anyone outside his circle of carefully acquired communist friends and acquaintances. Since he earned a good living as an accountant who sometimes took small bribes from influential government officials, the Agency had no need to provide salary or expenses directly; thus, there was no record of outside income, a fact sure to arouse suspicion. When the Soviet Union collapsed, Freddie, still in deep cover, called a pre-arranged telephone number. Expecting a summons home, he received instead a new assignment.

To the outside world, Frederic Benner—like many newly mobile Soviet citizens—pursued other employment opportunities. He gathered up his earnings, bid farewell to his circle of friends and then relocated to Vladivostok. There he resumed his dual professions: chartered certified accountant and cautiously illegal black marketeer, one who specialized in hard to find food items like upscale Russian vodka and Ossetra caviar. As did every minor criminal in the city, Freddie paid a weekly tribute to a local thug. In return, he was allowed to operate as he pleased, within agreed upon boundaries.

To anyone interested in their coffee shop discussion, it would appear that Cody and Freddie were negotiating prices and arranging for delivery of luxury edibles. That was the plan, anyway.

Cody said, "About your cover: Sasha has an envelope with documents and details. If you are polite and wipe your feet on the front doormat like a proper boarder, she might even feed you before the train leaves for Ussurijsk."

The field agent chuckled softly. "Under more pleasant circumstances, Sasha would be an old bachelor's dream: a handsome, mature woman, living alone in her own house, widowed; a magnificent cook who took in a boarder from East Germany to warm her bed during the long Siberian winter."

"A pleasant but necessary illusion."

"True," Freddie admitted a bit wistfully. "But the best illusions are based on reality, are they not?"

"They are, but only to the extent necessary to fool the audience."

"Sadly, that is indeed the case."

Cody finished his cappuccino. "Any other questions?"

Freddie shook his head.

"Okay. Get back to me in a week; earlier if you come up with something."

"I will call even if I have nothing interesting to say," Freddie promised.

Cody stood and placed rubles on the table. "My treat," he said.

Freddie uttered a derisive grunt. "If you really want to help my financial situation, buy a half-dozen Kobe steaks, not a lousy cup of coffee."

"I can't afford Kobe steaks."

"Not many can," Freddie admitted.

***

Cody watched the Aeroflot TU-154 lift off from Vladivostok's Knevichi airdrome, beginning the first leg of its long, multi-stop flight to Moscow. Barring mechanical or fueling difficulties, the Danilov file should reach the American Embassy in about eighteen hours. Cody, a veteran of five such flights, didn't envy the diplomatic courier's prolonged confinement inside a cramped, smoke-filled passenger cabin. Although he seldom, if ever, provided taxi services for the Consul General's couriers, the still-unfolding Danilov affair deserved special consideration.

Without really thinking about it, he reached for a cigarette but found a roll of Lifesavers instead. During the early stages of his campaign to quit smoking, Cody realized that his unconscious mind expected to find cigarettes in his left shirt pocket, their comforting presence a key element of nicotine addiction. Finding an empty pocket induced mild panic and intensified his craving. The presence of something tangible in that pocket, even peppermint flavored Lifesavers, was a helpful psychological crutch. He pinched one free and popped the chalky circle into his mouth.

Three months and counting, he mused.

Leaving the terminal building, Cody ambled across the street to a parking lot, unlocked and then slid into his automobile: a black, two-year-old Lada Samara in good operating condition. He started the engine, allowing it to idle for a minute, and then began the forty-kilometer drive back to the city, taking one of the few paved roads connecting Russia's major population areas.

A few miles beyond the airport, Cody drove past a wide, nearly flat field lined with row upon row of disused main battle tanks. Hundreds of armored behemoths lay rusting and neglected, their cannons locked in place, abandoned relics from another era hulking behind a dilapidated chain link fence. Dozens of military equipment graveyards speckled the Russian countryside, decaying monuments to the Soviet Union's distorted economic, social, and manufacturing priorities.

America had similar junkyards immediately following the Second World War, but few lay idle. Instead, workers quickly dismantled hard-edged war machines, melted down the scrap, and then resurrected the metal into calmer shapes. American optimism had forged a modern incarnation of swords into plowshares; turning bombers into aluminum siding that covered millions of new homes for returning veterans. Unfortunately, the military junkyards in Siberia lacked such energy. Mother Russia seemed exhausted, her purpose and spirit worn out by decades of mistreatment.

He rolled the Lifesaver to the other cheek and redirected his thoughts.

Although his initial reaction to Danilov's claim was outright skepticism, the old man seemed confident that fingerprint comparisons would prove his identity. The Russian's self-assurance cast doubt on the imposter theory, but Cody's reservations persisted, a flashing yellow light on a dark, deserted highway.

Cody knew he was forgetting an important historical detail, a critical piece of information that would alter the current situation in a significant way. The idea nagged at his consciousness, an annoying presence clouding his mind like the gauzy remnants of an unpleasant dream. He concentrated for a moment, his mind sifting through various word associations, all without result. Finally, he pushed the unresolved issue aside, knowing from experience it would eventually resurface.

Cody focused on another troublesome possibility.

If Danilov were indeed an American aviator, why would the Russians keep him around, in public, a political time bomb sure to detonate? Why harbor a potential diplomatic liability for *forty years*? Only one reason came to mind: Danilov had turned, had stayed voluntarily and Russian authorities had proof. Such evidence would provide the Yeltsin government with immunity from international criticism. In fact, governments favorably disposed toward socialism, along with their counterparts in the media, would view Russia's silence as benevolent—a humane gesture intended to shield an American turncoat from humiliation and disgrace.

On the other hand, Yeltsin and his cohorts might chose to conceal all evidence of Danilov's guilt. Admitting to an 'unfortunate' mistake, they could blame the incident on the bad old Soviet regime. Documentation validating the old man's collaboration with the enemy would be intentionally destroyed and thus unavailable for public scrutiny. Danilov the turncoat could then claim POW/MIA status and return home to a hero's welcome.

Cody's hand tightened on the Lada's steering wheel. That such a thing might occur was wholly repulsive and he refused to accept the possibility. A long-simmering outrage flickered and re-emerged, its intensity undiminished by the passage of time.

In 1968, 22-year-old Lieutenant Cody Ballantine had led a Special Forces search and rescue team into the A Shau, an enemy-controlled valley on Vietnam's northwestern border. A quarter century had elapsed since then, but the wartime incident remained clear in his memory.

***

Cody and his team eased along a fork of the Rao Lao, a muddy tributary that slithered between tropically jungled 5,000-foot-high mountains, their tops shrouded by mist and heavy gray clouds. They moved in a grid pattern, searching methodically for a downed helicopter, its three-man crew, and four wounded Special Forces troopers.

Early on the second day, Cody located the wreck in heavy forest, a crash site now abandoned and void of booby traps. The spot where the Bell UH-1 'Huey' came to earth was barely wider than the drooping rotor blades, mute testament to the pilot's remarkable skills.

The chopper sat upright but tilted, one skid bent; evidence of a hard but controlled landing. Beside it lay four med-evac stretchers, perfectly aligned in a single row. Each stretcher held the body of a dead soldier, their wounds still wrapped in temporary field dressings. Jungle rats had disfigured the corpses, but it was clear someone, presumably NVA regulars, had executed the wounded troopers, methodically firing a single bullet into each man's brain. The killers left the bodies in plain view beside the downed aircraft, disdainfully certain the atrocity would be discovered.

    Masking his outrage, Cody brushed away flies and helped his team wrap their dead comrades in shelter halves. They cut bamboo poles for makeshift stretchers and then carried the bodies to a larger clearing nearer the river. The effort took two trips. A short time later another Huey—accompanied by a gunship—airlifted the dead men to Lang Vei. Cody and his five-man team remained behind, determined to track and catch up with the murderers.

    Footprints, a mix of U.S. Army boots and NVA rubber soled sandals, made it clear the chopper crew were now prisoners. Supplied with fresh rations and new shelter halves, they tracked captors and captives for three more days, following a narrow game trail through heavy jungle, avoiding booby traps and patiently determined to ambush their potential ambushers.

    But all his focused outrage came to nothing. The jungle path widened and then disappeared into marshland bordering the Rao Lao, less than a mile from the Laotian border. Although Cody had no reservation about entering a technically neutral country, he knew it would do little good. The single path was no longer visible and what lay ahead on the far side of the river was the hopeless tangle of the Ho Chi Minh trail.

    The North Vietnamese had never acknowledged the atrocity, nor did they own up to capturing the three-man crew. That wasn't surprising. Admitting to one fact would confirm their culpability in the other.

    The four murdered soldiers, their bodies encased in flag-draped aluminum caskets, went home, their deaths providing closure, if not consolation. But the same was not true for the three-man chopper crew. They remained unaccounted for, an unfinished story, their fate a continuing, unsolved mystery to everyone except those who took them prisoner.

The missing helicopter crewmen were the first occupants in an expanding pantheon of ghosts that would haunt the corridors of his memory.

***

Cody relaxed his grip on the steering wheel. Don't get ahead of yourself, he cautioned. Settle down.

While he would never allow a turncoat to capitalize on American sympathies, neither would he pre-judge Danilov. He would let the evidence speak for itself.

It was also important to keep in mind what Jack Paraday had drilled into his head years ago. Under certain conditions, anybody could tell a lie—if not to friends, family or loved ones, then certainly to enemies—and sometimes to themselves. Those latter mistruths, sometimes characterized as rationalizations, were perhaps the worst kind. Still, if supporting evidence was not conclusive—and Danilov turned out to be a compelling enough liar—well, the old Russian just might succeed in perpetuating a major hoax.

Unfortunately, the infallible Mr. Paraday was no longer among the living; and, so far, no other individual had been able to match his uncanny ability to expose a deceiver.

But there were other, perhaps less reliable options Cody could pursue.

Earlier that day, shortly after his conversation with Zane, cryptographers had encoded and transmitted Cody's 'operational immediate' report, a heads up note to his boss in Langley, Virginia. Included in his message was a request for specific information from the Agency's historical research section. With luck, he would receive a response within twenty-four hours. Although State Department sources were usually trustworthy, corroboration obtained from multiple independent sources could better determine the validity of Danilov's improbable claim.

He cranked down the driver side window, took a deep breath and watched the distant, custard-yellow sun disappear behind heavily forested mountains. The tangy air was a prelude to a frigid season that arrived early and often persisted well into May. The prospect of spending a long, cold winter in Siberia was a reality too gloomy to contemplate. Maybe it was indeed time to explore another line of work.

Then again, perhaps he was too much the pessimist, his normally positive outlook tainted by an atrocity he had unwittingly facilitated. The Balkan incident had certainly changed him, but had it also prejudiced his ability to evaluate objectively the true character of individuals?

Maybe Danilov was indeed Captain Andrew Thompson, a bilingual, incredibly lucky survivor who managed to lose himself in Soviet Russia's cumbersome bureaucracy. If so, then the old gentleman might shed light on other missing Americans, including the other thirteen members of his aircrew. It was a remote but intriguing possibility.

He cranked the window up, shutting out the chill.

Or it could be the opening gambit of an elaborate, well-planned deception.

Chapter 4

The following day Cody walked up one flight of stairs to the consulate's cryptographic center. He pressed the buzzer and stared into the TV camera mounted above the six-inch thick metal door, a formidable barrier similar to those used on bank vaults.

A moment later a young man in civilian clothes opened the door slightly and asked to see ID. Apparently satisfied, he handed Cody a clipboard and showed him a red-bannered manila folder marked with a control number and the words TOP SECRET. Cody signed for the document and received a polite 'thank you.' Then the steel door closed with a resounding THUNK.

"You're welcome," he said to the steel door.

Although he held a top-of-the-chart security clearance, only cryptographers could enter their esoteric domain. It was not a personal thing. By federal law, sharing sensitive material, regardless of classification or category, occurred only on a 'need to know' basis.

Cody Ballantine, CIA officer and senior member of the consular staff, did not have the need to know.

He returned to his office and settled into his chair. He then broke the seal on the folder and removed a single page containing a typed list. Cody leaned forward and studied the eleven entries, noting one in particular.

Setting the list aside, he lifted the telephone handset and pushed a speed-dial button.

"Colonel Butler speaking."

"Cody here, Robert."

"Hi. What's up?"

"Well, a number of things, one of which you might find interesting."

"Really? And what might that be?"

"Late yesterday I asked the analysts at Langley to research certain historical information regarding our unannounced visitor. I have their uncharacteristically quick reply. Would you like to see what they came up with?"

"Are you kidding? If that means you are about to share a secret missive from the *sanctum sanctorum* in Spookville, then how could I possibly refuse? I'll be there in two minutes." The line went dead.

Cody replaced the handset, pinched loose another Lifesaver and waited, wondering whether he should take offense at the 'Spook' reference. The attaché's lighthearted tone convinced him he should cool it. Besides, Cody had enough people upset with him without adding to the list.

Two minutes later, almost to the second, Butler strolled in through the open door carrying a coffee mug. As usual, the young light colonel wore an immaculate suit.

"I got a wave in from Phyllis," Butler said.

"Then have a seat."

The attaché plopped into a side chair near Cody's desk. Blond and blue-eyed, the mildly handsome Air Force light colonel looked younger than his thirty-six years. Dressed in a gray pinstriped suit, crisp white shirt and rep tie, Butler could easily have passed for an alert, up and coming business executive, a man destined for a corner office.

"You have my undivided attention," Butler said. The crooked smile emphasized youthful features.

Cody slid the single sheet across his desk. "I received this a few minutes ago. Since you have the proper security clearance and a 'need to know' I thought you'd like to see this."

Butler's eyes narrowed slightly. Then he set his coffee mug on a coaster, took the page and studied the report.

TOP SECRET

Aerial Reconnaissance Incidents (Worldwide) – 1954

Date	Aircraft	Location	Disposition
27 Jan	RB-45C	Yellow Sea	Shot at by MiG-15s; escaped
12 Mar	RB-57A	Czech Border	Shot at by MiGs; 1 injured
29 Apr	RB-45C	Kiev	Shot at by MiGs; escaped
08 May	RB-47	Murmansk	Shot at by MiG-17s; 1 injured
15 May	RB-47	Kamchatka	Shot down by MiGs; 3 fatalities
27 Jul	PB-4Y	Guandong	Shot down by Chinese anti-aircraft fire; 9 fatalities
03 Aug	RB-50	Cape Gamov	Shot down by MiGs; 2 fatalities, 1 injured, 11 missing
12 Sep	RB-47	Bering Strait	Shot at by MiG-17s; 1 injured
09 Oct	P-4M	Wenchow	Shot down by La-9s; 10 fatalities
12 Nov	RB-50	Kamchatka	Shot down by MiGs; 12 fatalities
09 Dec	RB-47	Baltic Sea	Shot down by MiGs; 3 fatalities

TOP SECRET

Butler looked up. "According to this, we lost 39 airmen killed on those flights—and perhaps more—in 1954. How could we have kept such a thing secret, especially during peacetime?"

"Easy enough to do. Back in the Fifties, most people still believed what the government told them."

"In other words, we lied. Some government official attributed those losses to fictitious aircraft accidents."

"Probably."

"And if an aircraft was lost at sea, perhaps during bad weather, such an event might account for the lack of bodies."

"Also possible."

Butler remained silent for a moment. Then he said, "The Soviets shot down an Air Force RB-50 on August 3, exactly when and where Danilov said. That probably means he was telling the truth."

"Maybe he is, maybe not. That information has been around for almost forty years. It's practically common knowledge."

"Really?" Butler said, handing back the list. "Then why is it still classified Top Secret?"

"That was my idea. The list itself may not be classified, but our sudden interest in a forty-year-old shootdown isn't something I want known, especially since it presumably occurred a few hours drive from here. Classifying it Top Secret should keep overly curious busybodies out of our hair, for a while anyway."

"I never thought of it that way."

"I'm not surprised by that, Robert. Most military academy types are myopic and wholly untrainable. Nevertheless, I will try my utmost to augment your dismally narrow education."

Butler raised his right hand, displaying an Air Force Academy ring, and lightly tapped the desk's polished surface. "Knock, knock."

Despite himself, Cody chuckled.

He didn't know Butler very well, not yet anyway, but the military attaché should be someone he could rely on in a crunch, and vice versa. On the other hand, despite his joke, Butler might indeed be an Academy ring knocker with his eye on a general's star. A successful tour at a consulate, especially in Russia, would be a nice addition to his resume. Cody decided to learn a bit more about the military attaché. He would send another discrete cable at his first opportunity.

"So, what's next?" Butler said.

"I'll share this information with the Consul General, but I'd like to pick your brain first."

"About what?"

"I noticed the list contains two Air Force RB-50 aircraft, one of which Danilov claims was his. Both were shot down—the first in August and the other in November. My question to you is: What's an RB-50?"

Butler relaxed in his chair, obviously comfortable with the question. "That's an easy question to answer. Picture a World War Two Boeing B-29 Superfortress, the bomber we used to annihilate Japan: a beautiful airplane with a long, cylindrical fuselage, sweeping vertical stabilizer and four reciprocating engines.

"The B-50 bomber was an updated model with a more efficient wing design, more powerful engines and larger fuel tanks. The reconnaissance variant, designated with an 'R' prefix, came loaded with cameras and electronic sensing equipment in lieu of guns and bombs. It could fly higher and a bit faster than the bomber version."

"But it was still a four-engine prop job."

"Right, no match for a MiG jet fighter."

Cody studied the list again. "Almost a dozen incidents occurred in 1954, nearly one a month. The Soviets couldn't possibly have intercepted every mission. That means we were flying over Russia and China every week, more or less."

"Probably so."

"In secret, with obsolete aircraft."

"I'm afraid that's true as well. Look, we all know the Cold War was a misnomer. It's been rumored the Air Force would not award Silver Stars or Purple Hearts to deserving recon aircrews because it didn't want Congress nosing into the details of those missions, perhaps to discover why such decorations were justified. Curt LeMay could get away with it back then. Many in Congress believed he could do no wrong."

"He was also the archetypical bomber general. If memory serves, the air war in Vietnam turned his 'bombers can win any war' theory upside down. Without tactical air, our losses would have been much higher."

"I'll admit LeMay wore blinders when it came to fighter planes—as did most of the senior officers back then—but he made the Air Force what it is today."

Cody, a history buff, chose not to discuss the internecine warfare between bomber and fighter pilots during the Vietnam War. He returned to the original subject. "The RB-50 gone missing in August had fourteen crew members; the November shootdown listed twelve. Why the manpower difference?"

"Mission specifics dictated the number and skill set of aircrews. Photo recon ops required fewer crewmen than did electronic intelligence gathering."

"In other words the August flight—Danilov's—was probably an electronic surveillance mission."

"That makes sense given the number of airmen aboard."

"I presume they were looking for Soviet radar sites."

"Yes, but not only their locations. We also needed information on specific types of radar; that is: search, fighter control, or gun tracking, along with the frequency and range of each one. Back then, Russian air defense systems were a mystery to American military planners. We had no clue as to their capabilities. If the Russkies decided to launch an attack on the United States, our retaliatory bomber routes needed to bypass their strong points. The driving force behind those surveillance missions was our compelling need to develop a detailed map of the Soviet radar defense network."

"And the Russians, always paranoid about Western intentions, even during periods of cordial relations, reacted accordingly."

"They did exactly what we would have done under similar circumstances. Shoot first, talk later."

Cody offered a tiny smile, pleasantly surprised and satisfied with Butler's candor and willingness to share information. They were off to a good start. "Colonel Butler, despite your Academy-tainted education, I am duly impressed by the depth of your knowledge. How long did it take you to research all this?"

"A few hours. I got busy right after Danilov left the consulate."

Cody slipped the list back into the red-bannered folder. "Good work. We are making progress. Mr. Zane will be pleased."

"One should always strive to keep the boss happy," Butler suggested.

Cody checked his watch. "It's time for us to leave and get ourselves gussied up. Arriving late for the Consul General's grand opening soiree would greatly diminish his good spirits. Are you wearing mess dress?"

Butler shook his head. "Mr. Zane suggested I wear a tux. I'm pretending to be a civilian, remember?"

"I understand. However, you should wear your decorations tonight. Presumably you have miniatures?"

"I do, but may I ask why?"

"On formal diplomatic occasions," Cody explained, "like tonight for instance, most of our older male Russian guests will be medaled from tits to top hat."

"Is that so?"

Cody nodded. "Many of those distinguished gentlemen served in World War Two, what the Soviets call The Great Patriotic War. They have no qualms about exhibiting their personal role in defeating Adolph Hitler's Germany."

"Which means we must be similarly adorned," Butler suggested.

"Exactly. Our natural inclination toward quiet humility would be misinterpreted and deemed churlish by our guests. Besides, I have no choice. Although my official role is that of cultural attaché, the Russians think I'm part of the consulate's military section. I'm trying to reinforce what they already believe."

Butler's face registered mild amusement. "Subterfuge within a subterfuge."

"I do believe you are catching on," Cody replied.

Chapter 5

Cody's living quarters on Okeansky Prospekt—Ocean Avenue—comprised a full bath and four rooms: parlor, kitchen/dining area, and two bedrooms, one of which he used as a combination gym/study. The space, considered a *three*-room apartment by Russian standards—a measurement differential Cody had yet to figure out—suited his needs. He had no plans to entertain guests anytime soon, if at all.

He stepped from the shower, toweled dry and walked naked into the bedroom. An antique silent butler once owned by his grandfather held Cody's tuxedo. Usually, he eschewed outward displays of his Army service and avoided discussions about his involvement in that tragic war. Tonight however, was an exception.

Miniature versions of nine individual medals mounted in two rows hung from the upper left lapel of his jacket. Oak leaf clusters, 'V' devices and stars clung to several colorful ribbons. The medals would serve a deceptive purpose by re-enforcing what the Russians already believed. Officially, Cody was the consulate's cultural attaché. The always-suspicious Russians however, believed he was an unacknowledged member of the military section, or perhaps CIA. Keeping them guessing was all part of the game.

Like it or not, deception was a ploy both sides used but seldom acknowledged. The Russians believed everyone in the consulate was a spy and few in the Agency really thought the KGB no longer existed. Nevertheless, the old Soviet regime was history and the rules had changed. Although Cold War political maneuvering ended a few years ago, both sides continued to employ surrogates to achieve various ends. Ethnic groups who had personal agendas and centuries-old scores to settle served as indigenous proxies. Sometimes they did what we asked, but sometimes not, as Cody had learned from first-hand experience.

He pulled on underwear, shirt, trousers, socks, and glistening black shoes. Then he fixed onyx studs and cuff links to the shirt, adjusted the cummerbund around his waist, and then reached for his black bow tie. Getting the knot just right could be a pain in the ass, so he worked carefully. Satisfied, he slipped on the jacket, popped his shirt cuffs and, reluctantly, took one final look in the mirror.

The tuxedo and medals always reminded Cody of his wedding day and the astonishingly short-lived marriage: an aborted attempt to live a normal life with someone he loved. Staring at a formally dressed older version of himself rekindled the memory of his last encounter with Tessa.

***

After packing his uniforms and civilian clothes into a set of soft-sided luggage, Cody wandered through the ground floor rooms, admiring one last time the hand-polished millwork, high ceilings, and airy spaciousness of the house he had designed for Tessa, himself, and the children they would never conceive.

It was a grand manor, stone and steel and a steeply pitched roofline: a fine residence intended for a large family—generations of families—the children and grandchildren of Cody and Tessa. It was a dream not easily abandoned.

He and Tessa had spent many excited and pleasant hours over the architectural plan—one he had drawn in exacting detail. Seven rooms comprised the ground floor, including a master bedroom suite, which he now avoided. He paused several times at the entrance to other rooms, his eye measuring proportions, window orientation and color schemes. His gaze took in carpeting, furniture, paintings, and custom decorations. Despite his absence during construction, every detail turned out almost exactly as he imagined it would.

Commissioned through ROTC, Cody became Second Lieutenant Ballantine upon graduation from college. He completed the training required of those selected for Infantry, Airborne, and Special Forces. As customary, the Army granted Lieutenant Ballantine 30 days leave prior to his departure for Southeast Asia. It was during his time at home that he and Tessa agreed to begin construction. It might have seemed a risky proposition—building a house *before* getting married, but Cody had no doubts regarding his feelings for Tessa. Nor, it seemed, did she.

They exchanged long letters as the house took shape, sharing thoughts and ideas, happily determined to get every detail just right. Tessa sent photographs along with explanatory notes during each phase of the building process. That he might not survive a tour of duty in 1968—the most lethal twelve-months of that long, desperate war—had never entered his mind. Nearly seventeen thousand Americans would perish during that year alone, an inconceivable number he would later discover, but Cody did not doubt his survival. Was it precognition or merely the foolish confidence of youth?

An odd thought occurred as he walked through the quiet rooms: Was this magnificent house aware of his imminent departure, his self-imposed exile? Did the act of creation somehow imbue this inert object with an undetectable existence? If so, would it mourn his absence? The strange feeling passed. Without a loving family to shelter, this was merely real estate—a lifeless entity reflecting neither remorse nor happiness. The vast difference between a house and a home was never more evident to him than at that moment.

His brief house tour ended where it began, in the entry foyer where a furtive movement caught his eye. He turned toward the long, wide staircase.

Tessa stood at the top, one hand on the oak finial, the other massaging a Latin cross dangling from a golden neck chain. She wore a little makeup—faint touches of rouge, lipstick and powder—a sky-blue silk blouse, a darker blue skirt and comfortable shoes. The sight of her filled his chest with a bottomless ache, poking again the deep wound that might never heal. Their eyes met and he waited, expecting her to speak, wanting desperately to hear her voice, perhaps for the last time.

She continued fingering the cross, a nervous habit he recognized, a semaphore announcing her discomfort. Finally she said, "I'm sorry, Cody. We never had a chance. I realize that now. You deserved better."

He waited but knew she had nothing more to offer. They had traveled beyond any hope of reprieve and that knowledge resurrected a pointless resentment.

Tessa had withheld a great secret: one that could not withstand the intense intimacy of the newly wed. He wanted to ask her for an explanation but could not, for if he did, then Cody would also give voice to the despairing truth that would naturally follow. Even if she *had* told him, would he have accepted her word as truth? Might he have tried to convince her—and himself—that it did not matter? Yes, he would have done anything to keep her from leaving. But he also knew that whatever he promised or tried to do, his efforts were doomed. In the end, they would still be here, facing each other, unable to cross that vast chasm that kept them apart.

After a long moment, he turned away and reached into the side pocket of his trousers. He removed house keys and set them on the foyer table. Then, without looking back, Cody picked up his bags and closed the door on his way out, abandoning forever the possibility of spending the rest of his life with Tessa.

***

He stared at his image in the mirror.

After twenty-plus years, the pain of their separation still lingered.

There had been two others since Tessa: long, monogamous relationships with delightful, intelligent women. He had loved each one, but not enough nor in the right way, apparently.

At first, he had blamed the work: the frequent, unscheduled absences with little or no notice and long periods incommunicado. The nature of his assignments was part of it, yes; but in the end, each woman had finally realized she was competing with a phantom. Their departures saddened him, leaving a familiar void.

Years passed but memories of Tessa persisted, a lingering shadow that faded temporarily in the light of a new female companion, but never disappeared. Now, at age forty-six, he remained solitary and unattached; the not-so Perfect Spook.

Enough navel gazing, he chided himself.

He walked past the living room, picked up his keys and left the apartment. Waiting for the elevator, his thoughts turned to Cultural Minister Trushin and how best to broach the subject of Cold War shootdowns.

Once again, discomfort niggled its way into his mind, crowding out other thoughts. Danilov's claim troubled him a great deal, yet he could not determine the cause. What significant detail was he forgetting? What important fact was trying to elbow its way into his conscious mind?

The elevator pinged its arrival, breaking his concentration.

***

Late September weather in Vladivostok—frigid temperatures and increasing wind velocities—was similar to conditions in Chicago during January. Since he planned to park in the underground garage, Cody wore neither hat nor overcoat.

When he arrived however, Cody changed his mind and parked the Lada in a sheltered space behind the consulate, and then walked ten yards to the redbrick building. He exchanged a greeting with the U.S. Marine guard and passed through the rear entrance where a series of doors and passageways led to a richly carpeted, much wider corridor lined with paintings. Subdued lighting enhanced the artwork. To his left, oversized French doors opened to a brightly illuminated reception hall decorated with period furniture, heavy drapes and delicate vases bursting with fresh flowers.

He paused and scanned the gathering crowd. Classical music reached his ears, lilting chords rising above the silken murmur of polite conversation.

Cody strode past the French doors toward the main lobby fronting Pushkin Street. He stopped beside the heavy glass entryway and peered into the street. A line of black Zils, boxy Russian limousines resembling 1950s-era Packards, disgorged formally attired men escorting fashionably dressed ladies. Most he recognized from photographs, but Minister Trushin was not among them.

He returned to the reception hall.

Just beyond the entrance stood a tall, attractive brunette who welcomed each guest with a warm smile, an offered hand, and a greeting before directing them toward an adjoining group for introduction to the Consul General and his wife. He did not recognize the woman, which was not surprising. There were many on the consular staff Cody had yet to meet.

As he approached, Cody saw a momentary hint of recognition in her eyes. He searched his memory for clues to a prior meeting, but came up empty. She probably knew who he was from consular staff photos. He wondered if she also knew his actual versus his official function.

"Hi," he said. "I'm Cody Ballantine. I don't believe we've met."

"Good evening, Mr. Ballantine," she said, extending her hand. "I'm Anne Seymour." Her soft yet mellifluous voice revealed a slight accent.

Eastern boarding school, Cody thought.

Up close, her eyes were remarkable. Clear and perfectly formed, they lit her face with a quiet dignity common to well-rendered portraits. Her voice and manner evoked a faint reminder of someone, but he couldn't quite place who it might be.

"How do you do?" Cody said, taking her hand. Her grip was firm, but not intimidating. "Is Anne spelled with or without an 'e'?"

She smiled, exposing straight white teeth. "With an 'e', and pronounced Anne, not Annie." Anne Seymour's light brown eyes contained azure flecks, a strange yet tantalizingly familiar coloring.

"Then it's Cody, not Mr. Ballantine."

Anne leaned toward him and touched his arm lightly, her voice barely above a whisper. "I've heard all about you," she murmured. "You're the resident spook. Am I supposed to know that?"

He caught the floral scent of scandalously expensive perfume, probably Chanel, and felt something more. Her brief touch, friendly but not intimate, aroused feelings he'd nearly forgotten; a hesitant stirring like one emerging from deep slumber.

"No, you shouldn't know that," he managed to say. "I may have to take you into custody." With effort, Cody kept his voice at a normal pitch.

The covert nature of his work was certainly confidential. On the other hand, consulates—and most embassies—were notorious rumor factories. Like many closed societies, secrets were nearly impossible to keep. Did everyone also know about his Bosnian fiasco? That was certainly possible.

"And your job is?" He left the sentence unfinished.

"I am Director of Protocol. Mr. Zane's general gofer."

Cody turned away for a moment and studied the room. Ornate furnishings brought to mind the decadent elegance of Tsarist Russia.

"Is the décor your idea?"

"Mostly, but I had help."

"It looks very nice."

"Thank you. The style is a bit too First Empire for me, but our host country seems to prefer French-inspired anything, including drapes, brocade, and sixteenth century tapestries."

"And classical music," he added, nodding toward the string ensemble playing from a raised dais in one corner of the room.

"Yes, of course, but not Debussy or Bizet. Tonight's music is courtesy of Russian composers. I hope you like Tchaikovsky, Glinka, and Stravinsky."

"What? No Prokofiev?"

Their eyes met and Cody saw an expression he couldn't quite decipher. Although he was reasonably sure they had never met, she continued to remind him of someone and the nagging sense of familiarity was beginning to bother him.

"I don't think so," she replied. "Mr. Zane wants to keep our first official reception low key."

"And Prokofiev might have us dancing like ill-bred Cossacks, right?"

She laughed, a pleasant sound bubbling from deep in her throat. "Perhaps, but not tonight. Instead, we observe tradition: open with the Polonaise and close with the Mazurka." She extended her hand. "I enjoyed our conversation, Mr. Ballantine…Cody. Now I must see to our guests. Perhaps we can chat again, later?"

He wanted to check for a wedding ring, but couldn't without being obvious. "I look forward to it."

Anne Seymour glided away and melted into the crowd.

Cody took a minute to redirect his thoughts, and then walked deeper into the room. Waiters offered champagne and *hors d'oeuvre* from gleaming silver trays. He took a crystal flute and sipped the sparkling wine. Although not an expert, Cody assumed it was Dom Perignon. Whittier Zane would serve only the best: champagne from Moet et Chandon and beluga caviar from the Caspian Sea, all compliments of American taxpayers.

While Cody appreciated the value of diplomacy—honest discourse was always preferable to waging war—he also believed no amount of genteel bullshit could overcome inbred philosophical, cultural, and religious differences. Despite our practiced sophistication, he mused, we are hardly more than tribes—clannish gatherings of like-minded individuals or ethnic clusters, unwitting slaves to ancient social mechanisms and learned hatreds we have yet to fully understand let alone outgrow. Unbidden images from a Bosnian village tumbled into his mind. He pushed them away and forced himself to study the consulate's guests.

The room buzzed with subdued banter, mostly in Russian; idle chitchat about politics, art, and entertainment. He stopped now and then to listen, offering polite commentary when appropriate but preferring to remain on the periphery. As he strolled among the gathering, Cody shifted his gaze, noting the presence of each person. Consul General and Mrs. Whittier Zane—Ken and Barbie in their golden years—conversed with a Russian functionary and his lady companion, their lips forming words he could not quite discern.

Colonel Butler and his attentive blonde wife stood elbow to elbow with a small circle of Russian diplomats. Despite the formality permeating the room, everyone seemed to be enjoying each other's company.

The only off-key note, if one paid attention to such things, was the absence of the U.S. Ambassador and his entourage. That worthy gentleman had chosen to remain in Spaso House, the ramshackle yellow mansion that served as his official Moscow residence. It wasn't exactly a snub, given the great distance, but clear indication that dreary, provincial Vladivostok held little interest for those residing in European Russia.

Cody checked his Breitling. Nearly forty minutes had passed since he entered the reception area. The Cultural Minister was nowhere in sight.

Anne Seymour stood near the rear doorway talking with a waiter, a middle-aged Russian wearing a short white jacket over black trousers. She appeared calm and the waiter did not seem particularly distressed. Would she know if Trushin cancelled? Probably. Cody waited, politely out of earshot.

The Russian bowed slightly and disappeared through the doorway.

"Nothing amiss, I hope," Cody said as he approached.

She turned. "Not really. Yegor had a question regarding dinner arrangements. Are you enjoying yourself?"

"Not so much."

"Oh?" A tiny frown skipped across her face.

"It's a bit too proper."

He saw that odd expression again; the one he could not decipher. Then she said, "You don't like formal occasions?"

"Not really."

"May I ask why?"

He shrugged. "I'm not sure. Maybe it's the pretension. On the other hand, it's nice to see everyone all dressed up; especially the ladies, who seem to enjoy that sort of thing."

"Yes, we do. However, it seems most men prefer casual attire, so I think I understand your discomfort. Nevertheless, formality is often necessary, like tonight, for example. This is the consulate's first social event. Our guests and we are strangers. Formal attire, to some extent, makes everyone appear similar. It's like sharing a common uniform."

"You may have a point."

She smiled. "Give it time. Eventually, good food and ample quantities of champagne will ease the tension."

"Does that mean you've changed your mind about Cossack dancing?"

She laughed and her face glowed. "It might be worth it, just to see if you could."

Cody suddenly realized he liked Anne Seymour—very much. The feeling came without warning and he felt unsure of himself, a rare sensation, troubling and unpleasant.

She smiled and touched his arm again, a brief and warmly comforting gesture. "Relax. I was only joking."

Had she detected his unease? "That's a relief," he said, recovering his composure. He looked away, avoiding her eyes; afraid he would lose himself in their liquid depths. "Has everyone arrived?"

She followed his gaze. "I believe so. Minister Trushin might be late, but…well, here he is now."

The Honorable Aleksandr Petrovich Trushin, easily recognized by thick, fashionably long silver hair, strode into the reception hall like a tall, jovial conqueror. He was nearly seventy but Trushin, his posture militarily erect, radiated youthful vigor. An impressive array of full-size medals hung from his tuxedo in neat, colorful rows. The retired Air Force colonel turned politician escorted an attractive, much younger woman.

The Whittier Zanes approached the Minister and his female guest. The two men shook hands and then exchanged a traditional cheek-to-cheek greeting; left, right, left. Cody concealed his amusement. Zane appeared uncomfortable with public displays of affection. Nevertheless, he exhibited polite enthusiasm, more so it seemed when bussing the young woman.

"Have you met the Cultural Minister?" Cody asked.

"Yes, I have. As a matter of fact, it was he who suggested the decorating theme you seem to like."

"Really? That *is* a surprise. Trushin's an old-line communist. One would think French-tinged Tsarist décor would be anathema to someone like him."

Anne turned and he couldn't avoid looking into her eyes.

"People are seldom what they appear. That's why they're so interesting." She sipped champagne, holding the crystal flute delicately with both hands, a gesture Cody found incredibly feminine.

She wore one ring, a sapphire on her right hand. A larger sapphire surrounded by tiny diamonds hung from a pendant suspended from a gold chain around her neck. Delicate earrings, holding smaller stones, completed the exquisitely matched set.

It seemed she was unmarried and unengaged. Although Cody felt pleasantly relieved, a third possibility dampened his optimism.

What had she just said? *People are seldom what they appear.* A veiled clue, perhaps? She could be unmarried and unengaged, but living with someone; a suitably refined diplomatic type no doubt, a prospect Cody reluctantly conceded.

However, wistfully silent wondering was not part of his character. He said, "May I ask a personal question?"

A mischievous look danced across her face. "You may ask, but I reserve the right not to answer."

"Fair enough." He paused for a moment, searching for the right words. "Do you have a significant other?"

A faint wrinkle marred her smooth brow. "Did you actually say *significant other*?"

"Well, yes, but you know what I mean. Husband, fiancé, or a large, ill-tempered boyfriend?"

The friendly look cooled, matching the tone of her voice. "What makes you believe I would tolerate the company of an ill-tempered lout?"

"You wouldn't. It was a poor attempt at humor."

For a moment, Cody feared he might have lost whatever rapport they had established, but then a little warmth returned to

Anne's face and her voice softened. "I thought as much. Besides, you don't impress me as one easily intimidated by an ill-tempered lout."

Cody, unable to think of an appropriate response, said, "And the answer to my question is?"

She fingered the rim of the champagne flute for a moment, her eyes never leaving his. Cody felt the intensity of her scrutiny, as though she had placed his worth on a gigantic scale, the balance bar teetering first one way and then the other, slowly reaching equilibrium with whatever fate her judgment might reveal.

Finally, she said, "None of the above."

"I am very glad to hear that. Would you consider having dinner with me sometime next week?"

Her questioning look continued. "Are you married, Mr. Ballantine?"

The reversion to 'Mr. Ballantine' troubled him. It was a clear sign they were a long way from where he wanted them to be. He said, "I am not married, engaged, nor romantically encumbered. And please, it's 'Cody'."

Anne looked away, her gaze roaming across the reception hall. "I should get back to our guests."

Cody felt deflated, his enthusiasm hissing away like air from a leaky balloon. He knew what would come next, but managed to keep his voice cordial. "Yes, I understand."

She turned and faced him again. "Let me think about it. Call me next week and we'll see."

It was not the response he expected. She hadn't turned him down cold—not yet, anyway. "I'll do that."

"Until then." She drifted into the crowd, leaving behind a tantalizing aroma of spring flowers.

Cody took a deep swallow of champagne. What began as a promising possibility had quickly faded, leaving him perplexed and dispirited by the unexpected change in her attitude. He sighed, and once again allowed time for his thoughts to refocus.

A moment later, his disappointment fully submerged, he moved toward Minister Trushin, approaching indirectly, pausing several times to chat with people he knew. As Cody drew near, their eyes met and the Minister waved him closer.

"Ah, just in time." Trushin's voice boomed with good-humored enthusiasm. "I need a strongly biased opinion from another soldier."

"Good evening, Minister Trushin." They greeted each other Russian style and Trushin introduced Cody to Irina, the minister's lovely but silent companion.

"I assume you are acquainted with the Consul General and his beautiful wife?" Trushin said with a smile.

"Yes, we may have spoken once or twice." Cody shook hands with Zane and exchanged air-kisses with Laura.

"I was explaining our mutual failures," Trushin said to Cody. "Yours in Vietnam and ours in Afghanistan."

"How so?"

"Both, I believe, were political not military disasters. Our respective politicians were either unwilling or unable to establish and cultivate a firm national resolve. When such conditions prevail, the military mission, no matter how well planned or valiantly pursued, is doomed. Do you agree?"

Cody responded with what he believed was the truth. "Yes, I do. Both the North Vietnamese and Afghan Mujahideen succeeded because they captured and, most importantly, retained the good will and fighting spirit of their respective peoples.

"On the other hand, American political leaders blundered about without any clear idea of what they were doing. In the end, their constituents recognized incompetence and, appalled by the cost in lives, withdrew support."

Cody did not mention the myriad Russian atrocities inflicted upon the civilian population, savagery that fueled rather than quelled Afghan resistance. Nor did he comment upon the absurd arrogance of simpletons: American leaders, those elected and appointed, whose profound ignorance of military strategy and Asian history seemed limitless.

"Exactly so!" Trushin echoed. "And that allowed rebel political movements to prevail despite having inferior military forces.

The lesson is clear: absence of political resolve renders the soldier's effort moot."

Zane bowed good naturedly, "I yield to your argument, Mr. Minister. Now, if you'll excuse us, we shall leave you two to share war stories." The Consul General left them, his wife in tow.

Trushin sipped champagne and then eyed the delicate flute for a long moment, his expression a mixture of disdain and weary amusement. He turned to Cody. "War stories and Dom Perignon do not mix well, I fear. It may even be a sacrilege."

Had the aging Russian warrior read his mind? Zane had probably meant well, but his words came out wrong. One does not celebrate tragic wars and dead comrades with happy smiles and champagne. Cody said, "Yes, I agree. Perhaps another time?"

"An excellent suggestion. Do you know the Sapernaya bathhouse?"

"The gray building near the funicular?"

"Yes. Meet me there tomorrow morning at eleven o'clock. We will take steam together, talk of lost wars, and then toast our fallen comrades properly—with vodka. Afterwards, you may buy our lunch."

Trushin's suggestion was a good one. Ministers often discussed political and cultural issues with foreigners. Meeting an American at a public *banya*, especially during the initial phase of consular operations, would arouse little suspicion. And, with a little subtle prodding from Cody, it might provide a good opportunity for the retired Russian Air Force colonel to reminisce about the bad old days of the Cold War.

"I will be there," Cody said.

Trushin bowed slightly, his silver hair glittering beneath subdued lighting. "It is done then. Good. *Dos vadanya, tovarisch.*"

The Minister took Irina's elbow and drifted away, blending easily into the gathering.

Chapter 6

At ten-thirty, the following morning Cody passed through the consulate's glass doors, stepped onto the sidewalk, turned right and walked down Pushkin Street toward the funicular, Vladivostok's inclined railway station. A cold breeze tugged at his overcoat.

The Sapernaya bathhouse stood atop Eagle's Nest, the highest point in downtown Vladivostok. Getting there by car or taxi involved a slow roundabout drive up numerous hills. Alternatively, the cable-driven tram offered a faster, more direct route, ascending nearly six hundred feet in less than three minutes.

Cody's walk took him past several wounded buildings, their 19th century elegance sullied by age, indifference, and too much fractured stucco bleeding rust-tainted lime. Despite its unique European-style architecture, Vladivostok reflected the dingy exhaustion of an Appalachian mill town, its bustling glory days a dwindling memory. The former Soviet Union had spent little to improve civilian infrastructure and the result of decades-long neglect sprawled across the city like a frowzy cloak.

Whittier Zane, ever the diplomatic optimist, displayed great enthusiasm for the New Russia. He believed the end of the Cold War held great promise for Vladivostok. The port city and its magnificent harbor would become a magnet for savvy investors willing to explore the region's vast reservoir of natural resources.

Cody didn't think so. Without a major change in social attitudes and physical appearance, the world's businessmen would shun this polluted, crime-ridden city. Instead, they would funnel some of their wealth to Tokyo and Seoul, glittering national capitals anchored within bustling free market democracies. That was unfortunate. The long-suffering Russian people, whom Cody admired and respected, deserved a better deal.

He crossed the street near the Museum of the Pacific Fleet. The museum, converted to government use during Josef Stalin's reign, was once St. Paul's Lutheran Church, its demise a secular fate shared equally by church, mosque, and synagogue. Two granite sculptures representing *Shi-Tszy*, Manchuria's mythical lions, guarded the main entrance to the cable car station.

Ten minutes later the funicular eased to a stop. Cody stepped onto the platform and paused to admire the view. The city's terraced hillsides and dated buildings brought to mind San Francisco postcards from the 1950s. Boxy, Stalin-era structures, many festooned with spidery television antennas, swept down toward Golden Horn Bay. A brooding shroud carpeted much of the distant landscape. Only the elongated hump of the Egersheld Peninsula protruded above the fog and pollution, its blurred image reminiscent of an Impressionist rendering.

His panoramic vantage point high above the city filled Cody with a sense of omnipotence. He felt like a divine figure looming above the world, regally poised between vast layers of pale sky and slate blue earth, a modern Zeus reclaiming sovereignty over his mortal subjects who had lost their way. If given the power, would he gently nudge them back onto the path from which they strayed, or should he let them muddle along, stumbling into each other in high weeds? He was grateful the decision was not his to make.

Nearby, a church bell tolled the hour.

***

Minister Trushin, nude except for a white towel wrapped around his trim middle, tilted a copper dipper and poured warm water over a pile of hot rocks. A roiling cloud of vapor rose from the steamy sizzle. He hung the dipper beside the water bucket and joined Cody, who slouched on a wooden bench, his butt cushioned by a double layer of towels.

"Americans pretend at health," Trushin said, stroking himself with *venik*, a bundle of leafy birch twigs soaked in hot water, "but your people do not understand or appreciate the benefits of a good steam."

Cody took a deep breath before responding. "Maybe so, but sometimes a beneficial thing can be overdone." Perspiration gushed from every pore and it was difficult to fill his lungs completely.

"Use the *venik*," Trushin suggested. "The smell of fresh birch will clear your head."

Cody nodded and stroked his back and chest. It seemed to help.

"Is this too hot, Cody Wilhelmovich?"

Although they had known each other for several months, the Russian's not quite accurate use of the patronymic familiar was unexpected. Cody took it as a positive sign. "It's a bit warmer than I'm accustomed to," he admitted.

In fact, the *parilka*—steam room—was a hell of a lot warmer than he expected. Cody felt his body melting away, the toned muscles weakening with each passing minute. Before too much longer, he fretted, I'll be nothing more than two eyeballs staring up from a puddle of briny goo.

"You have become too used to American saunas," Trushin scoffed. "They are a weak substitute for a real steam."

Cody decided not to waste energy on a reply. Instead, he took a long drink from a water bottle.

"Ten more minutes," Trushin said. "Then we swim."

The bathhouse, contrary to the growing American trend of gender neutrality in almost everything, clung stubbornly to old world custom. Its men-only membership policy was strictly enforced—wisely, it seemed. Cody had not swum nude since his pre-teen days at the local YMCA, a practice American society had long since abandoned. He had always wondered if young ladies at the YWCA also swam in the nude. When he finally got the courage to ask, said young ladies had remained smugly mum on the subject.

The cold water shocked and refreshed his overheated body. Cody swam the length of the Olympic-size pool four times, pulling water aside with easy, powerful strokes. He emerged surprisingly rejuvenated, slipped into a terrycloth robe and joined Trushin at a poolside table.

"You swim well," the Russian said.

"Thank you. I learned at an early age."

Trushin poured mineral water into a clean glass and slid it towards Cody. "Here, drink."

He gulped it down and Trushin refilled the glass.

"Just what I needed," Cody admitted.

So far, their conversation was much like that in the steam room—casual and undirected—idle chatter between two old friends. Trushin had not broached the subject of Russia's war in Afghanistan nor had Cody volunteered anything regarding his service with the U.S. Army. For him, Vietnam was totally void of pleasant memories. Besides, his primary interest lay in Trushin's earlier experiences, those that occurred prior to Vietnam and Afghanistan. Cody wanted to explore the Russian's military service during the 1950s.

He decided to approach the topic indirectly. "When did you first join the Soviet Air Force?"

"In 1942. I was eighteen years old. My father was a major in the 12th Guards Tank Regiment. He and my mother were quite disturbed when I left university."

"I understand you became a double ace before you turned twenty."

"Yes, but most of my early victories were easy. The Nazi Heinkel bomber was no match for the Yak-3 fighter. The Messerschmitt however, was a very good dog-fighter and many of the Nazi pilots were highly skilled. While it is true I claimed ten enemy planes at an early age, I was also shot down three times before my twentieth birthday."

"I didn't know that. You were lucky to survive."

"Every combat soldier who survives war is lucky."

"True, but you may have been luckier than most. At war's end, you were officially credited with thirty-seven kills."

"It was really thirty-nine," Trushin said. "Two were disallowed. No clear evidence, they said."

"I will accept your count, Aleksandr Petrovich."

The old Russian smiled. "Thank you, *tovarisch*."

Cody sipped mineral water. He was getting close to the right time period but still chose to proceed slowly. Despite Trushin's clandestine role as a newly recruited but well-compensated informant, in Cody's mind the old colonel remained somewhat of a question mark. Although Trushin had provided background information on several local officials, benign stuff for the most part, Cody was not sure how far the Russian would go. On the other hand, Trushin might be playing him as well, looking for an opportunity to cause mischief for his young American rival.

Cody said, "What about after the war? Did you return to school?"

"*Da*. I attended Frunze Military Academy, near Moscow. After graduation and more training, I went to one of the new jet fighter regiments." Trushin smiled, as though reminded of a pleasant memory. "That was an exciting time for a young flyer."

"I'm sure it was. It's common knowledge that many Soviet pilots flew their MiG-15 jets against Americans during the Korean War. Were you among them?"

Trushin frowned. "Sadly, no. But like a good soldier I volunteered, along with many others." He sighed. "Only a few were accepted. All were veteran pilots, seasoned aviators much older than me."

Cody—eager to push the discussion into the post-Korean War era—paused, hoping Trushin would elaborate. However, the Minister seemed relaxed and not particularly interested in embellishing his achievements. How would the old man respond if Cody raised the issue of Cold War incursions into Soviet territory by American reconnaissance planes? There was one way to find out.

He swallowed more water and set the glass down. "I understand your enthusiasm to test yourself in those new fighters. It was a natural reaction, but political reality often dictates how we behave. During the Cold War, our two countries did not always act responsibly."

As he had hoped, Trushin rose to the baited question. "What you say is true, but your conduct was much worse than ours."

Cody suppressed growing anticipation. "How so, Aleksandr Petrovich?"

"You invaded my country many times. We never invaded America."

"By invasion, do you mean Powers and the U-2 flight?"

"Yes, Gary Powers the CIA spy pilot, of course. But there were also many other incidents."

"Really? Everyone remembers the U-2 affair. I've also heard about one or two other reconnaissance planes we lost over the Baltic, in international waters."

"Only one or two? In international waters?" Trushin waved a hand dismissively. "Bah! There were many transgressions, Cody Wilhelmovich. I was a young captain stationed at Nikolayevka. Frequent provocations occurred. Our orders were clear: Intercept and direct American intruders to land at the nearest airdrome. If they refused, shoot them down." He frowned and shook his head. "Naturally, the Americans refused to comply with our legitimate demand, so we attacked. Your big, swept-wing jets were very fast and difficult to hit, but we downed several. The older, propeller-driven planes were easy targets."

Cody noted Trushin's use of the collective 'we attacked' and chose not to ask whether the old aviator had personally shot down American planes. It wouldn't add much to the discussion and might well cause Trushin to become defensive. Instead, he asked what he hoped was a logical question. "What happened to the American air crews?"

"Most died in crashes. We returned all recovered bodies to American officials. Those who parachuted and survived were detained, then released or exchanged for political prisoners."

"Like the Powers exchange, one spy for another."

"Exactly so. But under International Law, such men could have been shot as spies or imprisoned for life."

Cody edged onto sensitive ground. "Did such things actually happen?"

Trushin didn't seem upset by the question. "I have no personal knowledge of those things, but in Soviet Russia, who can say for sure what did or did not occur?"

"But they were soldiers—soldiers not much different than you and me," Cody protested.

"No, not like us, *tovarisch*. They were criminals, invaders of a sovereign, peaceful nation."

"I do not agree, Aleksandr Petrovich. In war, hot or cold, there are always exceptions."

Trushin shrugged. "Perhaps. But we Russians were not as bad as you imagined, nor were you Americans as noble as you believed."

That wasn't exactly how Cody saw it. Although the U.S. was not blameless regarding certain unsavory activities, America did not condemn twenty millions of her citizens to death or a lifetime of slave labor in Siberian work camps. However, raising that issue would serve no purpose other than alienating a potential information source. Instead, he chose to weasel word his response.

"National goals and perspectives tend to be self-justifying. I concede that point; however, every country finds a way to justify questionable behavior."

Trushin merely shrugged. It was time to change the subject.

Cody's attention shifted to the pool and adjoining steam room. "I like this place," he said, admiring the glistening marble columns, Gothic arches, and Greek-inspired statuary. "Thank you for inviting me," he added, savoring the dank intimacy and muted echoes from a dozen quiet conversations.

"It was my pleasure to do so. I will leave notice that you are my guest, to be admitted at any time."

"That is very kind of you, but isn't that risky?"

The old man snorted in derision. "Risky? Vladivostok lies on the far end of the world. In Yeltsin's Russia, we might as well be on the moon. The KGB and MVD may not be dead, but most of the old guard is doing other things—bad things—for much more money. Those who remain here have little interest in civil affairs."

Cody didn't quite believe the latter, but he nodded.

Trushin rose, tightened the robe's belt and jammed his hands into floppy side pockets. "You may now repay my kindness, Cody Wilhelmovich, with a small lunch and a large vodka…or two."

"It will be my pleasure."

As they made their way toward the locker room, Cody again pondered the legitimacy of Andrei Danilov's unusual claim. In the hostile political atmosphere prevalent forty years ago, prolonged imprisonment for an unlucky few captives was more than possible; it was, in fact, part of the historical record. Given Russia's incredibly vast physical geography, much of it desolate and uninhabited, keeping certain prisoners far from public view would not be difficult.

However, Cody reminded himself, secret confinement in a remote location did not fully explain how Danilov managed to stay alive, and apparently well, for nearly four decades. There was much more to that story, and Cody intended to discover every detail, with or without Washington's permission. It was an exercise he did not relish, akin to walking blindfolded through a pasture—an unfamiliar field covered with freshly deposited cow pies.

Should he misstep, a shoe full of crap would be the least of his problems.

Chapter 7

After thinking about it for a day or so, Cody finally decided to call Anne Seymour on Tuesday, which happened to be today. Their last conversation the previous Saturday evening had ended on a not-very-promising 'let me think about it' note, so he did not want to appear too eager. With that on his mind, he reached for the telephone at the precise moment it buzzed.

"Yes, Phyllis?"

"Angela on line two."

He punched the flashing button. "This is Cody."

"Hi, Mr. Ballantine. Could you come up here, please? Mr. Zane said it was important."

"I'll be right there."

A few minutes later Cody joined Colonel Butler in the Consul General's office. At Zane's wave-in invitation, he took a chair next to Butler at a circular conference table in one corner of the spacious office.

"Sorry for the short notice, gentlemen," Zane began, "but I just spoke with Moscow about the Danilov business."

"Already?" Butler's surprise was evident. "I thought confirmation would take a bit longer."

"So did I," Cody admitted.

The expression on Zane's face was difficult to read but Cody sensed the consul general's apprehension. The yellow caution light clicked on once more, flashing a warning that Cody could no longer ignore. Damn it, what was bothering him about Danilov's claim?

"It is not confirmation," Zane said.

Cody's uneasy feeling increased. "Then it must be refutation. Is Danilov an imposter?"

Zane shook his head. "No one suggested that, at least not yet, but Moscow believes we may encounter difficulty verifying Mr. Danilov's claim to American citizenship."

Cody leaned forward. "What sort of difficulty?"

"Let me start at the beginning," the Consul General said. "First, a shootdown did indeed occur on August 3, 1954; this you already know. Second, a U.S. air defense radar station in Japan lost track of the aircraft at the exact location Danilov said it went down."

"So far, so good," Butler muttered.

"Maybe, maybe not," Cody said. "After forty years, that information is hardly a secret." He turned to Zane. "There's more, isn't there?"

"I'm afraid so. An American destroyer rescued one survivor, the navigator. Three days later, two bodies washed ashore on Askold Island. The Soviets notified U.S. authorities and returned the dead airmen shortly thereafter."

"I presume the other eleven crew members were listed as missing," Cody said.

"That is correct."

"Did the Air Force provide a crew list?"

Zane frowned. "Yes and no."

"What does that mean?" Butler said.

"Of the eleven missing crewmembers, six are listed by name, rank and serial number. The word 'REDLINED' appears five times. Captain Andrew G. Thompson is not among those identified by name."

"Then I presume Captain Thompson's name was among those redlined. Does that mean the Air Force is hiding something?" Cody asked.

"I don't think so. It's likely they sent the original 1954 crew list, concealing the identities of certain aircrew members, but it doesn't matter. We filed an official protest with the Soviet Union. Our note contained the names of all fourteen aviators, along with each man's rank and serial number."

"Are we getting a copy of that note?"

"Of course."

"Can you say when?"

"It may take a day or two. Anyway, the Air Force listed the remaining crew as 'missing, unaccounted for and probably lost' but they also kept the file open for seven years. In 1961, the missing eleven, including Captain Thompson, were declared dead and their individual files transferred to the National Personnel Records Center in St. Louis."

The yellow caution light inside Cody's head stopped flashing; it now glowed like a high intensity beam. When Zane mentioned the St. Louis Records Center, realization finally dawned, just as Cody knew it would. He sighed, wondering why such an important historical fact had remained beyond his recollection. "It was the fire," he announced.

Butler's confusion was evident. "What fire?"

Zane picked up a letter. "I'll read what Moscow sent. Quote. On July 12, 1973, a fire of unknown origin occurred at the St. Louis Records Center. The blaze destroyed seventy-five percent of the records for Air Force personnel with surnames from 'Hubbard' through 'Z'. Military records for officers and enlisted personnel discharged between September 25, 1947 and January 1, 1964 were lost. End Quote." Zane looked up. "The fax goes on to say that nearly eighty percent of Army personnel files were also destroyed. All told, approximately eighteen million individual military service records went up in smoke."

Cody desperately wanted a cigarette but suppressed the urge. After a moment, the craving subsided.

At the consulate's official ribbon-cutting ceremony, Zane—in a trendy and wholly out-of-character pronouncement—had declared the building a smoke free workplace. Smokers, Russian visitors excepted, could satisfy their cravings only at designated outdoor areas. Zane's No Smoking edict strongly reinforced Cody's determination to kick the habit. Going outside the office for a nicotine fix was out of the question, the equivalent to a public admission of weakness. Rather than acknowledging the obvious health benefits, he considered Zane's policy a challenge, one he intended to meet head on.

Cody said, "What happens now?"

"It sounds like we're dead in the water," Butler suggested.

"Not necessarily," Zane replied. "Before the fire, St. Louis sent millions of medical records to the Department of Veterans Affairs on loan. I don't know why that happened, but there is a slight chance Thompson's files might be among them."

"Were the original medical files loaned or were copies sent?" Cody asked.

"Loaned, I'm afraid. No copies were made."

"Then his records are probably gone. If they considered Thompson dead, why would anyone send his medical file to the VA in the first place?"

"I don't know," Zane admitted. "But it's possible St. Louis sent the records *en masse*."

"Possible, but highly unlikely," Cody said. "The probability of a dead veteran's records making it to the VA is miniscule."

Butler leaned forward, as though to make a point: "There is, however, another avenue we should explore. If Captain Thompson held a security clearance—and I presume he did—then his fingerprints might be on file with the OSI."

"OSI? Refresh my memory," Zane said.

"The Air Force's investigating authority is the Office of Special Investigations. It's the equivalent to the Army's Criminal Investigation Division or the Navy's NCIS. Among other things, the OSI coordinates background checks on individuals whose duties may require access to classified material."

"Do they keep copies, or is everything sent back to the requesting command?" Zane asked.

Butler shrugged. "I don't know."

Zane scanned the fax. "The OSI isn't mentioned specifically, but it's worth passing on to Moscow. Any other suggestions?"

Cody shook his head.

A few blocks down Pushkin Street, the bells of St. Nikolai's Cathedral tolled the hour. From habit, Cody verified the time: four o'clock. He said, "Meanwhile, what does Moscow suggest we do about Danilov?"

Zane set the fax aside and tapped his fingernails on the table. After several drum rolls he paused and said, "Danilov is supposed to return here Friday, three days from today. Between now and then we should prepare a list of questions, a script if you will, to extract as much personal information from him as possible."

"A debriefing?" Cody said.

"Not exactly. As I understand your term for 'debriefing', several interrogators are involved. One asks questions while others listen and observe, keeping out of sight. Then, sometime later, the observers ask the same questions, phrased differently, or different questions based on the subject's previous answers, taking note of inconsistencies or identically worded phrases. Is that correct?"

"More or less."

"I don't think we have time for that."

"So we just ask questions and hope for the best?"

"We will, of course, verify his answers." Zane shifted his attention to the attaché. "Robert, please develop questions relating to the military: unit assignments, commanding officers, friends; things like that." He turned and addressed Cody. "Your agency should work with the FBI and concentrate on the civilian side: hometown, schools attended, etcetera." He paused and offered a thin smile. "The devil, as they say, is in the details. Let's meet back here tomorrow to finalize our script. We can use Thursday to resolve open issues." He paused, his eyes moving first to Butler, then to Cody. "Do either of you have questions?"

The attaché shook his head slightly.

"Do we treat Danilov as hostile or friendly?" Cody asked.

Zane seemed to ponder the question, then he said, "Let's try for pleasantly neutral. I would prefer we give Danilov the benefit of any doubts we might harbor, at least in the beginning."

"I think that's reasonable," Butler offered.

Cody held his tongue. A career-conscious graduate of the Air Force Academy could afford to be reasonable, as could a close-to-retirement Consul General.

Colonel Butler's history and character were still question marks. Cody had not yet received an answer to his request for the attaché's personal file. On the other hand, Zane's professional tendencies were no doubt unchangeable as though deeply etched in granite. Career government bureaucrats had difficulty resolving unconventional issues. Lack of precedent or clearly defined guidelines often rendered them impotent when out-of-the-ordinary situations arose, especially when the probability of upsetting the status quo increased beyond mere chance and approached certainty. Sticking ones neck out was not a character trait of those who sought high office in America's Foreign Service.

And now, Cody reminded himself, was not the best time to roil diplomatic waters. His shaky professional situation notwithstanding, the American electorate would be choosing a president in less than six weeks. Ross Perot, a Texas billionaire and third party candidate, was drawing conservative support away from President Bush. Already down in the polls, anything remotely controversial might further erode the President's reelection chances. Although Cody never let politics affect his work or judgment, the same might not hold true for someone in Whittier Zane's position.

Nevertheless, Cody felt compelled to share information about the fire.

"I don't mean to poison the well, but there is something both of you should know," he began.

Butler looked interested but noncommittal. Zane merely raised an eyebrow.

"The Records Center fire occurred shortly after I joined the Agency. More than a few analysts believed it was the work of saboteurs. Absent our capability to verify military service, the thinking went, anybody could claim veteran status. It presented a major opportunity for illegals to pad their background stories."

Zane said, "By *illegals*, I presume you mean covert operators? Spies?"

"I'm afraid so. Such individuals would also receive veteran's preference when applying for government positions."

Butler looked puzzled. "What does that have to do with Danilov?"

"Maybe a little, maybe a lot. As you know, Boris Yeltsin and the reformers have stripped the KGB of authority. Many former KGB employees, agents and analysts from all levels, have left the government, either voluntarily or otherwise. Some found legitimate work elsewhere but the majority gravitated toward organized crime. Others became free-lance operatives, offering their services to anyone willing to pay the rent."

"What are you trying to say, Cody?" Zane asked, once again drumming his fingers on the table.

"Only this: Danilov might be ex-KGB or MVD; perhaps he interrogated the *real* Captain Andrew Thompson, maybe in prison or a work camp. Danilov is an accomplished linguist. He could have read about the Records Center fire in a U.S. newspaper. He probably knows we could never verify his identity. So, the worst-case scenario for Danilov is exposure as a fraud. So what? The guy vanishes and we never hear from him again."

Zane said, "It sounds like you're suggesting Danilov might be nothing more than an imposter looking for a free ticket to the United States."

"Or," Butler added, "more likely a criminal opportunist attempting to collect forty years back pay and a military pension."

"It's way too early to discount anything," Cody said. "We should certainly keep those possibilities in mind, but let's not prejudge the man. Absent a formal debriefing, one without hostile interrogators, our questions must focus on details only Captain Thompson would know: people and specific events whose existence we can easily verify."

Butler said, "Just a moment, Cody. If Danilov's an imposter, then what happened to the real Captain Thompson?"

"Who can say? He might have died in captivity, from wounds perhaps. Maybe he was executed as a spy and then buried in an unmarked grave."

The Gamov Incident

"Executed? Is that possible?" Butler's blue eyes reflected discomfort, perhaps disbelief.

"Yes, I believe so. Forty years ago, our two governments despised and distrusted each other intensely. American submarines lay hidden within missile range and long-range B-52 bombers, armed with nukes, flew station alert just outside Soviet territory. The Soviets deployed similar forces. Any one of a dozen hotspots—Berlin, Korea, or Taiwan for instance, could have easily triggered a nuclear exchange. It's a miracle we didn't blow each other away. Given that overtly hostile political climate, the secret execution or imprisonment of U.S. servicemen is not difficult to imagine."

Butler rubbed his chin and frowned slightly. "I suppose it could have happened that way."

"The fact is," Zane admitted, "If Danilov is an imposter, we may never know what really happened to Captain Thompson."

"Or to the other missing crewmen," Butler added.

Cody shifted his gaze from the attaché back to the Consul General. "Exactly. And not knowing their fate, leaving questions unanswered and wholly unresolved, might well be the end result of this entire affair."

No one spoke for a long moment. Then Butler muttered, "That sucks."

Indeed it did.

Chapter 8

Cody returned to his office, plopped into a high-back chair and swiveled toward the window. Beyond the glass pane, navigation lights glittered from dozens of ships: pleasure craft, fishing trawlers, and commercial vessels from a dozen countries plied the crowded bay. Almost every one carried illicit cargo of some kind: goods needed to sustain Vladivostok's flourishing black market economy. The busy harbor brought to mind the official rather than the punitive reason his superiors at Langley sent him here.

With the old Soviet Union moribund and no longer perceived as a major threat to America's security, the Agency had shifted its resources elsewhere. Without missing a beat, the Company switched its primary focus from Russia to China. Eyes and ears were re-tasked to gather intelligence about our newest old adversary.

Vladivostok, her population a mixture of Japanese, Korean, and Chinese residents sprinkled among the ethnic Russian majority, lay fewer than a hundred kilometers from the Chinese border. It was an ideal location from which to recruit, train and then dispatch covert operatives to the communist mainland.

That was the real reason for his posting to Siberia, or so went the story they fed him. It had little or nothing to do with how badly he had screwed up his previous assignment. In fact, his boss added, this was a ground floor opportunity to establish a vital intelligence network. The official tale, at best, contained an ounce of truth nestled within an odious pound of bureaucratic bullshit.

Cody had few illusions about why he had ended up in Vladivostok; or, more importantly, his prospects for meaningful success. Beijing was a thousand miles to the west. Any intelligence he managed to gather would be low-grade social and economic data: nice to have background material, but very little of military or political significance.

Nevertheless, if the Danilov situation consumed too much of his time, then the timetable established by Langley for recruiting local agents might be jeopardized. Agency bureaucrats, enamored of schedules and statistics, expected him to recruit and deploy 'x' new agents by 'y' date. Failure to meet or closely adhere to that arbitrary and meaningless calendar was a sure way to instigate an official inquiry, a thinly disguised witch-hunt followed by premature retirement or further banishment to an even more remote location. He envisioned his next assignment: Chief of Station, Antarctica.

Cody turned the problem over in his mind, examining options from different perspectives. He finally decided to make the only two recommendations that made sense to him: First, because of its potential political impact, the Agency should pursue the Danilov investigation to its conclusion; and second, adjust the schedule for establishing the new intelligence-gathering network accordingly.

Despite the soundness of his logic, the suggestion would no doubt result in much hand wringing at Langley. Wails of anguish and renting of garments was a distinct possibility.

He grunted—a soft echo in the quiet office. It was all a sham; a well-choreographed bureaucratic dance where one embraced or discarded a partner depending upon the melody. Cody knew he would have to fall in line, but he intended to add a few steps of his own.

With or without specific instructions, he would focus his efforts on Danilov, either to expose the Russian as an imposter or repatriate him back into American society. An appropriately worded letter containing his recommendations would cover his ass—for a little while anyway. When he needed the Company's research and analytical services, which was almost certain, Cody would make those requests openly. Sometimes, he reasoned, the easiest way to get inside the castle was through the main gate. When the bureaucrats finally arrived at a consensus decision, no doubt after lengthy discussion, the Danilov business would be concluded, or nearly so.

Likewise, recruiting the requisite number of covert agents within the original timetable was doable, provided he ignored quality and concentrated solely on quantity. Using funds available to him, Cody could flood the border with low-grade operatives of little or questionable value. He would thus adhere to the planned schedule, but any information those agents gathered would be proportional to his recruiting efforts. In other words, substandard.

Not pleased with subterfuge or his lousy attitude, he turned back to his desk. A moment later, he was busy at his computer, having convinced himself the former was necessary and silently promising to improve the latter.

***

As usually happened when he concentrated on a problem, Cody lost track of time. Hours later, he finally dialed Anne Seymour's number. He wondered if she, like many of her contemporaries, had fled the consulate at the stroke of five o'clock. To his surprise and delight, she answered on the second ring.

"Hello, Anne. Cody Ballantine. Sorry to call so late. I'm surprised you haven't left already."

It was nearly seven o'clock. The ass-covering letter was on its way, properly classified and encoded before its transmittal to Langley via satellite. Afterwards, he had spent two hours developing a first-draft questionnaire for Danilov's debriefing. The top of his desk was once again pristine.

"Not yet," she replied. "On most nights I'm here long after normal business hours. It's the best time to get things done."

"All work and no play?"

"Sometimes, but not always."

"I may have that same problem. Or so I've been told."

The Gamov Incident

She did not respond, so Cody pressed on. "If you're about finished for the day, would you have a drink with me? Perhaps a bite to eat?"

Her elastic pause told Cody that Anne Seymour was mentally framing a polite but negative response. Although it was what he expected, he was hoping for otherwise. Unfortunately, his initial instinct proved distressingly correct.

"I'm not sure that's a good idea," she said.

Cody, always selective in his occasional approaches to women, did not consider himself a ladies' man: a Romeo with irresistible charm. Yet, exploring a potential relationship with Anne Seymour felt right. Her calm rejection was a disappointment.

Determined to camouflage his chagrin with a pleasant tone, he said, "I think I understand. But, just for the record, is it me personally or are there other reasons?"

"It's not you personally."

"Is it me professionally?"

"Although I don't usually socialize with shady characters from the CIA, it's not that either."

Shady character? Did she know something about his botched assignment? Not sure, Cody decided to play it lightly. "Shady? *Moi?* Ms. Seymour, I haven't worn a trench coat in years. Besides, they're out of fashion."

"Thank God." Her voice reflected subdued humor.

"Well, if it's not me personally or professionally, then I assume there are other reasons."

"That would be a good assumption."

"Reasons you might like to share?"

"Not really, and certainly not over the telephone."

"I see. Then perhaps we *should* have a drink—in a quiet, comfortable place conducive to private conversation—in case you change your mind. Women have been known to do that on occasion."

A long pause followed, then she said, "Were you a used car salesman before your fall from repute?"

Fall from repute? Maybe she did know something after all. But then again, perhaps she was referring to the Agency in general.

Many consular employees resented the CIA's apparent disregard for diplomatic rules and distrusted everyone remotely associated with the Agency. Perhaps Anne was one of them. Still, he pressed on.

"You have found me out," Cody said. "Unfortunately, I had to leave the pre-owned automobile profession. Those gentlemen were much too upstanding. They resented my lack of scruples."

Her throaty laugh rang pleasant, even over the telephone. "I give up. I'm also in need of an after-work drink. Do you know the *Zolotoy Yakor*?"

The Golden Anchor, one of several new businesses opened during the past year, once again proved that crime and capitalism could happily coexist; not only in the United States, but also in Mother Russia, and in much the same way. The homey bar and grille, already a favorite among consular staff, served a mixed clientele. Legitimate businessmen, upper level government employees, and prosperous criminals frequented the *Yakor*, enjoying an amiable live-and-let-live relationship. Having a drink there also sent a clear message: Anne Seymour was not hiding from anyone.

"Yes, I know the place. We can walk there if you like."

"That's not a bad idea. I could use the exercise. Is it cold outside?"

"Anne, we're in Siberia. It's always cold outside."

"Even in summertime?"

"No. In July the temperature soars to maybe seventy-five degrees, but only during a hot spell."

"I need to buy more clothes," she muttered.

"Do women really need an excuse to buy clothes…or anything else for that matter?"

"Of course not, but needing to dress adequately for unpleasant weather is easy to rationalize."

"Well, bundle up and meet me in the lobby. Say, ten minutes?"

"Make it twenty," she said.

Chapter 9

"How did a young woman like you end up in a remote consulate nobody seems to care about?"

They were taking initial tastes of their first drink, a cosmopolitan for her and a scotch for him. Conversation had yet to progress beyond the mundane. The reticence Cody had detected in Anne's voice during their telephone conversation was still evident, although it did not seem nearly as pronounced. Going the bland-topic route seemed best, at least for openers.

"Not so young. I'm forty-two, but thank you for the compliment."

Her revelation surprised him. In the first place, she had the face and lithe physical characteristics of someone much younger. Furthermore, women seldom revealed their age, especially on a first date. It wasn't exactly akin to an unexpected melting of Siberia's permafrost, but perhaps a sign of warmer weather to come.

"What about you?" she continued. "I see a few strands of gray hair, but your face has a younger appearance."

"I'm forty six."

"A confirmed bachelor, I presume."

She was edging into sensitive territory, but Cody's defense mechanisms remained inert, perhaps because he felt comfortable and unthreatened in her presence. He also sensed a similar feeling from

Anne, small now but growing, almost as though they'd known each other all their lives.

"Not entirely by choice," he said.

"Really?" She waited, as though expecting him to elaborate.

"I was married for three weeks, a long time ago."

"Three weeks? Oh, my. I thought mine was brief."

"You were married?"

"Yes, for a whole year."

"What happened?"

She smiled. "We were talking about you, remember?"

He took a measured sip of his scotch. Could he explain his disastrous marriage objectively, without placing Tessa in an unfavorable light? No, he thought, that was not possible. Yet, sitting beside Anne Seymour and basking in her warm presence, Cody realized it no longer mattered. He had somehow moved beyond the need to protect Tessa, to guard against any attempt to sully his fond remembrances of her. In retrospect, his marital troubles seemed more like a poorly conceived episode from a second-rate soap opera.

"It didn't work out," he finally said.

Still smiling, Anne leaned forward. "Yes, I figured that part out. The three week duration of your marriage was a major clue."

"Ah, well, what I mean is, there were unexpected and rather unpleasant developments."

The smile froze and she eased back to her original position. "Did it involve abuse?"

Her question surprised him. "No, of course not. Why would you think so?"

She sipped her drink and looked away, not meeting his eyes. "It happens."

A memory filament glowed to life. At the consular reception, Cody had asked whether Anne had a husband, fiancé, or a large, ill-tempered boyfriend. He had meant it as a joke but her response was void of humor: *What makes you think I would tolerate the company of an ill-mannered lout?*

"Is that what happened to your marriage?" he asked.

She met his gaze and a sad half-smile curved her lips. "We're still talking about you. Let's keep on point—for now."

Cody realized he faced a significant decision. Her eyes seemed to convey an offer: We can take an important step forward, they hinted, but only together. Instinct told him she might be willing to share certain personal things with him, but only to the extent he confided in her. If he declined the unspoken invitation, their relationship would not progress beyond casual friendship. That dead-end prospect was far more unpleasant than all the ghosts lurking in the shadows of his mind.

"To begin with, I missed too many signs."

The half-smile vanished. "An affair? After only three weeks?"

Cody shook his head. "No, nothing like that. On the contrary. The marriage was never, ah, fully consummated."

"Oh…I see." After a moment she added, "What signs?"

He sipped more scotch and decided to volunteer a bit more. "We had a long, immaculate engagement. During that time we built a huge house, one designed to accommodate a half-dozen children. Our families are Catholic and, Planned Parenthood notwithstanding, we had the unspoken blessing from His Holiness."

"That isn't much of a clue. Many women choose to abstain from sex until after marriage."

"Yes, I know, but this was different. In those rare instances when we discussed sex, Tessa used phrases like 'wifely duty' and 'marital obligation'. There were other clues as well: no-touch rules regarding sensitive body parts, no heavy petting. Finally, she seemed immune to the natural tug of youthful passion. Clear hints, all of which I ignored."

"That's easy to do when you love someone."

"Maybe so, but this occurred in the late Sixties, during the Age of Aquarius and uninhibited free love. The mood of our relationship was out of synch with the times and, frankly, counter to my expectations. Still, I loved her and never questioned the unusual nature of our courtship. Instead, I convinced myself she was saving her virtue for the nuptial bed. That proved to be an illusion. In fact, the idea of actual physical love made her violently ill."

He took a long pull from his drink. "Believe it or not, the sight of your new bride upchucking at the prospect of having wedding-night sex is a real confidence killer."

"Oh, how awful. Did you try counseling?"

Cody realized he had already divulged much more than intended, but the words seemed to spill from his mouth of their own accord, escaping a moment before he realized they were gone.

"Tessa wouldn't talk about it: not to me, not to our priest, not to anyone. She was distraught and humiliated; I was shocked and frustrated. In retrospect, we were too young and inexperienced. Tessa could never bring herself to confide in me and I didn't have the patience or skill to understand what might be going on in her mind. After a couple of weeks, we gave up on each other and had the marriage annulled. It was an exhausting experience, an unpleasant memory I carried around for too many years."

Anne ran a finger across the rim of her glass, and then looked up. "Did you ever suspect childhood trauma—maybe a sexual thing?"

"I asked her about that several times, begging her to trust me, but she never could. Something like that might have happened, I suppose. But after our wedding night, pristine except for all the puke, sex was a topic she refused to discuss."

"There is another possibility, you know."

"Yes, of course. I once accused her of being a lesbian, but never believed it."

"Maybe you didn't want to."

"That's possible, I suppose. However, I later came to suspect something else; sexually related but quite different."

"I'm not sure that makes sense."

"What I'm trying to say is this: Tessa was very devout. Deep down, I suspected it had something to do with our religion."

"Really? In what way?"

"I think it was her educational background. Tessa attended girls-only parochial schools from kindergarten through high school. According to local lore, the nuns taught Catholic girls that sex was a necessary wickedness every woman had to suffer. Eve's lie to Adam about the apple had forever condemned women to endure the humiliation of sexual submission and the resulting agony of childbirth. Original Sin begetting more sin, so to speak. I think there was something in her mental makeup that led her to believe that nonsense, and it subsequently affected her psychologically—created a block of some sort."

He looked at Anne, expecting a response, but she remained silent.

"And yet," Cody said, not quite ready to abandon the subject, "we talked and exchanged many letters about having kids. I was in Vietnam during construction of the house, but our correspondence was crammed with details: nursery decor, kids' bedroom furniture—stuff like that. Where did she think our children would come from, the supermarket?"

"Denial can be a powerful emotion."

Anne's voice and the look in her eyes conveyed an undertone of bruised elegance, as though she spoke from firsthand knowledge and personal experience. He hesitated, wanting to pursue the unspoken implication. Instead, he shrugged. "I suppose so. Anyway, it's over and done with."

Anne sipped her drink. "What happened to Tessa?"

"She moved away. I lost track of her."

"And your big house?"

"I put it up for sale. I had accumulated six weeks leave, planning to take all of it for the wedding and honeymoon. With two weeks remaining before I had to report for duty, I just couldn't stay in town. Too much gossip and too many memories. I placed the house in the hands of a real estate agent and spent the rest of my leave wandering about the country aimlessly."

Cody had indeed left town and wandered about, but it wasn't a pleasant journey. Following the annulment, he went on an extended sexual binge, sleeping with any willing female, indulging himself in a boozy cavalcade of one-night stands. Although more vomiting did occur, there were subtle differences. First, he was the perpetrator; second, the cause was not sexual revulsion, but rather too much whiskey and not enough food.

It was a pathetic attempt to reaffirm his masculinity, to compensate for Tessa's profound sexual rejection. However, rather than salvaging his manhood, Cody had instead degraded himself, writing a sorry chapter in his life he would rather forget—one he was not about to share with Anne Seymour.

Or anyone else, for that matter.

"Is that how you ended up working for the government?"

He nodded. "The Agency first approached me in Vietnam, but I declined. After I reported for duty in the Pentagon, they contacted me a second time."

"When exactly did you arrive in Washington?"

"In early June of 1969."

"And here you are," she said. The pleasant smile had returned.

He spread his arms wide, palms upward. "In all my faded glory."

Cody felt relieved, purged of old phantoms and their debilitating effect on his social life. Exposing those troubling memories had been easier than he once imagined. Anne Seymour was having a strange effect on him.

He leaned forward, his forearms resting on the table. "Now it's your turn."

She finished her drink and Cody found his own glass empty.

"Can I have a rain check?" she asked.

He sensed their time together was nearly over. "For the drink or the life story?"

"Both."

"Does that mean there's a possibility for a second date?"

"It could."

"I'm not sure I understand."

She paused for a long moment before answering and her eyes narrowed slightly, as though studying him. Then she said, "You don't remember me, do you?"

The unexpected question shattered a seawall protecting his past behavior. Disgust and embarrassment arising from his post-Tessa binge flooded his memory like the heavy surge from an unexpected tide. Had Anne Seymour been one of those faceless women he had encountered soon after the annulment? Had Anne witnessed him at his worst? Quickly calculating elapsed time, Cody realized she would have been about twenty years old. It was possible, but he had no recollection of her—or any other woman he had used during that terrible interlude. Defying the laws of probability, it now seemed that Anne had been an unremembered part of the most shameful episode of his life.

Straining to quell the discomfort in his stomach, he met her steady gaze and replied in the only way he could. "I'm sorry," he said. "But I have no recollection of us ever having met."

Her reaction was rather nonchalant, not what Cody expected.

She said, "I'm not surprised, but now I understand your preoccupation. That was not a good time in your life."

Cody's insides continued to churn. Talk about past sins haunting the present. This was not how things were supposed to work out between them. The best laid plans…

"I'm curious," she continued. "How did you manage to get an invitation? Those coming out affairs are very exclusive events."

With effort, Cody managed to hide his confusion. Coming out affair? What in hell was she talking about? He picked up his glass, attempting to buy time, but there was nothing left to drink. He searched for a waiter, but they had somehow vanished, or were taking their break together.

"You must have known someone important," she added.

Comprehension glimmered. The coal from a long-forgotten event glowed and became hotter. Finally, it came to him. Of course! That stupid Thanksgiving Ball! The 'someone important' was his boss at the time; a well-connected senior officer who thought a society ball just might be the perfect venue to jolt a young captain out of his post-annulment depression.

The 'invitation' was, in fact, a thinly disguised order from a bird colonel to a recently promoted captain. Cody, having little choice, complied. Unhappy with the situation but shaved, bathed, and properly attired, Captain Cody Ballantine had attended and dutifully fulfilled his escort obligation. Although surrounded by nubile young ladies, the colonel's plan did not succeed.

Humiliated by his Free Love Tour of Uninhibited America, Cody had subsequently embraced the opposite extreme by committing himself to the monkish practice of self-examination and sexual abstinence. That unrealistic and unsustainable mindset prevailed during his tour in Washington, and was no doubt the reason why he ignored the enticing glances from all those lovely young debutantes, including Anne Seymour.

Just then, another tiny recollection glowed to life.

"Wait a minute," he began. "I *do* remember something."

Anne did not look convinced. "Really? Or are you just saying that to make me feel better?"

"No, it's true. I remember a tall, skinny girl who looked to be about fifteen years old. An expensively gowned deb who made fun of my dress uniform." Her eyes grew wide and Cody felt a huge grin spreading across his face. "Was that you, Anne?"

"Oh my God. Did I really look *fifteen*? How humiliating!"

"Well, maybe sixteen or seventeen."

"That doesn't help, Cody." Now she was smiling as well.

They continued to look into each other's eyes, but Cody's discomfort had fled, leaving a sense of time in suspension.

He recalled pleasant, nearly forgotten interludes like those wonderful summers in his uncle's vineyard. Those long-ago days, he finally acknowledged, were the best times of my life. Better than any that had occurred since. Were there more good days to come? Was it possible to recapture and re-experience an enjoyable fragment of the past? After years of believing otherwise, he sensed the answer might be yes.

"This is totally weird," he finally said. "You must have recognized me Saturday evening, at the reception. Why didn't you say something?"

"It didn't seem like a good time."

"That was perceptive. I had a lot on my mind."

"Did it concern Minister Trushin?"

Cody was about to deny any interest in Aleksandr Trushin, but then hesitated, reluctant to begin their relationship by telling a lie, even a necessary one. He finally said, "Let's not talk about work."

She nodded, perhaps sensing his dilemma. Then she said, "You never asked me to dance. I was very disappointed."

"You were busy, too," he replied.

"I meant back then, at my coming out party."

"Well then, it's time I made amends. Besides, you owe me a true-life tale. How about dinner Saturday evening, someplace fancy?"

"Fancy?" she said, tilting her head quizzically. "Are there really such places in Vladivostok?"

"Only one or two right now, but that will change."

"I see. Well, if I owe you a story, then you owe me a dance. It's long overdue, but I expect payment in full."

The almost-certain probability of spending more time with Anne generated a pleasant flush of curiosity and excitement; not because he wanted to hear sordid details about her marriage—he didn't—but for another reason.

Rather, there was a sense of unfinished business between them, a blank canvas touched by an unsure hand, and then abandoned. He was almost certain Anne felt the same way. Although their time tonight was near an end, Cody knew it was a temporary interlude, a situation much improved from their last parting. Despite a shaky beginning, the future thrummed with possibility.

"You can count on it," he said.

Chapter 10

Three days later, at nine-o'clock on Friday morning, Phyllis appeared in the doorway to Cody's office. "Your guest is waiting in the first floor conference room."

Cody rose and headed for the door. "Thanks, Phyllis."

Let the games begin, he thought.

Cody, Zane, and Butler had discussed, modified, polished and rehearsed the questionnaire *ad nauseam*. Now it was time to shake and bake.

Approaching the elevator, Cody took several deep breaths, forcing himself to relax. Yesterday, at nearly the last moment, the Consul General had decided the original plan regarding how they intended to conduct the Danilov meeting was more problematic than first believed.

"If we use three interrogators," Zane had explained, "then it might appear too much like a formal debriefing. Danilov might be less than candid if we treat him like a suspect in a criminal proceeding. Not only that, Colonel Butler and I have no practical experience questioning individuals under such extraordinary circumstances. Diplomatic negotiation is one thing; but cross-examining a specific individual—an accomplished liar, perhaps—requires different skills: expertise that, among the three of us, only you possess. Given this situation, I believe you, and you alone, should conduct the Danilov interview."

Although Zane's logic made sense, Butler's expression failed to disguise his silent disappointment. Clearly, the Air Force officer did not relish the prospect of standing on the sidelines like a spectator. That reaction did not surprise Cody, given Butler's personal history.

According to the background report provided in answer to Cody's query, Butler was the son and grandson of distinguished soldiers. His late grandfather Robert, obviously the attaché's namesake, had served in France as a surgeon during the First World War. The grandfather had then returned to active duty during the Second, temporarily forsaking his civilian medical practice. The attaché's father—a retired, highly decorated bird colonel—had also served in World War Two, as well as Korea and Vietnam.

Butler the younger, preferring the Air Force to the Army, had earned his wings and subsequently flew 53 combat missions during the Gulf War. The attaché, a third-generation military officer, would no doubt look forward to an eyeball-to-eyeball discussion with a man who might indeed be a long lost colleague.

But that was not going to happen. Cody suspected the Consul General, after thinking about it, had decided he wanted no part of the Danilov interrogation. Excusing himself alone would have been too obvious; excluding Butler as well left the single interrogator scenario. Although Cody empathized with the attaché, the issue was out of his hands. However, their physical absence would not preclude Zane or Butler from detailed knowledge of the proceedings.

Cody had spent the previous evening memorizing Butler's list and formulating an approach using both questionnaires. He had also checked and re-tested the electronic bugs, tiny devices sensitive enough to capture and record every whisper from any spot inside the conference room. There was little doubt Zane and Butler would take the opportunity to eavesdrop on his conversation while remaining out of sight.

In any case, their physical presence in the room did not matter, so Cody refocused his mind on the coming interview.

When the elevator door slid open, he walked down a short hallway and entered the conference room. Zane and Andrei Danilov turned at the sound.

Danilov's expression revealed little and body language offered few clues into his emotional state of mind. Beyond a noticeable hint of apprehension—a natural reaction given the circumstances—Cody detected nothing unusual or deceptive in the man's demeanor. Finally, even though he did not expect to see it, the absence of Danilov's briefcase triggered a mild sense of disappointment.

"Ah, there you are," Zane said. "I was explaining to Mr. Danilov our bureaucratic dilemma. Because we have yet to hear from Washington, we are without specific instructions on how to proceed. He informed me that administrative procedures at the Primorski Agricultural Institute are likewise victim to standard operating procedures and are thus equally cumbersome. As a cooperative gesture, he has agreed to answer whatever personal questions you have in mind."

While Washington's bureaucracy grinds our request to fine powder, Cody silently added. He said to Danilov, "That is very kind of you, sir."

The Russian, apparently feeling more comfortable, seemed amused. "Although I hoped otherwise, this development is not unexpected."

"Oh?" Zane said.

"Yes. Allowing only one week for a response from Washington was far too optimistic. All government bureaucracies thrive on the tedious predictability of mundane routine. Unusual situations run counter to those expectations."

An old axiom popped into Cody's head: The measure of another man's intelligence increases proportionately to the extent he agrees with you. Although pleased with the Russian's observation, Cody remained silent. Concurring with Danilov's rather low opinion of government bureaucrats, especially in the Consul General's presence, was a roguish impulse he managed to control.

"Perhaps you are correct," Zane offered without enthusiasm. His gaze moved from Danilov to Cody. "Well, I'll leave you two alone for a while. If you need anything, please let me know. When you are ready for refreshments, please call Angela, my assistant."

Zane turned, shook hands with Danilov, exchanged a cordial glance with Cody and then left the conference room.

When the door closed, Cody motioned to one of six padded armchairs placed around the highly polished oak table. "Let's make ourselves comfortable, shall we? Would you like coffee, some breakfast perhaps?"

"Actually, I prefer tea," Danilov said, settling in. "A habit necessitated by the near absence of coffee during my long sojourn. I took breakfast at the hotel."

Cody lifted the telephone handset and punched numbers.

"Hi, Angela. Would you ask someone to bring us tea and coffee, please?" He listened for a moment. "Sure, a few crumpets would be nice. And thanks." He cradled the handset.

"Crumpets?" Danilov asked. "As in English crumpets?"

"Not really. It's a term I use to categorize pastry in general. For some reason it caught on. I may have inadvertently contaminated the consulate's fastidiously correct vocabulary."

"Ah," Danilov smiled.

Cody took a chair opposite the Russian. He had decided to treat Danilov as a Federation citizen, possibly KGB, and therefore a potential threat—at least for the time being. If asked, he could not have articulated his reasons. Danilov's eyes mirrored gritty wisdom—perhaps unwillingly acquired—and something else: a hint of retained memories from a darker, less civilized time. Although Cody's questions and outward demeanor would seem benign, he would be attentive to any hint of deception.

"Are you CIA?" Danilov asked.

A direct and rather unexpected question, Cody thought. Was it an idle inquiry or a natural KGB assumption? He said, "As you saw from my ID, I am Mr. Zane's advisor on cultural affairs. I also work closely with the military attaché. However, having vaguely defined responsibilities does not necessarily equate to membership in the CIA."

That wasn't exactly a lie, Cody reasoned. After all, it was customary for the Agency to work closely with other consular departments, including various advisors and attaché staff. Customary, yes—but not necessarily a hard and fast rule. Let Danilov make from that whatever he chose.

"Then you are Mister, I mean Colonel, Butler's colleague?"

"Exactly."

"I see." His eyes took in the room. "I presume listening devices are operating?"

"It's standard procedure. Is that a problem?"

"No, of course not." Under the circumstances, it is a reasonable precaution, a situation I fully expected." He smiled, perhaps to assure Cody that he harbored no ill feelings. Then he said, "Well, shall we begin?"

Cody had already begun by paying special attention to Danilov's speech patterns and voice inflections. As their discussion progressed, he intended to mimic, in a subtle way, Danilov's phrasing and conversational style. Early in his career, Cody had picked up that particular interrogation technique from a grizzled Agency field operative. Without being too obvious, the lesson went, try to sound like the other guy. If you eliminate tonal dissonance and provide familiar feedback sounds, the subject will unconsciously relax. In other words, become a cohort, not a threat.

Since he did not want to appear threatening, Cody would not ask the major question troubling his mind. Namely, how did a captured American military officer survive for nearly forty years inside Soviet Russia? He would save that discussion for another time; perhaps when Danilov was more relaxed. Instead, he approached the interrogation from a more traditional angle.

"Let's begin with some personal background," Cody suggested. "Where were your born and raised?"

"Pittsburgh. In the Birmingham neighborhood."

An interesting detail, Cody thought. Not exactly up there with the Manhattan Project, but it was something. "Is that where you attended school?"

"Yes. South Side School until the ninth grade. Then we moved to Natrona Heights, about twenty miles away."

"What year did you graduate from Natrona High School?"

"I was in the class of 1946. And Natrona's high school is called Har-Brack." He spelled it out.

"That's an odd name."

"Yes, it is. When first built, they combined the school's old designation with the county name: Harrison County and Brackenridge City Union High School; thus, Har-Brack. That's the story I remember, anyway."

"Did you receive a yearbook?"

"Yes, but I left it with my parents. It could be anywhere—or even lost."

Yearbooks always contained an array of class pictures, but any resemblance between a high school photograph and the same man nearly fifty years later was remote. Still, it was a starting point. Lost or not, someone would have a 1946 class yearbook from Har-Brack and that yearbook would have a photo of young Danilov, or Thompson.

Cody continued probing high school memories: buddies, girl friends, teachers and neighborhood hangouts, paying particular attention to Danilov's pronunciation and word usage. Western Pennsylvanians had a unique vocabulary. Once Danilov relaxed, perhaps he would lapse into a provincial expression or phrase. That, however, was unlikely. After thirty-eight years in Russia, all traces of Danilov's childhood lexicon would have long since disappeared.

The old man had little trouble remembering details from his youth and Cody paid special attention to the chronology. Memorized stories tended to follow a sequential timeline, with little deviation. However, Danilov's narrative bounced through his early years, back and forth, exactly as one might recall past events.

Cody tried not to be overly impressed. On the down side though, someone might have extracted every remembrance from the real Captain Thompson, via one or more interrogations like this one, or perhaps under duress. Afterwards, Thompson's recollections, carefully reconstructed in a seemingly haphazard manner, might prove useful to someone like Danilov.

A knock interrupted the conversation.

Cody rose from his chair, opened the door and then stepped aside, surprised to see Angela wheel in a serving cart. The Consul General's personal assistant seldom delivered coffee. There were, however, exceptions to every situation. Apparently, this was one of those rare occasions.

"Tea and crumpets," she said, smiling.

Danilov stood, his body relaxed, hands at his sides. Cody wondered: Did he rise in the presence of a lady from habit, as befitting an officer and a gentleman, or did he merely want some tea?

"This looks great," Cody said.

Angela smiled at him, obviously pleased.

The top shelf held two Pyrex pots—coffee and plain water on separate hotplates—a sugar bowl and creamer, cups, saucers and silver, all affixed with the Great Seal of the United States. A tin box containing a variety of teas stood nearby. Mixed pastries on a china plate rested on the bottom shelf. She eased the cart close to the wall and inserted plugs into receptacles.

"Thank you, Angela. We can help ourselves."

"You're welcome, Mr. Ballantine." She lingered for a moment, placing napkins and china just so, and then closed the door on her way out.

"She seems like a pleasant young lady," Danilov said, pouring hot water over a tea bag.

"Yes, I think so."

Cody set the pastries on the table and poured coffee for himself. Had Danilov seen Angela's 'I'm interested' look? Did he notice her coy demeanor towards Cody? Probably. The old guy didn't seem to miss much.

Weeks before the consulate's official opening, the young woman had made several subtle advances, inviting Cody to reciprocate. As was his practice, Cody demurred. Angela had all the physical attributes, but she was much too young—late twenties, he imagined. Old enough for a fling, he admitted, but far too young for a serious relationship. Besides, Cody felt compelled to obey his Primary Work Rule: No Office Romances.

He stirred cream into his coffee and tried not to think about Anne Seymour.

"When and where did you learn to speak Russian?" Cody asked, taking his seat.

"I could always speak Russian. My grandmother taught me. She was born in the Ukraine, near Kiev. Her family emigrated to America when she was fifteen." Danilov paused, sipped his tea, and then continued. "I learned the Cyrillic alphabet long before my ABCs."

Now *that* was a surprise. Cody had not expected a Russian connection so quickly. "Tell me about her."

"She married at nineteen, a ceremony arranged by her father of course, a common practice back then. Her husband, my grandfather, was also Ukrainian—a steelworker. They had three children, all girls. My mother is the eldest."

"Did they also live in Birmingham?"

"No. Their house stood closer to the mill, on Mary Street."

"And your grandfather worked in the steel mills?"

"Yes, at Jones and Laughlin, in the foundry. He died there in some sort of industrial accident nobody would talk about. I was three or four years old, so I have little memory of him. A short time later my grandmother moved in with us."

Cody formed a mental picture of the woman: middle-aged, widowed, passing time while teaching her young grandson Russian, telling the boy about his grandfather and their family's origins in the Old Country. It was a familiar story, consistent with those times, the eldest child taking in a widowed parent, everyone adjusting their lives as best they could. They were, after all, family.

The story sounded authentic, maybe even heartwarming, but Cody refrained from making a judgment. Although Danilov demonstrated great mental capacity, the skills necessary to remember specific events were identical to those required to memorize obscure details unrelated to one's own life. So far, the man had revealed nothing that one could not glean from a prolonged, intensive, and persistent interrogation.

Cody continued with his questioning, allowing Danilov to talk freely about his friends and family, seldom interrupting the narrative. An hour passed, then two.

Danilov seemed to have an endless supply of his grandmother's stories. This sort of thing is not unusual, Cody reminded himself. In fact, mixing generic recollections from two different lives was tradecraft practiced by every deep cover agent. Some of those stories could easily have come from Danilov's 'real' life—that is, personal incidents blended seamlessly into someone else's life story, the two combined to form a single, coherent fabrication.

They paused for a bathroom break, refreshed their cups and then continued.

"What happened after high school?" Cody asked.

"I attended Pennsylvania Military College."

Cody searched his memory. Several states had military colleges: Virginia Military Institute in Lexington, the Citadel near Charleston, South Carolina. Cody had never heard of Pennsylvania Military College. "That's a new one on me."

"Really? I am surprised. Penn Military has existed for a long time. The first school opened in Delaware, around 1821. It moved from its original location to Pennsylvania during the Civil War."

"Is it close to Pittsburgh?"

"No. In Chester, on the other side of the state, a few miles south of Philadelphia."

"How did you end up in a military college?"

"My high school history teacher, Mr. Caruthers, graduated from PMC. He was someone I respected. He suggested it so I did some research."

"I assume Penn Military is all male, much like VMI and the Citadel?"

"Yes, it is."

"If memory serves, VMI freshmen are called Rats. Their counterparts at the Citadel are Knobs. Did PMC have a special name for freshmen?"

Danilov did not answer. Rather, he examined the pastries and then carefully lifted a miniature apple Danish from the plate.

"This is quite tasty," he said between bites.

Cody selected a cinnamon roll. "Yes, they are, but I shouldn't be eating any."

Danilov chuckled. "You are a young man and can easily work it off. For myself, I am too old to worry about such things." He finished the Danish, wiped his fingers on a linen napkin and sipped tea. "Now then, let me tell you a little about my life at PMC."

Cody chewed the cinnamon roll while the old man reminisced, apparently from memory.

"To answer your question, freshmen are called Rooks. Upperclassmen taught us to march, shine our shoes, adopt a military bearing and loudly recite silly prose about clocks and cows, all from memory and without pause or hesitation, of course. Later, I studied mathematics, engineering, history, and military leadership. For some reason, I enjoyed every minute of it; from my first day until graduation."

"Is that so?"

"Yes. PMC felt natural and completely familiar, like returning to a pleasant, long-forgotten childhood place."

As he spoke, Danilov's expression softened and his eyes became glazed and distant. Listening to the recollection, Cody visualized the cadet battalion, untried young men wearing immaculate dress gray uniforms, marching in perfect unison, drill commands echoing across the athletic fields behind Old Main. Like a shared ancestral memory, he could feel the critical eyes of upperclassmen focused upon Danilov as the young man erased demerits by walking punishment tours, rifle at shoulder arms, parading with his fellow miscreants in the quadrangle while other cadets enjoyed free time.

"In 1949, during my junior year, Penn Military joined the National Association of Pershing Rifles. Eighty seven cadets applied; twenty-five or so were selected for the drill team."

"Did you make the cut?"

"Yes. It was the proudest moment of my life."

"I can believe that."

"Our chapter, Company Q-5, entered various drill competitions, but PMC didn't place very high. We were too new at the time. Nevertheless, it was a great experience, almost as much fun as the summer war games."

"What were those like?"

"The fourth classmen traveled to Indiantown Gap, near Harrisburg, and participated in the National Guard's annual field exercise. About three thousand cadets from military schools up and down the east coast attended. Reserve Army sergeants were the enemy, officers served as advisors or umpires, and real airplanes dropped flour sacks. It was great fun."

Some fun, Cody thought, remembering his Special Forces training and nightlong treks through Georgia's snake and alligator infested Okefenokee Swamp. "Did you have time for a girlfriend?"

"Two or three, actually. In my senior year I dated a young lady from Swarthmore College, a few miles north on state route 320. My buddy Tom Foster had a '47 Chevy Coupe and we took a drive almost every weekend. The ladies were delightfully friendly, no doubt impressed by our snappy cadet uniforms."

Cody tried not to smile. Liberal, anti-war, and patronizingly elite Swarthmore College *friendly* toward military uniforms? My, how times have changed. "Was it a serious relationship?" he asked.

"Not really. She was nice, but her family was much too wealthy. After graduation, we went our separate ways."

"What else do you remember?"

"The school's history is difficult to forget. Colonel Frank Hyatt was the third consecutive Hyatt to command PMC's cadets, preceded by his father, General Charles and his grandfather, Colonel Theodore. Their combined tenure spanned nearly a hundred years—since before the Civil War. It gave Penn Military a unique atmosphere of continuity and timelessness."

Once again, a seemingly innocuous question produced interesting results, information that might reinforce or diminish the authenticity of a human lifetime. It confirmed Cody's belief that no question was unimportant. For the first time, he acknowledged an unlikely possibility: Danilov might indeed be Captain Andrew Thompson.

"I presume you graduated in 1950, right?"

"Yes, that is correct. I was offered and subsequently accepted a Regular commission in the Air Force."

"A Regular commission? Isn't that unusual?" Cody tried not to sound defensive. When he graduated from college as one of three ROTC distinguished graduates, the Army had offered him a *Reserve* commission.

"I think it was about half and half," Danilov said. "Half Regular, half Reserve. A few opted for graduate school; some pursued civilian careers."

"I see." Graduation meant another class photograph, but this time of a young man in his early twenties. Absent unexplained fires in Natrona Heights and Chester, those photographs should be available in school archives. It occurred to Cody that the old man was either solidifying his case or painting himself into a corner. He said, "Why did you choose the Air Force?"

"I wanted to be a pilot. Unfortunately, I am slightly colorblind and tend to confuse specific shades of blue and green. It is a minor flaw, but sufficient for disqualification. The news came as a complete surprise."

Cody wondered if the real Captain Thompson was or had been colorblind. If so, could one fake a test for colorblindness? Was that even relevant?

The door opened, disrupting Cody's train of thought. Whittier Zane strolled in, a pleasant smile on his face.

"Sorry, to interrupt your conversation gentlemen." His facial expression changed slightly, matching his apologetic tone. "But I promised not to monopolize Mr. Danilov's entire day, especially on such short notice. It's nearly two."

"Two o'clock?" Danilov said, checking his watch. "My Goodness. I had no idea we talked for so long."

"We neglected to provide lunch," Zane admitted with a slight frown. "And I apologize. I promise to rectify that shortcoming when next we meet. May we reconvene at another time?"

"Of course," Danilov replied.

Cody stood and stretched. "Thanks, we appreciate your cooperation."

From his perspective, it had been a good session. There was much for him to review and the promise of actual photographs, while not conclusive proof, excited him.

"Then it's settled," Zane said.

Danilov stood. "And now I shall take a long walk followed by a short nap before having my dinner."

Cody said, "Mr. Danilov, could we get together tomorrow morning for a few hours? There's still a great deal to cover and I'd like to hear more about your experience in the Air Force."

"Certainly. Nine o'clock?"

"Perfect."

"Very well," Zane added. "And I'm sorry to further intrude on your weekend. By this time next week however, we should have received Washington's response to our query."

Danilov massaged the back of his neck with the fingers of his right hand. "No apology is necessary, Mr. Zane. I have been waiting nearly forty years for this opportunity. I can wait a few days longer."

"Nevertheless, thank you for your patience."

"And thank you for agreeing to come back in for a little while tomorrow," Cody added.

"Think nothing of it," Danilov replied.

As the old man slipped into his overcoat, Cody thought about their first meeting. The brown leather briefcase filled with a 'thick document' continued to intrigue him. Without question Danilov considered it germane, otherwise why did he bring it with him.

Cody hid his curiosity behind a pleasant smile. "Until tomorrow then," he said, extending his hand.

Chapter 11

After Cody escorted Danilov to the rear entrance of the consulate, he returned to the conference room, closed the door and turned to Zane who was waiting for him.

"What do you think?" the Consul General asked.

"It went okay, I suppose. Our guest has either a great memory or remarkable powers of memorization."

"I agree. An impressive performance, if indeed it was."

"You were listening?"

"Yes, as was Colonel Butler. He too was impressed."

"How long before I can see a typed copy of our conversation?"

Zane frowned slightly. "He talked for nearly five hours. It may take a while." The Consul General did not sound optimistic.

"But I don't have a while. Why not copy segments of the tape onto four separate spools. Have reliable staff people type and proof each spool. That way, four typists could work on a different time-period of our meeting. Afterwards, combine the word processing files before final printing."

"Why the hurry?"

"I'd like to review the transcript before tomorrow's meeting. Perhaps I can spot an inconsistency or two."

"Yes, of course. Well, I'll see what can be done."

Cody moved to another subject. "Have you received correspondence naming the five REDLINED crewmen?"

"No, not yet."

"Without it, we're playing guessing games. Can you pull a few strings?"

"I have no strings, Cody."

"Don't underestimate yourself, Mr. Consul General. You may be living the ultimate Cold War story. If so, the *New York Times* will eagerly publish excerpts from your best-selling memoir."

"Or, perhaps, they will instead publish an exposé of the ultimate Cold War hoax, naming you and me as primary buffoons—gullible dupes taken in by the KGB." He fixed Cody with a hard stare. "What do your instincts tell you about Danilov?"

It was a timely question, one that Cody had posed to himself while the old man unraveled his story. He said, "Like you and Colonel Butler, I am trying very hard not to be impressed. If this guy is not Captain Andrew Thompson in the flesh, then Danilov has done a masterful job assuming his identity."

"What's your next step?"

Cody had already formulated what he planned to do. Danilov graduated from high school and college. FBI and/or Agency researchers could locate yearbooks from each institution. When Cody got a copy, he would study class pictures for any resemblance to Danilov's current appearance. He might even ask the old man to identify and describe classmates by name.

Those pictures would also be invaluable for another reason.

Human features changed over the years, a natural process of time and circumstance. Some elderly people were hardly recognizable from their youth. Others appeared older, but still looked more or less the same. How one matured and aged was a matter of genes and lifestyle. Nevertheless, youthful photographs also represented the starting point for a rather interesting computer simulation process.

The Agency's forensic scientists were expert at facial reconstruction and computer modeling. Cody remembered a lecture on that very subject—a rambling dissertation filled with eye-glazing terms like 'shape vectors' and 'texture parameters'. Properly defined and applied, a computer program could digitally represent aging human features by dynamically manipulating data points in three-dimensional space, and then visualizing the results by generating a series of photographs, each one aged by a specified number of years.

Or so they said.

Still, adding decades to someone's face, even with the world's fastest computer, would take a bit more time.

After sharing those thoughts with Zane, Cody said, "I think we should also make an effort to locate the lone survivor from Thompson's RB-50 crew. Maybe Butler could look into that: get a name, current address, and then fly him over here if necessary."

"That occurred to me as well. Anything else?"

Cody shook his head.

Zane turned toward the door. "It sounds like a good plan. I'll notify Colonel Butler and then get the Word Processing department started on the transcript."

***

When Cody stepped into his office, the first thing he noticed was the red Message Waiting light blinking on the secure telephone. He sat, lifted the handset, punched in his access code and listened to the standard preamble.

"Message received Friday, eleven-ten A.M."

A slight pause followed, then: *"Hello Cody, this is Hal."*

He felt a twinge of anticipation. Hal was Harold Bates, an Assistant Deputy Director for Operations, a senior intelligence officer who also happened to be Cody's current watchdog and/or boss; perhaps both. Had the bureaucracy arrived at a decision already?

The voice message continued.

"Regarding your unexpected visitor; We agree with your recommendation and strongly suggest you devote full time to the Danilov business. In fact, consider it a very special project. Tell us what you need and I'll make sure you get it promptly. A few of us older hands always suspected the Soviets of detaining American POWs and downed airmen, just as they did with captured German prisoners during World War Two. If your man is the genuine article, then it will confirm what we have long believed. If we can

authenticate one survivor, then surely there must be others. Keep me informed and good luck."

The recorder clicked off.

Well, Cody thought, the ADDO just offered me the keys to the kingdom, resource wise, and called the Danilov affair a *very special project*.

Cody checked his watch. Hal Bates had called three hours ago, at eleven A.M. Friday, Vladivostok time. That meant he had placed the call from his Langley office at eight P.M. Thursday, Washington time. Cody smiled. You are forcing the brass to work through the cocktail hour. That is *not* a good idea.

Although the full transcript would travel by diplomatic pouch, Cody knew it was important to provide Hal with immediate feedback. He fired up his personal computer and summarized his meeting with Danilov. He also recommended the Agency locate the shootdown survivor. Finally, he made a high-priority request for graduation photographs from Har-Brack High School, Natrona Heights, and the Pennsylvania Military College for the years 1946 and 1950, respectively. He concluded with a strongly worded suggestion the Agency use their facial aging and reconstruction computer program to simulate what young Thompson might look like after four or five decades.

He edited and then reread the final draft. It would do for now. Later, if necessary, he would share other details. He saved, printed and stamped the hard copy TOP SECRET.

Cody started for the crypto center, but then paused as an idea popped into his mind. Next to his computer, resting beside his Roget's Thesaurus, stood a copy of Webster's Ninth New Collegiate Dictionary. Following a hunch, he found the section entitled *Colleges and Universities,* an appendix located in the dictionary's end papers. He flipped to the entries that started with the letter 'P'.

Although he checked several variations and alternative spellings, he could find no listing for the Pennsylvania Military College.

***

After delivering his memo to the code room, Cody saw Angela standing outside his office, apparently waiting for him. She carried a letter-sized manila envelope. Phyllis was nowhere in sight.

"Hi, Angela. Is that for me?"

"Yes. It just arrived by secure fax. Mr. Zane said you needed to see a copy immediately." She handed Cody the envelope.

"Thank you." She continued looking into his eyes, as though reluctant to leave. He recognized her behavior but refused to pursue the unspoken suggestion. He offered what he hoped was a neutral smile. "Was there something else?"

Her facial expression changed from coyness to youthful determination. "Yes. I was wondering if we could have a drink later, after work."

Angela was an attractive young woman, but it was time to curtail whatever thoughts she might have regarding any sort of close personal relationship. "That might not be such a good idea," he said. Belatedly, he realized Anne Seymour had used those same words during their first telephone conversation.

"Why? Are you seeing someone else?"

Cody did not answer immediately. Was Anne *someone else*? The idea did not sound absurd—not at all—but admitting to that possibility would surely cause a titillating quiver of office gossip which, Cody suspected, defied Einstein's theory and travelled far faster than the speed of light.

Choosing to avoid the topic, he said, "How old are you, Angela; twenty-five?"

"More or less. Is that what's bothering you?"

"Why shouldn't it? I'm forty-six years old. May-December relationships succeed only in the movies or ditsy romance novels. Sometimes, not even there. Besides, we work in the same office. The consular staff might find older-man/younger-woman a topic of enduring interest, but I would not. In fact, it could be a hindrance, making my job more difficult than it already is."

His response did not answer her question directly, but Cody hoped it would suffice.

The determined look faded and her cheeks became flushed. Her embarrassment was obvious. "I see. Well, I'm sorry to have bothered you, Mr. Ballantine."

He tried to ease her discomfort. "You didn't bother me, Angela. Not at all. Actually, I'm more than a little flattered. Being approached by attractive young ladies is not something that generally happens to me."

Cody thought how easy it would be to take advantage of her youth and inexperience. Lord knows, she was physically desirable, and he would certainly enjoy her company—for a while. But having indiscriminate sexual liaisons was an unpleasant characteristic of his much younger self. Since the post-Tessa debacle, he had avoided short-term encounters—especially one night stands. It was, he told himself wistfully, a just penance for all his prior bad behavior.

She gave him a half-smile. Then she said, "I'd better get back to work."

"Me, too," Cody replied, waving the envelope.

Chapter 12

Inside his office Cody sat, loosened his tie and extracted ten, single-spaced pages from the manila envelope, taking note of the title:

February 24, 1955

Memorandum from the American Embassy at Moscow to the Soviet Foreign Ministry Regarding the Incident at Cape Gamov

He scanned the first page and then quickly flipped to the second where he found the crew listed by name, rank, and serial number. Captain Andrew George Thompson was fifth on the list. Unexplainably, Cody felt relieved.
His mind focused, he settled into his chair and began to read.

The Government of the United States of America refers to the destruction on August 3, 1954 by Soviet fighter planes of a United States Air Force B-50 aircraft off Cape Gamov in the international air space over the Sea of Japan.

On January 21, 1955, following an intensive investigation, substantiated by an eyewitness account, the United States Government concluded and takes this opportunity to place solemnly upon the record, the relevant facts as set forth below.

Early in the morning of August 3, 1954 a four-engine B-50 aircraft belonging to the United States Air Force was dispatched from its base in Japan by proper authorities to perform a routine navigational exercise in the air space over the international waters of the Sea of Japan, then returning to base in Japan upon mission completion. The officers and crew were instructed prior to departure that under no circumstances was the aircraft to fly closer to the Soviet-held landmass than twelve nautical miles.

Upon its departure, the B-50 aircraft had on board a crew of fourteen persons, all members of the United States Air Force and all nationals of the United States, as follows:

     Cody again studied the list, noting the crew mix: nine officers, including Captain Andrew George Thompson, and five enlisted men. He also noted the difference with regard to aircraft designation: B-50 as opposed to RB-50. Was this merely a typo or a subtle attempt by the State Department to conceal the 'R' and therefore the 'Reconnaissance' nature of the aircraft?
     Unable to determine the answer, he continued reading the State Department's forty-year old, ponderously diplomatic prose.

The B-50 aircraft proceeded on a westerly course of approximately 280 degrees from the Japanese island of Honshu. When it arrived in the airspace over the international waters of the Sea of Japan, approximately 50 miles from the Korean coastline, the aircraft turned right to a north-northeasterly course of approximately 40 degrees. As instructed, the crew continued to carry out the navigational exercises given them as above stated.

The aircraft had reached a point in the air space over the international waters of the Sea of Japan approximately 30 miles south of Cape Gamov, flying a heading of approximately 40 degrees at an altitude of 20,000 feet when suddenly, at approximately 7:00 A.M. local time, and without any prior warning whatever, Soviet MiG-15 fighter planes intercepted and then fired upon the United States aircraft.

One MiG-15 commenced the interception by attacking from below and to the left of the B-50, and shooting the Number 2 (left inboard) engine, rendering it inoperative. One or more additional MiG-15 fighters thereupon appeared behind the B-50 and directed fire on the left wing and the fuselage. Another MiG-15 approached from above and to the right and directed additional fire on the Number 3 (right inboard) engine and upon the right wing of the aircraft. These latter attacks set the Number 3 engine on fire.

Immediately upon being hit by gunfire, the aircraft dived sharply, losing altitude rapidly, again turned right and assumed a southeasterly course of approximately 120 degrees. Subsequent attacks by MiG fighters tore off the right wing and the tail section causing the aircraft to disintegrate. The component parts of the B-50 aircraft hit the water at approximately the same position at which the interception and attack took place. The total time elapsed between the commencement of the initial attack until the component parts of the B-50 aircraft hit the water was approximately five minutes.

Upon the B-50's first becoming disabled, in consequence of the actions of the MiG-15 fighter planes against it, the members of the B-50 crew were directed by the aircraft commander to abandon the aircraft and to seek safety by bailing out. The United States Government believes that most, if not all, members of the crew parachuted into the Sea of Japan, all coming down at points within an area approximately 30 miles south of Cape Gamov.

When the B-50 failed to return to its base at the time expected, and could not otherwise be contacted or accounted for, United States authorities commenced and conducted a meticulous and thorough search of the area by aircraft and by surface vessels.

The search of the Sea of Japan off Cape Gamov succeeded in the sighting in international waters of several survivors and disclosed the active presence in the same area of Soviet Patrol-Torpedo (PT) type boats and trawlers. One of the search aircraft belonging to the United States dropped a lifeboat but only Captain Eugene R. Phillips, the navigator, was able to reach it and climb aboard. Intermittent surface fog hampered the rescue efforts and no other personnel could be rescued by the United States at that time.

When the weather in the area cleared, by dawn of August 4, 1954, rescue aircraft could see no evidence of survivors, other than Captain Phillips. Subsequently, Soviet authorities turned over the remains of two crewmen, Captain Archibald T. Edmunds, the co-pilot, and Master Sergeant Leland P. Cupp, the flight engineer, which, according to Soviet authorities, had washed ashore on Askold Island sometime during August 6, 1954.

The Gamov Incident

The United States Government finds, and charges, that in direct consequence of the Soviet Government's actions above described, the following took place:

1. The B-50 aircraft was totally destroyed.
2. Captain Archibald T. Edmunds, the co-pilot situated on the flight deck, succeeded in bailing out from the aircraft into the waters of the Sea of Japan, was badly injured as a direct result of the attacking MiG-15 fighter planes, and died as a result of these physical injuries, from shock, and from his exposure for approximately twenty hours in the Sea of Japan.
3. Master Sergeant Leland P. Cupp, the flight engineer, situated on the flight deck, succeeded in bailing out from the aircraft into the waters of the Sea of Japan, was badly injured as a direct result of the attacking MiG-15 fighters, and died as a result of these physical injuries, from shock, and from his exposure for approximately twenty hours in the Sea of Japan.
4. Captain Eugene R. Phillips, the navigator, situated in the nose of the aircraft, was thrown headlong into the body of the B-50, suffered numerous injuries as a direct result of the attacking MiG-15's, and succeeded in bailing out from the aircraft. Despite climbing aboard the air-dropped lifeboat, Captain Phillips suffered wounds, shock, and exposure in the Sea of Japan from about 7:05 A.M. local time, August 3, 1954, to approximately 1:00 P.M. local time, August 4, 1954. He was subsequently rescued from the waters of the Sea of Japan by a United States Naval search vessel.

5. The remaining eleven crewmembers have not so far been accounted for. The United States Government finds, however, that all of them suffered bodily injury and shock as a direct result of the shooting by Soviet MiG-15 aircraft. It finds further that several, if not all, successfully parachuted to the surface of the Sea of Japan in the area above described. The United States Government must also conclude that these airmen were either picked up alive by surface vessels of the Soviet Government, or in due course, dead or alive, were carried by prevailing sea currents to Soviet-held territory and into the Soviet Government's custody. Those dead, the United States Government charges, were brought to their death by injuries caused in the course of the attack on the B-50 aircraft, by shock, and by exposure in the waters of the Sea of Japan. Those that were alive when they came into the custody of the Soviet Government suffered additional injuries and anguish caused by their long detention at the hands of Soviet authorities.

The above noted conclusions are soundly based on the following considerations:

The note went on to reiterate, in slightly different terms, much of what Cody had already read. There was, however, one additional fact: In the hours immediately following the shootdown, American search aircraft had observed two, perhaps three, Soviet PT boats departing the crash site at high speed.

The last few pages summarized the not-unexpected Soviet response: a claim that the B-50 had crossed into Soviet airspace; and, that it attacked first by firing on the MiGs, whereupon the Soviet pilots reacted in self-defense. In other words: It Wasn't Our Fault. The Soviets also denied knowledge of Americans other than the two whose bodies they had previously returned.

Cody leaned back and considered what he knew so far. First, both Russia and the United States had confirmed Danilov's version of the incident. Second, the U.S. believed most, if not all, the crew bailed out before the aircraft disintegrated. Third, if Soviet PT boats sped *away* from the crash site after the shootdown, then they probably had one or more downed American flyers on board, presumably alive.

The State Department memorandum provided details that only the parties involved should know: specifics about the crew and the shootdown itself. The document would be another way to verify information surrounding the incident; details Danilov could not avoid sharing during the interview process. The possibility that the old man had prior knowledge of the diplomatic protest note and its contents was remote.

Cody also mulled the troubling question surrounding Danilov's supposed graduation from the Pennsylvania Military College, an institution not listed in his Webster's dictionary. There could be a logical explanation for the omission, but Cody's mind considered another possibility.

Did the 'real' Captain Thompson, perhaps sensing what might be happening to him, intentionally feed his interrogators misinformation? If so, should Cody be alert for other inconsistencies as well? It was another layer of complexity he expected, but hoped not to encounter.

Finally, and most perplexing of all, was the lingering question: If Captain Andrew Thompson, aka Danilov, was pulled from the sea alive by Soviet sailors manning PT boats, how had he endured—perhaps even thrived—all those long decades in Russian captivity?

Cody stood, stretched and yawned. It was past seven o'clock and his stomach produced a hollow, growling rumble. Breakfast and the late-morning cinnamon roll were distant memories. Once again, he had worked through lunch but was no closer to solving the riddles posed by Andrei Danilov's unexpected appearance. What he needed was a substantial dinner and an equally substantial alcoholic beverage, not necessarily in that order.

The telephone buzzed and he picked up, reluctantly.

"Good evening, Mr. Ballantine. This is Ms. Jamison in the Word Processing department. A final copy of your interview transcript is ready."

It would take him several hours to go through the document. He could leave the office now and grab a quick bite before starting his review; or, he could stay, finish the job, and eat at home. The refrigerator in his apartment contained cheese, cold meats, and a half-loaf of not-quite stale bread.

"Thank you, Ms. Jamison," he said. "I'll be right there."

His desire for food could not overcome the discomfort at leaving an important task undone.

Chapter 13

The following morning at precisely nine o'clock, Andrei Danilov stepped from the basement elevator into the Pushkin Street lobby of the U.S. Consulate.

Because he had indicated discomfort at visiting the consulate on a regular basis, which now seemed likely, Cody had arranged for Danilov to be picked up and dropped off at prearranged locations throughout the city. As instructed, Cody's man drove one of several Agency cars, all nondescript Russian-made sedans, and used the consulate's rear access into the underground garage.

"Good morning," Cody said, extending his hand. "You're right on time."

Despite the weekend, consular staff occupied their regular posts, coping with start-up tasks common to newly established administrative functions. That issue aside however, working a couple of hours on Saturday was hardly an inconvenience. Other than a few modest cultural venues, Vladivostok offered little in the way of weekend diversions.

Danilov removed his gloves and took Cody's hand. "Punctuality is a common courtesy. Sadly, many consider it an option."

"Assuming they consider it at all," Cody added.

"Indeed."

It was difficult not to like Danilov. Polite and articulate, he exuded quiet charm and old-fashioned mannerisms, like standing when a lady entered the room. Although Cody wanted to accept Danilov's claim and quickly repatriate a long-forgotten cold warrior, the central question remained: If he was actually Captain Thompson, what had happened to him during all those long years behind the Iron Curtain? Today, Cody intended to find out.

They helped themselves to tea and coffee and settled around the conference table once again, occupying the same chairs as before.

Cody said, "Do you visit Vladivostok often?"

"Not exactly often. Perhaps once or twice during a month, primarily to attend concerts or to shop the GUM department store. Ussurijsk doesn't offer much along those lines."

"I suppose not." Cody sipped coffee, set his cup down and decided there was little more he might gain from small talk. He said, "When we left off yesterday afternoon, you were telling me about your slight color blindness."

"Yes, I remember," he began wistfully. His eyes seemed to focus somewhere in the middle distance. "During my fourth year at Penn Military, the Air Force's newest jet fighter, the F-100 Super Sabre, was just coming into service. It was an incredibly sleek and beautiful airplane. Even parked with its engine shut down, it seemed poised for immediate flight. I dreamed of strapping myself inside this machine and zooming off into the wild blue yonder, my white silk scarf fluttering in the slipstream while love-struck young ladies swooned on the tarmac."

Cody smiled. "If I'm not mistaken, fighter jets have closed canopies; ergo, no fluttering scarves."

"A minor detail," Danilov said, reaching for his tea. "Reality seldom inhibits youthful fantasies."

"What happened then?"

"I was given options. I could translate Russian documents in the Pentagon, teach others to do likewise, or use my language skills in ways the Air Force was not yet prepared to divulge. The latter option, I was told, included specialized technical training and, upon graduation, interesting flying duties of great national importance."

"Naturally, you chose the latter."

"Yes. The Air Force sent me to Keesler Air Force Base in Mississippi. There I studied radar systems and learned how to detect and classify specific electromagnetic signatures. Back then, what I did was called ELINT—Electronic Intelligence."

"It's still called ELINT," Cody volunteered. "You were stationed in Mississippi when the Korean War broke out?"

"Yes."

"When did you leave Keesler?"

"October, 1951. After technical school, the Air Force assigned me to Alaska, Ladd Air Force Base, near Fairbanks. My unit, the 72nd Strategic Reconnaissance Squadron, occupied Quonset huts on a remote part of the field. I spent a year there."

"Doing what?"

"Trying to stay warm."

At Cody's suggestion, Danilov identified his commanding officer, friends, and local hangouts, apparently recalling everything from memory, including the Totem Club, a popular watering hole the size of a two-car garage.

"An old timer, Tom 'Dirty' Black, frequented the Totem. After a few drinks, purchased by us of course, he would recite poems about Alaska's gold rush days, ballads like those written by Robert W. Service. My favorite was *Dangerous Dan McGrew*."

"The title sounds familiar," Cody said.

"I used to know it complete, but not anymore. I seem to have lost a few stanzas with the passage of time."

"Haven't we all."

"We flew RB-50s, an updated version of the World War Two B-29 bomber. Pylons mounted underneath each wing, outboard of the engines, allowed us to carry two seven hundred gallon fuel tanks. The additional fuel gave us significantly more range. We did not carry bombs, however. Instead, engineers reconfigured and extended the bomb bay aft. The entire area, from behind the flight deck extending to just beyond the wings, was enclosed. Unlike those on the flight deck, the rest of us worked in a windowless compartment. Our six-man group sat at consoles, jammed together like sardines, so cramped we could not wear our parachutes while working."

"I presume parachutes were there, somewhere."

"Fortunately, they were stowed nearby."

Cody revisited a prior comment. "Yesterday you mentioned a fourteen man crew. What were their functions?"

Danilov paused before answering, as though mentally counting heads. "Up front, on the flight deck, were the pilot, co-pilot, and the flight engineer. The naviguesser had a perch in the nose." He chuckled softly, "That is what we jokingly called the navigator."

"Why was that?"

"His technical gear, primitive by today's standards, made navigating around the North Pole a challenge. The Pole's magnetic characteristics affected sensitive electronic equipment, especially the directional compasses. Erratic winds also caused the airplane to drift off course. The navigator's job was quite difficult and involved a certain amount of speculation. The navigator called the procedure 'dead reckoning'; we called it 'guessing'…thus naviguesser. Still, our playful anecdotes about being lost in the Arctic were never vindictive, always in jest."

"I see. Who else made up the crew?"

"The rear compartment housed the six ravens, a radioman, a tail gunner, and two cryptographic operators. That makes fourteen, I believe."

Cody leaned forward. "An actual *tail gunner?* Really?" He pictured a scene from a World War Two black and white newsreel: German fighter planes zipping through American bomber formations as gunners returned fire, their expended brass casings glinting in high sunlight.

"Yes, but it is not what you think. He had a station behind us and operated the guns remotely, using an optical sight. It was like playing an arcade machine, one without the little steel balls."

"I see."

"A poorly designed arcade game, I should add. The twin fifty-caliber machine guns were almost useless. The effective fire cone was limited to about fifteen degrees aft and the system often malfunctioned."

Cody wondered if a malfunction had occurred over the Sea of Japan on August 3, 1954, but another question aroused his curiosity. "Why were two cryptographic operators aboard?"

"That was a security issue."

"I don't understand."

Danilov shifted in his seat. "I suppose it is okay to talk about this now. After all, the information is forty-years old."

"You must be the judge of that."

Danilov did not answer immediately. He stared at Cody for a long moment. "In for a penny, in for a pound," he finally muttered. A tiny shrug followed, as though he'd left an internal dispute unresolved.

Then he continued. "The cryptographic technicians carried two highly classified coding machines on board, each housed in an aluminum container about the size of a regular suitcase.

"The machines had a keyboard and a series of eight independently adjustable rotors. Each rotor was a three-inch circular disk about a half-inch thick; all eight were stacked together and encased in a horizontal metal cylinder attached to the keying device. Each rotor could be manually set to one of twenty-six positions, corresponding to the alphabet, and each had fifty-two electrical contact points, twenty-six on either side. The settings changed daily." Danilov paused. "Mr. Ballantine, what do you remember about your college mathematics?"

"Enough to be dangerous. It sounds like you're suggesting statistical probabilities."

"A permutation, I think. Or maybe something else. No matter. When encoding specific characters, a system that employs polyalphabetic substitution can replace a double 'r', as in the word 'borrow', with two different characters, say 'ng'. The system might then replace the next occurring double 'r' with another double character: 'ee' for example. In fact, it might also replace an 'r' with another 'r'. How a system substitutes any particular character depends upon the number of rotors used, and how each is initially set to one of twenty-six alphabetic positions.

"A system having eight rotors, each containing twenty-six characters, means the probability for predicting an exact mathematical pattern, thus breaking the code, is miniscule. I have forgotten the exact formula, but the number of possible outcomes for any particular word or character is astronomically high, thus nearly impossible to predict."

"It sounds like a very secure system," Cody said.

"Back then, it was. Nowadays, using sophisticated computer technology, I am not so sure."

Cody, his presence banned from the consulate's crypto center, felt a jealous twinge. "How do you know so much about cryptography? I thought you needed a special security clearance for that stuff."

"You do. I had a Top Secret/Cryptographic clearance. In addition to my regular duties, I was also the on-board Cryptographic Security Officer."

Cody recalled Colonel Butler's remark about background checks and the possibility of duplicate records within the Air Force's Office of Special Investigations. He made a mental note to follow up. "I see. Sorry for the diversion. You were discussing the on board cryptographic systems."

"Yes. Our standard procedure was to transmit radar findings immediately, in code. After the senior ELINT officer drafted the text, one cryptographer would encrypt the message using his machine. The other would do what they called a 'check decryption' on the second machine, to make sure the first device worked properly."

Not sure of what he meant, Cody asked, "If the machines were identical, why wouldn't they perform identically?"

"Theoretically, they should. However, the crypto equipment drew power from the on-board electrical systems. The slightest fluctuation could affect the machine's performance and perhaps make the code easier for the Soviets to break. If they could break one message, then the entire cryptosystem might be compromised. The practice of using two machines, one checking the integrity of the other, practically eliminated the chance of that happening."

Cody nodded understanding and Danilov continued.

"The check decryption also verified the first operator's work. If everything looked okay, the senior cryptographer took the message, now a series of meaningless five-letter alphabetic code groups, to the radioman who then transmitted the encrypted message to squadron headquarters using standard Morse code.

"Obviously, the encryption devices were a closely guarded secret, so crypto operators carried side arms and powerful incendiary devices on board. If it seemed likely we would be forced down in unfriendly territory, we had orders to melt the equipment and burn the codebooks first, and look out for ourselves second. If we were forced down over the sea, then the codebooks and equipment would sink to the bottom along with the airplane."

Cody knew from personal experience that individuals who chose military service also accepted a certain measure of personal danger. Wartime, either hot or cold, only exacerbated those risks.

"I take it you also had ELINT duties."

"Yes, I was Raven Five, the most junior among the electronic warfare officers. When I left Alaska however, I functioned as Raven Three."

"Why were you called ravens?"

"Probably because we were flyers engaged in secret, or black, operations. In other words, black birds."

"Of course. What, exactly, did you do on those missions?"

Danilov finished his tea, rose and made a fresh cup.

"Several things, but first I shall have another of your delicious crumpets."

"Please be my guest," Cody said, rising, "but I hate to see anyone eat alone." He warmed his coffee and took a Danish. Although he had augmented last evening's meager supper at home with a huge breakfast, Cody felt no guilt. From his perspective, he was still playing catch-up, calorie-wise.

Danilov finished the small pastry and continued. "Are you familiar with radar properties?"

"Let's assume that I am not."

"Then we shall keep to basics. The usual way to identify radar is by its operating frequency, in megacycles, much like a radio station generates. However, radars do not transmit a continuous wave, but rather a series of pulses. Radar units must pause a few microseconds to receive the return echo, seen as a blip on a radarscope. The *rate* of transmitted pulses is called the pulse repetition frequency, or PRF. When it is operating, a radar's unique PRF produces an audible sound, either a low frequency hum or a higher frequency whine, ranging across the entire electromagnetic spectrum.

"A skilled raven can identify specific radars by the sound in his earphones, much like a musician recognizes the difference between say, b-flat and a-sharp. On a recon mission, we recorded every sound emitted by Soviet radars on reels of magnetic tape. We also monitored an oscilloscope, a round, green cathode ray tube that visually captured the radar's electronic shape. When we detected a PRF, we noted its geographic location and then took a photograph of what we saw on the scope. Later, presumably at designated bases within the United States, analysts and engineers could see and hear exactly what we saw and heard. That information allowed them to develop countermeasures or jamming devices."

"Photographs? You used flashbulbs?" Cody didn't think so. The flash would wash out the image on the scope.

"No, of course not. We had 35-millimeter Leicas with a big lens and highly sensitive black and white film. The f-stop and shutter speed were pre-set. All we had to do was focus and shoot."

"I see. Please go on."

"During a mission, each raven took a specific operating band. As Raven Five, I monitored early warning radars operating at the lower frequencies. And, because of my Russian language skill, I also monitored the voice channels. More seasoned ravens took the medium and high frequency bands; that was the range where most intercept and ground control radars functioned. Raven One covered the airborne intercept radars that guided Russian fighters to their targets."

Cody knew the answer, thanks to Butler, but he asked anyway. "And why was all this necessary?"

Danilov fiddled with his teacup for a moment. "We had an interesting map at Ladd, our base in Alaska: a view of the earth from a point in space high above the North Pole. From that perspective, distances between the United States and the Soviet Union were much less.

"Should war come, Soviet bombers would take a polar route, track south over Canada and then disperse across the United States. We would do likewise, in reverse. To limit combat losses, American bombers needed to bypass Soviet air defenses. Our job was to identify and locate Russian gun laying, aircraft tracking, and fighter intercept radar stations. I also eavesdropped on conversations between Soviet ground controllers and fighter pilots. Knowing their language and procedures allowed us to avoid their interceptors."

"Where did those missions take you?"

"We usually flew west from Fairbanks, over St. Lawrence Island to the Gulf of Anadyr. From there, we turned south and followed the Soviet coastline, approaching Kamchatka from the north or northeast. We nosed around Petropavlovsk and sometimes crossed the Kuril Islands so we could monitor stations along the Sea of Okhotst.

"Some missions took us the other way, over Wrangel Island. A few times we went as far as Novaya Zemla, a Soviet nuclear test site. We carried special equipment on those missions—paper filters and vacuum bottles—so we could collect particle and air samples." Danilov shifted in his chair. "It was common knowledge that prolonged exposure to low-level radiation could render a man sterile. Naturally, we called those missions 'neuter flights'."

"Was ambient radioactivity a major concern?"

"I suppose not. At our flying altitude the levels were probably too low to cause real harm. But Novaya Zemla is a five-thousand-mile round trip from Fairbanks. In an RB-50, that is twenty-four or twenty-five hours in the air. In winter, the temperature at twenty thousand feet was fifty to sixty degrees below zero, Fahrenheit. Although our radar tracking sets generated heat from vacuum tubes, it was never enough to keep us warm. The coffee in our Thermos jugs would freeze solid if we didn't drink it early in the mission."

Cody tried to imagine conditions aboard an obsolescent aircraft forty years ago. He pictured himself in bulky flying gear, cramped beside his fellow crewmen inside a dimly lit, windowless compartment, periodically wiggling his toes and fingers in an effort to stave off the intense cold. His buttocks felt the constant vibration produced by the airplane's four reciprocating engines while his ears picked up the telltale whine of enemy search radars and the crackling voice of an approaching MiG fighter pilot. He felt the tension build, one gloved hand pressed against his earphones, the other manipulating dials and switches.

"It doesn't sound like a very pleasant environment."

Danilov fingered his teacup. "After a while, you become accustomed to it."

Cody tended to agree. Human beings, especially soldiers, were highly adaptable creatures, often finding comfort and humor in savagely primitive environments. "It appears your aircraft routinely intruded into Soviet territory."

"That never happened, officially. We had instructions to fly no closer than twelve nautical miles to the Soviet mainland. Unofficially however, we were told to do whatever was necessary to locate and catalog their radar stations, regardless of territorial boundaries."

Cody recalled Cultural Minister Trushin's remark about the United States 'invading' the Soviet Union. "Was this a common practice?"

"As I said, not officially, but it happened." One corner of Danilov's mouth ticked upward in a tiny half-smile. "When it did, our instructions were always verbal, never written."

"I presume you were challenged by the Soviets."

"Bad weather often limited our flying activities. It also constrained the Soviets. Back then, they had few all weather interceptors in service. Still, I logged fifty-seven missions: long, exhausting flights in cramped quarters. In my year at Ladd, MiG fighters intercepted our aircraft four times. We exchanged gunfire twice. Fortunately, we were all terrible shots and nobody hit anything."

Cody realized he had been drawn into Danilov's story; had become excited and fascinated by a little known aspect of the Cold War. "Russian MiGs notwithstanding, did you enjoy the work?"

"Yes, I did…at first. However, it did not take the Soviets much time to determine our intent. After a while, they began using older devices to track our flights: mostly Dumbos and Whiffs."

"I have no idea what you just said."

"Sorry. The Dumbo was a stationary, C-band, P-3 early warning radar; the Whiff was a mobile, SON-4 fire control E-band radar linked to an anti-aircraft battery. Both devices were copies of American equipment developed during the mid to late Forties. Their newer gear operated in the higher frequency bands—100 to 150 megahertz."

"I'll take your word on that."

"After a few initial successes, the missions settled down to long, boring flights with few discoveries."

"How did you manage to stay awake?"

"Lots of coffee and Benzedrine tablets."

The use of amphetamines by aircrews did not surprise Cody. In Vietnam, Special Forces troops routinely took stimulants during extended covert missions. He said, "Did you actually believe we would go to war with Soviet Russia?"

Danilov's eyes again took on a distant look. After a moment, they refocused. "Yes, I did. Most of our Air Force commanders had flown and fought in the Second World War. To them, the Soviet Union's post-war occupation of Eastern Europe was a prelude to future land grabs. The rest of the world, exhausted by the war, did not seem to concern themselves about Soviet ambitions to seize control of other countries. Only the United States had the means and the resolve to stand in their way.

"Pearl Harbor was still fresh in the minds of senior American military officers and they were determined to prevent another surprise attack. That is the reason we built a string of early warning radar sites in Alaska and along the northern Canadian border. The Soviet government was ruthless and paranoid. They viewed our defensive actions as a preamble to a nuclear attack." He shook his head slightly, as though in disbelief. "Nuclear conflict seemed inevitable. Few of us planned for a long, pleasant life."

Danilov's comment about the future raised another question. "Were you married?" Cody asked.

"No, but I became engaged later, after my return to the States."

"Where were you stationed?"

"Lockbourne Air Force Base, about twelve miles southeast of Columbus, Ohio. When I arrived, Lockbourne was converting to the new RB-47 jets, another bomber derivative. I was assigned duties as an instructor, teaching new ravens what we learned in Alaska."

"Is that where you met your fiancé, in Columbus?"

Danilov nodded.

"When did you become engaged?"

"A few months before my assignment to Japan."

"What was her name?"

"Sophia Marie Lombard," he replied, his face creasing into a melancholy smile. "She was beautiful and Italian and Roman Catholic. I was half Russian, half English and all Lutheran. Our developing love relationship was an undisguised embarrassment to her family." Danilov sighed. "As you may already know, Martin Luther and his eternally damned Protestant followers are anathema to many devout Catholics."

"So I've heard," Cody said, not ready to pursue a religious discussion. "Tell me about Sophia."

He listened while Danilov told a familiar serviceman-meets-girl, parents-disapprove story, impressed once again by the old man's remarkable grasp of detail.

The old man's credibility was growing as he spoke. Yet, a number of unanswered questions continued to nag at Cody's consciousness, issues voiced by pesky little inquisitors unwilling to sit quietly without being satisfied. Have patience, he told himself. Let the story develop naturally.

Danilov's cultured voice softened. "I wanted to get married before going overseas and take her with me, but Sophia's parents convinced her there was insufficient time to plan the huge, formal wedding everyone seemed to want. Everyone except me, that is."

He paused, as though forming his next thoughts. Cody sensed that the old man had something deeply personal to communicate. Was his obvious passion sincere, or was it merely rich frosting on a counterfeit confection?

After a long moment, Danilov finally spoke. "Women believe men are insensitive about weddings. In truth, we are not. It is merely that we have a different perception of the marriage event. In our minds, there is a significant difference between the *ceremony*, a largely commercial and social exercise, and actually voicing the marriage vow—giving our word to the woman we love, the two of us standing together in a holy place before God, family, and friends. Instinctively, we understand and embrace the *vow*, our sacred word of honor, while relegating ceremony—the social event—to a less important realm. To a woman, that point of view reeks of male insensitivity. Or, worse, disinterest."

He stared at his empty teacup. "When she decided to wait, I sensed our wedding might never happen. Two years is a long time to be away from your fiancé. I had no idea it would be closer to forty." Danilov paused and looked away, as though remembering a simpler, fonder time. Then, wistfully, "I wonder what became of her."

Cody sipped his coffee, now lukewarm.

I wonder what became of her.

A similar question had once haunted him, an interrogative posed by a persistent inner voice who had easily dampened the false exuberance gleaned from alcohol and too many unremembered women. Although his particular circumstance differed, someone special had also vanished from Cody's life, a woman he had loved with all the fiery passion that youth willingly exhibits but can seldom control or restrain. What, indeed, had become of Tessa?

Surprisingly, the question no longer roiled his insides or taunted him with might-have-been scenarios. That life, and some of the residual guilt, was behind him. He had endured a terrible hour and survived to middle age. Scarred but intact, he was again ready to explore the possibility of romance, to accept whatever God or fate or circumstance might present.

Anne Seymour's image filled his mind. She had re-appeared unexpectedly, a long forgotten encounter from an earlier time, a woman who presented an opportunity to re-experience the old magic—a wiser version, certainly—but a magic still vibrant and untarnished by unpleasant memories. It was, perhaps, one last chance to enliven the melancholy tempo that now seemed so much a normal part of his life.

Danilov's voice brought Cody's mind back to their conversation.

"You must forgive an old man his reminiscences."

"Of course," Cody replied.

A brief silence followed, and then Danilov said, "An odd thought just occurred to me regarding vows."

"What do you mean?"

"Well, once our own marriage vows have been exchanged, it seems to me that men become less interested in the vows of others and more inclined toward the social aspects—a reversal of attitude, so to speak. What I am trying to say is this: After our own wedding, most of us dislike attending the marriage ceremonies of others. Yet, we seldom decline an invitation to the reception. I am not sure I understand why that happens."

"Really? What don't you understand about free booze and food?" Cody replied.

The old man smiled. "Ah, of course. How obvious."

The discussion of marriage gave rise to another question: If Danilov was indeed Captain Thompson and wanted to return home, would Cody need to arrange for additional passports? Despite his long captivity, it seemed unlikely that Danilov/Thompson had become a monk.

Cody said, "Since you mentioned it, are you married now? Do you have a family in Ussurijsk?"

Danilov hesitated slightly and his eyes betrayed a quality Cody immediately recognized.

"No," Danilov said, "I have no family."

He's lying!

Cody's suppressed doubts re-emerged, boiling to the surface like a breaching whale. He felt like standing up, pointing to the old man and shouting 'Aha!' Instead, he kept his expression and emotions in check. Jack Paraday's admonition regarding lies had once again proven itself, validating Paraday's Conjecture, a human condition so named in his honor.

It was the first rift in the old man's discourse, but Danilov quickly recovered from his momentary lapse. "I live alone."

"I see," Cody said, expertly veiling his disbelief. "Another confirmed bachelor," he added with a knowing smile.

The obvious lie was a subject Cody knew he must revisit, along with the mysterious, perhaps non-existent, Pennsylvania Military College. For now, it seemed better to let those two issues languish, at least for the time being. He would find another way to extract the truth from Mr. Danilov.

"Well," Cody said, "shall we move on?"

"Not just yet," Danilov said. He rose to his feet, an inquisitive expression on his face.

Cody stood quickly, his mind and body immediately alert, a condition triggered by Danilov's clearly false response regarding family.

"I drank too much tea," Danilov admitted sheepishly. "I must visit the toilet."

Chapter 14

His suspicions aroused by Danilov's misstatement, partial truth, or outright lie, Cody anticipated something more dramatic than a request to visit the restroom. Still, the power of suggestion notwithstanding, it was not a bad idea.

"So must I," Cody said, relaxing slightly.

Noting the empty coffee and hot water pots, he reached for the telephone, but then hesitated, reluctant to call Angela. After a moment, he keyed a familiar extension.

As they washed their hands following the bathroom break, Cody surreptitiously eyed Danilov's wristwatch, a moderately priced stainless steel Vostok with a black face and white Arabic numerals. He also checked for a circular depression or a fading tan line on the old man's left ring finger, but saw none. Despite tradition however, some men never wore a wedding band, so its absence was not a foolproof indicator of marital status.

In response to Cody's telephone call, Phyllis—a silver-streaked brunette in her mid-Fifties—had brought fresh pots filled with coffee and hot water. She also tidied up their mess, gathering up used napkins, soggy tea bags and pastry-crumbed saucers.

"Thank you, Phyllis" Cody said, as she left the conference room.

Cody was acquainted with a number of Russians. Most chain-smoked foul smelling cigarettes, but Danilov either did not smoke or chose to abstain. Either way, there were no ashtrays to empty, nor did a stale haze taint the air, its presence hovering near the ceiling like a vile blue cloud.

Absence of smoke gave rise to a mischievous thought.

Presumably, Danilov was a Russian guest. Therefore, Whittier Zane extended smoking privileges to guests who visited the consulate. As they settled in, Cody wondered: If Danilov the Russian guest could smoke in the conference room, and it was later determined he was truly Captain Andrew Thompson the American, would Zane re-impose the No Smoking rule and prohibit Thompson from lighting up? He almost wished the old man smoked, so he could discover the answer.

"I imagine leaving Sophia was difficult," Cody said voicing the obvious, not yet ready to pursue the bothersome issues in Danilov's story.

"It was. I thought she might consider eloping, so I asked her to accompany me, without a chaperone of course, to Travis Air Force Base, my embarkation point. I told her we could marry in California—use an Air Force chaplain, a priest—but she did not like the idea of sneaking off or going against her parents' wishes. In any case, they would never allow their unmarried daughter to accompany me across the country, with or without a chaperone, and Sophia chose not to defy her family. At the station, we kissed goodbye and made promises we would never keep. Then I boarded the train to San Francisco, alone." Danilov fixed Cody with a baleful stare. "I know what you are thinking."

"Oh?"

"Yes. You imagine a dejected serviceman sitting alone in a dome car, drinking himself into oblivion as the countryside rolls by, the distance between himself and his betrothed increasing with each passing minute."

Dome car? Had Danilov actually ridden one of those relics from the glory days of rail travel? He said, "Maybe something like that."

"It did not happen that way. I accepted her decision and behaved myself."

"That's unusual…and commendable."

I sincerely mean that, Cody silently acknowledged. Years ago under similar emotional circumstances, a younger version of yours truly had taken a high dive into the shallow end of the pool, a fact he chose not to share. The young Danilov/Thompson however, seemed made of sterner stuff. Cody continued his questioning.

"When did you arrive in Japan?" he asked.

"It was the beginning of May, 1954. I am not certain of the exact date. On the flight over we crossed the International Date Line so it was either the second or third."

Losing or gaining a day while crossing the Pacific Ocean was another detail an imposter might forget to memorize. Nevertheless, Cody's skepticism persisted, a state of mind aroused by Danilov's 'no family' comment. While he still tended to allow some benefit for doubt, Cody knew he could not accept the old man's citizenship claim without conclusive proof, especially now.

"So," he said, calculating elapsed days, "you were in Japan exactly three months before the shootdown."

"Yes, that seems right. The Air Force assigned me to another strategic reconnaissance squadron, the 91st, at Yokota Air Base. We flew the same type aircraft, the G-model RB-50. It was almost like homecoming week."

"How do you mean?"

"Recon aircrews were a small, select group of aviators so it was not unusual for us to run into each other now an again. A few comrades from my old squadron at Ladd likewise ended up at Yokota, but on different aircrews. We met frequently at the Officer's Club for drinks or one-dollar steak nights. Our Alaskan reminiscences covered the usual subjects: terrible flying weather and twenty-five hour missions, or the Totem Club and Dirty Black's poetry recitations."

"I assume Yokota had nicer facilities than Ladd."

"Without question."

"Did you get into Tokyo much?"

"Yes, on several occasions. There was a popular nightspot called the Albion Club. It occupied the top floor of the Nichigeki Theatre, a circular, nine or ten-story building in the Ginza district. A band provided live music—Japanese singers and musicians imitating American Rock and Roll stars—and lovely, well-dressed hostesses offering polite company in exchange for expensive cocktails."

"Real booze?"

Danilov smiled. "Iced tea at whiskey prices."

"Naturally."

Some things, including the well-polished practices of pretty girls working in bars, never seemed to change. A decade earlier in Saigon, other ladies had used the same modus operandi on a younger generation of American soldiers. Hustling overpriced drinks, Cody mused, must be the world's fourth oldest profession, immediately behind soldiering, prostitution, and politics. He couldn't remember which came first.

"If the girls were 'lovely' as you put it, were you tempted to stray?"

"Is that an important consideration, Mr. Ballantine?"

"No, of course not." Cody returned to the original subject, secretly pleased with Danilov's non-answer. Discussing one's sex life with a stranger would have been inappropriate conduct, especially for an Officer and Gentleman. He returned to the original topic. "Did you fly the same kind of missions?"

"Yes, but not initially. Newly assigned aircrews flew several training flights to familiarize themselves with the general area and local weather conditions. We completed five round-robins along the Japanese and South Korean coastlines before our first 'real' mission."

"More flights over and around the Soviet Union?"

"Not at first. You probably do not remember this, but the American military establishment was not in a very good mood back then. Although the United States signed the Korean Armistice a year earlier, nobody had forgotten the Chinese intervention, an aggressive act prolonging a miserable war that eventually ended in stalemate. For that reason, our initial electronic intelligence-gathering missions targeted China, specifically Dalian. If you are familiar with political geography, then you know that Tsar Nickolas called Dalian Port Arthur. Russia used it as a warm water outlet to the sea. It was also where the Russian Fleet first battled the Japanese Navy in 1904."

From his readings, Cody recalled that Port Arthur was the initial engagement of the Russo-Japanese War, a conflict Tsarist Russia lost. It was Japan's first military victory over a Western power. That success, a shocking surprise for many Europeans, vaulted the island nation to world recognition. As recompense, Russia ceded the port to Japan in 1905. China, an American ally during World War Two, took control after Japan's defeat.

"That sounds like a long flight," Cody remarked.

"It was. Three thousand miles round trip, more or less. From Japan, we would first bisect South Korea thus gaining access to the Yellow Sea. We would then head north to eavesdrop around the Liaodong Peninsula. There was little to discover but the Chinese were very aggressive when it came to defending their territorial boundaries. Fortunately for us, they still flew Russian made La-11s, a World War Two propeller driven fighter. Their newer MiG jets, provided by Josef Stalin, were not yet fully deployed. However, most of our flights probed Soviet not Chinese air defenses."

"Not to belittle your efforts," Cody said, "but it sounds like business as usual."

"Yes, I suppose it was. Except for the weather, which was much better than what we experienced in Alaska, our tactical situation had not changed. The Soviets refused to engage their most current early warning radars, so we were unable to locate or identify recently installed air defense systems."

"It sounds like stalemate of another kind."

"Indeed. And that is why new tactics were devised."

"You flew deeper into Soviet territory?"

"Not necessarily. We took a different approach."

Cody waited for an explanation.

"It worked like this: On a typical mission we would leave Yokota and climb to our normal cruising altitude, usually twenty thousand feet. At a predetermined point over the Sea of Japan, the pilot descended to approximately two hundred feet above the water. From there, we would approach our target, say Petropavlovsk on the Kamchatka peninsula, at very low altitude; that is, underneath the Soviet radar. When we were thirty miles out, still in international waters, the pilot would add power, haul back on the control column, and quickly regain our original altitude. From a Soviet radar observer's perspective, we appeared from nowhere, an unknown intruder bearing down on them at high speed."

"That sounds provocative."

"It was. The Russians assumed we were attacking."

"And so they switched on their latest air defense systems in response," Cody suggested.

"Exactly. The onboard consoles lit up like Christmas trees and our earphones buzzed with new pulse frequencies. Later, we used the tape recordings and oscilloscope photos to categorize the new radars. As they did with all Soviet air defense systems, Air Force analysts assigned them unique codenames such as Cross Fork, Knife Rest, and Token. For us, it was like discovering an electronic gold mine."

"Taunting the Russian bear is a dangerous game, especially in a poorly-armed, outdated airplane."

"Yes it was, as we later discovered. In response to our incursions of Kamchatka, Soviet air controllers often scrambled fighters from the MiG airfield at Nikolayevka."

Cody frowned. "Just a minute." After his bathhouse talk with the Cultural Minister, Cody had researched the probable location of young pilot Trushin's airbase. "I thought Nikolayevka was near Odessa in the Ukraine."

"That may be. It is a frequently used place name, much like Springfield, U.S.A. But Nikolayevka village on the Kamchatka peninsula is located a few miles beyond the Avachinskaya inlet from Petropavlovsk. The Soviet MiG base was nearby."

"I see." Cody had not considered Kamchatka. He assumed Minister Trushin's service occurred in the Western Soviet Union. It was a stupid oversight, adding to the mixed emotions he now experienced. Did young Trushin serve on Kamchatka in 1954? Did he and his fellow pilots intercept American reconnaissance flights? Did he actually fire upon American planes? It was an intriguing set of questions. And quite irrelevant to the present situation.

"Please go on," Cody said.

"I could hear Soviet controllers talking to MiG pilots, directing them to our location. It was good for us that those early MiGs did not have airborne radar. Our pilot merely turned away from their pursuit path and flew a few hundred feet above the water on our way out. After a half hour or so, the pilot resumed normal cruise altitude. In the meantime, the radioman transmitted our coded findings back to squadron headquarters at Yokota. And thus ended another productive mission."

Cody had analyzed numerous deep-sea cat and mouse confrontations between American and Soviet nuclear submarines during the Sixties and Seventies, naval exercises designed to gauge each country's war fighting capabilities. Both sides had lost submarines and sailors, through accident, design, or miscalculation.

Land forces had also tested each other but Cody never realized the extent to which similar activities had once occurred in the skies. The knowledge re-enforced his belief that the Cold War had been a deadly, three-dimensional chess game complete with soldier-knights, politician-bishops, kings, queens, and the entire human race serving as pawns. This old gentleman could very well be a forgotten casualty of that war—a lucky survivor from a dangerous era now thankfully past.

Cody said, "Tell me what happened on the day you were shot down."

Danilov frowned, no doubt recalling unpleasant memories. "Ferret mission aircraft commanders always filed two flight plans. It was standard operating procedure. On that particular day, our public and therefore fictitious plan described an exercise to test navigational equipment over the Sea of Japan. Our real, highly classified mission was briefed as a low-level penetration run on Vladivostok, similar to those previously flown to the Kamchatka peninsula and Sakhalin Island."

Cody recalled the State Department's protest note to the Soviet Union, a claim that the American aircraft was merely conducting routine navigational exercises over the Sea of Japan. The U.S. note echoed the public flight plan. Danilov's revelation coincided exactly with the official—that is, public—record.

"Ferret mission?" Cody asked. "Is that what they were called?"

"Yes," Danilov replied. "From an operational perspective, we were directed to 'ferret out' what the Soviets were trying to hide from us."

"Of course."

Ravens and ferrets. Cody recalled his Army service and the military's penchant for devising snappy metaphors.

Danilov continued. "We took off at 0300 hours and climbed to altitude—twenty thousand feet—then flew toward North Korea. Previous flights had reported unusual electronic activity near Wonsan harbor. Our first task was to verify and record those emissions on our way to Vladivostok."

"I assume you used the low level approach technique?"

"Yes, but we did not discover anything new, so we regained altitude and proceeded northeast."

"How close were you to the North Korean mainland when you turned toward Vladivostok?"

"Fifteen miles, maybe a bit more. Ravens had a mission map and we could follow the flight path based on elapsed time and pre-arranged navigational checkpoints. We were scheduled to start our low-level run on Vladivostok at exactly 0700."

"What happened?"

Danilov fixed Cody with another baleful gaze. "We never made it that far."

Cody held the old man's stare. "So it seems."

Chapter 15

Danilov pushed away from the table, stood, stretched and then poured hot water over a fresh tea bag. Cody waited until the old man re-seated himself.

"Evidently," Danilov began, "our approach to Wonsan harbor became known to Soviet air defense authorities, information no doubt furnished by the North Koreans. The Russians estimated, correctly it turned out, our arrival at several potential landfalls, including Vladivostok. Of course, we knew nothing of those developments. About an hour away from the city, Craig—Major Howard—descended to two hundred feet."

Cody remembered Major Craig Allen Howard's name from the diplomatic note he'd read earlier, primarily because the major seemed to have no given name, but rather three British family names. He also recalled something else.

"I believe you mentioned being stationed with Major Howard in Alaska."

"Yes, I did. Although most of my comrades from Ladd were assigned to different aircrews, Craig was the lone exception." An appreciative smile crossed Danilov's face. "He knew about my eyesight problem and the aborted flying career. Sometimes, usually on our way home from a mission, I would request permission to visit the flight deck. Craig always granted access. The RB-50's nose and upper portion of the flight deck were made of clear Plexiglas; curved plastic panels, each one surrounded by an aluminum frame. It reminded me of a greenhouse."

"The view must have been incredible."

"Indeed. But it was also quite warm at times."

"Who were the other crew members?"

Danilov recited a list of first and last names, including rank, pausing now and then to note an individual characteristic or idiosyncrasy.

Satisfied the names matched those contained in the protest note, Cody brought them back on subject. "You were saying Major Howard flew about two hundred feet above the sea on your way into Vladivostok."

"I did. That may not sound like a significant accomplishment, Mr. Ballantine, but the RB-50 is a huge airplane. Flying at low altitude requires a great deal of skill and concentration. Variable air currents rising from the sea made for a bumpy ride. But Craig was a superb pilot, more than equal to the task."

"How long did he fly at that level?"

"About fifty minutes, more or less. When we were thirty miles out from landfall he alerted the crew and then climbed to ten thousand feet." Danilov paused, obviously preparing himself for an unpleasant task. "As my earphones filled with radio chatter from Soviet air controllers, I remember thinking how routine this was going to be. Once the MiG fighters became airborne, I would alert Craig and he would avoid making contact, just as he had so many times before in Alaska." Danilov paused again and frowned, slightly. Then he shifted uncomfortably in his chair.

Cody waited while Danilov composed himself.

"Only this time, it was different. Seconds later I heard the voice of a Russian pilot talking to his controller: 'Yuri, we have the intruder in sight. Eleven o'clock low, three thousand meters above the sea. It is an American B-29 bomber.'" Danilov paused, as though realizing an explanation was necessary. "The Soviets often misidentified the RB-50. To a casual observer, the two aircraft were nearly identical in appearance."

Thanks to Colonel Butler, Cody had viewed photographs of both aircraft. Except for the external fuel tanks hanging from each wing outboard of the engines, he could see very little difference between the two.

"I couldn't believe my ears," Danilov continued. "The Russian pilots actually *saw* us, had our plane cleanly spotted, and that unpleasant knowledge came as a complete shock. You see Mr. Ballantine, if our airplane was at their eleven o'clock low, that meant *they* were at our five o'clock high."

Cody quickly pictured the relative positions of the RB-50 and the fighter planes. "In other words, the Soviet MiGs were above and behind you and a bit off your right side."

"Exactly; and, given our heading, the Russians were also hidden in the sun's glare, invisible to us. Realizing that, I said, 'Major, hostile aircraft, five o'clock high. They have us in sight.' Craig acknowledged, banked immediately, turned away from the mainland, and climbed. We were probably fifteen miles from Vladivostok, still in international waters. Since our compartment had no windows, I assumed Craig was trying to obtain a visual sighting or maybe hide in a nearby cloud.

"There followed more chatter between the Soviet air controllers and MiG pilots. Evidently, they were unsure what to do. Then I heard: 'Captain Sergei Nagorski, you have permission to fire weapons. Bring the intruder down!'"

Danilov absently scratched an earlobe. "I could not believe what I had just heard. They were actually going to shoot. Not only that, the weather was clear, allowing the MiGs unobstructed approach angles. I relayed the controller's words to Craig and told him to prepare for an attack."

As Danilov spoke, Cody imagined the crew's state of mind. Except for those up front, most could not see what was going on outside the aircraft. Blind to the action, adrenaline surging through their veins, they were bystanders, impotent observers unable to alter whatever outcome Fate had in store for them.

Danilov continued. "Next came a string of abrupt, high pitched popping sounds, like pebbles hurled against the aluminum skin of our airplane, only much, much louder. It was unbelievable.

They were trying to kill us, really *kill* us, I mean." Danilov paused. "Have you ever been shot at, Mr. Ballantine?"

In Vietnam's central highlands, war's reality had edged up on Cody, beginning with a smattering of short-duration firefights with few casualties—engagements that slowly increased in frequency and violence. That perverse good fortune had allowed his mind and body to become somewhat, but never completely, acclimated to the din and random fury of close contact with a seasoned enemy. Those early clashes spared Cody the bowel-voiding embarrassment that sometimes accompanies a sudden, ear shattering, first-time combat engagement.

"Yes, unfortunately."

"In Vietnam?"

"Mostly. It is not something you ever get used to."

"No, I suppose not." A moment of silence passed between them before Danilov resumed where he'd left off. "By this time, Craig was maneuvering to evade the MiGs, yawing and banking violently to spoil their aim. Despite his efforts, it did not do much good. Another series of explosions produced smoke inside our compartment. I disconnected my earphones, unfastened the seat harness and used the fire extinguisher. Some of the monitoring equipment had shorted out and there were several electrical fires. The pilot's evasive maneuvers made it difficult to maintain my balance and I had difficulty directing the extinguisher's flow. It was a bad situation but, despite wide eyes and concerned looks, everyone seemed in control of themselves."

"Did you return fire?" Cody asked.

Danilov snorted. "Our tail guns were not much of a threat, Mr. Ballantine. The gunner tried, but the mechanism failed—again. Although he attempted to fix the problem, we did not expend a single round."

Murphy's Law, Cody thought. Critical equipment always fails at the worst possible time.

"To me it seemed like hours, but only a few minutes had passed. Then I heard the most frightening sound of all. The bail out alarm reverberated throughout the interior, shattering any hope that we might escape the fighters. It was the worst moment of my life, or so I thought at the time. Despite the situation, I never seriously believed we would not make it back to base. To think otherwise was to acknowledge far too many unpleasant possibilities: crashing, a failed parachute, drowning in the sea; or capture, confinement, and perhaps torture and execution. Not many crewmen believed we would be rescued before the arrival of Soviet vessels.

"When the alarm sounded, I set aside the fire extinguisher. Everyone had parachutes clipped to their harnesses and were forming up near the escape hatch. I did likewise."

According to the State Department protest, the U.S. believed most, if not all, the crew managed to bail out. Although Cody was intensely interested to hear Danilov's version of how many crewmen actually escaped, he hesitated to ask, unwilling to interrupt the old man's narrative.

"That was another surprise," Danilov said. "I have no recollection of leaving our compartment or hooking on my parachute, but there it was, properly fastened to my chest harness, the metal 'D' ring visible, ready for use."

His characteristic smile, self-deprecating and sheepish, seemed a bit strained and embarrassed, like one attempting to explain the unexplainable. Finally, he uttered a tired sigh. "Sometimes, the will to survive overpowers our nobler intentions. Perhaps it was an unconscious response, an action honed by hours of survival training. In any event, some of us used the rear belly hatch, which was now open. Presumably, others were exiting through the forward hatches. I followed the tail gunner out."

"Who was that?" Cody asked.

"An older crewman, Sergeant Ed 'Grizzly' Baer. He was a veteran of the Second World War. European Theatre, I believe."

Cody recalled Baer's name from the State Department's missing crew list. "What happened next?"

"I have several vivid recollections of that moment. The first was the roar of rushing air when the escape hatch popped open. It was like a deafening announcement that all this was real, that I might actually die. Next was tumbling forward and being sucked violently into space.

"I do not remember pulling the ripcord, but I felt the jolt when the canopy snapped open. When I looked down, I saw a string of six parachutes, each white disk proportionately smaller, like aerial stepping stones descending in a long curve towards a distant blue sea."

Danilov bowed his head for a moment, then resumed. "I was probably the last man out. As I counted parachutes, a monstrous *crack!* filled the air. I caught sight of our plane just as the right wing buckled. The ruptured fuel tanks ignited, the wing separated from the fuselage, and the plane nosed down into a tight spin, trapping those who remained aboard. I could see it rotating as it fell: black underside, then unpainted aluminum top flashing in the sun; once, twice, three times. Then the tail section tore off, breaking the fuselage in two."

Cody pictured those long, final moments. The remaining crew, pinned by enormous G-forces to the inside bulkhead of the rapidly spinning aircraft, would have been unable to reach an escape hatch, even if one stood ready and open a few steps away. Their bodies immobilized by the inflexible laws of physics, those final seconds of life would have seemed like forever. In a way, they were.

"Although fog patches covered large portions of the sea, the airplane hit the water in a sunny spot; three big splashes followed by considerable debris sprinkled across the crash site. The biggest pieces sank almost immediately, but burning gasoline marked the spot where they went in."

Danilov paused, his eyes glazed as though in a trance.

"I have no memory of actually hitting the water," he said, his voice now a monotone. "Suddenly I was floating, held up by a Mae West, the parachute discarded, slowly becoming waterlogged and sinking. A mile or so away, four MiGs circled the burning gasoline, pirouetting around a black smoke column." He blinked several times. "Maybe they spotted bodies floating in the debris field, perhaps not. A few minutes later, they formed a loose 'V' and flew toward the mainland.

"Right about then I drifted into a thick fog patch and everything vanished, totally depriving me of spatial orientation. Time and motion stopped. I was blind and weightless, floating in the naturally buoyant salt water, surrounded by absolute silence. Death had claimed me, or so I thought at first. God had weighed my soul and then passed judgment. I was in Purgatory, doomed to a gray existence; one without sight, sound, or physical sensation—a sinner condemned to an eternal emptiness midway between Heaven and eternal damnation.

"But then I detected the faint odor of burning gasoline. Despite my befuddled state of mind, I suddenly realized that Craig had died with his airplane. He was one of those 'last man out' aviators and would have stayed at the controls until everyone safely abandoned his doomed aircraft."

The old man blinked again, clearing his eyes. Then his voice softened, as though in prayer. "Of all those men with whom I flew, Craig Howard is the one I miss most of all, even to this day. During my darkest hours in the Svetloye mines, the memory of Craig's irrepressible sense of humor and unassuming courage kept me going long after I decided it would be easier to give up and die. I owe him much more than my life. I owe him my sanity."

Danilov paused and took a deep breath, leaving Cody to ponder the 'Svetloye mines' reference.

"Eventually, the fog burned off. Under a sunny blue sky again, I thought about the six others who had bailed out ahead of me. If my parachute count was correct—and I have no assurance it was—then seven of us got out. That left the other seven crewmen unaccounted for. I also wondered, selfishly, if Craig had sent a distress call before the plane disintegrated. Absent a mayday signal, it would be late afternoon before our squadron organized and dispatched a search effort. If we were not rescued or captured before dusk, then we were destined to spend the night floating in the sea, an ordeal we could not survive."

"Was the water that cold?"

"According to the mission briefing officer, summer water temperatures in the Sea of Japan ranged from sixty-six to sixty-eight degrees; not exactly frigid, but not warm enough for a man to survive indefinitely either. Eventually my body temperature would equalize to the sea. After eighteen hours or so I would succumb to hypothermia."

Cody ran the numbers in his head. Danilov went into the water around seven in the morning. Eighteen hours later meant he would die, alone and in darkness, sometime between midnight and one o'clock the following morning.

"Not a pleasant prospect," Cody said. "Did you spot any of your crew?"

Danilov shook his head. "The sea was calm with less than one meter swells. But my chin was only a few decimeters—a little more than a foot—above the surface, so I could not see very far. I shouted several times, but never heard a reply. I kept at it for a while, and then gave up."

The old man paused and swallowed more tea, an obvious attempt to retain his composure. "Hours passed and the sun climbed higher. My white flight helmet offered some protection, but the August sun was unrelenting. My lips cracked and my tongue kept sticking to the roof of my mouth. I was tempted to rinse with seawater, but that would have made it worse, so I tried to conserve moisture by breathing through my nose. It did little good.

"But grinding, unrelenting thirst was only part of it. The profound silence was palpable, almost like a sentient being, and its voiceless presence nearly overwhelmed me. I was utterly alone: an insignificant, solitary speck floating on a vast, watery expanse beneath an empty, sun-shot sky. It was easy to believe that I was the only person on earth, desperately alive yet forgotten or abandoned by an unconcerned God."

Danilov's recollection gave Cody a momentary feeling of déjà vu. His mind flashed back to a dark mountaintop in Vietnam. There, resting against a limestone outcrop, he stared into the unusually clear sky, a black dome alive with countless stars seamlessly woven into the Milky Way's lacy magnificence.

From his vantage point near the Equator, Cody recognized his favorite constellation hanging in the eastern sky. On that particular night, Orion was not standing erect. Rather, the constellation tilted ninety degrees to the left, as though the Great Hunter lay resting on his back, having grown weary from chasing the Pleiades.

What Cody saw in those brief moments—grand and glorious and undimmed by artificial light—encompassed but a miniscule fraction of Earth's home galaxy, itself a spiral pinprick tumbling through an ever-expanding universe.

In the dark solitude of Vietnam's central highlands, Cody realized that the entirety of the human race, when compared to such vast, incomprehensible magnitudes, was hardly more than a rambling string of ciphers far to the right of a cosmic decimal point. Why, he remembered asking himself, would God concern himself with such vain, frivolous, and inconsequential beings? The answer had come to him almost immediately: Maybe He didn't.

"I know the feeling," Cody volunteered.

Danilov acknowledged Cody's admission with a nod, and then continued. "Sometime that afternoon I experienced what some might call an Epiphany; perhaps it was only a hallucination; delirium brought on by shock and dehydration.

"Suddenly I realized my life was over. Death would surely come for me, and when it did, my body would rejoin the sea, the source of all life on Earth. My corporeal self would nourish ocean creatures and they, in turn, would feed others in an endless cycle. Yet, my spirit would survive physical death. The essential *me* would go on, perhaps in some mystical continuum just beyond the realm of human comprehension, to join other souls in a timeless, ever flowing stream of existence.

"It was a comforting thought, consistent with religious beliefs learned in childhood but ignored as an adult. I thanked God for my life; croaked dry, thick-tongued goodbyes to Sophia and my family, and then waited for the end.

"A while later I heard the distant rumble of a motor boat. That sound was not a delusion; it was real. I could almost feel the vibrations. At that instant, everything changed." The old man paused, then rose, stretched and checked his wristwatch.

"I've arranged to have a cold lunch sent in," Cody said. "It should arrive shortly. Will that be okay?"

Danilov nodded agreement. "But I must catch the last train to Ussurijsk later this afternoon. I have a luncheon engagement tomorrow with an old friend. We meet every Sunday to eat, drink wine, and reminisce about our days in prison."

The question of Danilov's long survival inside Soviet Russia was never far from Cody's thoughts. He recalled the earlier reference. "Was Svetloye a prison?"

Danilov nodded. "Yes, and more."

"Will it be possible for you to share those memories with me today?"

Danilov took his seat and fingered the teacup. "Some, but not all. There will not be time."

That's probably true, Cody acknowledged. He would try to get the essentials today; tomorrow or next week would have to take care of itself.

"You said everything changed when you heard the motor boat. What does that mean?"

Danilov's eyes took on the now-familiar distant look and his voice seemed to come from deep within. "Sea water had soaked though my flight suit. My feet were cold and I could feel the wet chill creeping up my legs. The sun was midway down the Western sky and I knew the coming sunset would be my last on earth. I would not survive the night. Adrift and alone, the stark reality of my own death became a little easier to accept. In that overpowering silence my ego driven self-importance revealed itself as a comical absurdity."

He paused, and then asked, "Mr. Ballantine, are you familiar with the poem *Thanatopsis*?"

Cody thought for a moment, recalling the title from his school days. "I know it's a poem, but not much else."

"It was written by William Cullen Bryant. I first read it at Har-Brack, but promptly forgot it."

"High school literature," Cody said. "I may have read and forgotten it too, after the exam, of course. Now that you mention it, the poem was probably required reading at most high schools back then."

"I imagine so. Anyway, when I was a cadet at Penn Military, old Doc Johnson made us memorize the last stanza. We were required to stand and recite it aloud in class."

"That sounds a bit odd. Why memorize only the last stanza?" Cody asked.

"Doc Johnson believed the poem's final lines conveyed an important reality, an unavoidable truth soldiers should always remember. In retrospect, I believe he was right. I have never forgotten that stanza."

Cody, genuinely interested, posed the obvious question. "Do you still remember how it goes?"

"Of course."

The old man recited from memory:

"So live, that when thy summons come to join
The innumerable caravan which moves
To that mysterious realm, where each shall take
His chamber in the silent halls of death,
Thou go not, like the quarry-slave at night,
Scourged to his dungeon, but, sustained and soothed
By an unfaltering trust, approach thy grave
Like one who wraps the drapery of his couch
About him, and lies down to pleasant dreams."

Danilov continued. "So there I was: a soldier in a good cause, a warrior vanquished in battle, but one who now stood prepared to 'wrap the drapery of my couch around me, and lie down to pleasant dreams.'"

"But the unexpected sound of an approaching boat resurrected the possibility of rescue, and with it a swallow of fresh water. I could almost taste its wet coolness. At that moment, the prospect of continued survival filled me with a frantic desire to live." He paused and appeared mildly embarrassed. "I no longer wanted to become one with the fishes."

"Hope can be a two-edged sword," Cody offered.

"Indeed it can. Ancient Greeks considered Hope a curse. I never understood why until that moment. In a split second, my mental state switched from calmly accepting death to desperation and near panic. Suddenly, thirst became a crushing, unbearable presence. I could not face being alone with my misery. Had the boat passed by, I am not sure what I would have done."

"But they didn't pass, did they?"

Danilov shook his head. "Their approach angle was about twenty degrees, easily within visual range. We spotted each other at about the same time. When I raised my arm, the pitch of the motors changed immediately."

"Was it a trawler?"

"No, it was much smaller. It looked like a World War Two torpedo boat, but one flying a Soviet flag. They tossed a life preserver. I managed to slip into it and they pulled me from the sea. Once on deck, I tried to stand but the effects of prolonged submersion was debilitating."

"Had you been wounded?"

"Other than a few painful bruises, presumably from being tossed about during the last moments of flight, I was unhurt."

"You were lucky."

"Much luckier than most of my crew. When I tried to stand my knees buckled and I ended up sprawled on the deck. The boat crew appeared sympathetic to my condition. A sailor helped me regain my feet and one of them said: 'Bring him water.' I assumed he was the captain.

"Right then, I had a decision to make. If I concealed the fact I understood Russian, it would probably reinforce their already strong belief that I was a spy. If I actually spoke Russian, it would no doubt *convince* them I was a spy."

"Not much of a choice."

"Exactly. After I gulped down my drink, I looked at the boat captain, a man in his forties with green eyes. Something told me to tell him the truth, so I formally thanked him, in Russian. I also complimented his crew, more to let him know that I was more than just a little conversant in their language. That caught them off guard and everyone grew silent."

"What happened then?"

"He acknowledged my thanks and asked if I was hurt. When I said no, he ordered his men to confine me to the storeroom. Two sailors took me by the arms and escorted me below. They provided another cup of water before locking me up. A minute later the boat moved off at high speed."

According to the State Department report, American search planes had spotted Soviet PT boats speeding away from the area. Was Danilov in one of them? If so, then it was the worst kind of bad luck. Had the Soviets not happened by when they did, American search aircraft might have located and rescued the downed flyer, sparing him a four-decade ordeal.

"I take it there were no other Americans on board?"

"I do not believe so; it was a small boat. But before they took me below I inquired about my crewmen."

Cody had been thinking about the crew as well. Of the fourteen on board, Danilov and the navigator survived; two bodies were returned. Assuming the seven who could not bail out died in the crash, that left three men unaccounted for.

"What did the captain say?"

Danilov shifted in his chair. "He ignored my question."

Chapter 16

A soft knock sounded. Cody rose, opened the door and stepped aside as Phyllis wheeled a food-laden cart into the conference room.

"Just in time," he said. From the corner of his eye, he saw Danilov rise. "Thanks again, Phyllis."

She nodded acknowledgement and then arranged various plates—buffet style—at one end of the rectangular oak table. Her work done, Phyllis smiled politely at Danilov and then closed the door on her way out.

"Among God's many blessings," the Russian said, "are quiet, competent women."

"I wouldn't share that thought aloud in public," Cody advised. "At least not in cosmopolitan America. It seems we have entered an age where certain women take offense at every opportunity, no doubt in protest against our historic oppression of the fairer sex."

Danilov looked startled for a moment but then waved a hand dismissively. "Social activists and professional complainers take themselves much too seriously, especially those whose minds are insufficiently occupied with more serious matters. Russians have no time for such self-aggrandizing activities. They are too busy trying to make a living in a difficult world. What I said was intended only as a respectful compliment to an attractive, efficient woman."

"I'm sure you did," Cody said, "and Phyllis would not be one to take offense. However, her views are not common among the majority of modern American women."

"I have much to learn, it seems," Danilov replied.

They built sandwiches by stacking cold meats, cheese, lettuce, and tomatoes on slices of dark and light bread, and then slathering mustard and/or mayonnaise on the top layer. Cody also managed to fit pasta salad on his plate.

"Those look familiar," Danilov said, pointing to a cellophane-wrapped saucer brimming with chocolate squares.

"They're called 'brownies'."

"Yes, of course. Now I remember."

"Phyllis makes them once in a while. They don't last very long. Does Russia have an equivalent?"

Danilov shook his head. "I don't believe so. Not in Siberia, anyway."

"Then take the entire batch with you. I'm sure Phyllis wouldn't mind. In fact, she'd consider it a compliment."

"You are very kind. I might even share one or two with my associates at the Institute."

As though by mutual agreement, both men ate in comfortable silence. After so much intense conversation, Cody welcomed the interlude, using the time to absorb what he had heard that morning. He also wondered where Danilov would take him next. Reliving details of the shootdown had clearly taxed the old man. He seemed worn out and less energetic than during their previous meeting.

I still think of him as Danilov, Cody admitted, munching on a dill pickle. Yet, despite his aroused sense of caution, earlier doubts were subsiding.

Was it possible to memorize another man's entire lifetime in such vivid detail? Possible perhaps, but not probable. Yet, the human mind, ripe with paradox and contradiction, had also proven itself capable of staggering intellectual achievement. The old guy was certainly intelligent. Did he also have the mental acuity of a savant? Instead of being a math or music wizard, could Danilov absorb the memories and persona of another man and then co-opt them as his own? To be wholly convincing, such an individual would have to sacrifice his own personal experiences and unique characteristics—a difficult achievement, but not impossible.

Cody set his empty plate on the cart.

"A bit earlier," he said, "you spoke about having regular Sunday luncheons with a fellow ex-prisoner. I take that to mean you spent time in the Gulag with this gentleman. Is that so?"

Danilov wiped his fingers on a napkin and sipped tea before responding. "Yes, unfortunately."

"Tell me about it."

"First, let me offer some background information. As you may or may not know, Gulag is an acronym. The full phrase, *Glavnoye Upravleniye ispravitelno-trudovyh Lagerey*, means Main Labor Camp Administration."

"You make it sound benign, like a summer work program. I always thought Gulag meant concentration camp."

"No, that word is *kontslager*, a term invented by Leon Trotsky soon after the October revolution in 1917. However, time and usage have given 'Gulag' a broader meaning. It now describes the entire Soviet slave labor system: arrest, interrogation, transportation, and finally imprisonment in various work camps. Within that wider definition, Mr. Ballantine, I have acquired first-hand knowledge and personal experience."

"I take it you were placed under arrest."

"Not at first. After we docked, I was turned over to the local *Ministerstvo vnutrennikh del*. As I mentioned earlier perhaps, the MVD's secret police had charge of political prisoners and associated confinement facilities.

"Evidently, the boat captain had radioed ahead with news regarding the capture of a Russian-speaking American flyer; one who had been aboard the downed spy plane. MVD officers, accompanied by a half-dozen uniformed guards armed with automatic weapons, took me directly from the torpedo boat into a canvass-topped truck parked nearby."

Cody listened as Danilov described a mostly silent, hour-long truck ride over rough, unimproved roads.

"In addition to water-logged boots, I wore a standard flight suit over my suntans. That was our summer uniform—khaki-colored gabardine; Army Air Force issue left over from World War Two. My clothing had not dried much and I shivered in the late afternoon chill. The guards ignored my discomfort. I asked where they were taking me. 'You will find out soon enough,' one of them snapped.

"Based on where I thought the attack occurred, along with the duration of the boat ride, I assumed we were in the vicinity of Vladivostok or possibly Nahodka. The former proved to be accurate."

Danilov described his arrival in a quasi-military camp; a drab cluster of wooden barracks surrounded by a high chain-link fence topped with barbed wire. Twenty-foot high guard towers complete with spotlights and machine gun crews stood at fifty-yard intervals.

"We got there an hour or so after dark. Once inside the main building, a guard gave me a bundle of dry clothing: work boots, socks, underwear, shirt, trousers, cap and a long coat. He said my boots, flight suit, and gabardines would be dried out and returned. They never were, of course. The MVD also confiscated my wallet and dog tags."

"So there you were: in Soviet Russia, without proper identification, wearing civilian clothes."

"Hindsight is always perfect. I should not have relinquished my dog tags, wallet and ID so quickly."

"Surrounded by armed guards, you probably didn't have a choice."

"Perhaps not, but I made it too easy." Danilov checked his watch again. "To shorten a long story, they flew me to Moscow via military transport, a two-day trip requiring numerous fuel stops. In Lefortovo prison, Soviet officials questioned me at length over a period of several weeks. During that time, I described our mission as a routine navigational exercise conducted entirely over international waters. When asked to explain my specific function, I told them I was a linguist, assigned to monitor Soviet fighter-control voice channels. 'For what purpose?' they asked. 'To avoid confrontation,' I replied."

"Did they believe you?"

"Not at first. Then I repeated the conversation between the Soviet air controller and the interceptors; I even remembered the name of the MiG fighter pilot: Captain Sergei Nagorski, and the controller, a man the MiG pilot called 'Yuri'.

"Although they brushed aside my knowledge of such details, I could tell they were unsure how to proceed." Danilov paused, as though for emphasis. "Remember this: I possessed sensitive information regarding our electronic intelligence and cryptographic systems. I hoped to convince them my duties were militarily benign. Failure to do so left suicide as my only remaining option. Believe me, I harbored no illusions regarding my ability to withstand prolonged torture or to resist drugs like scopolamine."

"You're here, so apparently your ruse worked."

"Yes, finally. They wanted to know where I learned to speak Russian and I told them the truth: from my grandmother. I even repeated some of her old stories about growing up near Kiev, naming specific villages like Hoholiv and Bobryk, along with relatives who lived there and the people her family knew. They used several interrogators, in pairs, each asking questions about my previous answers, but in a different way. After a while I think they accepted my story, reluctantly."

"Tell me about the rest of your air crew. Were they undergoing similar interrogations?"

"I don't know. I never saw any of them again and the Russians ignored my queries along those lines. I was persistent but they steadfastly refused to provide any information in that regard."

"I see." It was standard practice to keep detainees separated and then compare their stories. "Sorry for the interruption."

Danilov continued. "About a month after my capture, guards marched me into a courtroom to face three judges. The prosecutor charged me with violating Article 58 of the Soviet criminal code. My defense counsel, a man in his sixties, appeared competent but he had little to refute the so-called evidence: my uniform complete with rank and insignia, dog tags, ID, Mae West, and some floating debris obviously gathered from the crash site—oxygen bottles, sleeping bags—stuff like that. All with U.S. markings."

"Should I even ask about the verdict?"

"You may ask, but you already know the answer. The court found me guilty of spying and sentenced me to fifteen years hard labor and *ssylka*, Siberian exile. My protests and demands to see American diplomatic consul were rejected out of hand. 'A convicted criminal does not have rights or privileges', the chief judge informed me. At the sound of his gavel, Captain Andrew G. Thompson became *zek* Danilov."

"*Zek?*" Cody said. "I'm not familiar with that term."

"It is a word derived from *zaklyuchennyi*—prisoner. Andrei is the Russian version of Andrew and John is my father's name. My grandfather's family name is Danilov. So, putting all that together, the Russians issued new identification papers on October 1, 1954. I became *zek* Andrei Ivanovich Danilov: a contrived name for a prisoner who existed only on paper."

The old man laced his fingers together and placed both hands on the table. "At Ladd and Yokota, I had heard stories about Americans captured during the Korean War; soldiers and airmen who had simply disappeared. Most of us believed that some POWs had survived and were being held secretly in China or the Soviet Union. No one knew when, or whether, they would be acknowledged and subsequently returned to United States custody.

"And now I found myself prisoner in a hostile country, forced to dress in civilian garb, and my true identity expunged. Did the Air Force list me as missing or dead? I did not know. Either way, I had become invisible—a non-entity. As far as the outside world was concerned, the Russian prisoner Andrei Danilov existed; Andrew Thompson, the American aviator, had simply vanished."

Danilov's eyes flashed and Cody sensed a weary anger; an irate lassitude fired by life's vagaries and tempered by the bitter reality of unalterable events. A life had been stolen and, intuitively, Cody knew exactly what the old man was thinking and feeling.

"When you're twenty-five," Cody suggested, "fifteen years seems like forever."

Danilov shifted in his chair. "Indeed. It is an immense amount of time—your entire remembered existence—everything from adolescence through adulthood. To me it was a long dirt road stretching across the vast Russian steppes, dwindling away toward a distant, unreachable horizon. Surviving the journey into middle age was far from certain."

"But you did survive," Cody reminded him.

"So I did. A week later, about fifty of us, all convicted of various crimes, were herded into military trucks. We were a disparate group: Poles, Estonians, and a few Lithuanians. Our ranks included a common thief from Moscow and a Ukrainian political leader convicted of 'anti-Soviet activities.'

"Other than cautious eye contact, we did not speak to each other except when necessary. Nobody knew who among us was really going to prison or who might be a spy, an informer planted to glean additional incriminating information.

"After an hour or so, we stopped at a railroad siding. Guards ordered everyone out and then marched us into transport trains. Not passenger trains, Mr. Ballantine, but cattle cars. Straw covered the wood planked floor. About thirty of us occupied each car. We ate, sat, and slept on that floor. A wooden half-barrel in one corner served as a communal washbasin; in the opposite corner, another was used as a toilet. After bowel movements, we wiped ourselves as best we could, usually with straw.

"It took nearly a month to reach Vladivostok. The train stopped each day so we could eat and replace the barrels. Once a week or so, guards ordered us to clean the cars and put down fresh straw. They also boarded more prisoners. By journey's end, our car held nearly fifty men. As you can no doubt surmise, traveling conditions were primitive, unsanitary, and foul smelling. Later, if you like, I can provide more details."

"Later will be okay."

"Upon arrival in Vladivostok guards marched us to a transit prison. Once there, we were allowed to bathe and wash our clothes. Afterwards, cooks fed us black bread and soup. Then guards loaded us into trucks once more and drove to the same dock where the torpedo boat put me ashore three months earlier. Now, a large ship was moored there."

"Are you sure it was the same dock?" Cody asked.

Danilov nodded. "Like an unwitting participant in a surreal nightmare, I had come full circle. For the next five days, the ship slowly filled with arriving prisoners. My contingent was among the first to board. Assigned to the ship's hold, we took the upper bunks, which allowed slightly more headroom. Since it was the middle of November, full winter in Siberia, we also wanted to be closer to the ceiling where the temperature was slightly warmer.

"Once at sea and despite the cold, small groups were ordered on deck. There, an MVD political officer spoke through a small megaphone and informed us of our destination: the Magadan Oblast, a political subdivision two thousand kilometers to the north. Most of us would work the Svetloye gold fields at Susuman, a mining town near the Arctic Circle; a few might be assigned elsewhere.

"The MVD officer extolled us with inspirational slogans like 'Work is honorable and courageous; Work is the surest and fastest way to freedom'. But the hidden message was clear: 'You are prisoners of the State. No work, no food.'"

Danilov brushed a blue-veined hand across his face, perhaps trying to dispense the unpleasant memory.

"Would you like to take a break?" Cody offered.

Danilov shook his head. After a moment, he continued with his story.

"It was worse than a bad dream. In high school, we jokingly compared two-a-day football practices to the Siberian salt mines. Now, here I was—an American citizen, a military technician who had never fired a shot in anger—on my way to a mining camp in Siberia. *Siberia!* Can you imagine my state of mind?"

Prior to his banishment to Vladivostok, Cody had studied CIA reports that described, in grim detail, the Soviet Union's penal system during Josef Stalin's reign. The Georgian dictator had sent thirty million people to concentration camps; so many in fact, that slave labor costs eventually became a significant drain on the chronically anemic Soviet economy. Many prisoners ended up in graves, a drastic but effective way to reduce operating cost.

At first, the horrifying personal recollections from former inmates had been difficult to accept. But there were too many corroborating witnesses and, like the Holocaust, the Gulag had become a fact he could not dismiss. Nor could the rest of the world.

Officially published two years ago, Aleksandr Solzhenitsyn described a terrible reality that transformed whispered rumor into shouted truth. Cody had read an underground copy of *The Gulag Archipelago* nine years earlier. Although Solzhenitsyn's narrative had been compelling, Cody was about to hear a first-hand account from a presumably reliable source.

"No," he replied, "I cannot possibly imagine how you felt."

"It took about a week, maybe more, to travel from Vladivostok to Magadan, the provincial capital. As the ship sailed north, the weather got progressively colder. We arrived in late November 1954. The temperature was minus ten degrees Celsius, not exactly the autumn weather I was accustomed to in Ohio or Pennsylvania."

Cody did the conversion. "Fourteen degrees, Fahrenheit. That's pretty cold."

"Yes, but not as cold as our ultimate destination. A military convoy transported us to Susuman—a dingy, depressing settlement about six hundred kilometers farther north."

Danilov spent the next few minutes describing his arrival, orientation, barrack number assignment and labor detail. "The shipboard MVD officer advised us that most prisoners would be assigned work in the underground gold mines. He was correct."

Cody said, "I thought an American might get special treatment or perhaps better accommodations. That didn't happen, did it?"

"Absolutely not. After my conviction and sentencing in Moscow, I was quietly warned by the Soviet prosecutor to keep my identity and nationality secret."

"Why was that?"

"I have no idea, but it was clearly a veiled threat. In any case, I never saw another American, so I decided to heed his warning and speak only Russian. When asked by other prisoners, I claimed my grandmother's hometown as mine. I provided few other details. That was not unusual. Prisoners shared little about their previous lives. Anyway, I had the foolish notion that, after fifteen years, the MVD might forget I was an American military officer and set me free."

Cody could almost feel a much younger Danilov's hopeful desperation, a frantic grasp at any proposition offering the possibility of survival. It was an understandable human reaction. Unfortunately, hope and logic are incompatible bedfellows.

"How long did you work in the gold mines?"

"Slightly more than five years. It was the worst period of my life. I say that without the slightest hesitation or doubt. And I would not have survived without help from a German prisoner of war."

The presence of captured German soldiers in the Gulag was not altogether surprising. POWs from the Second World War had been a contentious issue between the Soviet Union and their former enemies. A decade after hostilities ended, Soviet authorities finally acknowledged their existence and began returning survivors to West German authorities. By then, there weren't many left.

"How so?" Cody asked.

"Ernst Klaus was taken prisoner when the German Sixth Army surrendered at Stalingrad. That was in January 1943. When I first met him, eleven years later, he was thirty years old but looked fifty. Despite confinement in Siberia for nearly half his life, Ernst considered himself lucky. He said to me, 'I was a nineteen-year-old private, a common soldier. When the Russians captured my unit, Soviet officials separated German officers from enlisted men. The officers were either shot immediately or worked to death. A few survive to this day, but most did not last six months.'

"It took a while, but I eventually came to trust Ernst enough to reveal my true nationality. I did not, however, tell him my real name, rank, or other background information. I let him believe my airplane had strayed over Soviet territory by mistake. Ernst found it amusing that the two of us, both soldiers and former enemies, were now prisoners of an ex-ally. Hitler had betrayed Stalin, and Stalin had betrayed Roosevelt. 'Such is the way of dictators and politicians', he told me. Ernst took me under his wing and taught me the unwritten laws of camp survival."

Cody knew that rules of behavior are common throughout the animal kingdom, but none were more rigidly enforced than those within a closed prison society. He said, "Were they difficult or complicated?"

"Quite the contrary. The rules were very simple: Never inform; Work less; Eat more; Live until tomorrow."

"That sounds overly simplistic."

"No doubt. The best rules are exactly that: clear and unambiguous. However, those who survived also relied on luck, youth, and inner strength."

At Cody's urging, Danilov described how prisoners worked the narrow gold vein, manually freeing the precious ore from Jurassic shale and siltstone. Working deep underground, they chipped away with hand picks and chisels, sometimes on their knees, dusty gray gnomes confined to a cramped, gloomy circle of Hell; a domain reeking of clammy earth, unwashed bodies, and forsaken dreams.

"My transformation from healthy young man to scrawny survivor did not take long, less than two months. One day, Ernst looked at me and said: 'You have become a walking *vogelscheuche*; you are now one of us.'"

"*Vogelscheuche*?" Cody said. "What does that mean?"

"Ernst was raised on a family farm in Westphalia. He said the prisoners reminded him of scarecrows."

Cody nodded but remained silent.

Danilov continued. "Ernst showed me how to conserve energy, to dig slowly but steadily so I was never idle when the mine foreman appeared. Idleness meant less food in our bellies, which resulted in poor health, a condition usually followed by sickness and possibly death."

Cody said, "I've read accounts of mass starvations in the Gulag, primarily during the Thirties. Did you experience anything like that?"

"No, not really. We were fed enough to maintain working strength, but not much more. Our diet consisted of porridge, bread, and vegetables; salted fish and a strange mélange—a mystery stew of sorts. Once in a while, it contained tiny meat chunks: lamb or goat, I think. But it could have been dog. One never asked."

"I can understand why," Cody offered.

"Indeed. However, as bad as I thought it was, long-serving inmates informed me that, since Josef Stalin's death the previous year, life in the camps had improved considerably. That might have been so, but I never accustomed myself to the casual, detached cruelty. Nor did I look forward to the long, sunless Arctic winters when temperatures fell to forty-five degrees below zero, Fahrenheit."

He hesitated and his eyes glazed for a moment, but then he continued. "There is something strange about the far northern latitudes, especially in August and September. The light is strangely different; an effect probably caused by the acute angle at which photons strike the earth. As winter approaches, the sun's daily arc slips closer and closer to the Southern horizon. During that half-lit interim, the world takes on a more somber appearance. The wind rises and seems to murmur a warning: 'prepare yourself.' The dwindling light seemed to hint at an inevitable end to humanity's existence in the universe. Finally, a morning comes when the sun does not rise. Its absence is like an end to all hope.

"That unsettling phenomenon happened every year, but—and this is the unexplainable part—it did not happen to *me*, not at first anyway. All those dreadful experiences were happening to someone else, to another being who lived on a distant planet circling a faint star—or so it seemed. During that long arctic darkness, life in the camps was at its worst. Cruelty became commonplace. It was three years later, during one of those bad times, when I finally accepted the truth: The life I led was *real*; all this was happening to *me*, right here, in a location far worse than the empty landscape of an alien world. The utterly impossible had somehow occurred: I, the real me, was a slave laborer wasting away in Siberia."

For a transitory moment, Danilov's eyes revealed a wounded, desperate pleading. Believe what I tell you, they seemed to say. Accept as truth mankind's limitless aptitude for brutality and its selective indifference to misery. Acknowledge the bestiality lurking just beneath our civilized veneer. Recognize that Hell exists, not only within the ethereal realm of religious dogma, but also here on Earth. Once you accept that, then you can also understand why the dogged persistence of a single human mind can offer the only hope for salvation.

Danilov's calm, guarded intelligence quickly returned and the old man shrugged, as though mildly embarrassed by its sudden and unexpected absence.

Cody recalled Dante's epic poem *The Devine Comedy* and the poet's description of one circle of Hell: an eternally frozen world, a place where human souls lay gripped in rigid ice. He could not remember the specific mortal sin warranting that level of punishment, but that did not matter. Danilov had clearly suffered a similar fate and, against all odds, survived the experience.

Nevertheless, the original question lingered: How could a man ascend from such hellish depths to achieve not only freedom, but prosperity as well? What did he offer to his captors that might warrant such treatment?

An earlier response tugged at Cody's memory. "Mr. Danilov, you told me the Russian court sentenced you to fifteen years at hard labor."

"Yes, that is correct."

"But a few minutes ago you said that only about five were spent working in the mines."

"Also true."

"I don't understand. How did that happen?"

An amused look crossed the old man's face, as though recalling a long-forgotten practical joke. The weight of years seemed to fall from his shoulders.

"How did that happen?" he repeated. Then he added, "Through the Grace of God, remarkably good luck, and John Steinbeck."

Cody wasn't sure he'd heard correctly. "Do you mean John Steinbeck, the American writer?"

"None other," Danilov acknowledged.

Chapter 17

Cody leaned back in his chair, unsure how to proceed. Was the reference to Steinbeck some sort of inside joke? If so, then Cody did not understand the premise let alone the punch line. The old man's amused silence offered no clue.

Finally Cody said, "John Steinbeck, the famous author, rescued you from the Svetloye gold mines?"

The question seemed to re-invigorate Danilov, further brightening the old man's demeanor.

"Yes, he did; in a rather odd manner of speaking."

"What manner was that, exactly?"

"It happened like this: On the fifth anniversary of my imprisonment, sometime near the end of November 1959 as I recall, guards escorted me to the camp commandant so that I might receive my annual lecture."

"Around Thanksgiving?" Cody asked. It was not a casual question.

Danilov returned a blank stare. "Thanksgiving? Oh, my. I have not thought about that in years." His eyes focused on the middle distance and he seemed lost in thought.

"Of course not. My mistake."

Perhaps the trick question was too obvious. A smart guy like Danilov would surely know the Thanksgiving holiday was uniquely American. He waited while the old man recaptured his train of thought.

"Anyway," Danilov continued, "the commandant informed me that my conduct and work productivity had been exemplary. Should my efforts continue in like manner, I could look forward to joining the *pridurki*—prisoners who have easier jobs.

"By then I had learned to play the game. I thanked him for the opportunity to remedy my crime against the Soviet State by performing such difficult but important work. As I continued to grovel verbally, I happened to notice a copy of *The Grapes of Wrath* on his desk. At that moment, an outrageous idea seemed to grow inside my head, from a tiny bud to full bloom in an instant."

Danilov paused for a moment, as though reliving the experience. Then he said, "Mr. Ballantine, as you probably know, there are a series of frescoes on the ceiling of the Sistine Chapel in Rome."

"You mean those painted by Michelangelo?"

"Yes, but there is one in particular: the section called *The Creation of Adam*. It depicts God reaching out to Adam, their fingertips almost touching. It is without doubt the single most recognizable portion of the entire composition."

"I know the one you mean. What about it?"

"When the idea occurred to me, it seemed that God had reached out and touched my forehead with His fingertip. It was that sort of feeling; there and gone in an instant, leaving behind a fully-formed idea."

"Like a Divine Inspiration," Cody said.

Danilov smiled. "I understand your skepticism. Nevertheless, it was as real to me then as this conversation is now."

"I'm sure you believe that," Cody admitted. "So what happened next?"

"I looked at the commandant. 'Did you enjoy that book?' I asked. He sneered at the suggestion. '*Nyet!* I do not read decadent works produced by simpering, weak-minded capitalists.' The book, he added, had been confiscated from an incoming prisoner who understood the English language; he intended to burn it in his stove. 'It will serve a better purpose by keeping my ass warm this winter,' he declared.

'But Comrade Commandant,' I said politely, 'John Steinbeck is not a capitalist. This work is a paragon of progressive socialist thinking.'

"At first he thought I was mocking the system. Anger clouded his eyes. 'Explain yourself,' he demanded.

"I quickly sketched the plot, adding a bit of dramatic license. The commandant seemed fascinated by the Joad family and how greedy bankers had forced good and decent people from their forty-acre tenant farm.

"So what if the farm was not theirs *legally*? What about *morally*? The Joad family had worked that land for generations; had sweated over, died upon, and were buried in it. I continued, describing the Joad's forlorn struggle to find a new home in California, detailing the family's travels across the dusty American Southwest, driving along in a beat up, overloaded truck."

Not for the first time, Cody wondered where Danilov was taking him. Rather than interrupt, he waited while the old man took more tea.

Danilov set the cup on its saucer and then continued.

"In that book, Steinbeck elaborated on several themes key to what I now considered my idea.

"The first reinforced a common socialist argument, namely: greedy capitalist bankers routinely oppress the common worker for no reason other than to gain more wealth. The second was Tom Joad's spiritual philosophy, one he acquired from Jim Casy, the fallen preacher who accompanied the Joads. Casy, a presumably God-fearing man, was nevertheless unable to control his passionate desire for young ladies. Do you happen to remember what Casy's philosophy was, Mr. Ballantine?"

"I'm not sure. Refresh my memory."

"Jim Casy was on a pilgrimage, a man searching for his lost soul. On that long and difficult journey to California, Casy finally discovered what he perceived as the ultimate truth: Human beings do not possess an individual soul. Rather, each person owns a tiny piece of a larger, collective soul. That unbreakable spiritual bond connects each of us to all others.

"Tom Joad's acceptance of Casy's philosophy struck a responsive chord in the commandant. 'You mean, like the State is the collective soul of its people.' he said. 'Exactly, sir.' Then I added the clincher." Danilov paused. "Mr. Ballantine, have you ever read *The Grapes of Wrath*?"

"In college, I majored in ROTC." Another half-truth, Cody thought, remembering a much less bellicose interest; an academic passion long since abandoned. "Reading John Steinbeck was not a requirement, and social philosophy held little interest for me." He smiled, slightly ashamed of youthful ignorance too often disguised as bravado.

"Then you have no knowledge of how the novel ended, do you?"

"I remember the movie more than anything. Henry Fonda played Tom Joad, Jane Darwell was Ma. I think it won an Academy Award."

Danilov shook his head. "A good film, but the climax was a travesty, a peace offering to satisfy American Puritanism."

"Why do you say that?"

"In Steinbeck's novel, a pregnant Rose of Sharon, abandoned by her husband, gives birth to a stillborn baby; not in a hospital but in an empty railroad boxcar during a flash flood. Unable to afford burial, her uncle reluctantly deposits the baby's corpse into a raging river. Soon afterwards, the destitute remnants of the Joad family seek shelter from a thunderstorm.

"In a dilapidated barn they come upon a man and his small son. The man is near death from starvation. Intuitively, both women know what has to be done. After Ma Joad sends everyone outside, Rose breast-feeds the starving man, giving him mother's milk, life-sustaining nourishment intended for her dead child."

"That explains why the movie's ending was changed," Cody suggested.

"Yes, I suppose so. But what Rose did in the novel gave me the idea for a social metaphor. In my interpretation, Rose became Soviet Russia, the mother country selflessly feeding her starving people; starvation created by Tsarist excesses and capitalist greed.

Rose's unspoken moral authority shined like a beacon, an unselfish personal sacrifice, one meant to serve a greater, higher good."

Cody raised an eyebrow. "And he bought it?"

"Why not? My interpretation was close enough to the truth. Steinbeck believed capitalism would eventually create its own demise. The accumulation of too much wealth in too few hands inevitably leads to working class revolt. Those themes permeate *The Grapes of Wrath*. It also happens to be a key element of Marxist-Leninist philosophy."

"But Steinbeck wasn't a communist."

"That did not matter. He wrote the book during the Great Depression, when socialism first took root in America. Did I stretch a point or two? Probably. But remember this: I was desperate to get out of those mines. A year earlier, MVD guards took Ernst and a dozen other German POWs from the camp. I cannot say what happened to them. Maybe they were released, but maybe they were taken someplace else and shot.

"In ten years, the guards would come for me, or so I presumed. Since I had no knowledge of my official U.S. status—missing, incarcerated prisoner, or presumed killed—I did not know what fate awaited me after completing my sentence. But I knew one thing for certain: I did not want to toil in those lightless mines like a forgotten drone and then quietly disappear into an unmarked grave. Such an end was unthinkable! Life without purpose or hope is not worth living."

"I agree, but what were you trying to achieve?"

"Achieve, Mr. Ballantine? Survival, nothing more."

Perhaps now, Cody thought, is when the Great Question will be resolved. "But I don't yet understand how."

"Then let me finish. My interpretation of Steinbeck's novel left the commandant flabbergasted. 'I had no knowledge of this,' he told me. 'Nor do most Russians,' I suggested. 'It is a shameful episode of American history not easily admitted. If you like, I would be honored to translate the book. Let all Russia know the truth. I am, after all, a qualified linguist.'

"For a moment I thought I had overdone it. His eyes became guarded and suspicious. 'Of course,' I added, 'you would receive full credit for shedding light on the oppressive nature of life in America.' I could see he was interested, but unsure how to proceed. 'We shall see,' was all he said."

Cody now understood the intent of Danilov's plan. Once again, he was impressed by the old man's quick intelligence. He found himself captured by the story, eager to learn how the scheme unfolded.

"I went back into the mines, back to chipping into the hard earth, to hawking up thick clots of mucus laced with gray rock dust; a macabre existence with no past and no future, only a grueling present filled with mindless labor. Ernst was no longer there to help me through difficult periods. I was alone. It seemed my life had begun and would surely end in that murky cave populated by weary shadows, a realm echoing with sodden coughs from the eternally condemned.

"Two weeks later the commandant summoned me again. This time he had company: an MVD colonel from Magadan. 'Tell me your theory,' the colonel insisted. Having had time to refine my thoughts, the second presentation went much smoother. 'And you would be willing to create a translation reflecting these ideas?' he asked."

"And of course you would," Cody interjected.

"I was given three weeks to translate *The Grapes of Wrath*. The rules were very clear. The camp commandant would review each translated chapter. If the story was not as I had described to them, then the work would stop and I would spend the remainder of my sentence in the mines."

"Was it a large book?"

"Thirty chapters."

Cody mulled the proposition. "Ten a week. Isn't that a lot?"

"If one is writing from scratch, it is an impossible task. But I was merely reading in English and typing in Russian, on a typewriter with a Cyrillic alphabet."

Cody tried once again not to be impressed. "Wasn't that difficult?"

"Very much so. I learned to type at PMC, but getting my mind and fingers used to a different keyboard layout was the hardest part of that entire exercise. It is true what they say about old habits."

"But you succeeded."

"I did. Those three weeks were heaven. I ate two meals each day with tea and good black bread in between, food similar to what they served the commandant and his administrative staff. At night, I slept on a clean bed in a warm room. For the first time in five years I could shower regularly and use the *banya*—steam room." He paused momentarily and then added, "Being physically clean is an incredible luxury most people do not appreciate."

"I suppose not. What happened then?"

"The commandant sent the completed work to the MVD colonel in Magadan. In the meantime, he gave me copies of newspapers, usually the *New York Times* and *Washington Post*, and a few magazines too. Certain articles and editorial opinions had been circled for translation. By then, I had mastered the Russian typewriter and my productivity was much improved."

"How was the translated book received in Magadan?"

"Quite well. The colonel sent the published work to Moscow. After that, my translating duties expanded to include mining journals and other technical magazines, mostly those originally published in the United States or Great Britain."

"And thus began your new career as linguist."

"So it would seem."

"Did you serve your full sentence in Susuman?"

"No, ten years."

"And afterwards?"

"I was offered relocation options; none included returning to the United States. Neither was I permitted to live anywhere near a major population center. But that was not unusual. Many political prisoners, including native Russians, were not allowed to return to their homes, for various reasons.

"My situation however, was double-edged. On the negative, I was a foreign military officer; a man who had been arrested, tried and imprisoned, probably in secret. But I had served my sentence without complaint. I also provided valuable services to the State. When given the opportunity, I even expressed sympathy for certain socialist ideas. With those positives, they were willing to release me early, something like a parole, but only within a specified area and without total freedom of movement, ever."

"That sounds like a life sentence."

"It was, but the unspoken alternative was far worse. Still, I had succeeded in attaining my primary objective: survival. My next goal, returning home, proved much more elusive." Danilov checked his watch. "And now I must go or I will miss my train."

While Danilov retrieved his hat and coat, Cody reached for the telephone, punched a series of numbers and waited. When a voice answered, Cody said, "Our guest is ready to leave."

"I appreciate the use of your car and driver," Danilov said.

"It's the least we can do. Anyway, by next Friday we should have confirmed your identity and made arrangements for your return to the United States."

"This has been a long time coming," Danilov sighed, obviously tired. "I find it difficult to believe it is almost over."

Cody felt a surge of emotion for the old aviator. Despite the lie about not having a family and the mystery surrounding the Pennsylvania Military College, both of which Cody vowed to resolve before their next meeting, he now believed Danilov might indeed be Captain Andrew G. Thompson. During the past three meetings, Cody had studied Danilov's every word, gesture and facial expression. If the old man was a liar, then his acting skills were truly awesome. Nevertheless, Cody's training and conscience demanded that every detail be verified.

A knock sounded. "Your transportation has arrived," Cody said, extending his hand.

"*Dos vadanya, tovarisch,*" Danilov said.

As they shook hands, Cody felt a twinge of discomfort. Why had he offered the traditional Russian farewell? Why not something more American, like: *See ya later, alligator?* Was it an automatic response, ingrained during forty years of semi-captivity? He wasn't sure.

***

Cody returned to his office, plopped onto his padded swivel chair, leaned back and took several deep breaths. Prolonged concentration on Danilov's narrative had nearly worn him out. He would rest for ten minutes and gather his thoughts before summarizing today's interview for Hal Bates at Langley.

He would have preferred a short nap, a breather to refresh himself prior to setting out for his long anticipated dinner date with Anne Seymour. A little snooze would rejuvenate his mind and body, but it was not to be.

Cody experienced mixed feelings about today's revelations.

Had a younger Danilov given 'aid and comfort' to the Soviet Union by voluntarily serving as a translator? Probably. On the other hand, it seemed Danilov had not revealed his true military function nor anything related to America's electronic intelligence gathering activities. One could argue he had provided a relatively unimportant service while keeping secret an array of information vastly more significant and potentially damaging to United States security.

Danilov's behavior had been necessary to assure survival in a hostile land. The old man had endured ten long years as a slave laborer, isolated and imprisoned in a remote corner of a foreign country, plodding numbly toward a future that might not exist. Under those conditions, his conduct was difficult to condemn.

Part of him desperately wanted to believe Danilov's story and Cody yearned to repatriate Captain Andrew Thompson, a forgotten warrior from a conflict unlike any in history. Another part demurred, not yet willing to consider another, more disturbing question that must logically follow; a question he was unable to ignore because it clamored for resolution, a persistent nagging that began soon after Danilov walked through the consulate's front entrance nearly two weeks ago.

If the man was indeed Captain Thompson, the voice inside his brain asked, then surely there must be others; not only Cold War shootdown survivors, including those from Danilov/Thompson's RB-50, but also MIAs from Korea and perhaps even World War Two. How many could there be?

Cody believed the majority of those still listed as MIA were dead, perhaps tromped underfoot on a muddy battlefield; their bodies concealed in knee-deep goo like countless Union and Confederate soldiers, or washed away in rivers and streams. Some may have vanished in trackless jungle or suffered total incineration by bomb or artillery blasts.

Most perhaps, but not *all*. Had other survivors endured similar or worse depravations? It was an issue Cody did not wish to consider, not yet. He first wanted to resolve Danilov's troublesome statements about family and Penn Military. Why would the old man conceal or misrepresent something so easy to verify? It didn't make sense.

Cody's mind sifted the possibilities.

The first seemed obvious. Danilov had a Russian family and lied about it. Again, why would he claim otherwise?

Two scenarios came to mind: First, Danilov's 'coming out' was an inherently risky venture and he felt it necessary to protect them. The second scenario was less flattering: Danilov planned to abandon his family; leave them behind. While Cody might help with the first—secreting a small group of people out of Russia was not an impossible task, especially these days—all it took was enough money placed discretely in the hands of a few key individuals. The second scenario—abandoning his family—was a matter of conscience, something only Danilov could resolve.

The other possibility was less obvious. Danilov once had a family but no longer. That would explain the 'I have no family' response. While technically a true statement, it also qualified as misleading, thus requiring further examination.

Likewise did the minor mystery surrounding the apparently non-existent Pennsylvania Military College.

Cody yawned.

Despite those as-yet unanswered questions, he took a measure of comfort from knowledge that Agency responses to his numerous research queries should arrive early the following week, perhaps by Monday.

The Agency's feedback would clarify the situation—or so he presumed. He was growing weary of flying blind, so to speak. At their next get-together, Cody was determined to settle the unresolved questions raised by the unexpected appearance of Andrei Danilov.

As his body relaxed, his mind conjured the image of Anne Seymour. Visualizing her, Cody could not help but wonder about matters of a more personal nature, and whether or not they too might be moving toward a satisfactory resolution.

Chapter 18

"Please don't get the wrong impression," Cody said, parking his Lada on Naberezhnaya Street, nosing into a spot a half block away from the Amursky Zaliv. "Although this is a hotel, it also features one of the city's better dining rooms."

Anne Seymour faced him and cocked her head. "Does that mean your intentions are entirely honorable?"

"Absolutely," Cody said, raising his right hand, three fingers extended as though reciting the Boy Scout oath.

"How disappointing."

Cody noted the twinkle in her eye and responded with an exaggerated sigh. "I know, but it's not my fault. When I was a boy, an old priest suggested that I should endeavor to rise above earthly temptations."

"Oh, God!" she said, smiling and rolling her eyes.

"I had no idea what he meant," Cody added.

Andrei Danilov took a room at the Amursky Zaliv during his weekend visits, but they would not be running into him this evening. According to the watcher assigned to Danilov, the old gentleman had boarded the last train to Ussurijsk late that afternoon, exactly as planned.

Cody pushed those thoughts from his mind. He wanted to forget about Danilov, at least for a while, and concentrate exclusively on Anne Seymour.

Built into the rocky side of a steep hill facing the bay, the street level entrance to the Amursky Zaliv was actually the top floor.

The *Maître d'* escorted them past a Dutch tiled foyer and into the main dining room, a comfortably furnished space with subdued lighting. Several Impressionist-style paintings hung from oak paneled walls and classical music purred from hidden speakers. Forest green carpeting muffled their footsteps.

"This is fantastic," Anne said, taking the seat offered. Their table, located next to a large window, provided a magnificent view of Amursky Bay.

"I'm glad you like it."

When their waiter appeared, Cody said to her, "What would you like to drink?"

Anne wrinkled her nose, an expression he found both impish and charming. "I'm not sure. Perhaps something different for a change."

"Feeling adventurous, are we?"

"Maybe a little."

Cody addressed the waiter. "*Zelyonye Glaza*," he said, nodding toward Anne. He ordered a Stolichnaya martini for himself. "Without an olive."

"Green Eyes? Is that what I'm drinking?" Anne asked.

"We'll find out shortly, won't we?"

She poked his arm playfully. "Tell me."

"It's a dry white wine with two large drops of Crème de Menthe."

"In other words, green wine."

"I suppose," he admitted, "but like a well-made kir, the whole is greater than the sum of its parts."

Her eyes took on a knowing look. "Too much cassis and the kir becomes cloyingly sweet, wholly unfit for human consumption."

"Absolutely true. A waste of good wine or champagne."

It was a pleasant beginning, unlike the guarded tone of their most recent departure. Anne had promised to tell him about her short-lived marriage, reciprocating what Cody had previously revealed about his aborted relationship with Tessa. Given Anne's earlier reaction to his innocent query, he suspected some variation of spousal abuse. Nevertheless, he kept his curiosity in check.

The waiter arrived, set their drinks before them and backed away. Anne lifted the glass by its stem and examined the contents. Two iridescent green cones descended into pale golden wine. "It looks pretty," she said. "Weird, but pretty."

Cody extended his drink and their glasses touched with a crystalline ping. "To new adventures."

Anne took a sip and her face registered mild astonishment. "This is wonderful!"

"I think it's a house specialty."

Cody relaxed as Anne surveyed the dining room, her delicate fingers absently stroking the stem of the wine glass, avoiding the crystal bowl that was lightly fogged with condensation. A tiny smile lifted one corner of her mouth, secretive and content, as though recalling a fond memory. Her quiet manner gave no hint of apprehension or unease. Likewise, he felt no need to perform, no compulsion to offer witty banter or, worse, a pontifical dissertation on Important World Events. Cody, always comfortable with silence and inner reflection, sensed the presence of a kindred soul.

Anne, clearly pleased with their surroundings, turned to him and said, "I am impressed. We could be sitting at a fine restaurant anywhere in the world."

"If you could choose a different location, where would you like it to be?" he asked.

"This will do, for now." She studied the nearest painting. "Are you familiar with French Impressionism?"

He was, and said so. "The works of Claude Monet are my favorite."

"Claude Monet is everyone's favorite," she added.

The proverbial ice, if any was present, seemed to be broken. Yet, he felt no need to fill the pleasant silence with meaningless banter.

At the exact right moment their waiter reappeared, order pad at the ready.

For an appetizer, Anne suggested mushrooms baked in sour cream. "Most people believe Russia's national dish is either cabbage or borsch," she told him.

"And it isn't?"

"I think it's mushrooms."

Her remark triggered a recollection, an idle observation he once made and then filed away in the archival portion of his brain. Almost every restaurant he frequented in the city, even sandwich shops, offered mushrooms in some form, especially in late summer and early autumn.

"You could be right about that," he said.

The chef was probably an immigrant; if not, then he must have been reasonably sober or at least in a good mood because dinner was an exceptional affair. Like a long-married couple, they shared a taste from each other's entrée, comparing relative merits.

Anne had *Morskaya Fantaziya*, Marine Fantasy, a lemony seafood thermador served from an elegant silver chafing dish prepared tableside. Cody chose beef tenderloins topped with a red whortleberry and vodka sauce.

They ate slowly and chatted, exploring common interests including pet peeves: chief among them being consular customs and practices they could easily live without.

As he first suspected, Anne came from the East Coast. While attending Bryn Mawr, she wrote articles for *College News*, the student newspaper. She did not mention her year-long failed marriage, the presumed reason for their date tonight, nor did she seem particularly inclined to broach the subject. It didn't matter. He was content to relax in the soft glow of her presence.

"Do you still write?" he asked.

"Not really. I think it was a Seventies thing. You know: angry, enlightened young woman proclaiming her independence from a male-dominated society."

"Did you burn your bra?"

"I *knew* you were going to ask me that," she chided good-naturedly.

Cody offered a fake frown. "I hate being predictable."

Her smile radiated light and warmth, filling the narrow space between them with a tentative intimacy. Cody felt himself smiling as well, a goofy grin creasing his face, an expression more suited to a love-struck boy than a mature man firmly ensconced in middle age.

"So," he said, "how did you get from liberal, bra-burning Bryn Mawr to Foggy Bottom's boring conventionality?"

The smile faded and her eyes became guarded, as though recalling an unpleasant memory. His innocent question had somehow tainted the atmosphere, aborting whatever potential the future might have held.

Cody realized he had blundered into a minefield, a rookie lieutenant screwing up on his first patrol. He desperately wanted to take it back, to retrace his steps and reenter the enchanted domain he had unwittingly abandoned. But her expression told him it was too late.

"That is a rather long story," she said.

"It's not one I need to hear," he countered, touching her hand, still searching for a way to recapture the lost mood. He grasped a fleeting idea. "Unless it's about kinky sex," he added. "I wouldn't mind hearing about that."

His attempt at humor failed. The wariness in her eyes persisted and remained impenetrable, a perfectly constructed barrier, and he realized it would not come down unless she chose to lower its protective shield.

"Regardless," he continued, his tone once again serious, "I'm here to listen."

They finished their meal in silence. She met his eyes every now and then, as though gauging the nature of an unspoken truce. Cody allowed her time to think about whatever it was that bothered her, hoping to convey attentive interest while giving Anne the first option to pursue any topic she chose.

It was not in his nature to sit and remain quiet in the presence of female company, but he sensed there was little else he could do in this situation.

Finally, over coffee, Anne's words—hesitant at first then tumbling out in a steady coherent stream—described her brief marriage to Jason Talbot Craig: a bright, handsome man, smugly educated at Harvard like his father and grandfather, and sole heir to the sizeable results of their labors.

"We met just after graduation, at one of those pretentious gatherings the financially comfortable seem to prefer, way too full of ourselves and determined to reshape the world to match our idyllic visions. As is often the case, our views were based on ignorance and dreamy ideas—a common malady afflicting most Ivy League and Seven Sister graduates. Fact, however, seldom overcomes zealotry."

"So I've heard." Cody smiled, trying again to lighten the mood.

"News of our engagement and subsequent marriage was carried in the *Washington Post's* society pages, as were details about our month-long European honeymoon. After we settled into our home, Jason became CEO of Talbot Electronics, one of his family's privately held companies, a nice little firm in Annandale, Virginia. Although not a huge operation, it was sufficient to prepare him for bigger things: a stepping-stone to Talbot Industries, the family's largest and most profitable business. That's when the fun began."

"Let me guess," Cody volunteered. "Jason wasn't much of a businessman."

Anne's pained expression confirmed his assessment. "Back then, computer and telecommunication ventures were providing an array of exciting new opportunities. Jason decided it was a passing fad. He avoided risk and continued to rely on old, established technologies. The company's products quickly became obsolete. Sales plummeted. In less than a year, he took the business from a profit position to an operation that hemorrhaged cash.

"There soon followed a series of frequent and private family meetings which, I gathered, were mostly unpleasant affairs. Afterwards. Jason would shut himself in our study, blame others for his failures, and drink himself into a mumbling stupor. I tried to help him get through it but that only made things worse."

Anne sipped her coffee, using the same delicate mannerism Cody first noticed at the consulate's reception two weeks ago. Now comes the bad part, he told himself.

"Finally, the family acted. His father assumed leadership of the electronics business, replacing Jason as chairman of the board. Although Jason kept the president's title, Craig Senior made it clear his son could make no business decisions without family approval. My husband became a figurehead, the imbecile offspring who could not measure up to his old man. The social humiliation and loss of prestige worsened an already touchy situation."

"How do you mean?" Cody asked, not sure what to make of Anne's noncommittal expression.

"Jason's nature was never docile. He spoke, acted and even played aggressively. I always assumed he was being a tough competitor, always striving for a win. That's what first attracted me to him. The reality was much less flattering. Jason was not tough; he was just mean. He took cheap shots at people, both verbal and during sporting events, like intramural football and hockey.

"The day Jason lost the chairmanship of Talbot Electronics was the turning point in our marriage. As usual, he came home seething. The family was against him, he bellowed, as was the entire management team that was supposed to be on his side. Together they had plotted to assure his failure. Naturally, none of it was his doing.

"I can't recall exactly what I said to him, but it was the wrong thing." With a steady hand, Anne swallowed another sip of her coffee. "In hindsight," she continued, "anything I said would have been wrong."

She fixed Cody with an unwavering gaze. "I ended up in the hospital with broken ribs, one eye swollen shut and numerous contusions. At first, I didn't know how to react. Except for the normal bumps and bruises encountered while growing up, I had never experienced serious pain. But there in that hospital bed, bewildered and aching, I also felt something else—a sensation far worse than painful discomfort.

"What I experienced was an overwhelming sense of shame and utter helplessness. Prior to Jason's attack, I had never been physically struck in my life—not by my parents, not by an angry girlfriend or sister. Never. That beating was the most shocking, humiliating, and degrading experience of my life."

Cody shifted in his seat. A red rage simmered just beneath the surface, but he remained outwardly calm, employing the mental discipline honed during years of clandestine operations. "Afterwards," Cody offered in a subdued voice, "I bet he apologized. Maybe even cried a little."

"Were you hiding nearby?" she asked.

Her tiny, incredibly sad smile dampened Cody's quiet rage. He felt a sudden urge to protect Anne, to forever safeguard her from life's unknowable trials. Yet, he remained still, controlling the inner fury that threatened to overwhelm his better judgment. He flexed his back muscles, primarily to release tension.

"I wasn't hiding nearby," he replied. "Jason's behavior was predictable." He sensed there was more to the story. "What happened next?"

"A few days later, Dad's attorney showed up at the hospital and asked if he could help. By then, the swelling in my lips had gone down enough so I could speak without too much discomfort. I told him to begin divorce proceedings, to make it quick and to assure it was uncontested. He also arranged to have my belongings moved from Jason's house, since I no longer considered it my home."

"That took determination," Cody said. "Most women would have rationalized the beating as a one-time aberration."

"Maybe so, but I couldn't. The beating forced me to accept my husband as he really was. Jason was not the hard-nosed competitor he would have everyone believe. That image was a fraud. His violent nature revealed deep-seated cowardice; it exposed him as a man unable to face his own shortcomings. Beating me was the act of a bully who preyed only upon the weak."

She studied the coffee in her cup for a moment, then met his eyes and continued.

"Wanting to avoid scandal, Jason's family tried to talk me out of it, but I threatened to press domestic battery charges and then blab everything to a sympathetic gossip columnist. They persisted, dropping by frequently, bringing flowers and other peace offerings. That's when my father called in a favor.

"During my last two days in the hospital, one of Dad's associates—a retired D.C. policeman named Leon Jones—stood guard at my door, refusing entry to anyone named Talbot or Craig but especially to Jason Talbot Craig." Anne smiled. "Mr. Jones, a rather large black man, was the perfect choice. Unless one happened to be a doctor, lawyer, or high government official, my soon to be former in-laws went out of their way to avoid such people."

Cody pictured the scene in his mind: A career police officer built like a Pittsburgh Steelers offensive lineman, barring the door with his massive body, arms folded across his thick chest, a scowl knuckled into his face. Such a man would have intimidated all but the frivolously insane. His effect on Anne's sheltered, Afro-phobic in-laws must have been dramatic, perhaps even humorous.

"When I left the hospital, I moved back with my parents. A week or so later, Jason was mugged by several unknown attackers. Interestingly, his money and valuables were untouched. The authorities called it a 'wilding'…teenagers beating someone up for the fun of it. In any case, the police made no arrests. Jason ended up in the hospital and was a long time recuperating. I never heard from him or his family again. My father refused to discuss the incident. He said some matters were better left alone."

"I think I'd like your father," Cody said.

Her eyes glowed, a combined effect that erased the sad undertones permeating her recollections.

"I think he'd like you, too."

Cody sensed Anne's relief, a musty burden shaken from her spirit, leaving behind a clean sheet snapping in the warm breeze beneath a high, bright sky.

"What happened next?" he asked.

"Like you, I needed to get away for a while. The Foreign Service had always appealed to me so I applied and took the exam. One thing led to another and here I am, posted to a remote corner of Russia, drinking coffee and green wine, sitting next to a man obsessed with kinky sex." The smile persisted.

"Hardly a step up, I suppose."

"Too early to say," Anne replied. Then, "Want to hear something interesting?"

"What I've heard so far was not boring. Is there more?"

She leaned forward and Cody caught a familiar, tantalizing scent of her perfume. "It's about you."

"Is that so?" he replied. The ever-alert sentinel inside his head began to wave yellow caution flags.

Her smile eased, giving way to something akin to a wistful reminiscence. "To begin with, I was always determined to do something different with my life, to go my own way, regardless of what anyone thought. Never, I told myself, would I slavishly marry the 'right' man, a fellow of means who belonged to the 'right' family; nor would I send our children to the 'right' schools and spend my idle hours embracing all the 'right' causes.

"My friends could follow that path, but not me. I was going to be Amelia Earhart, daring aviatrix and breaker of boundaries—the female counterpart of Lucky Lindy. In her day, the comparison to Charles Lindbergh was common. Many newspapers even referred to Earhart as Lady Lindy. In any case, she was my role model and, like her, I was determined to conquer new worlds."

"And did you?"

Anne shook her head. "I turned out to be a counterfeit rebel. In the end, I did exactly what I promised never to do. One moment I was Lady Lindy up in the sky, the next I was a battered wife, wondering what had gone so wrong. Recuperating in a hospital bed wasn't necessarily a surprise: the life of a daredevil adventurer is not without risk. I expected my share of lumps. But the actual cause for my ending up bruised and battered came as a shock."

Cody knew exactly how she felt. His life had likewise turned out much different than he once imagined. He was tempted to share his days of debauchery, to tell her of his own shortcomings, but then thought better of it. Some parts of our lives, he reflected, are better left in the past.

"This is where you come in," Anne said.

"Have I forgotten this part, too?" he asked.

"Hardly. You weren't even there."

"In that case, please go on."

Her cup was empty and Cody refilled it from a silver carafe, refreshing his own as well.

"Nearly ten years had passed since my divorce became final," she began. "I was back in Washington, on vacation and visiting family. By then, I was approaching my mid-thirties: an unattached, childless woman with no prospects for remedying either condition."

"Did you enjoy diplomatic work?" Cody asked.

"Yes, very much. But something was missing from my life. I thought it might be that 'nesting' thing women are supposed to have, or maybe I was just unhappy with the state of my personal life. Anyway, I was taking a morning walk, thinking about such things, and found myself on the Mall near the Vietnam Memorial. It was cold and not many people were around."

"When was this?"

"Early 1983, February."

The Memorial's dedication ceremony had occurred the previous November, a time when Cody had been at Langley, waiting for a new assignment. For some unknown reason, he felt compelled to attend the event.

The pre-ceremonial parade seemed rather odd to him: a procession where marchers—Vietnam veterans—gave a 'welcome home' tribute to each other. While friends and relatives cheered or cried from the sidewalks, most bystanders—those untouched by the war—shuffled uncomfortably and exchanged bewildered glances, as though unable to comprehend the moral of a tragic fable. Their confusion did not surprise Cody.

Most Americans were oblivious to how deeply their rejection had wounded the spirit of those returning from Vietnam. Worse, a great many citizens still harbored no regrets whatsoever regarding their shabby treatment of soldiers. This latter group of influential zealots then proceeded to infect young minds with their own warped version of history. For them, America would always be the villain.

Although he had opted to watch the parade, Cody skipped the speeches. A few days later, after most of the crowd had dispersed to other parts of the country, Cody returned, alone.

He had not approached the Memorial during that initial visit, but stood on a small rise facing the center of that long black chevron, not quite ready to view the names of friends and comrades etched into black granite.

That would take a little more time.

Memories of the war and its aftermath still evoked quiet outrage. In response to Ho Chi Minh's military aggression and South Vietnam's political corruption, two American presidents had surrounded themselves with the best educated incompetents ever assembled and then followed their counsel. The Memorial Wall stood as mute evidence of their collective ineptitude.

"I didn't mean to interrupt," Cody said, forcing his mind back into the present. "What happened next?"

"This is going to sound weird," she began, "but the Memorial brought to mind my coming out party and the tall soldier who escorted me across the ballroom floor. A soft-spoken young man who advised me to discover what I truly believed and then live my life accordingly; advice I first ignored but now followed with passionate enthusiasm."

"I actually said that?"

"You actually did. Anyway, as I thought about it, a compelling question popped into my mind, one that demanded an answer. Suddenly, I just *had* to know if your name was among those listed on the Wall."

"You remembered my name?"

"How could I possibly forget Wild Bill Cody? The Ballantine part was almost as easy to recall."

"I'm sorry I asked."

"The urge to know if you survived was overpowering—like nothing I had ever felt before. Almost without realizing it, I found myself approaching one of the National Park attendants."

"You were going to check the book of names."

Anne nodded.

"Mine isn't there," Cody volunteered.

"Yes, that's what he told me. It was then that I knew you were probably alive and okay. Somehow, that knowledge made me feel better. Yes, I had unresolved questions and personal problems, but so did everyone else. Knowing Vietnam had not claimed your life made me want to continue searching for whatever I thought was missing from my own. The assurance that you survived gave me courage." She paused and shrugged. "Isn't that the silliest thing you ever heard?"

Cody did not respond immediately as the old guilt rose up in him once again. It was true: he had survived while others had perished. An unexceptional young man had made it through the fire while other young men—perhaps more deserving of life—had not. Like them, he had put himself at risk, but Fate had decided to spare him and he could not fathom why. Cody still felt like he owed something to someone. He was willing to pay but he did not know the what or the how or to whom he owed.

Then, to his relief and astonishment, the familiar sense of listless remorse ebbed. As the unsettled frustration waned, a long suppressed gratitude finally took root and blossomed. He was glad to have survived—for whatever reason—and thankful to have lived long enough to end up here in this quiet room sharing company with the most beautiful woman in the world.

Yes, Vietnam and his aborted marriage would remain part of him for as long as he lived. That was certain. But to be whole and well in the here and now was an incredibly precious gift, and the reason for it, if indeed one existed, no longer mattered.

He reached for her hand.

"No," he said. "That isn't silly at all."

Chapter 19

On Monday morning, Cody's first incoming telephone call was from Freddie Benner, the man he had dispatched to Ussurijsk. He listened for a moment and then said, "Okay, Freddie. I'm on my way."

Cody replaced the telephone handset, walked to the closet and slipped into his overcoat. After a moment's hesitation, he reached for a black fur cap. On his way out, he spoke to Phyllis.

"I'll be gone for a while, perhaps two hours, not more than three," he told her, stuffing the soft flat cap into an overcoat pocket.

She gave him a tight smile. "Be careful."

"Always," he said.

Cody had arranged to meet Freddie at his boarding house, Sasha's place, located near the city's Dolphinarium, about two kilometers away. During his visit, he would pick up a few black market items, thereby reinforcing their fictitious and clearly illegal buyer-seller relationship.

He stepped outside. Although eager to discover what his covert operative had learned about Andrei Danilov, he also opted for his usual caution.

He ambled down Svetlanskaya Street, past the Post Office and toward the GUM department store, stopping frequently to gaze into shop windows, checking to see if anyone followed, which was likely. Old habits, it seemed, died slowly, so he performed the expected ritual of shaking his followers.

Cody stepped inside a coffee shop and reemerged ten minutes later with several others, his head now covered by the fur cap. Then he caught a local bus and rode six blocks before getting off. He did this several times, always keeping within a group of people, using different busses and shops where he casually reversed the overcoat, switching the color from charcoal to gray, and wearing or not wearing the cap.

It was basic tradecraft, generally successful when deployed against a lackadaisical effort, which he also suspected might be the case. Satisfied he was alone, Cody finally headed toward his real destination.

Freddie's boarding house, a somber gray Victorian once owned by an Uzbek miner who had abandoned Vladivostok when his gold vein petered out, was a Company-owned facility. Following his usual routine, Cody walked beyond it, turned down a side street, and then into an alley that ran behind the house. He entered the back yard though a gate in the high wooden fence, climbed the rear stairs, and pulled the bell chain. Sasha, a somewhat older American woman of Russian extraction, answered the door.

As had Freddie, Sasha Rodnova had likewise moved to Vladivostok soon after the Soviet Union's economic collapse, posing as a widow of ample financial means, presumably resulting from an inheritance left to her by a fabricated late husband. Using Agency funds, she had purchased the house along with an interest in a local fishing boat and settled into a quiet existence.

Freddie had arrived a few months later and took up residence as a boarder. In his role as a very small operator in a gigantic black market, he moved small amounts of contraband items brought in by Sasha's fishing boat partner, a Korean immigrant family who also happened to be Agency employees. Everyone made enough money to live comfortably, but not extravagantly. They also paid regular tribute to a local crime boss, and generally attracted little or no attention.

"Good Morning, Cody," she said, taking his cap and overcoat. "Freddie's in the library."

The air in the rear entryway, located adjacent to the kitchen, quivered with the aroma of warm, fresh bread. He smiled at the thin, pleasant-faced woman. "Good Morning, Sasha."

"Would you like coffee?"

"No, thank you. I'm trying to cut back."

She shook her head in obvious disapproval. "First cigarettes and now coffee? You are beginning to worry me."

"Sometimes I worry myself."

Cody walked through the kitchen and down a hallway. He slid open two massive pocket doors, stepped into the library, and then pulled the doors closed.

"Hello, Freddie," he said to the man perusing a nearly full bookshelf. "How was Ussurijsk?"

Freddie turned and uttered a barely audible grunt. "If Vladivostok is a backward, thoroughly depressing city, then Ussurijsk is much worse," he replied, taking Cody's offered hand.

"Really?"

"I'm afraid so. Ussurijsk reminds me of a Depression-era town in West Virginia, two years after the mines shut down and the last grocery store went belly up. Only West Virginia was much more pleasant."

"That bad, huh?"

"Yes, it is. Consider this: Today, sixty years after the Great Depression, many Russian homes lack indoor toilets."

"Really? I didn't know that. Where do you find such arcane but interesting statistics?"

"Those which I cannot verify I fabricate in my spare time."

"I see," Cody replied.

Fredric Allen Benner was a typical covert operative; that is, the opposite of Ian Fleming's fictional hero, James Bond It was a characteristic Cody appreciated.

An oddly moral and rather plain featured man, Freddie's motivation did not arise from a deep-rooted hatred for an enemy, but rather contempt for a political system that routinely subordinated human well-being to a high-sounding but ultimately ruinous social philosophy.

Freddie was expert at internalizing his outrage, easily assuming the guise of an obedient, quietly oppressed citizen who glumly accepted the subtle indignities endured by his fellow sufferers. Like many of the best operatives, Freddie's local associates considered him a trusted companion: rabbi, priest, and privy counselor rolled into a single persona.

"When did you get back into town?" Cody asked.

"A little past midnight. The train was six hours late."

"Mechanical problem?"

Freddie raised both hands, palms up. "Who knows?"

"Have you had breakfast?"

"Yes. Sasha fed me eggs, oven-browned potatoes, and too many of her marvelous biscuits."

The kitchen aromas came to mind. "Good." Cody motioned toward a pair of facing leather settees separated by a coffee table. "Sit down and tell me about our friend Mr. Danilov."

Freddie eased into a sofa with a quiet sigh. "Where shall I begin?"

Cody took a seat opposite his field agent. "First off, was it difficult gathering information?"

"No, not really. The Primorski Agricultural Institute isn't involved in military projects; therefore, the working atmosphere is subdued, even relaxed. As per your excellently forged credentials, I posed as a technical writer doing research for *Geologika*, a properly obscure European scientific journal. My former colleagues at Cal Tech would have been impressed by the vita sheet I presented."

"I'm sure. Did you happen to bump into Danilov?"

"Not during my fake interviews, but I did see him in the library once. He did not see me, though."

"How long has he worked there?"

"According to city housing records, since about 1973. That's when he arrived from Magadan and assumed his new post at the Institute. Shortly thereafter, he moved into his two-bedroom apartment on Blyukher Prospekt."

"Two bedrooms?"

Freddie nodded, holding up two fingers.

Cody felt certain Danilov had not been totally honest about that aspect of his life. A single individual occupying a two-bedroom apartment back in 1973 was a rarity in Soviet Russia. Freddie's news tended to reinforce a strong suspicion that Danilov had been less than candid regarding a family.

He rubbed his chin with thumb and forefinger. If his guest had hidden one fact, perhaps he had obscured other things as well, such as his attendance at the still-undiscovered Penn Military College. But why had he done so?

"Two bedrooms?" Cody repeated. "If the local bureaucracy allowed Danilov to occupy a scarce two-bedroom apartment twenty years ago, then it stands to reason he had a family, and probably still does."

"I don't think so," Freddie said.

Cody blinked. "What do you mean?"

"Danilov seems to be a loner. I followed him all last week. He leaves for work at the same time every morning and returns home in the evening, seldom deviating more than a few minutes either way. When he left his apartment to eat or shop, he was always alone, except for one occasion. On Sunday last he took a long lunch with another fellow about his own age. Other than that, he pretty much kept to himself."

"I see," Cody said. But he didn't, not really. "Tell me about the lunch companion. Did he look official?"

"Hardly the type," Freddie answered. "He seemed at ease and much too cordial. I assumed they were old friends."

Freddie's analysis, although based on personal observation, did not feel right. Danilov was hiding something. In that one instance, the expression in the old man's eyes had been unmistakable. The more he thought about it, the more Cody became convinced Danilov was concealing important personal facts.

If a family existed, then where could they be? Sequestered somewhere, perhaps involuntarily, pending the outcome of Danilov's claim to U.S. citizenship? Was the KGB involved? If not, then why the charade? Furthermore, if Danilov was indeed Captain Andrew

Thompson, then he surely knew his entire family would be welcomed to America, happily and without question.

Unless, of course, the Russian government objected.

From the beginning, Cody had focused primarily on the veracity of the old man's improbable tale. He had not fully analyzed the potential diplomatic repercussions attending Danilov's miraculous resurrection as Captain Andrew Thompson.

Suppose everything he said was true. Suppose Danilov was indeed a cold warrior long presumed dead, a Gulag survivor and, most disturbing of all, a captured U.S. military officer tried, convicted and imprisoned by Soviet authorities, in secret, for thirty-eight years.

Trying to guess how the Russians would react under those circumstances was a futile exercise. Always suspicious of Western intentions, they would probably deny everything, circle the diplomatic wagons, re-arrest Danilov and then squirrel him away somewhere, this time for good. Without conclusive proof—Moscow would deem an official affidavit inadequate—the U.S. claim would die a soundless death.

On the other hand, the Russian government might readily acknowledge known facts about the affair and then allow Danilov and his family to leave the country. Unfortunately, that pleasantly uncomplicated outcome seemed altruistic and not very likely to occur.

Cody had already considered several methods to extract Danilov/Thompson from Russian territory, legally or otherwise, should it become necessary. However, moving a family of unknown size, including grandchildren perhaps, all Russian nationals, loyal citizens who might not desire to accompany their patriarch to America, was a much more daunting problem.

But not impossible.

"Something on your mind, Cody?" Freddie asked.

"I was sure Danilov had a family."

"That may be, but I saw no evidence of such ties. Is that important?"

"Too soon to tell."

Cody could not sit still. Abruptly, he stood and walked toward the double doors.

"I need to check a few things. Do you have anything else for me?"

Freddie shook his head.

"I'll talk to you later this week," Cody said.

Sasha had coffee already poured when Cody entered the kitchen. "When I heard the doors opening and your heavy footsteps," she explained, handing him a full cup on a saucer, "I knew you needed this."

He took the coffee and returned a sheepish grin. "So much for cutting back," he said lamely.

***

Cody approached the reception area and saw Phyllis seated at her desk.

She tilted her head toward his office. "You have unopened mail." It was her way of telling him classified material had arrived from Washington via diplomatic courier.

"Thanks," he said, concealing his rising excitement. The material probably contained replies to his earlier queries: answers, no doubt, accompanied by a note from Hal Bates. At least, he hoped so.

She peered at him over nanny glasses. "Did Sasha feed you lunch?"

He paused near her desk. "I had coffee."

"And she didn't offer lunch?"

"Freddie was bending her ear."

"Again?" She stood and reached for her purse. "I'll get you a sandwich from the commissary."

"What would I do without you, Phyllis?"

"Starve, probably."

A Halliburton stainless steel briefcase lay atop his desk. He retrieved keys from a concealed safe inside the closet, seated himself behind his desk and then inspected the locks. Because it came directly from Washington via courier, tampering was unlikely. Nevertheless, he checked from habit before using two separate keys to open the briefcase.

Inside lay a red-bannered envelope marked TOP SECRET.

He broke the seal and slid the contents onto his desk. As he suspected, Hal Bates had written a lengthy cover letter, which he firmly affixed to the quarter-inch thick packet with a steel pressure clip.

Cody intended to skim Hal's letter, but the wording in one paragraph caught his eye. As he read, a smile crossed his lips.

"Well, I'll be damned," he mumbled.

Hal had unknowingly solved the minor mystery surrounding Pennsylvania Military College.

He removed the clip, set the letter aside and studied a series of black and white photographs. The first group, reproductions from Har-Brack High School's 1946 yearbook, along with a five-by-seven inch blowup, revealed the untested face of eighteen-year-old Andrew G. Thompson. The resemblance to one Andrei Danilov nearly a half-century later, while possible, did not satisfy Cody. The second group, taken from PMC's 1950 yearbook, was remarkable.

Four years at Penn Military had turned Andy the hapless teenager into Cadet Sergeant Major, soon to be Second Lieutenant, Andrew G. Thompson: a handsome, sharp-eyed young man brimming with self-confidence. Despite shorter hair, youthful features, and the cadet uniform's high collar, the resemblance was unmistakable.

Cody set the enlargement aside and studied the reproduced page of class photographs, eight cadets in all, including Thompson. Listed beside each picture were the cadet's extracurricular activities, along with a brief sentiment from his graduating class. The legend beneath Cadet Thompson's photograph read: *An iron gentleman from the Steel City.*

The next several pages contained both a forensic and computer generated comparison of young Thompson's facial characteristics to a photograph of Danilov taken the day he first arrived at the consulate. Both analyses agreed: Based on the Agency's unique and finely honed aging algorithms, the probability that Cadet Thompson and Andrei Danilov were the same man approached ninety-seven percent.

Cody then read a letter from the 4th District Office of Special Investigations, Washington, D.C. The note informed him that the OSI had completed a thorough background check of Second Lieutenant

Andrew G. Thompson on 12 June 1951. Despite having Russian relatives, said officer was granted a Top Secret/Cryptographic clearance. The district office did not retain file copies of photographs, fingerprints or other identification.

The last few pages, typed on Agency letterhead, contained nearly a dozen bullet points highlighting the current status and last known whereabouts of several individuals Danilov had mentioned during interviews. Cody had also made several specific interrogatories, all of which were answered.

With a mixture of relief and chagrin, he turned and stared out the window toward the busy harbor. It now seemed, despite the unresolved family issue, that Andrei Danilov was indeed Captain Thompson, late of the United States Air Force. One of America's missing soldiers had turned up unexpectedly, and that was an event one must celebrate. Nevertheless, two unanswered questions remained.

To Cody, the family issue was most pressing. Danilov wanted to return to the United States, which was his due, but getting an entire family out of Russia would take careful planning. He was inclined to use Sasha's fishing boat—a fifty-foot vessel operated by a trusted Korean family—as transport for Danilov and his family. Cody would arrange for the boat to rendezvous with a U.S. Navy ship in international waters.

The remaining question, *how* Danilov managed to survive all those years, assumed secondary importance.

A light sound interrupted his thoughts. He turned as Phyllis pushed the door open with her shoulder and then walked in, carrying a small serving tray.

"Turkey and Swiss cheese okay?" she asked.

"Perfect."

"And an oatmeal cookie," she added.

Phyllis set two small plates and a glass containing iced tea on his desk, using a napkin as a coaster.

The photographs lay in plain view and Cody made no effort to conceal them. Phyllis had been his assistant for nearly seven years, voluntarily accompanying him from post to post, including his current tour in the Agency's penalty box. With calm efficiency, she kept the paperwork goblins off his back, allowing him to concentrate on what he believed was his *real* job: keeping track of the bad guys. It was a comfortable, older-sister/younger-brother relationship born of mutual respect.

"Look familiar?" Cody asked, handing her the enlargement of Cadet Thompson's class picture.

Phyllis studied the photograph. "Nice looking kid. He reminds me of our recent visitor." She handed it back. "Is there a story here?"

He motioned toward a side chair and waited while she sat. "Yes, there is. I thought you might be interested in hearing about it."

"Really?" she said, folding her hands.

"I think so."

In 1969, a few months before Captain William Cody Ballantine had escorted Miss Anne Teasdale Seymour to her table in the Washington Hilton's ballroom, Major Frank Townsend, Phyllis's 36-year-old fighter-pilot husband, had ejected from his disabled F-105 'Thud' over the just-bombed iron and steel works at Thai Nguyen, North Vietnam. Four years later, when Hanoi released American prisoners, Major Townsend was not among them. Although he had waved to his wingman from a good parachute, Hanoi never acknowledged his capture. As did the downed helicopter crew Cody had tried but failed to rescue, Major Townsend had likewise disappeared from history's yearbook.

Phyllis had raised their two children, sent them off to college, and then applied for an administrative post at the Agency, hoping to learn more about her husband's fate. But nothing ever surfaced: no sightings, no rumors, and no reports of newly discovered remains. Twenty-three years had passed since Major Townsend's plane went down. She had never remarried.

Cody did not want to resurrect old memories, nor did he wish to inflict pain or discomfort on this good woman. Still, given the option, Phyllis would have chosen to hear about Andrei Danilov, and Cody knew this instinctively.

Without preamble, he told her the substance of his interviews and the highly improbable outcome arising from a forty-year-old Cold

War incident. As he spoke, hints of an old hurt resurfaced in her eyes, an expression that nearly broke his heart.

I have made a terrible mistake, he thought. But it was too late to rectify his error so he plowed on, telling her the essence of Danilov's incredible story.

He finished and the room grew silent.

Finally she said, "And, after four decades, you believe this Danilov character is really our long lost Captain Thompson?"

"It looks that way."

Phyllis did not respond immediately. Instead, she picked up young cadet Thompson's college graduation picture and studied it for a long moment. "I'll bet you never thought life would turn out this way," she said, addressing the photograph. Then she added, softly, "Well, neither did I."

Cody reached for her hand. "I know this brings back old memories and I am truly sorry. I never intended to upset you."

She raised her eyes, now slightly moist, her expression a bittersweet mixture of long-controlled grief and fervent hope undiminished by the passage of time.

Phyllis had always reminded Cody of an ancient Greek myth. To him, she was the modern-day embodiment of Homer's Penelope, a remarkable woman yearning for the return of her own special Ulysses.

In Homeric legend, Penelope the Greek queen was lucky: her wandering soldier-king finally came home. In real life, Phyllis the American housewife was not; Frank Townsend, her soldier-aviator husband, never did.

She said, "Oh, Cody. We have lost so many good men. Not only the thousands killed and more thousands permanently disabled, but also those who simply vanished from our lives, like my Frank did so long ago." She set the photograph aside. "Most of us, myself included, now realize they won't ever be coming home. It's a sad reality we have come to accept. Yet, unexpectedly, one of our lost soldiers from a long-forgotten time has turned up alive and well. Despite our personal loss, his return is a miracle, a joy beyond words."

Phyllis stood and placed both hands on the chair's backrest.

"You have nothing to be sorry about, Cody. *Not* telling me would have been wrong and we both know it. Someday, God willing, my family might learn the truth about what really happened to Frank. If not..." She shrugged. "Then we'll live with it, just like we have all these years."

He wasn't sure how to respond, so he nodded.

She turned to leave then paused. "Get him out of here safely, Cody. See to it he makes it home, back to where he belongs."

He swallowed, determined to control his voice. "I intend to," he promised.

Although he had no clear plan, Cody knew he was prepared to do whatever was necessary to make his promise a reality.

Chapter 20

"How much should we tell Danilov?" Cody asked, looking first at Zane, then at Colonel Butler.

"You are, I presume, referring to Captain Thompson," the Consul General replied.

They sat in Zane's office, grouped around a low coffee table. Gray clouds filtered late-morning sunlight and the gloom beyond the window matched Cody's unsettled mood. He had not slept well, waking regularly from brief catnaps, unable to quell the pesky issues demanding resolution.

"Yes, Captain Thompson, of course. For some reason, I still think of him as Andrei Danilov."

Butler frowned slightly. "Does that mean you have doubts?"

"Only two and neither relate to his identity."

"Go on," Zane said.

Cody massaged the back of his neck. "First, despite what he told us about living alone, having a two-bedroom apartment suggests otherwise. I believe our man has a family somewhere. Having said that, I can't come up with a sound reason why he might conceal their existence. Second, how did he manage to stay alive all those years, and do as well as he obviously has?"

Zane said, "I understand your concern about family—getting them out could be challenging—but why worry about the other? It sounds to me like he did what was necessary to survive, largely without compromising himself. Perhaps he did play the collaborator. What does that mean, really? His actions and work products were benign, perhaps even harmless. It wasn't like he translated important documents of a military nature."

"So he claims," Cody interjected.

Zane ignored the comment. "Under identical conditions and circumstances, I'm convinced each of us would have acted in much the same way."

That was probably true, Cody silently admitted. Nevertheless, doubts remained, and leaving issues unresolved was not something he could easily accept.

"To answer your original question," Zane went on, "I believe we should be candid and tell him everything we know, including the fact his official records no longer exist. Perhaps Dan… I mean Thompson, will expand upon what he's already told us. Either way, once we offer him passage home, he will decide either to leave his family, if indeed they exist, or demand we get them out as well."

"I cannot imagine this man voluntarily leaving his family members behind," Cody said. "That would be totally out of character. Unless, that is, the prison story is complete fiction and I've been faked out of my socks."

Like once before, he thought, remembering Mirko Zanic, a charismatic political leader and the worst kind of terrorist: one who fervently believed God condoned the murder of innocents. Zanic had cleverly masked profound hatred for Orthodox Serbs and Muslims with soft-spoken platitudes, a cruel deception Cody failed to detect—a mistake that led to disaster and his eventual exile to Vladivostok.

He looked at Butler. "Any word on the other survivor?"

"Yes, but the news is not very encouraging, I'm afraid. Captain Eugene R. Phillips, the rescued navigator, remained in the Air Force and retired as a light colonel after twenty-two years of service. He died in 1981 from lung cancer."

"In his later years did he add anything to the original story?" Cody asked.

"Not according to the Air Force."

"What about family members?"

"He kept both a diary and a military journal but neither contains anything new. His family considers him a hero."

"Which he was," Zane added.

"They all were," Butler suggested.

"Even our man?" Cody posed the question, waited a long moment, but received no answer. Then he said, "To recap, it appears we have a second survivor from a forty-year-old shootdown, along with an official record that lists him and ten others as *missing*; a man who may be a hero, a traitor, or a little of each. Have I overlooked anything relative?"

"Naturally, I would like to know what happened to the other crew members," Butler said.

"So would I," Cody replied, "but unless our recently resurrected MIA reveals something new, it seems we might never discover what actually happened to them."

"That may not be entirely true," Zane said. "Earlier this year Russia and the United States established a joint commission to explore issues related to POWs and MIAs. Work is just getting started but the Russian Federation has agreed to open its files, even those dating back to World War Two."

"That sounds encouraging," Butler said.

"Unless it's another snow job," Cody suggested. "All sizzle and no steak. It wouldn't be the first time."

"It's much too early to make that judgment," Zane cautioned.

"Perhaps."

"What's our next step?" Butler said to Zane.

The Consul General did not answer immediately. Finally he said, "The photographs and facial analyses, while not one hundred percent conclusive, offer persuasive evidence that our guest's claim is valid. Based on that, we should officially confirm Thompson's identity and offer him a diplomatic passport along with a first class airline ticket on the next available flight to the United States."

"Escorted?" Butler asked.

"Of course," Zane replied.

"And if he accepts?" Cody asked.

"Then we must assume our man will travel alone. Otherwise, he will either provide a reason to delay his leaving or ask for additional accommodations."

Cody tended to agree. The diplomatic passport would expedite Danilov's departure and force him into a go-or-no-go decision. That would bring the unresolved family issue to a head. It was not a perfect plan, but 'good enough' would do for now.

"Suppose he isn't prepared to leave here immediately?" Cody asked.

"Let's cross that bridge if and when we have to," Zane replied.

***

When Cody returned to his office, Phyllis pointed to the telephone. "Call the boss," she said.

Hal Bates probably wanted an update regarding Danilov's status. Cody checked the time: Six-thirty P.M. in Washington.

"Thanks, Phyllis."

Once comfortably seated behind his desk, Cody reached for the secure telephone and keyed in a series of numbers. Not surprisingly, the Assistant Deputy Director for Operations answered before the second ring.

After exchanging pleasantries, Hal said, "I can't tell you how pleased we are with your efforts, Cody. It looks like you may have struck gold."

"I'm not sure what you mean," Cody replied. The chair no longer felt comfortable. He searched his shirt pocket for a Lifesaver, worked one free and popped it into his mouth.

"Do you read the newspapers we send?" Hal asked.

"Every page."

"Then you realize the president's re-election is at risk. According to a recent poll, Governor Clinton could win the White House with a plurality."

"Is Ross Perot that much of a factor?"

"By most accounts he's captured nearly twenty percent of the president's regular constituency, enough to deny Mr. Bush a second term."

Cody's unease grew. "And the president views the return of a long-lost cold warrior as an opportunity to regain his conservative base?"

"No, of course not. But his chief political advisor does and that gentleman has spoken to the director, without the president's knowledge I'm told." Hal paused and Cody knew what was coming. "So," the ADDO continued, "how long before you can put our long-lost aviator on a plane to Washington?"

"I'm not sure. There may be a complication." When Hal did not respond, Cody knew his boss was waiting for an explanation. "Danilov, Thompson told us he has no family."

"I remember that from the transcripts. What's complicated about that?"

Cody took a deep breath. "I believe he's lying. Either the family is hidden away somewhere, or the KGB has them in custody."

The silence told Cody his boss was considering the possibilities. After a long moment Hal said, "If your hunch is right, this could be an elaborate ruse."

"That is a possibility."

"To what purpose, Cody?"

"I haven't figured that part out yet."

"Do you doubt Danilov's claim?"

"No, I believe he is Captain Thompson."

"Then you must also believe Danilov, or Thompson, is part of whatever game the Russians are playing."

"I'm not sure what to believe, Hal."

The ADDO seemed to consider Cody's words. Then he said, "That's not like you, Cody. How do you intend to resolve this?"

"The Consul General suggested, and I agreed, to offer our guest a diplomatic passport and immediate transportation out of Russia. Danilov…Thompson… will either accept or stall for time."

"A direct approach. I like that. When will you make the offer?"

"He's scheduled to be here again Friday."

"Two days from now. Can anything be done sooner?"

"The gentleman asked us not to contact him directly."

"Yes, I remember that, too. It made sense then, but now I'm not so sure."

"Welcome to the club."

Another long pause followed. "Cody," Hal began, his words coming slowly, "if you pull this off, and I have every confidence you will, then your little *faux pax* in Bosnia will vanish like it never happened. Needless to say, your once-rising star within the Agency will resume its ascendancy."

Cody's fist tightened around the handset.

Only someone like Hal Bates, a man who had spent his entire CIA career in analysis rather than field operations, would consider the destruction of a Muslim village and the murder of sixty-seven men, women and children a 'little *faux pax*'. Cody took a deep breath, let it out slowly and relaxed his death grip on the telephone.

"Hal, I'll make this happen. He is definitely our guy and it's the right thing to do. I was merely informing you of potential complications."

The ADDO's mood seemed to brighten. "I knew we could count on you, Cody. Do you have anything else?"

"That's enough for now, isn't it?"

"A little more than I expected, but nothing you can't handle. Keep me posted." The line clicked dead.

Cody replaced the receiver and crunched the Lifesaver between his teeth.

What had occurred in the Balkans was never far from Cody's mind. Banishment to Siberia was just penance for his role in that bungled operation. Nevertheless, Hal's mention of Bosnia resurrected a flood of unpleasant memories.

※※※

Cody had personally recruited Mirko Zanic, an amiable Croatian schoolteacher turned political activist—a man who professed to seek a just and lasting peace for Bosnia's diverse cultures, a patriot who dreamed of creating a "tiny America" where children of every faith could live without fear of harm. In Mirko's vision, Ivanjska—his home village and ancestral birthplace—would become the shining model for a post-Soviet Europe, an ideal society every nation would envy.

Political reality, as it often did, placed the schoolteacher's dream at risk. Memories of old wounds and ancient crimes still festered among population groups. Ethnic Balkans, like most people living in that part of the world, could never forgive an insult or forget a blood feud.

At Mirko's urging, Cody provided the schoolteacher with enough Czech-manufactured AK-47 automatic rifles and ammunition to arm an infantry squad. Such weapons were necessary, Mirko told him, to discourage violence by similarly armed Serbian militants who believed every Croat was, either directly or indirectly, associated with a despicable organization called the Ustasa, a murderous quasi-political group infamously known for its eager collaboration with the Nazis a half-century ago.

Mirko's argument sounded plausible. There were indeed Serbs—Orthodox Christians and Muslims—who focused solely on exacting revenge for past wrongs, some dating back three hundred years, some more recent.

In fact, many Croatians had allied themselves with Hitler during World War Two. With Nazi help, they had gained political power in the former Yugoslavia and then attempted to convert Muslim and Orthodox Serbs to Catholicism. Those who resisted were imprisoned or murdered. Post-war reports estimated that a half-million Serbians, along with thousands of Jews and Gypsies, had died in Ustasa extermination camps.

Now, Mirko claimed, vengeful Serbians from his own village were threatening to take reprisals against innocent Croats in retaliation for long-ago crimes committed by others. The weapons were a defensive measure against out-of-control Serbian thugs.

Unfortunately, as Cody was about to experience first-hand, Paraday's Conjecture once again proved true: Everybody lies.

Mirko and a dozen of his friends, now armed with automatic weapons thanks to Cody, attacked and destroyed a Muslim village near Babici. After setting fire to the mosque, they killed everyone—everyone, that is, except a dozen young women whom they raped multiple times. Afterwards, Mirko's men branded each girl's forehead with a stylistic 'U', an unmistakable calling card. Finally, like a macabre ritual, the renegade Croats cut each girl's throat and then arranged their bodies head to head in two rows.

The hated Ustasa was alive and well, and Mirko was its newest champion.

Kneeling beside the desecrated bodies, Cody stared into each bloodless face. Even the perfect relaxation of death could not conceal the horror of their last moments. Once again, Cody questioned God's decision to allow mankind free will. It seemed naïve, perhaps criminally so, to rely wholly on spiritual faith to produce righteous human conduct.

If it were up to Cody, he would instantly mete out terrible punishment to anyone who dared commit such unholy atrocities. Public condemnation followed by an unpleasant death would alter the concept of divine retribution; religious theory would become undisputed fact. Pillars of salt, liberally distributed across the world, would no doubt improve mankind's behavior toward one another. Or so he believed.

In response, Cody had enlisted a platoon of Serbian military police and, together with a half-dozen U.S. Army Special Forces soldiers—the latter unshaven and dressed as local civilians—captured Mirko and his gang of murderers.

"Those young girls," Cody said to a handcuffed Mirko. "What crime did they commit?"

"They were Muslims," the schoolteacher explained, "an insult to Jesus Christ and his holiness, the Pope."

Infuriated by Mirko's lunatic reply, Cody then compounded his initial misjudgment with an act of calculated negligence.

He ordered American SF troops into their borrowed BOV-VP—an all-wheel drive armored vehicle—and then spoke with the Serbian lieutenant in charge of the MP platoon.

"Return to the village and care for the dead," Cody instructed, in a voice loud enough for everyone to hear. "Then I suggest you deliver these criminals to the proper authorities."

The Serb commander nodded, his eyes filled with tacit understanding. "As you wish," he replied.

Cody climbed into the beat up vehicle and prepared to leave.

Mirko, knowing exactly what was about to happen, screamed at Cody: "God will not forget what you have done to us!"

That is probably true, Cody had silently admitted. Nor is He likely to forget my part in what you and your friends did back in that little village. Exchanging a final glance with the villainous schoolteacher, he motioned the driver to move out.

The next day, an early rising farmer had discovered the tortured and emasculated corpses of Mirko and his associates hanging by their feet from trees just outside Babici. A sign on Mirko's body branded the group as *Murderers of Innocent Muslims*. The rogue Croatians had taken a long time to die, their suffering perhaps as cruel as the young girls whom they had raped and murdered.

In Cody's wishful I-am-God universe, it was a fitting end. Run of the mill immorality was one thing: a disappointing but generally tolerable human characteristic. On the other hand, malevolent evil had no conscience, no saving qualities with which it could redeem itself. Mirko and his cohorts, unlike their innocent victims, got exactly what they deserved.

European newspapers however, had downplayed or ignored the massacre and rape of Muslims, choosing instead to publish photographs of Mirko and his comrades. Outraged editorials suggested American involvement, albeit without offering proof. Ultimately, the murderers became martyrs and the murdered innocents forgotten. A wave of sectarian violence followed, resulting in a dozen more deaths on both sides.

Just as he expected, the Agency recalled Cody to Langley. They soon issued a formal reprimand and then banished him to a tiny office where he spent the next two months shuffling intelligence summaries. It was during this hiatus when it occurred to him that he might be in danger of becoming what he despised. It was the first instance where Cody questioned his choice of professions. But not the last.

As far as the Agency was concerned, Cody's posting to Vladivostok was a way station, a minor purgatory from which restoration to grace or involuntary retirement would ensue. His past contributions and letters of commendation counted for little. They were, in fact, ignored, as one might disdain wearing an unfashionable necktie.

However, a third possibility existed.

Voluntary resignation and a fresh start doing something totally different; work he once enjoyed as a young man. The idea lurked in the back of his mind, a tantalizing siren crooking her finger, a golden-haired Lorelei inviting him toward an unseen shore.

***

Cody pulled himself away from the moody recollection and speculated on Hal's comments regarding the upcoming presidential election, and what might be happening at Langley.

George H. W. Bush had once served as CIA Director under the Reagan administration; that was common knowledge. CIA, the ultimate old-boy network, would be eager to assist their former boss in every way possible, especially since their distinguished ex-colleague also happened to be the current President of the United States.

The promise of another victory dance over the Soviet Union's corpse would play well in conservative quarters. Hell, it would ring positive in all but the most strident left-wing constituencies.

However, such a possibility could not persuade Cody to believe that the president, a decorated wartime aviator, would ever take political advantage of any situation involving military veterans.

There were, however, many others on both sides of the aisle who had no qualms about using whatever means necessary to further their political agendas.

In any case, getting Danilov—Thompson—out of Russia was far from being a done deal.

Despite wishing otherwise, Cody now occupied center stage, a reluctant actor bereft of good lines, and thus unable to affect the play's outcome.

It was a situation he did not enjoy, but one he intended to rectify.

Chapter 21

Cody stood by the picture window looking out at the narrow bay, its waters roiled by an approaching late afternoon squall. The scudding gray clouds reminded him once again that winter in Vladivostok came early, stayed late, and seldom offered extended periods of sunshine or hope of an early spring.

The door opened and he turned at the sound.

"Welcome home, Captain Thompson," Zane said, extending his hand to a seemingly bewildered Andrei Danilov, who still wore hat, overcoat, and gloves.

The greeting, uttered from inside the consulate's first floor conference room, tended toward the melodramatic but Cody smiled amiably, content to relinquish the limelight to the Consul General.

"Oh?" Danilov said, removing his gloves before taking Zane's hand. He shot a glance at Cody. "You have found my records?" he asked, directing his question to Zane. "You are satisfied?"

"Yes, we are indeed. Although not entirely conclusive, the evidence strongly suggests you are precisely who you claim to be."

Concern skipped across Danilov's face. "Not entirely conclusive? What does that mean?"

The Consul General brushed the question aside. "Mr. Ballantine will share our findings with you in a moment. For now, I wanted to be the first to welcome you back into America's fold."

"That is very kind of you, sir."

Cody remained silent while Zane's gaze slid towards Cody, a frozen smile on his lips. The Consul General seemed out of words.

His lines spoken, he seemed like a stage actor waiting for a tardy response from his inattentive associate.

"Thank you for your time, Mr. Zane," Cody said.

He had expected a lengthier, more rousing welcoming speech from Zane, a 'stars and stripes forever' soliloquy laced with kudos and gilded rhetoric about the triumph of perseverance over despair. Instead, the Consul General had been uncharacteristically succinct. He now appeared ready to leave.

"I will brief Mr. Danilov, I mean Captain Thompson, on what we have so far discovered."

His relief evident, Zane's smile unfroze and he rubbed his hands together, the procurator Pontius Pilate reincarnated, once again absolving himself of whatever irksome consequences that might follow.

"Excellent. If you need anything, please let me know."

The Consul General's departure seemed more like an escape. Clearly, Zane's persona did not flourish in unusual situations. Cody had a sudden insight.

Huge bureaucracies—the State Department certainly fit that category—abhorred out-of-the-ordinary situations. At this very moment, working away in some obscure Washington office, Cody suspected that a committee of nameless Washington procedure writers was no doubt composing an exhaustively detailed protocol to guide other consulates should untold numbers of sixty-year-old MIAs suddenly emerge from captivity.

Danilov removed his fur cap and overcoat. He looked at the hat and coat rack. "Something has been added," he noted, making use of the newly installed furniture.

"Yes. As you already know, we are still in the process of moving in." Cody motioned toward the sideboard. "Tea? Crumpets?"

"Not just now. Later, perhaps."

As in all but their first meeting, the brown leather briefcase did not accompany Danilov. Cody would eventually find a way to raise that issue—but, not yet.

"Then let's talk," Cody said, concealing his disappointment. He took his usual seat and set a large manila envelope near his elbow.

Danilov eyed the envelope then joined Cody. "I gather from Mr. Zane's comment that my military records were inconclusive."

"Yes, they were."

"I find that completely surprising. What difficulties did you encounter?"

"Your personnel file no longer exists."

Danilov looked confused. "I don't understand. Were they confiscated? Have they been secreted away?"

Cody shook his head. "Not exactly." He then related essential facts surrounding the 1973 St. Louis Records Center fire, omitting any mention of arson, real or otherwise. "In all," he concluded, "approximately eighteen million military personnel files were destroyed, including yours and those of your crew members."

Danilov leaned back, his expression a mixture of surprise and chagrin. The reaction appeared spontaneous and genuine, void of theatrics.

"There were no copies made?" he asked, finally. "No backup files or microfilm stored offsite?"

"Neither, I'm afraid."

"How can such an oversight be possible?"

"I can't answer that."

Danilov stared at the table for a moment, and then re-established eye contact. "And no official record of my military service exists?"

"I'm afraid not."

"Nothing of my training, the missions I flew, or the decorations I earned?"

Until this moment, Danilov had not mentioned awards or decorations, nor had such a possibility occurred to Cody. Yet, the revelation wasn't a complete surprise. Personal modesty seemed perfectly in tune with the old man's character.

Cody said, "What sort of decorations?"

I received a Bronze Star and an Air Medal for the missions we flew while stationed at Ladd, as did others. Craig also got a DFC."

"I see. Unfortunately, the fire probably claimed those records along with everything else. What happened to your personal copy of the citations?"

"I sent them home to my parents." Danilov tilted his head to one side, a troubled, inquisitive gesture. "Tell me: are they still alive?"

Cody had no choice but to answer. "No, I'm afraid not. They passed away six years ago—within a few months of each other."

The old man nodded slowly then asked, "Natural causes or disease?"

"As far as we know, they died of natural causes."

Danilov swallowed once, then folded his hands together, fingers interlocked. When he finally spoke, his voice was subdued. "I suspected that might be the case. When the probability of returning home after nearly four decades became more than wistful hope, I thought about many things, including the likely passage of friends and loved ones. Although I hoped otherwise, I prepared myself for the worst. Were they still alive today, both would be in their nineties—possible but unlikely. Still, the actual death of parents, no matter the circumstance, is not something one easily accepts."

"I understand."

Danilov studied his hands for a moment, then looked up. "My parents were good people. I have missed them."

Having nothing to offer, Cody did not respond.

Danilov continued. "They had two children, a boy and a girl—my sister. Losing their son—never knowing what really happened to him...to me—would have been a terrible burden to carry all those years."

"I'm sure it was."

The old man's attention wandered, as though his mind had drifted back to childhood and happier times. Then his eyes, now slightly moistened, refocused.

"What about my little sister? What happened to her?"

"I have better news. She is alive and well—married with children. You are an uncle, three times over."

"An uncle? Imagine that," Danilov formed the words through a half-hearted smile. Then he raised an eyebrow. "Boys or girls?"

"Two boys and a girl. Actually, they are adults now—grown men and women with children of their own. That makes you a great uncle or something. Genealogy was never my strongest suit; too many 'once or twice removed' designations, a concept that baffles me." His attempt at light humor had little effect. "By the way," he added. "Your oldest nephew is called Andrew."

"Really? That was my paternal grandfather's name."

Cody shook his head and smiled. "I don't think he was named after your paternal grandfather."

The old man's brow furrowed, then comprehension seemed to dawn. "Oh, I see." After a moment, he said, "Are they well?"

"Yes. As far as we can determine, your sister and her family are pretty much living happy, normal lives."

"That is good to hear." Danilov resumed staring at his folded hands, moving his thumbs against each other, rubbing the pads in a circular motion, apparently lost in deep thought.

Finally, he looked up. "And Sophia?" he asked. "Did you also discover what became of her?"

"I did," Cody said, recalling the bullet points in the Agency's letter. "It seems your fiancé married someone else."

"Of course she did. Sophia was too attractive to remain a spinster. There would have been many suitors. Do you know when that happened?"

"About two years after your plane went down."

"Two years? A respectful interval, don't you think?"

"Yes, I do."

"I presume she then married a Roman Catholic gentleman of impeccable Italian lineage?"

"A dentist named Grimaldi. They have children *and* grandchildren."

"Grandchildren? Oh, my. Life *does* move on, doesn't it, Mr. Ballantine?"

"So it would seem."

His thumbs paused and Danilov's quizzical expression returned. "If my military records were destroyed, how can you be reasonably certain that I am not an imposter? After all, locating relatives and a former fiancé proves nothing."

Cody did not reply. Instead, he fingered the manila envelope and extracted an eight-by-ten-inch photograph, a single sheet containing eight youthful faces—including that of Cadet Thompson—copied from PMC's 1950 yearbook.

"Do any of these young gentlemen look familiar?" Cody asked, sliding the photo across the table.

Danilov took the photograph.

For the first time that morning, his face creased into a wide, delightful expression. "Oh, my goodness." His eyes moved from face to face and he shook his head slowly, the smile never fading. "Were we *really* that young?" he muttered, obviously to himself, yet clearly enjoying the moment.

"Apparently so," Cody offered.

"I remember every one of these cadets," Danilov said, without looking up. "Military school classmates tend to form much stronger personal bonds than students who attend traditional schools."

"Yes, I know."

Danilov now seemed more relaxed and at peace, his initial despondency eased perhaps by warm recollections. He continued studying the photograph, obviously lost in old memories. After what seemed like a long time, he passed the picture back to Cody.

Still smiling, he said, "How is my alma mater these days? Have there been many changes?"

"I'm afraid so."

The smile went rigid and then vanished. Danilov's eyes narrowed and hints of his earlier discomfort reemerged. "In what way?"

Cody took a deep breath. "Like your military records, the Pennsylvania Military College no longer exists."

Danilov stiffened in his chair. "It burned as well? That seems highly unlikely."

"No, nothing like that."

"What, then?"

"Penn Military became another casualty of the Vietnam War. Weekly demonstrations by students from nearby colleges—including Swarthmore no doubt—and increasing popular disgust with the war caused an immense social upheaval. Public pressure and rapidly declining enrollments took their toll. In 1972 the Corps of Cadets was officially and permanently disbanded."

Danilov's eyes grew wide and his jaw sagged. Then he said, his voice barely audible, "Disbanded? Permanently?"

"Yes. To survive as an institution of learning the school became coeducational, changed its curriculum to focus on liberal arts, and assumed the name of its new benefactor. What you knew as Pennsylvania Military College is now called Widener University. Old Main still stands, as do the dormitories, now refurbished and expanded to accommodate a mixed student body. But I'm afraid the college you remember is gone."

Danilov swallowed several times, his distressed gaze moving around the room as though searching for a precious object, now irretrievably lost.

Cody rose, poured water into a glass and handed it across the table. "Drink this."

It took a few minutes for Danilov to compose himself. Then, in the same quiet voice, "How very ironic."

Cody sensed the old man had something specific on his mind. "In what way?"

"I find it strange that a distinguished military college, one having a hundred and fifty years of scholastic history, should become a casualty of war. Akin, I would think, to closing Harvard's law school due to a corrupt legal system, or Wharton shutting its doors because a financial or accounting rule proved fallacious and allowed corporations to cheat their shareholders." Danilov smiled—a familiar, weary upturn of his lips. "Why should one occur and not the other?"

It was an interesting question and Cody took a moment to answer. "Perhaps," he suggested, "it's because society places a higher value on lawyers and accountants than it does on soldiers."

"Probably so, but why? Would a lawyer risk death to uphold a legal principal? Would an accountant endure incredible hardship or confront grave personal danger to preserve the sanctity of debits and credits? I think not."

"And I agree," Cody said. "But soldiers are a tiny segment of American society. Those in military service wear uniforms, not suits. They stand out in a crowd. In difficult times, they and their institutions are much easier to ostracize and condemn.

"Furthermore, soldiers and policemen are living proof that we live in an imperfect world; one filled with malevolence and social dysfunction. Without guardians, the general populace would become easy prey to the world's bullies, a fact difficult for many to accept."

"How shortsighted. Without soldiers and policemen, who will protect lawyers, accountants, and so-called intellectuals from the world's barbarians?"

Cody sensed the question was rhetorical, and he remained silent.

Danilov turned and stared out the window. Cody followed his gaze. A cold rain spattered against the windowpane and droplets slithered down the glass, partially obscuring the view of Golden Horn Bay.

He turned back to Cody. "So what happens now?"

"That's an easier question to answer. We send you home," Cody said, extracting a gold colored booklet from the manila envelope and sliding it across the table. "This is a diplomatic passport. We can have you on the next commercial flight to Tokyo. Once there, you can continue on to San Francisco or to another major U.S. city, depending on the most convenient airline departure schedule." Cody paused, anticipating a reaction.

Danilov opened the passport to a photograph purporting to be that of an American diplomatic envoy; a man named Andrew Thompson.

"This picture was taken the day I arrived."

"Yes, two weeks ago."

"It seems much longer." Danilov turned several pages, pausing now and then. He seemed interested in the entry and exit stamps, some applied carelessly—intentionally so, per Cody's instructions—from various countries during the past four years. The booklet's exact center, marked by staples, contained a Russian visa fitted neatly inside the passport.

Danilov again paused to read the entries. "This says I arrived in Vladivostok two days ago."

"That isn't unusual. Special diplomatic envoys seldom spend more than a few days in any one location."

"I see. Well, everything looks quite authentic. My compliments to you or to whoever did this."

"Thank you."

"What about airline tickets?"

"Once we select a flight, Phyllis can obtain tickets in less than an hour. Then you will be on your way, escorted of course. America has changed a lot in forty years."

"So I have read and been told."

Danilov closed the booklet and held the passport in both hands, staring at the embossed Great Seal of the United States. Without looking up, he asked: "Mr. Ballantine, what happens to me once I return to the United States?"

"Several things. First, you will be welcomed home properly; you might even get another medal. And, since you never officially left the service, I imagine the Air Force will correct your records, including, perhaps a retroactive promotion to major or maybe lieutenant colonel. Then you will receive back pay, lots of it, but I am not sure how much. Lastly, the government will provide a monthly retirement check commensurate with your final rank and whatever years of military service they deem appropriate."

He looked up. "That sounds quite generous. Anything else?"

"Of course, there will be questions regarding the fate of your crew. Other than that, I don't expect much political fallout. After all, we have *glasnost*. The shootdown, your capture and subsequent detention will be blamed on Cold War tensions and the bad old Soviet regime. The world will view your repatriation as tangible evidence that we now live in an age of cooperative enlightenment."

"How nice to think so."

Cody detected an uncomfortable edge to Danilov's voice, so he decided to proceed on a lighter vein. "You will also be in great demand as a talk show guest, another source of fame and potential revenue."

Danilov's expression soured, as though he'd swallowed something distasteful. He said, "Followed, no doubt, by a lucrative book contract for my memoirs." The disdain in his voice was unmistakable.

"All entirely up to you, but I don't believe complete anonymity is an option. That would mean concealing your existence. Why, after all this time, would you choose to become a hermit in your own country?"

Danilov broke eye contact and stared at the passport. A moment later, he shrugged. "That is not a realistic expectation, I suppose."

"Anyway," Cody said, "after the dust settles you can live wherever you like, close to your sister and her family perhaps, and begin a new life."

Danilov stared at Cody. "A new life? At my age? That is not a particularly comforting thought." The edginess had returned to his voice.

"But you'll be home, among family." Cody shifted in his chair. Was Danilov—Thompson—getting cold feet at the last minute? Or was he afraid that a return to the United States might ultimately reveal old secrets best left undiscovered?

"Home? Hardly, Mr. Ballantine. Not after forty years. Family? Yes, but estranged." Then he sighed and his voice softened, returning to its normal tone. "In any event, I cannot leave immediately. There are certain matters I wish to resolve—letters to friends, the gathering together of a few personal effects—that sort of thing. But I can be ready to leave Monday morning."

Cody sensed hesitation, a palpable reluctance on Danilov's part to suddenly uproot himself from less than perfect yet familiar surroundings, to rejoin an American society frenzied beyond what he might have read or imagined. After spending nearly four decades in Siberia, his reaction was understandable. But Cody's doubts persisted.

There was something important Danilov had not yet divulged, an undisclosed detail hinted at by a barely detectable whiff of uneasiness.

Now that the former aviator was on premises and technically on United States property, Cody felt it important to keep him close. However, those options were limited. To the rest of the world, Danilov was a Russian citizen. Short of forcibly restraining him, Cody could do little to prevent the old man's departure.

Still, he had to try. "If you like, one of our people will collect your personal items. And you could write letters here."

Danilov shook his head. "I prefer to handle those things myself."

Cody disguised his simmering anxiety. "Of course. Is there anything I can do in the meantime?"

"Nothing comes to mind. But in case you're wondering, I would prefer you not contact my sister until I am back on American soil, or at lease enroute." Danilov handed the passport back. "And it is probably not a good idea for me to carry this until I am ready to leave."

Cody returned the passport and yearbook photograph to the manila envelope.

Danilov stood and extended his hand. "I appreciate all you have done Mr. Ballantine. I am looking forward to going home. Still, after all these years dreaming of little else, the actual reality of that prospect is more than a little intimidating."

Cody rose and shook hands. "I'd be surprised if it was otherwise. May I ask: Are you returning to Ussurijsk immediately?"

"Unfortunately, no. The train does not leave until later this evening."

"Then why wait? It's only a hundred kilometers or so. Let our driver take you there. That way, you could get an early start on finalizing your affairs."

Danilov's face reflected gratitude. "How very considerate of you, Mr. Ballantine. If that would not be an inconvenience, then I accept."

Cody reached for the telephone, satisfied with a minor victory. "It's no trouble at all."

Tapping in a phone number, Cody wondered if, among his belongings, Danilov would include the contents of a brown leather briefcase, a 'thick document' seen by the Duty Officer on that first day, but not since.

Chapter 22

Later that evening, the soft buzz from Cody's mobile telephone interrupted a pleasant conversation with Anne Seymour.

"Pardon me," he said, reaching for the instrument. "I've got to answer this." Without looking, he knew it was 10:00 PM, local time.

Cody stood and walked a few steps away. "Ballantine."

Freddie's voice responded. "Good evening, Cody. Our friend is at home, apparently tucked in for the evening."

"Anything else going on up there?"

"No, that's it for now."

"Thanks. Keep me posted."

"Always," Freddie replied.

Cody disconnected the call.

Soon after Danilov's departure, Cody had dispatched a surveillance team—Freddie, Sasha and another couple—to Ussurijsk. Using two vehicles, they had bracketed Danilov, traveling a few miles ahead and behind the consulate car transporting the man Cody now believed was Captain Andrew Thompson.

He returned to Anne's living room sofa and inhaled her familiar perfume: warm and feminine and flowery.

"Sorry," he mumbled.

"Is this how you usually spend your evenings?" She turned slightly to face him, her lips forming a wry smile.

"What do you mean?"

"Taking furtive, late-night calls from your spooky associates; clandestine meetings with dark-eyed Mata Haris who appear at your door in the wee hours, begging to be rescued from evil pursuers."

"Her name was Margaretha Zelle."

"Who?"

"Mata Hari.'

"Zelle? I thought she was from India or Sumatra—somewhere in the Orient."

"The public name and birthplace were fictitious, used merely to embellish her show business biography. She was Dutch."

"Dutch? Show business? You mean like an actress?

"No. Like an exotic dancer."

She poked his arm playfully. "No!"

"Scout's honor, but don't feel bad. Most people believed the show biz version."

"You mean, people like me."

Cody shrugged.

"What happened to her?"

"She was executed by a French firing squad in 1917."

"How awful."

"That isn't the half of it. Zelle actually spied for France and many believed she was innocent, a victim of French paranoia and German disinformation."

Cody reached for his drink, a buttery Chardonnay from California's Dry Creek Valley, and took a long sip.

He felt like an idiot. Here I am, sitting beside the most desirable woman I have ever met, and all I can talk about is Mata Hari? Where is your suave *patois*, your *beaux mots*? The answer was obvious: You *have* no suave phrases, he reminded himself, and sweet talk was never part of your conversational repertoire.

She was looking at him, the same wry smile on her lips.

He set his glass on a coaster. "Do you like your job, Anne?"

The smile grew wider. "You need to work on your segue technique."

"One of my numerous flaws."

"Oh? How numerous?"

"Enough, I hope, to keep you interested." He wondered if his comment expressed too much interest, perhaps too soon.

"I see."

Not exactly a wild rush into his arms, but neither was it a rejection.

"So, how do you like being Director of Protocol?"

"It's fine. The work is challenging and it keeps me busy. On the other hand, life and circumstance pay little attention to youthful intentions. I never learned to fly an airplane, so Amelia Earhart's legacy remains unchallenged—at least by yours truly. Neither did I change the world. What about you?"

"I wanted to be Captain America, righter of wrongs…or maybe an architect."

She chuckled softly. "Captain America I can believe, but architecture? Really?"

"Really."

An inquisitive expression replaced the smile. "What type?"

"Residential."

She cocked an eyebrow. "Is there more?"

He relaxed a bit more, glad to be back on relatively safe ground. "When much younger, I happened upon an oversized book filled with color photographs—grand English manors…ostentatious estates built in the 17th and 18th centuries. That book created a desire in me to build fine houses. Not hundred-room mansions nor little brick boxes, but something in between: individually designed homes, each with a unique character."

"Like the one you designed for Tessa."

"Something like that, more or less."

"Instead, you became a spook."

"A semi-spook. I don't do much field work these days."

"Is that really true?"

It is now, Cody felt like saying. Instead, he nodded slightly. "I think so. In either case, until it actually happened, working for the Agency was an occupation that never occurred to me."

"Do you like being a semi-spook?"

Anne had deftly turned his question about her diplomatic service around. He shrugged, and opted for an honest answer. "I did once. Now I'm not so sure."

"Then why continue?"

"It's important work that needs doing. Besides, I've never had a good reason to pursue alternatives."

She did not answer immediately, as though considering her response. Then she said, "I see. Well, if you actually did—consider alternatives, I mean—would it be architecture, or something similar to what you're doing now?"

Cody searched her eyes. There he found quiet curiosity and guarded interest.. He also saw the look of one who had suffered a great wound. Yet, despite unforgotten pain, Anne seemed willing to re-travel a similar path, hopeful that life would offer a more pleasant outcome this time around.

For his part, Cody's mind and spirit had shed the restrictive bonds imposed by post-marital conflict, sloughing it off like an old shirt. In Anne's presence, Tessa's memory no longer mattered. That sexually frigid young woman, along with their failed marriage, became hardly more than a cheerless recollection from a stern, unchangeable past.

But the future was different—it was malleable: white-hot metal awaiting the blacksmith's hammer. The choice was his. He could allow it to cool and darken, retaining its old form, or he could fashion something new—a shape not yet clearly discernable.

"Maybe both," he answered. "But with a difference."

"Oh? How different?"

He took a deep breath. "I own a fifty acre vineyard in the Alexander Valley, not far from Healdsburg, in Northern California."

Anne seemed surprised. "How on earth did you end up owning a vineyard?"

"By accident and good luck, mostly. My uncle passed away a few years ago; he left it to me. Charles Ballantine—Uncle Charlie—lost his wife to cancer. He never remarried."

"How sad."

"It is. Connie was the love of his life. He often reminisced about how they met at the Rendezvous Ballroom in Balboa just after the war."

"Balboa?" she asked. "In Panama?"

He shook his head. "California. It's a little island near Newport Beach. The Rendezvous Ballroom was a popular dance hall back then."

"Oh, I see. Please go on. I didn't mean to interrupt."

"According to Uncle Charlie, it was mutual love at first sight. Although they were not blessed with children, he still wanted someone in the family to continue what he started. I suppose that's where I came in. During high school and college, I spent seven pleasant summers living in their house and working for him. He was a very perceptive man and probably sensed my unspoken interest."

"Are you serious?"

"Absolutely. I loved spending time with him in the vineyards. My uncle believed tending vines was an art form, an act of creation, a constant striving to balance two needs: the biological and the aesthetic."

"I'm not sure I understand that."

"It has to do with shaping and pruning the vines; leaving just the right number of buds to prevent overproduction. Vines with abundant fruit clusters produce grapes of marginal quality. Reducing the number of clusters intensifies and concentrates the flavor. The result is higher quality grapes. During the growing season, we matched each grape cluster with the proper number of leaves. That exercise channeled energy into the fruit instead of excess greenery. Judicious pruning not only makes the cordon look attractive, it also provides an optimum balance between fruit and foliage."

"It sounds complicated."

Cody shrugged. "Maybe a little."

***

"Vines are like people," Uncle Charlie once told him. "Put them under stress and the strongest among them will always meet the challenge. Difficult conditions: climate, marginal soil, and heartless pruning will test a vine. As is true in all nature, plants and creatures that prove adaptable will prevail; the weak and inflexible languish and eventually fade from existence."

Cody was usually gone by late August, forsaking his uncle's vineyard and those patient lessons taught under cloudless skies, reluctantly heading for indoor pursuits, primarily academic. Leaving when he did, just before harvest, Cody missed the sharp, fruity aromas that characterized the first crush, a time when grapes yielded initial clues about the character and potential of its wine—a season of joy and promise and yet to be discovered potential.

Years later, after his graduation from college, Cody finally experienced what he had so often missed. In that promising spring of his life, he silently vowed to return; to spend his days in the vineyards, filling a vacuum in his life he never knew existed.

That was before Tessa, and the Army, and Vietnam, and Bosnia—before all the humdrum and havoc that cluttered his life with the messy residue of living.

***

"Nowadays," Cody continued, "my little enterprise sells grapes to the major wine producers; Gallo and Mondavi, among others. It's a fascinating business, close to nature and fairly profitable too, despite my current status as absentee owner."

Anne's mildly surprised expression became inquisitive. "Am I to understand you'd consider being an 'on premises' owner?"

"More than that. I'd like to expand and update the residence using my uncle's old stone house as a starting point. The building is sited perfectly, slightly below a knob of higher ground overlooking the vineyard, which slopes down toward the Russian River. I might even try my luck at winemaking—small batches for personal use."

Anne shook her head, a look of wonderment on her face. "You're full of surprises, aren't you?"

"It's not a venture I would attempt on my own," he added cautiously, trying to gauge her feelings without being too obvious. "I would need a partner; someone cultured and refined to keep me on track."

"And to wash grape stains out of your clothes."

"A little of that, too."

She stared at him. "And you'd really leave the Agency?"

"Yes," he said, surprised at how easily the answer came.

He now understood that getting Danilov/Thompson out of Russia was an absolute necessity. While it would never erase the guilt and shame he carried regarding Mirko Zanic and his band of renegades—nothing ever could—it would allow him to leave the Agency on his own terms, to perhaps recapture a tiny portion of a youthful dream he once had.

"I'd have no choice," he added. "One thing I learned from my uncle: Operating a vineyard requires a full-time effort. As my Uncle Charlie used to say: Anything worth doing is worth doing to excess."

"Is that so?"

He moved his head toward her and she leaned forward to meet his kiss.

Anne's lips felt warm and soft and when they parted slightly he felt the light, explorative touch of her tongue. A pang surged through his body, an electric charge reverberating deep in his groin, a sensation that nearly overloaded his mind with a searing jolt of long suppressed desire.

She pulled away gently and then smiled into his eyes.

"I would have liked your Uncle Charlie," she whispered.

Chapter 23

Their spontaneous passion carried them through a long, rambling weekend, an interlude marked by lovemaking, laughter, and quiet talks about the future; two wounded souls cautiously re-exploring the boundaries of a realm they had once forsaken.

The mobile telephone, buzzing at regular twelve-hour intervals, was Cody's only reminder of another life that continued to demand his attention.

"My, aren't *we* in a good mood this morning," Phyllis said as Cody strolled into the reception area on Monday. "Have we misbehaved?"

"Is it that obvious?" he asked, stopping near her desk to pour coffee.

"Other than the schoolboy grin, you remain inscrutable. Nevertheless, there are rumors, which I won't repeat, regarding you and our Director of Protocol. I presume what I've heard isn't merely catty chatter?"

Cody felt an uncomfortable twinge. He had always avoided office romances, believing them contrary to professional conduct. Yet, except for the Danilov situation, which he intended to pursue to its conclusion, Cody realized he no longer had much interest in Agency rules or practices.

The discovery filled him with an unexpected sensation. After more than twenty years, the prospect of leaving his arcane occupation generated neither remorse nor melancholy—only patient anticipation and muted exuberance.

Another thought occurred. He said, "Maybe it's time you latched on to a new boss. I have a feeling this could be my last assignment."

"How sweet," Phyllis replied. "I'm so happy for you, Cody." Then she waved a hand dismissively. "But don't concern yourself about my future. You're looking at a fifty-five plus female, the wife of a decorated Air Force pilot who probably died while a POW. The Agency wouldn't dare let me go. In fact, I may demand a promotion." Then she smiled and said, "After all, look at what I've had to put up with all these years."

Another smile creased his face. "Now that you mention it, that's not a bad idea. You deserve one for tolerating my neurotic behavior for so long."

"My sentiments exactly." Her eyes reflected warm affection. "Now that we understand each other, get to work. You have another briefcase. More special mail from Langley."

Cody nodded. "Coffee first, mail second."

Seated at his desk, Cody eased the coffee mug onto a coaster. Then he opened the briefcase, slit the sealed envelope with a letter opener and removed several pages: short paragraphs neatly typed on Agency letterhead. Since he had not asked for additional information, his curiosity was aroused.

Attached to the pages was a note from the boss.

Cody:

I thought you might find the enclosed material interesting, particularly Item 1, which adds credence to our guest's story. The excerpts come from various confidential sources.

Regards,

Hal

He set the note aside and turned to the first page.

CONFIDENTIAL EXTRACT
Reports of American Prisoners in Eastern Siberia
DISSEMINATION FORBIDDEN

LOCATION:Svetloye Camp #5 (Susuman)
SUMMARY:A repatriated German POW who worked in the Svetloye gold mines from 1944-1958 claims to have befriended a Russian-speaking American aviator who would not or could not reveal his real identity. 'Andrei' reportedly told the German POW that Soviet fighters shot down his aircraft over international waters in the late summer of 1954. The German ex-POW described Andrei as "a tall, nice-looking young man with brown eyes and a pleasant disposition."

Cody read the paragraph twice, slowly.

Without question, the Agency's source for the Susuman report was Ernst Klaus, Danilov's mentor and confidant when both men worked the Svetloye gold mines. That meant the former German soldier was alive, or had been when he gave his information to U.S. authorities. Danilov—Thompson—would be pleased to learn that his old comrade had returned safely to Germany.

He continued reading.

LOCATION: Spornoe Camp #3 (Kolyma River Basin)
SUMMARY:A Lithuanian prisoner who worked at this coal mining camp in 1954 claims to have seen six or seven Americans confined to "zapretchdelanki" [roughly, 'isolated plots']. Every few days or so, one or two were taken from the camp until none remained. When asked how he knew they were Americans, the Lithuanian replied: "It was common knowledge."

Cody rubbed his chin. Were those Americans at Spornoe part of Thompson's RB-50 crew? Absent a specific date, Cody could not be sure.

He read on.

LOCATION: Military Hospital 315 (near Nahodka)
SUMMARY: A Ukrainian medical technician reported treating a prisoner being held under guard in late 1954. The patient—a blond man of average height, about 25 years old—wore a gray flying uniform, suffered from severe burns and was unable to communicate in Russian. After treatment, MVD guards removed the patient from the hospital.

Nahodka, another port city, wasn't very far from Vladivostok. Could this be one of Thompson's crew? The timing seemed right. Cody desperately wanted more detailed information, but realized Hal had sent all that was available.

As he read similar accounts, more than a dozen in all, Cody searched for other possible correlations between the Gamov shootdown in 1954 and eyewitness reports, hoping to discover the fate of Danilov's fellow aviators. But he found nothing definite.

He also attempted to maintain a running count, also to no avail. How does one tally 'a few' or 'several' or 'a large/small group'? Still, the total number of prisoners sighted was much higher than Cody imagined—nearly a hundred, he estimated. Were all those captives American servicemen?

Disturbed, he set the documents aside and checked the time: 10:05 A.M. Danilov said he would be ready to leave 'Monday morning.' Technically, he had about two hours remaining, but Cody felt an acidic knot forming just below his breastbone. He slipped fingers underneath his shirt and massaged the spot gently.

His initial light mood became anxious and unsettled, much as quiet summer air trembles when a thunderstorm first approaches. On impulse, he reached for the telephone and punched a mobile telephone number.

"Benner," a familiar voice answered.

"Hello, Freddie. What's happening with our guest?"

"Mr. Danilov took a morning walk, then returned to his apartment where he remains."

"He's supposed to be on his way here."

"Then I'm afraid the gentleman has missed the morning train."

The knot tightened. "Is there a rear entrance to his apartment?"

"Of course."

"And you're sure he didn't slip out the back door?"

"Not unless he used the garage. Does our guest own an automobile?"

Cody reached for a Lifesaver, wishing it were an antacid tablet. "I don't know, Freddie. Have you seen any official-looking cars hovering near the building?" Cody refused to believe Russian authorities had snatched Danilov without Freddie's knowledge.

"I haven't, but let me check with the others. Call you right back." A soft hum filled his ear as the line went dead.

Cody drummed his fingernails against the desktop, trying not to count the seconds or dwell upon tired axioms about watched pots never reaching a boil. Danilov was still in his apartment, Cody assured himself, packing a few things for his long trip home or perhaps writing those letters he mentioned. Leaving Russia after four decades would be a tumultuous upheaval in the old man's life; he was merely running behind schedule, nothing more.

Although he expected it, the telephone's distinctive buzz startled him.

"Yes?"

"Negative on the automobiles, official or otherwise. We're confident he's still inside."

"How confident?"

"We're on top of this, really."

Cody leaned back, breathed deeply and forced himself to relax. The acidic knot eased.

Of course Danilov is still inside the apartment. Stop behaving like Chicken Little. He said, "I know you are, and I appreciate your efforts."

"Neither rain, nor snow, nor gloom of night...how does that go again?"

"Keep in touch, Freddie."

***

Despite Cody's attempts to occupy his mind, the morning seemed to stretch endlessly toward a distant afternoon. To fill the time, he read a tract on how local Chinese triads—organized criminals trafficking in drugs, prostitution, and illegal exportation of raw materials—transferred large amounts of cash electronically, primarily through syndicate-owned travel agencies, to similar locations throughout China and Russia. However, the esoteric intricacies of *fei chien*, flying money, failed to hold his interest. Long minutes expanded like a rubber band under increasing tension.

Around lunchtime, Cody decided to take a break. The knot in his stomach had given way to a hollow growl. He stood, stretched and slipped the mobile telephone into the side pocket of his suit jacket.

"I'm going down to the commissary for a quick bite," he told Phyllis. "Let me know if anyone calls. Can I bring you something?"

She wrinkled her nose and squinted. "You're actually taking time to eat lunch?"

"I need to keep my strength up."

Her expression told him Phyllis wasn't fooled by the banter. They had worked together too many years for her not to sense the pressure he felt.

"I'll get something later," she said.

Downstairs in a secluded corner, Cody spooned corn chowder into his mouth, studiously ignoring sly glances from consular staff. Damn! He'd completely forgotten about the rumor mill. He should have taken a walk instead.

The phone buzzed. "Yes?"

"Call Freddie on his mobile," Phyllis said.

"Thanks."

He rose and walked casually toward the exit. Once in the hallway, he punched numbers into his phone.

"It's me," he said when Freddie answered. He stopped beside the elevators and pushed the UP button.

"We're on our way, boss."

Cody did not respond immediately. What was Freddie talking about? "On your way? What does that mean?"

"We are driving back to the consulate. Our guest is riding in the other car, just ahead."

Cody raked fingers through his hair. He said, "Tell me how it happened, Freddie."

"About twenty minutes ago our man came out the back entrance to his apartment carrying a brown valise. He approached our second car and asked for a ride back to the consulate."

The elevator door slid open; it was empty. Cody stepped inside and pushed '3'. Then he said, "In other words, Danilov made the surveillance team."

"Apparently."

"How did that happen?"

He heard Freddie's tired sigh. "It's a small town, Cody. Not many cars and few strangers about. As I reported earlier, he took several long walks this weekend. It occurs to me our guest has been shadowed before, perhaps many times, over extended periods. Given that experience and his familiarity with the local scene, we probably weren't difficult to spot."

Freddie's logic made sense. Furthermore, Danilov had correctly assumed Cody would monitor his activities after leaving the consulate.

"I see. And now he's a passenger in the second car?"

"He is, indeed."

"And the five of you are on your way here?"

"Not five, four. Your concern about a potential family and the possible arrival of government officials got us to thinking. As a precaution, Sasha volunteered to remain in Ussurijsk and keep an eye on the apartment."

"That was a good idea," Cody suggested.

"Later, she plans to take the evening train back. Or I can pick her up sooner if you like."

The elevator door opened and Cody strode toward his office. "No, the train sounds fine. How long before you and Danilov arrive?"

"Less than two hours. I'll call you when we're back in town."

Cody mulled Freddie's information. It sounded much too easy. "You said he was carrying a brown valise; not a suitcase, not a duffle bag."

"That's correct."

"In other words, a leather briefcase."

"Something like that, yes."

"And he's alone?"

"Also correct."

According to Freddie's weekend reports, Danilov's long walks were solitary events. If he had contacted anyone, like a family member or other confidant, then Danilov probably used the telephone.

Despite his concerns, Cody tried not to ignore the positive aspects. Getting a lone man out of Russia—along with whatever he had in the briefcase—would be absurdly easy, especially if said individual carried a genuine diplomatic passport and an authentic-looking visa. Cody would let the diplomats handle whatever adverse repercussions that might arise from his use of forged documents.

The bottom line was clear: Danilov was coming back in, voluntarily. However, he was also traveling light. Either he was taking few personal possessions, or had something else in mind. Neither mattered now; the old guy was enroute and solidly in American custody.

With luck, Cody's backup operation—reluctantly put in motion—would prove redundant.

Cody nodded to Phyllis on his way into his office.

"Thanks, Freddie. Call me later."

Chapter 24

Danilov settled into the same chair he had occupied on previous occasions. Then he sighed and gave Cody a tired smile. "I apologize for my tardiness and any inconvenience it might have caused."

Freddie and company—minus Sasha—had traveled from Ussurijsk without incident. They had parked both cars in the underground garage and then escorted their passenger to the now familiar confines of the first floor conference room.

"It wasn't an inconvenience," Cody replied, "so no apology is needed."

Danilov nodded appreciation.

Cody continued. "I have arranged for you to stay in one of our guest rooms tonight. The food in the consulate's commissary is better than average, but the décor isn't as nice as the Amursky Zaliv's dining room.

"I also took the liberty of getting you a new suit of clothes, garments more in keeping with your new identity as an American diplomatic courier. In the morning, you will board the first scheduled Aeroflot flight to Tokyo, fully credentialed as a U.S. diplomatic courier. Later today I will introduce you to your traveling companion."

"You seem to have thought of everything."

"We'll find out soon enough."

Danilov continued to smile, but then shook his head. "Unfortunately, none of that will be necessary. I have given this a great deal of thought, Mr. Ballantine. Despite my long-held desire to return home, I simply cannot leave Russia."

The surprise announcement re-awakened Cody's latent suspicions. The old man was clearly hiding something, but what? Cody masked smoldering doubts and responded, keeping his voice steady and measured. "I don't understand. How can you *not* want to return home? What's changed since our last discussion? Is there something you're not telling me?"

"I have told you all that needs to be told."

"Sorry, but I don't believe that. In fact, I suspect you might be hiding something—an incident that occurred in the past; a disloyal act perhaps, one you're reluctant to tell me about."

"No, it is nothing like that."

"Is your family being threatened?"

Danilov's brow furrowed. "I have no family. Don't you remember?" Then, perhaps to clarify his previous answer, he added: "I had a family once, but no longer."

Cody reflected on that bit of news. It could explain Danilov's odd reaction when first asked about family; body language Cody interpreted as a lie.

"*Had* a family? I don't understand. What happened to them?"

"That is quite a different story."

"Different? How so?" Cody continued without pause, adopting the tone of a concerned, frustrated friend. "I cannot think of a single reason why you'd want to remain here, of all places, rather than America. Why not finish what you started? Tell me what happened. What's bothering you?"

"It is a personal matter; one I intend to keep so."

Cody's intuition told him Danilov's family was key to the old man's decision, but he chose not to approach that issue directly. Instead, he decided to pursue a more provocative line of inquiry.

"Then I must assume your decision has to do with what occurred during imprisonment. Maybe you provided questionable services to the Soviets, acts that might cast you in an unfavorable light. What other logical reason could there be? America is your home, the country you once served and defended. You have a family *there*, as well."

Danilov nodded silent acknowledgement, then he said. "All true except for one important difference."

Cody waited while the old man formed his response.

"Mr. Ballantine, the America I remember no longer exists in reality, but only in memory. *My* America vanished—as did my youth—not immediately, but in slow dribbles, like sand passing through an hourglass. All my memories of home and popular culture, the public personalities, songs and movies, the very essence of American life in the 1950s—all those things occurred in an era long gone and mostly forgotten.

"After the passage of forty years, everyone I knew back there is either dead or has become a stranger, including my sister and any living relatives. To them, and everyone else as well, I do not exist. Even Penn Military, a venerable institution where I gladly abandoned my childhood, a special place whose traditions and memories sustained me through difficult times, has not survived."

"I understand that," Cody said. "But, PMC's unfortunate demise notwithstanding, did you expect otherwise?"

"Of course not. But consider this: Russian culture and its social infrastructure have not changed significantly since the day I arrived. In many ways I have been living in stasis…an unchanging state of existence.

"When someone emerges from a time capsule into an advanced society, the passage of four decades is more than a lifetime; it is a quantum change in custom, public discourse, and societal mores. America and its people leaped forward while I marched in place. Upon my return, I would be instant history, a curiosity, a dusty anachronism: an old man who might never be able to re-acquaint himself with modern society. In short, an object of pity.

"Mr. Ballantine, I lack the courage to abandon my safe existence, despite its less-than mediocre comforts, and therefore choose not to risk what little of my dignity remains." He paused and again smiled; a sad, slow upturning of his lips. "Perhaps old age makes cowards of us all."

The explanation was easy to understand: Fear of the unknown was a universal human trait. The challenge of adapting a staid 1950s mindset to accommodate a volatile, technology-rich America would be daunting.

Danilov would step from a social environment not much different than one he left forty years ago into a dynamic society preparing to shoulder its way into the twenty-first century: A nation whose people shopped gigantic malls rather than quaint neighborhood stores; where television entertainment ended the exclusive reign of local movie theaters and Saturday afternoon serials.

But there were other, deeper alterations that would quickly become apparent: changes in national attitude, subtle and otherwise. Danilov would discover a creeping narcissism in the American character: a belief that feeling good takes precedence over common courtesy and self-discipline. Such attitudes, nurtured by an equally self-absorbed national media, produced far too many citizens wholly unaware of their appalling ignorance. And what would he make of activist judiciaries—judges who assumed control over political and moral issues, arrogantly usurping constitutional powers they were never meant to have?

Cody tugged his ear lobe. The phrase 'culture shock' popped into his mind.

Yet despite its faults, America was unquestionably the greatest country in the world; a nation populated by decent folks willing to share what they had, or to sacrifice their lives and wealth for a noble cause; a land of promise and hope.

Cody said, "There is truth in what you say, but don't underestimate yourself. You've survived much worse."

"Indeed I have, but the sad truth is, I may not survive life in my native country."

Cody sensed more than natural aversion to change. Danilov was feeling sorry for himself. It was time to change the rhythm.

He leaned toward the old man. *"Bullshit!"*

The word cracked through the air like a whip, a sharp rebuke unlike their previous, mutually cordial exchanges. Danilov's eyes grew wide and he opened his mouth, but Cody continued.

"Pardon my French, but I don't believe you'd freely choose to remain in Ussurijsk, a shit hole according to some, rather than returning to America, no matter how difficult. What haven't you told me? What are you *really* afraid of?"

Danilov's face reddened slightly, reflecting an expression Cody had not seen before: calm, controlled outrage. "Mr. Ballantine, mmy wife and sons are *buried* in that shit hole. And, despite your contemptuous opinion, Ussurijsk was the best home we ever had."

"I am truly sorry about your wife and sons, and I meant no disrespect," Cody said, now more determined than ever to discover the fate of Danilov's family. "But I believe your main reason for staying in Russia has little to do with dread of modern American society. After what you've been through, I'd be astonished if that was the case. There is an underlying issue here, an aspect to your story I don't understand, and I believe it relates to your Russian family. Am I correct?"

The look of indignation receded from Danilov's eyes, the anger slowly replaced by childlike vulnerability. He sighed and massaged the bridge of his nose with thumb and forefinger. Looking up he said, "Are you correct? Perhaps, but also not quite so correct."

"Tell me about it," Cody urged.

Danilov sighed, a weary gesture of resignation. Then he rose to his feet. "If you insist. But first I shall have some tea."

***

"Where did you meet your wife?" Cody asked, sipping his coffee.

"In Magadan. She was a librarian, among other things."

Among other things? What did that mean? Cody did not ask that question, but said, "How did you end up there?"

"I never returned to the mines after translating *The Grapes of Wrath*."

"You mentioned that."

"But I was still in Susuman, within the main work camp, albeit in nicer quarters. They assigned me to a secluded corner inside the administration building and gave me a wonderful old desk, one with an attached typewriter-stand jutting off at right angles, its surface slightly lower than the desktop."

"I know exactly what you mean," Cody said, remembering an antique oak secretary's desk his father still owned.

"So there I worked, translating English language documents of every kind: newspapers, magazines, university monographs; even selected chapters from certain books."

"What sort of books?"

"Everything imaginable; novels, histories, textbooks. I could not detect any specific pattern."

"Go on."

"In addition to my new duties, it seemed I was now a candidate for political rehabilitation. Along with two-dozen other prisoners, none of whom were American, I attended lectures, was given reading assignments, and participated in discussion groups, all designed to educate us about the joys of modern socialism."

"And did you become enlightened?"

"Like all effective propaganda programs, 're-education' was based on fifty percent fact and fifty percent misinformation delicately applied, sometimes with humor, other times with pious outrage. But to answer your question, I let them believe what was necessary to keep my easy job. In that regard, I behaved exactly like everyone else."

"When did you leave Susuman?"

"In January 1965. In all, I spent slightly more than ten years there."

"Were you paroled?"

"Not exactly. It seems someone else had taken an interest in my work and rehabilitation progress."

"Let me guess: The MVD colonel from Magadan; the officer who approved the original Steinbeck translation?"

"Very good."

"He was still there?"

Danilov smiled. "I was told, in confidence of course, that my benefactor had once displeased a highly placed political commissar in Moscow. As punishment, said highly placed official banished the colonel to his current post in Magadan. I also learned that most MVD officers assigned to the Russian Far East remained there until retirement. Obviously, this particular colonel had other plans; he was using me and my work to re-establish his reputation. It seems he, too, had hopes of returning home."

Cody, mindful of his own banishment, shifted uncomfortably in his seat. "What was your colonel's name?"

"Yablonov. Arseny Gregorovich Yablonov."

"And it was Colonel Yablonov himself who got you out of Susuman?"

"Yes. He wanted more control over my work and Susuman was six hundred kilometers to the north. Apparently, moving me bodily to Magadan was a lot easier than communicating with the camp commandant via long distance telephone." Danilov paused to sip tea, holding the saucer in one hand and raising the teacup with the other, pinkie extended, a refined gesture, like one enjoying High Tea in his favorite English club.

"That makes sense," Cody said. "As a translator, I presume your work took you to the library on occasion."

"It did."

"Were you allowed free rein, or did you have an escort?"

"A little of both. I could move freely within the general vicinity of my apartment and workplace but was ordered to keep away from train or bus stations. However, after I started seeing Ulyana, the escort became less visible."

"Ulyana. That's a lovely name."

"She was a lovely woman."

"What happened next?"

Danilov's eyes narrowed and Cody sensed a return to his previous reluctance, as though retreating once again behind a stone fortress.

"As I said earlier, Mr. Ballantine: that is a personal matter; one I am unwilling to discuss further."

Cody shrugged. "In that case, since you won't tell me about your family, I can only assume your reasons for remaining behind lay elsewhere."

"What do you mean?"

Cody leaned forward and his voice took on a harder edge. "Did you provide the Soviets with military secrets? Do they have documentation proving you committed treason? Is that why you are refusing repatriation?"

"I have committed many sins, Mr. Ballantine. But treason is not among them."

"Then perhaps it's something less obvious."

"Oh? What do you mean?"

Cody's manner changed slightly and voice softened. "You spent ten years in Susuman, the first five in the mines, but the latter period in relative comfort. Tell me: How does a vigorous young man cope with sexual deprivation?"

Danilov set the teacup on its saucer—his hands did not shake—and then locked eyes with Cody. "Despite segregation and confinement, sexual conjugation was not an insurmountable problem."

"There were female criminals in camp?"

"Criminals? Our camp housed many prisoners, Mr. Ballantine, but few committed actual felonies."

"You believe that?"

"I absolutely *know* that. When a nation criminalizes political disagreement, it must then incarcerate common citizens whose only crime is dissent. In such a society, everyone becomes a prisoner, eventually."

"Are you telling me there were no murderers, rapists, or thugs in Susuman?"

"There were more priests and pastors in our camp than all the murderers, rapists and thugs combined. The real criminals were confined in a separate part of the camp."

"More clergy than criminals? I find that difficult to believe."

"And I am surprised to hear that, especially from an educated man."

Cody thought for a moment. Then he said, "I understand the moral conflict between communism and Christianity, and I'm not surprised by the imprisonment of clergy and others. But were there really that many?"

"Yes, absolutely. When Constantinople fell to the Muslims in the 15th century, the spiritual center of Eastern Orthodox Christianity shifted to Moscow."

"Really? I didn't know that."

Danilov nodded before continuing. "Four centuries later, the communists banned religious orders and sent many of the clergy to gulags. Susuman's population was typical of most camps. It housed petty thieves, larcenists, political dissidents, and far too many of those imprisoned for nothing more than their religious beliefs."

Cody decided to believe Danilov and he acknowledged the point with a shrug. "Then let me rephrase: There were female *detainees* in your camp?"

"Yes, quite a few. They had separate living quarters, but a man meeting privately with a woman, if both were so inclined, seldom posed a problem."

"I see."

"Of course, working in the mines left little time or energy for such pursuits. Besides, as a mine worker I had little to offer in the way of recompense."

"Then sexual favors were for sale?"

"Please do not delude yourself, Mr. Ballantine. Life in the Susuman camp was a bleak, humiliating existence, much worse than my words can describe. In such an environment, one acquires few human comforts without payment or condition. Although language specialists like myself were given a few extra rubles, food and fuel were far more valuable commodities, especially in wintertime.

"Yet despite our dismal situation, sexual unions were not always based on a mutually beneficial commercial arrangement. Sometimes a woman took kindly to a man, further evidence that mutual desperation can often reveal the best in human beings."

"Did you have someone special?"

"In Susuman, every personal encounter was special. But the answer to your implied question is 'no'. Further, I did not engage in homosexual acts; nor did I participate in depraved situations involving sadism or children or anything remotely lewd. In plain language: There exists no sexual affair so repulsive that I would choose permanent exile rather than leave this place and risk exposure. Is that what you really had in mind?"

"Something like that."

"Are you disappointed? After all, that would provide an easily accepted explanation for my decision."

"I never seriously considered that possibility. However, given your sudden change of heart, it was an area that had to be explored."

"And so it has," Danilov said. "Presumably to your satisfaction?"

Cody realized that he had lost the initiative; they were back on equal footing, much like their previous conversations, and that was a problem. Somehow, he needed to find a way to get Danilov talking about his family. They, Cody now believed, were the sole reason behind Danilov's decision to remain in Russia. "Yes and no," Cody replied, intending to press the issue.

A soft knock interrupted his train of thought. Cody rose and opened the door. Freddie, his expression composed but not without concern, motioned for him to come outside.

Cody turned and looked over his shoulder. "Please excuse me for a moment."

Danilov nodded and Cody stepped into the hallway, closing the door behind him. "What's up, Freddie?"

"Sasha just called from Ussurijsk," he replied, keeping his voice low. "We may have a problem."

Chapter 25

Cody felt a quiver of anticipation. "What kind of problem?" he asked.

"A half-hour ago," Freddie continued in the same quiet tone, "two official-looking Zils pulled up alongside Danilov's apartment, one behind the other. A pair of rough-looking men—Sasha's description—stepped from the first car. She thinks they were MVD, possibly KGB."

"Were they in uniform?"

Freddie nodded. "Identical dark suits, black leather coats and fur caps."

That wasn't really a uniform in the normal sense, but KGB-types seemed to dress alike, announcing their presence as would a large sandwich board hanging from their shoulders.

"What happened then?"

"The first two went inside Danilov's apartment building and returned about five minutes later. After speaking to those who remained behind, they got back into their car and drove off. The other two repositioned themselves about a half-block away, facing the apartment's main entrance."

"And the first car?"

"Sasha took a roundabout walk. The other team parked in the rear, on the same street where our backup car was stationed earlier. The Russians were chain-smoking black Sobranie cigarettes and seemed to be waiting for something…or someone."

Cody's initial flush of anticipation vanished, replaced by a sense of detached guilt. He quickly submerged the uncomfortable feeling.

"Tell Sasha it's time to come home, Freddie."

"Already done, boss. She's on her way to the station, just another *babushka* carrying a worn shopping bag."

"I hope you're right."

"She'll make the evening departure with time to spare," Freddie said. "Sasha promised to buzz me from the lavatory as soon as the train moves beyond Ussurijsk."

"Let me know when she calls."

"Of course." Freddie cocked his head. "Are you surprised by this development?"

"Not really. Our man took one too many out-of-town strolls on consecutive weekends. It was bound to raise suspicion. One of his die-hard commie pals at the Institute probably passed the word to an interested party."

Freddie smiled, an expression without humor. "The more the world changes, the more it stays the same."

Cody didn't answer. He tugged an ear lobe and considered his next move. "Have you checked outside? Is the consulate under surveillance?"

"Not that anyone can determine. Everything looks normal, whatever that means these days."

"Maybe normal at this moment but not for long," Cody suggested. "Russians have long memories. Someone in the MVD or KGB still keeps an eye on Danilov. Their objective seems clear: Take him into custody."

"Perhaps, but you never told me why you and the Russians are so interested in Mr. Danilov. Even though his cover is blown, if indeed he has one, shall I presume it remains none of my business?"

As usual and absent fanfare, Freddie and his team had willingly placed themselves at risk, never asking why. Withholding certain operational knowledge was always difficult. Cody's decision to exclude everyone from certain aspects of his plan to extricate Danilov from Russia was a choice he had to make. In that regard, only four consular staff members knew Danilov's true identity. And things would have to remain that way for a while longer.

He met Freddie's inquisitive gaze. "Later, when this is over, we will get together in Sasha's library and have a nice chat."

"Fair enough. What now, boss?"

"Take a ride over to the Churkin neighborhood and get in touch with Mr. Pak. Tell him we are going fishing tonight, regardless of weather conditions, and he should invite several of his closest relatives."

***

Danilov stared out the window, saucer in one hand, the other holding the teacup's thin handle. He turned as the door opened.

"Sorry for the interruption," Cody said, taking his chair.

Danilov remained standing. "No apology is necessary. You have been most generous with your time."

"As have you," Cody said. "Which raises an important question: Prior to your first visit here, how often did you travel to Vladivostok?"

"Once, perhaps twice a month. I mentioned that earlier."

"Yes, I remember. I assume that most of your friends or colleagues at the Institute were aware of your visits?"

"Of course. I shop for them occasionally—mostly small items or personal necessities. It is a common courtesy. Ussurijsk does not offer much in the way of quality products or variety. Why is this important?"

Cody ignored the question. "Earlier today, you approached my surveillance team outside your apartment and asked for a ride back to the consulate. Do you recall the exact composition of that team?"

Danilov took his seat at the conference table, his expression reflecting concern and mild suspicion. "Yes, I do. There were two middle-age couples, each couple in a separate car."

"How many of those individuals accompanied you on the way here?"

"Three. One lady remained behind."

"Her name is Sasha. She just telephoned. That's the reason we were interrupted. About a half-hour ago, four men in two Zils visited your apartment. Your place is now under surveillance."

Danilov paled slightly. "How were they dressed?"

"Dark suits, leather coats. Sasha described them as unpleasant-looking men." Cody paused to let Danilov absorb his words. Then he said, "To answer your first question, the increased frequency of your trips here probably aroused suspicion."

"But why should it? Nobody at the Institute knows who I really am."

"What about your wife? Did she know?"

Danilov hesitated, then nodded slowly.

"When did you tell her?"

"I never did. She already knew." Danilov rubbed his face with both hands and color slowly returned.

Cody said, "Earlier, you told me she was a librarian, *among other things*. Might one of those 'other things' include working for the MVD?"

"You are very perceptive."

"When did you find out?"

"The day she passed away, almost one year ago."

"And she kept it from you all those years?"

"Ulyana was a True Believer," he said, his voice betraying hints of long-suppressed bitterness. "She devoted her life to the communist cause. Our sons, like the offspring of all loyal Party members, joined the Children of October, Young Pioneers, and the Komsomol, moving from each organization as they grew older.

"Against my wishes, she encouraged them to join the Army before attending university, which they did—eagerly, as exuberant young men are wont to do—seeking excitement and freedom from parental supervision. The fact that Russians were fighting a war in Afghanistan did not seem to bother her. Ulyana had no concept of war, of its brutality and the relentless abrasion of the human soul until only the primordial beast remains. Nor did she have much respect for the Afghan Mujahideen. She considered them backward savages; no match for Soviet military power."

"What happened to your boys?" Cody asked gently.

"They, like so many other young men, were killed in the Panjshir valley."

Cody recognized the location. The Valley of the Five Lions was home to a large concentration of Tajiks, a mostly Persian-speaking people who migrated to Afghanistan from Iran more than two centuries ago. Fierce fighters, they had been armed and funded by the Pakistani Intelligence Service, an organization that served as middle-man in a clandestine CIA program dubbed 'Cyclone'. Undoubtedly, Danilov's Russian-born sons were the victims of a covert American operation designed to help Afghan freedom fighters defeat the Soviets. The sad irony was impossible to ignore.

Cody said, "I'm sorry, truly I am."

Danilov nodded once. "Thank you."

"When did that happen?"

"In 1987. Two years later, the Soviet Union admitted defeat and withdrew all its troops from Afghanistan. Shortly thereafter other Soviet republics rebelled. The central government eventually collapsed.

"Ulyana refused to believe what was happening. 'A temporary setback,' she told me. 'All great nations suffer short-term declines.'

"As more time passed and the truth became clear, Ulyana finally realized she had sacrificed everything—her entire adult life, our sons, and perhaps the chance to find happiness with a man she truly loved rather than one she accepted—all for a cruel illusion. That is when she told me of her long association with the MVD and revealed knowledge of my true identity."

"I take it she was your assigned watcher."

Danilov checked his cup. He rose and poured hot water over a fresh teabag.

"Watcher? Yes. Deep down, I probably knew or suspected such might be the case. But Ulyana was a lovely young woman who seemed genuinely attracted to an unimportant linguist saddled with an unpromising future. As far as I knew, she was a devoted wife and mother, a woman who gave me two wonderful sons: children whom I loved and spoiled shamelessly."

He returned to his seat. "Maybe we were not exactly lovers in the truest romantic sense, but we were certainly compatible. Ulyana and I seldom argued. Instead, we laughed at the same jokes and shared mutual interests in art, music, and literature—and, of course, our children."

"Sometimes, that can be enough," Cody suggested.

"Given the harshness of my experiences over the previous ten years, it was more than enough. Ulyana offered hope for a better life, one without cruelty or deprivation or endless labor in cold, dank places. She was indeed my watcher, Mr. Ballantine, but I became her willing subject."

Cody's suspicions, always lurking beneath the surface, reawakened. "Does that mean you compromised yourself with her? Shared confidential information about your military duties?"

Danilov shook his head wearily. "You still do not understand, do you? Except for Ernst Klaus, I never told anyone about my real life, not even Ulyana. For nearly forty years I maintained the fiction about once living in my grandmother's village near Kiev, putting into practice a propaganda tactic I learned from my re-education lectures: Tell a lie often enough and people will eventually accept it as truth. Perhaps I wanted to believe the fiction myself. It was, after all, a much kinder story than reality.

"Did I enjoy special privileges? Certainly. Ulyana's still-secret position afforded her certain luxuries; benefits she claimed were due to her long service as a State librarian. I accepted that explanation and savored the fruits of her dishonesty without question. After Susuman, would you have behaved differently?"

"Probably not," Cody admitted. They sat in silence for a moment, then: "You said your wife died about a year ago. What was the cause of death?"

Danilov's expression reflected deep sadness and his eyes took on a faraway look. "It happened last year, on a cloudy Saturday in mid-November, the 16th. By then, former Soviet republics had declared independence from Moscow and the unexpected collapse of the old regime was nearly complete. Late that morning she finally confessed her involvement with the MVD.

"Oddly, I was not surprised by the revelation, nor did I condemn her. I still mourned the deaths of Pyotr and Vasily in Afghanistan and Ulyana's news seemed unimportant.

"Instead of recrimination, I spoke of our sons, their young lives wasted in a vain attempt to maintain a corrupt political regime; a system that ignored the best interests of a good and decent people. We also spoke of other, more intimate things. Afterwards, around noon, Ulyana left the apartment. 'I must confess my sins,' she told me."

"She actually said that?"

"Yes. Her words surprised me as well. In all our years together, Ulyana had never mentioned God or religion, except in derogatory terms. But churches were re-opening throughout Russia, evidence of widespread religious reawakening. Ulyana was a good person—really—and I thought she had discovered some inner light, a faith long repressed or dormant. I let myself believe she sought God's forgiveness as a way to soften a mother's grief over her dead children.

"Although I offered to accompany her, she shook her head. 'Dear Andrei, this is something I must do alone.' Two hours later policemen knocked at my door. A passer-by discovered Ulyana's body slumped beside the graves of our sons. She had swallowed poison."

Despite Danilov's personal tragedy, Cody felt a sense of conclusion, a mental state similar to those who finally acknowledge a loved one's death. He said, "Once again, I am truly sorry."

The issues of family and Danilov's access to luxury items were now resolved to Cody's satisfaction. Although pleased, one final item remained: the reason behind Danilov's decision to remain in Russia. Cody sipped coffee and waited for the answer.

"It seems everyone who was ever close to me is either dead or beyond reach," Danilov said.

"Perhaps not," Cody suggested, seizing an opportunity to lift the old man's spirits. He took Hal's letter from an inside jacket pocket. "Listen to this." Cody read the key entry. *"A repatriated German POW who worked in the Svetloye gold mines from 1944 to 1958 claims to have befriended a Russian-speaking American aviator who would not or could not reveal his true identity. Andrei reportedly told the German POW that Soviet fighters shot down his aircraft over international waters in the late summer of 1954. The German ex-POW described Andrei as a tall, nice-looking young man with brown eyes and a pleasant disposition."*

Danilov's dour expression vanished, replaced by wide-eyed astonishment. "Ernst Klaus is *alive*?"

Cody returned the letter to his pocket. "Apparently so, at least when he gave his report. I don't know exactly when that was, nor do I know if he's still among the living, but the point is this: Ernst Klaus made it back home; he reunited with friends and family. What about you, Captain Thompson? Are *you* going home, or have you decided to take your chances with the MVD goons watching your apartment?"

Danilov seemed not to hear. "Ernst is alive," he muttered. "How remarkable." His eyes remained glazed for a moment longer, then cleared. "Do you remember the first day I arrived here?"

Cody nodded.

"I never intended to ask for asylum. That day I acted on impulse."

"I'm not sure I understand," Cody said.

"Don't you see? By remaining here, close to the graves of my wife and sons, I hoped to rectify my craven acquiescence to Ulyana's wishes; to somehow atone for the needless deaths of my family."

Realization dawned and all the misshapen puzzle pieces fell into place. "A noble sentiment, but one without logic. What's done is done. Your wife and sons are beyond the reach of your guilt."

"No matter. I was prepared to stay."

"*Was?*"

Danilov's expression became determined. "I told you I was a coward, Mr. Ballantine. What I am about to do proves it. Remaining here risks re-imprisonment. The prospect of spending the rest of my life in a place like Susuman is too unbearable to contemplate. I presume your offer of a diplomatic passport and visa remains open?"

Cody didn't bother to hide his relief. "It is, but our original plan probably won't work. When you fail to show up at your apartment later tonight, the alarm will sound. Russian authorities will quickly cover every train station, airport, and embarkation point. Even with a new suit and special passport, you and your escort run the risk of being detained."

"Wouldn't that cause a diplomatic incident?"

"Probably, but why should they care? You'd be in custody and the United States would have to prove or otherwise validate your false identity. And the MVD would know your diplomatic passport was a fake. By the time things got sorted out, you'd be a non-person again, lost in a wilderness of mutual deceit. Check and mate."

Danilov's concerned expression returned. "Do you have an alternative plan?"

"I do, but understand this: I cannot risk sending someone into your apartment while it's under surveillance. Whatever is there must remain there."

The concerned look changed to one of desperate longing. "What about the photographs of my family; the keepsakes of our lives together? Those items are irreplaceable."

"I'm sorry, but you'll have to leave them behind."

Danilov sighed and his attention returned to the rain-streaked window. "Then all my personal possessions will surely be confiscated and probably destroyed." He rubbed his eyes with the fingertips of both hands. "It seems God or fate has decreed that no record of my life on this earth shall survive." He looked at Cody. "A life without mementos is one void of purpose or meaning."

Cody said, "I agree. However, when this is over, perhaps I can buy them back. In Russia these days, few things are beyond the reach of hard cash, especially large amounts of U.S. currency discretely offered. After you're safely on your way, I will pass the word to some of my unsavory acquaintances."

"You would do that?"

"If it's possible, I'll get it done."

Danilov smiled, the look of a father pleased with his son's achievements. "I believe you will, Mr. Ballantine."

Cody reached for the telephone and punched numbers. "Hi, Phyllis. Could you come down here, please?" He listened for a moment. "Thank you," he replied, and then replaced the handset.

"I have some work to do and not much time to get it done. While I'm busy with that, Phyllis will escort you to the executive lounge. There you can relax, have a drink, and get something to eat if you like."

"I take it we will not be leaving immediately?"

"Not immediately, but as soon as I can arrange it."

The door opened and Phyllis stepped in. Both men rose.

Cody said, "Phyllis Townsend, may I present Captain Andrew Thompson, late and perhaps still of the United States Air Force." He turned, "Captain Thompson, Phyllis Townsend."

Phyllis smiled, and extended her hand. "A pleasure to meet you, Captain." Her eyes reflected warm attentiveness, an expression Cody found interesting and unexpected.

Danilov bowed slightly and took her hand. "The pleasure is mine," he said. Then an inquisitive look appeared on his face. "Is it Missus or Miss Townsend?"

Phyllis didn't reply immediately. As Cody watched them linger over an extended handshake, another idea took shape in his mind.

"You may call me Phyllis," she said.

Chapter 26

Three hours later Cody addressed three members of his rather small staff. The group stood in one corner of the consulate's underground garage. Darkness had fallen and the all-day rain had slackened to a misty drizzle. Cold, damp air swirled through the open doors.

"We'll use four vehicles," Cody said to them. "I will take our guest out in the third car. Later, I'll switch to the Kamaz which, hopefully, is already parked near the yacht club." The fact Cody planned to drive a dilapidated Russian-made truck to the rendezvous point instead of a nearly new consulate car did not seem to surprise anyone.

"What's our departure protocol?" Freddie asked.

"Everybody goes out together, more or less. You and Sasha will take the first two cars and head for the airports, Vladivostok and Nahodka. You can decide among yourselves who goes where. Phyllis will drive the last car to the Dolphinarium and then cruise the waterfront for about fifteen minutes." He looked at Phyllis. "Don't do anything dramatic—just out and back."

She smiled. "Yes, father."

Cody spent the next five minutes reviewing mobile telephone procedures. One by one, he met the eyes of each person.

"This should not be very difficult or dangerous. Everyone drive low and slow and try not to run over any pedestrians." He paused for a moment. Then he said, "Are there any questions?"

Silence and wry smiles greeted his query. "Okay, then. We leave in five minutes."

"Be sure to wear your boots," Freddie said.

***

Except for a few nighttime lights, the Vladivostok Yacht Club—a grandiose designation for a shabby main building and a mostly sorry collection of private boats anchored in Sportivny Cove—appeared deserted.

Cody stopped his consulate car a few feet behind the Kamaz and killed the engine. He paused for a moment, gauging the silence. Then he turned to the old man. "It's show time," he said to Danilov, and then opened the door. The drizzle had stopped but thin clouds remained, partially obscuring all but a few stars and softening the moonlight to a creamy glow.

Inside the truck, a beat up eight-year-old vehicle slightly larger than a Ford pickup, Cody found two sets of old clothing, including rubber boots.

"Put these on," he said.

Danilov took the offered bundle, sniffed, and then quickly pulled his head away. "These smell like dead fish and sea weed."

"That's the idea. We're supposed to be fishermen."

They changed quickly in the cold air. Cody locked their street clothes and shoes inside the car's trunk.

"Ready to go?"

Danilov fingered the collar of his fisherman's coat, sniffed lightly and then made a sour face. "Is it too late to change my mind?"

"What, and miss all the excitement? Where's your pioneer spirit?"

"Resting peacefully in a comfortable chair, precisely where *I* should be."

They climbed into the truck and Cody turned the ignition, waited for the diesel glow light to come on, and then brought the engine to clattering life. After a brief warm up, he followed another roundabout course, constantly checking the rear-view mirror. Forty minutes later, he turned off the paved highway and drove down a sloping road toward the Egersheld Peninsula, a rocky finger jutting into the silky black waters of Cape Tokarevsky. A half-mile short of his destination Cody pulled over, engaged the parking brake and killed the engine. The Kamaz sputtered and died, its clatter replaced by an abrupt stillness; a near perfect silence disturbed only by waves lapping against the unseen shore well below their location.

"More pioneering?" Danilov asked in a low voice.

Cody did not reply. Instead, he pointed down the road toward a narrow pathway leading out to where a lighthouse stood, a ghostly white column perched on the peninsula's southernmost tip. The beacon flickered, a cyclic arc that swept the seaward approach to the bay.

"Is that where we are going?"

Cody shook his head. "We'd have to pass too close to where the lighthouse keeper lives. Our boat will meet us about twenty degrees east of there." He nodded toward the glove compartment. "Hand me the flashlight."

They walked carefully down the steeply pitched lane, turning their feet sideways to keep from slipping in the mud. When the road flattened, they turned left. About a hundred yards later their boots crunched on smooth stones littering the shoreline.

At a spot near a sharp-edged granite outcropping Cody stopped and squatted, facing the water. "Now we wait."

Danilov crouched beside him, leaning against the rock's vertical surface. "For how long?"

"Less than twenty minutes."

"I presume you are coming with me?"

"Right."

"And where might we be going?"

"With luck, to where a U.S. Naval vessel is cruising the Sea of Japan, by way of a fishing boat operated by a friend of mine. Which reminds me. When we rendezvous with the Navy ship, probably by first light, be sure to request permission to come aboard. The Squids appreciate stuff like that."

"Squids? I thought sailors were called Swabbies?"

Cody smiled. "One of the many changes you'll be encountering."

"I see." Danilov remained silent while Cody searched the blackness, then he said, "I assume you will be coming back here sometime later?"

"No. I'll stay with the fishing boat until it docks tomorrow evening, hopefully with a nice catch."

"What about the truck and car?"

"They'll be picked up later."

"You have done a lot of work in just a few hours. I am impressed…and grateful."

"All part of the service. Be sure to recommend me to your friends."

"I will, should any turn up." Danilov's slight frown was visible in the faint moonlight.

"Is that likely?" Cody asked.

"I don't know, but I would like to think so."

Cody returned his attention to the open water.

"Where will the Navy take me?" Danilov asked.

"To the Japanese port of Yokosuka. From there, our original plan takes effect. A State Department escort will come aboard, provide new clothes, an updated American passport and then accompany you to Tokyo International Airport at Narita. From there: one long flight and you're home at last."

Danilov didn't respond immediately. Finally he said, "Home. How strange that word seems to me. It is difficult not to conjure images of Ulyana, my sons and our cozy apartment in Ussurijsk. Despite its imperfections, those were the happiest days of my life."

He turned to Cody. "Perhaps my first visit to the consulate was a foolish gesture, the action of an old man wishing to recapture his youth. Did I suffer for a time? Yes, without question. But, except for the terrible loss of my family, the last quarter-century was not so bad. We lived comfortably; I enjoyed my work and was a respected member of the Institute. And I had one good friend, a man whom I have now abandoned."

"The gentleman you meet on Sundays?"

"Yes."

Sitting with his back against the rock, dressed in shabby fisherman's clothing, Danilov looked like a vagabond in his dotage, an unwanted burden long-since abandoned by heartless relatives. It was an image Cody refused to accept.

"You are still feeling sorry for yourself and it's starting to get on my nerves. What's done is done. It's time to forget the past because, sooner or later, your late wife's MVD pals would have knocked on your door, just like they did today.

"Maybe they'd only ask you for a signed statement, something to the effect that your stay in Russia was voluntary, an axe to hold over your head or perhaps a document to cover their butts. After that, who knows? Maybe they'd let you live in your comfortable little apartment with all your privileges, or maybe you'd be on the next boat to Magadan. Anyway, it's all conjecture, not worth an ounce of gourmet horseshit."

Danilov chuckled and his face brightened. "Is that a popular item in America these days?"

A light flashed in the distance, one long followed by two short; precisely from the spot in the bay Cody expected it. He pointed the flashlight and replied with the prearranged signal. The acknowledgement, two long and two short flashes, came almost immediately.

He turned toward Danilov. "For all I know, it very well could be. Idiotic fads emerge and vanish as quickly as popular music. What might become trendy in America these days, including gourmet horseshit, is beyond prediction. In any case, you will find out soon enough."

"You make it sound awful."

"Do I?"

"Yes, absolutely. All joking aside, what is American popular culture really like these days?"

Cody slouched against the rock.

"What's America's pop-culture *really* like nowadays?" Unbidden, a scene from one of the funniest Woody Allen movies he'd ever seen popped into his head. Without hesitation he paraphrased the lines. "Do you remember the mystery-critter stew they served at Susuman?"

Danilov nodded, warily. "Of course."

"Pop culture is something like that," Cody replied, "only worse."

A black rubber raft scraped ashore, its slick curved shape glistening in the moonlight. Four kneeling men, their oars planted on solid ground, held the raft reasonably steady as it rose and fell in light surf. Cody recognized the faces of Pak Kwang Ho and three of his five sons. He grasped Danilov by the shoulder.

"That's our ride to the fishing boat," Cody said. "Let's go."

Chapter 27

Three days later, Cody took a small penknife from his trouser pocket and sliced the wide tape securing a cardboard box. The container, about eighteen inches square, had arrived that morning, as expected. Shortly thereafter, the Duty Officer delivered the package to Cody's office.

It's almost over, Cody reminded himself. Two loose ends to tie up, then you can follow the same advice you offered to that long lost aviator: leave the past behind and begin a new life.

However, exactly when that new life would begin remained a question only Anne Seymour could answer. Cody smiled. About midway through the coming winter, Anne would realize she preferred Northern California to Siberia. That realization would signal the end to his days as a spook.

He folded the tiny penknife and returned it to a trouser pocket. He then pried open the box and removed crumpled newspaper used to keep the contents from shifting. The extra packing was a conscientious touch, the act of one who understood the importance of her task.

Cody removed several photographs mounted in identical five-by-seven-inch frames and a dozen or so keepsakes, placing each one carefully on his desk. He focused on the keepsakes first: athletic ribbons—some with a medal attached—merit certificates, a dozen letters bound with a crimson ribbon, and a small batch of student report cards.

Then he studied the three photos: the first showed an attractive, fair complexioned woman—presumably Ulyana; the second, two teen-age boys; the last was a group shot of Danilov…Thompson…with his family, each in a separate frame.

The boys—smiling, vigorous looking young men—appeared to be seventeen or eighteen years old. Cody studied the faces of the two young men and saw both parents reflected in their features. The loss of their sons must have been devastating.

Cody set the pictures aside and removed the last items: two nearly full leather-bound albums. One contained programs, mostly from school events, and a few clippings from local newspapers. The second held family snapshots, the first half in black and white, the remainder in color; apparently mounted in chronological order.

He placed the box on the floor beside his wastebasket, stuffed the crumpled newspapers inside, and then returned to the albums.

As he slowly turned pages, Cody realized he was viewing a family's life in compressed form. In the narrow black spaces between each photograph lay every human emotion and countless exchanged words: fond and fierce, remembered and forgotten, all forever silent now. He studied their mostly happy, sometimes goofy expressions, and recognized the photos as cherished snippets from one man's unique voyage through time.

Cody paused and stared out the window. Light snow whispered against the glass, adding to his sense of moody introspection. How many snapshots and personal mementos existed to mark his often-furtive passage through the last quarter-century? Not many. Perhaps two-dozen, he guessed. Less than one per year. Had his life been that empty of warmth and passion? It didn't seem that way at the time, but now he wasn't so sure.

Despite captivity, depravation, and agonizing personal tragedy, Captain Andrew Thompson had managed to live a reasonably full life, in many ways far richer than one might have expected. Cody, a free man with unfettered access to the world's resources, felt an unreasonable twinge of envy for his former guest.

He almost regretted the subterfuge—an unfortunate but necessary deception.

Ten minutes later he stacked the albums, framed photographs, and other mementos neatly on his desk.

They took up very little space.

He walked to the office closet and removed the brown leather valise Captain Thompson had carried from Ussurijsk a few days ago. Inside were nearly five hundred typed pages, a personal memoir of his life in Siberia. No wonder he could recall past incidents with such clarity. By his own admission, Thompson had spent the last year recollecting and writing.

Cody recalled a portion of their last conversation, a half-hour before they left the consulate to meet Mr. Pak and his sons.

***

"I was going to smuggle the manuscript out of the country before the MVD re-discovered who I was, if they ever could, given Russia's post-collapse disarray. Then the new consulate opened unexpectedly so I decided to hand it over personally. As I told you earlier, asking for asylum was a last-minute decision. That is why I held on to the manuscript."

"Still having second thoughts about your decision to leave Russia?"

"None whatsoever." He then passed the valise to Cody. "Take care of this for me."

Cody promised he would.

"There is one more thing Mr. Ballantine," he added. "A request. I am due to have lunch with my old friend on Sunday. We meet at the same place every week, a restaurant called Kafe Briz, at our usual table near the window. It is only three blocks from my apartment. When I do not show up, he will worry and wonder what happened to me. Would you see that my friend gets this letter?" He removed a sealed envelope from an inside suit pocket. The name 'Gregor' was scrawled across the front.

"You haven't been overly candid, have you?"

"No, of course not. I wrote only that I had to leave Ussurijsk unexpectedly and that all was well. I promised to contact him as soon as I could."

Cody took the envelope. "In that case, I will have Sasha deliver it after we are out of here."

***

And she had, giving it to an older gentleman as he sat alone by the window, a glass of wine near his hand. Prior to handing off the letter, Sasha had picked the lock to Danilov's apartment and filled her shopping bag with those keepsakes she deemed important. Returning to her house in Vladivostok, she packed each item carefully in the box now filled with crumpled newspapers and then gave it to another agent for delivery to the consulate.

Cody opened the briefcase, a large leather affair with gussets and wide straps. Then he carefully inserted the photographs and other mementos, easing them alongside the bound manuscript. Everything fit without difficulty so he fastened the straps, retrieved his overcoat, and stepped outside his office.

"Phyllis," he said, setting the valise on her desk, "how would you like to deliver an important package to an old friend of ours?"

She raised an eyebrow. "Which old friend might that be?"

"Captain Andrew Thompson. You two seemed to get along well during the time I was off arranging for his departure. Right now, I imagine he'd welcome the sight of a friendly face."

"He might." Her expression remained uncharacteristically guarded.

Cody raised an eyebrow and waited for her answer.

"Will I be traveling as a diplomatic courier, exempt from searches, etcetera?"

"Of course."

"When should I leave?"

"As soon as you can arrange it."

She hesitated before asking the next question. "Will I be coming back here?"

Cody slipped into his overcoat. "I wouldn't think so, but that's entirely up to you, Phyllis."

***

As happened on his first visit to the Sapernaya Baths high atop Eagles Nest, the mention of Cultural Minister Trushin's name granted Cody immediate and courteous access into the white, four-story townhouse situated behind mature trees at Number 14 Aleutskaya.

"Sir, please come this way. Minister Trushin is in the lounge."

Cody followed his escort into a spacious room near the back of the house. Traces of cigarette and cigar smoke hung suspended just below the elegantly corniced high ceiling. Trushin, partially screened by a large indoor plant, sat beside a picture window, facing the winter garden. He was alone.

"Thank you," Cody said to the escort, and approached the silver-haired Russian.

Trushin turned, smiled and rose to his feet. "Cody Wilhelmovich, how good to see you again." They shook hands and brushed cheeks; left, right, left. "How do you like my club?"

"It's extraordinary, Aleksandr Petrovich, and very well preserved. I presume the architecture is noteworthy?"

"Absolutely," Trushin said, motioning to an easy chair then seating himself beside Cody. "It was designed and built in 1910 by Junghandel, a German, for Julius Bryner."

Cody shrugged. "I'm not familiar with either gentleman."

"Of course you are!" Trushin boomed. "The great Russian-American actor, Yul Brynner, was born in this house in 1920. Old Julius, Bryner spelled with one 'n', was his grandfather."

"Really?" Cody said, pleasantly surprised. "And now it's a private club for worthy gentlemen such as yourself."

Trushin nodded, his silver hair glittering in morning light slanting through the window. "Times change. Fortunes are made and lost and sometimes regained. It does not matter; the world moves on." A waiter appeared. "Cody my friend, have you ever tasted Cuban coffee?"

"I'm not sure."

Trushin held up two fingers. "*Kuban kaffe*," he said. The waiter left.

"What will I be drinking?" Cody asked.

"Sweetened espresso. It is quite enjoyable."

A folded newspaper lay on a low table between their chairs. Cody retrieved a white envelope from his suit jacket. Inside were fifty crisp one-hundred-dollar bills, the denomination of choice for drug dealers, various criminals, and part-time CIA informants. Feigning a stiff neck, he swiveled around and then unobtrusively inserted the envelope within the newspaper's folds. They were alone but the large, spreading plant screened his movements from potential observers, such as waiters or club staff.

"So, *tovarisch*," Trushin said, retrieving the envelope and tucking it away, "what little mischiefs have you been perpetrating on my country?"

"Mischiefs? None that I can remember. Not recently, anyway," he added with a smile.

"Oh? Then why did I send four ex-KGB men to Ussurijsk to watch an empty apartment?"

Why, indeed? Cody mused, his eyes taking in the balanced geometry of the winter garden. The answer nagged at his conscience, whispering in his ear like a tattletale aunt: To convince an emotionally wounded American aviator it was time to go home, the voice murmured, and to keep those intentions secret from everyone in the consulate—including Sasha.

Although her suggestion to remain in Ussurijsk was an important part of Cody's deception, Sasha knew nothing of his arrangement with Trushin. The ex-KGB types, instructed to watch the apartment for three hours, had followed their instructions perfectly. Sasha, as he knew she would, had reported their presence to Freddie.

Cody had then passed the staged information to Captain Thompson, continuing the ruse designed to jolt a spiritually exhausted man from his guilty malaise; to re-awaken haunting memories of imprisonment and harsh deprivation. A necessary deception, yes, but not one he enjoyed.

Jack Paraday's pessimistic observation came to mind, words uttered many years ago. "Lies have many flavors and textures: some are vile and rancid and clearly obvious; others are sweet-smelling like vanilla extract, yet bitter on the tongue. But the most convincing lies are complex, one piled upon the other like layers in a Dobos torte, interweaved veneers of cake and icing artfully arranged.

"Still others are benign: Santa Claus, the Easter Bunny, the Tooth Fairy—all deceptions in the strictest sense of the word, but not malevolent or mean-spirited. Like the sweet Hungarian dessert, they exist to satisfy a craving: the parental desire to prolong the brief, happy magic that is childhood.

"Nevertheless," Paraday had cautioned, "lying in a noble cause is still a lie. The inherent nature of certain ventures, once initiated, invariably leads to less than perfect outcomes. If you cannot accept that, if you are unwilling or unable to weave a convincing falsehood, then you must find another occupation."

Cody's fabrication had clearly succeeded, but therein lay the conundrum. Did a good end, such as Drew Thompson's repatriation, justify deceitful means? He examined his conscience and realized it was a riddle he could not solve.

He kept those thoughts to himself, masking his doubts with an easy smile.

"Call it a trial run," he said, turning toward the Russian. "A little test."

Trushin raised a bushy white eyebrow. "What kind of test?"

"A check of capabilities, nothing more."

"You do not trust me?"

"Of course I trust you, Aleksandr Petrovich. We're friends, are we not?"

"I truly hope so."

Their coffee arrived. Trushin lifted the tiny cup from its saucer and raised it to eye level.

"To mutual trust."

"And to friendship," Cody added.

The espresso was smooth and sweet and possibly the best Cody had ever tasted.

Epilogue

Near Healdsburg
Sonoma County, California
May 1995

"How on earth did you find this place?" Phyllis asked.

"It belonged to my uncle," Cody replied. "I used to spend my summers here, working in the vineyards. He died 'without issue' as they say, so he left it to me."

"It's beautiful!" Her eyes roamed across the landscape. "I can't get over your grapevines; they look so perfect, like a page from a Bordeaux travelogue. You must have good soil up here."

"Not really. It's mostly poor benchland—Franciscan gravel along with a few veins of sandy loam and residual clay. But it's perfect for growing grapes."

"Don't get him started," Anne warned, "not unless you want a lengthy dissertation on soil geology and Northern California microclimates. Trust me, he will put you into a deep coma."

"A short version might be interesting," Phyllis said, smiling.

"Please, Phyllis. Don't encourage him or we'll be having our dinner at midnight," Anne cautioned.

Drew Thompson frowned and shook his head, a sly twinkle in his eyes. "That is out of the question. My aging constitution can tolerate only so much stale cheese and cheap wine."

They sat in light shade beneath a portico on a bluestone-paved verandah, relaxing on cushioned wicker chairs grouped around a low table. A soft breeze lightened the pleasantly warm air.

The vineyard lay just beyond the sloping lawn, perfect rows marching down the hillside, each gnarled crucifix alive with fresh growth. In the middle distance, its shallow waters nearly hidden by scrub and willow, the Russian River meandered through the Alexander Valley.

Cody had always hoped to end up here. Anne was the missing key that made it happen. "Speaking of cheap wine," he said. "I'm going to have a bit more. Anybody else need a refill?"

"If you insist," Drew said, draining the last swallow from his glass.

"Sure," Phyllis said.

Anne slid her nearly empty glass towards him.

"It appears we have unanimous consent," Cody suggested.

Cody poured a golden Ferarri-Carano chardonnay into each goblet.

Not only was he basking in the warmth of Anne's presence, a feeling still fresh as the first day they met, he also had the added pleasure of hosting two people he admired and respected. The task however, of persuading the former Phyllis Townsend and Major Andrew G. Thompson, now retired from the United States Air Force, to leave their home in Pittsburgh had been more difficult than he imagined.

"Tell me the latest," Cody said. "Is the book selling well?"

A Raven's Tale, Drew's memoir of the shootdown and his imprisonment in Siberia, had received good reviews. Cody found the book's additional details fascinating, and the straightforward prose made for an effortless read.

"Pretty good, I guess. According to my publisher, folks are buying nearly two thousand copies a week."

"That's great," Cody said.

Except for his long, agonizing years in the mines, Drew's book painted a generally favorable picture of the Russian people and his life in Siberia, thus muting much of the diplomatic fallout.

Nevertheless, politics being what it is, there were still those who demanded reparations for the shootdown and some measure of accountability regarding those still listed as missing. As far as Cody could tell, nothing much seemed to be happening in that regard.

After a brief flurry of interest, the issue of MIAs once again disappeared from the news. He said, "I particularly enjoyed the epilogue. Your hoped-for reunion with Ernst Klaus in Westphalia, after all those years, set the stage for a perfect ending."

"Thank you," Drew said. "I sincerely appreciate that."

Cody paused for a moment, not sure how to frame the next question. Just ask, he told himself.

"Although you didn't mention it in your book, I was told you also had a passing reunion with Sophia at one of your local homecomings. Curiosity overwhelms my natural modesty and social refinement. So tell me, how did *that* go?"

Phyllis smiled slightly. Unlike her husband, she seemed unbothered by the question.

"She is not at all like I remembered," Drew said. "In fact, we have nothing whatsoever in common. Our brief get-together was a borderline disaster."

"Now I understand why you omitted that part," Cody said. "Old loves are better remembered when reality doesn't intrude into our fantasies."

"So it would seem," Drew admitted.

"Nevertheless," Anne said, "it's a wonderfully uplifting story, just the way you wrote it."

Drew smiled. "You are very kind."

Anne leaned forward. "Did you know Cody never mentioned your meetings in Vladivostok until the book came out? I had to *read* about it. Can you imagine keeping such deep secrets from your wife?"

"It wasn't a secret," Cody said innocently. "Not really. You never asked me about my work."

"But how was I supposed to *know* enough to ask?"

"Forget about him volunteering information," Phyllis said. "It's a waste of time." She looked at Cody. "In seven-plus years, you told me very little about what you were doing."

"That's how it's supposed to be," Cody replied. "Besides, keeping secrets allows the Agency to declassify and divulge only those operations that make it appear more heroic than it really is."

"A policy that also buries unsuspecting taxpayers in piles of bullshit," Phyllis added.

Under which we can conveniently hide our mistakes, Cody wanted to add. Instead, he smiled and nodded. "Exactly. Ample quantities of bovine excrement is the universal lubricant that prevents government agencies from getting hung up on unpleasant facts."

"Now *that* I believe," Anne laughed.

It was true, Cody thought, remembering Mirko Zanic and his innocent victims. What had occurred in Bosnia was a ghastly tale the Agency had quietly buried in an underground vault.

There was another personal aspect to that awful tragedy, a shameful truth he would never share with anyone. Yes, he had certainly provided Mirko and his cohorts with automatic weapons—arms that resulted in the rape and murder of innocents. Likewise, Mirko had betrayed a solemn trust.

There was, however, more to the story than deception, betrayal, and murder. The worst part, the part he hated to admit even to himself, was that he *knew* what Mirko had in mind and could have done nothing to prevent it.

On the night they uncrated and handed out the assault rifles, compliments of Cody Ballantine and the CIA, a fleeting expression danced across Mirko's face: a cold narrowing of the eyes and the hint of a malevolent smile—unmistakable clues to a seething ethnic and religious hatred undiminished by the passage of centuries. In a flicker of gut-churning insight, Cody realized he had made a terrible mistake, and he knew with unshakable certainty what Mirko intended to do.

Standing in their midst, watching them clean and load their weapons, Cody also understood he was powerless to change what he had unwittingly put into motion.

The crystal-clear premonition passed: the schoolteacher re-assumed his false pastoral guise and his followers smiled and joked among themselves.

That awful foreknowledge had seared his mind with an indelible brand, a wound that would ache until the moment of his death. He had armed a group of religious lunatics, and what he had initiated could not be slowed or stopped or otherwise derailed.

What he could do however, was clean up afterwards, and take his own measure of revenge. After the carnage, Cody had enlisted the Serbs, who promptly captured Mirko and his cohorts. Handing Mirko and his gang of murderers over to the Serbian military police had assured a slow, agonizing death for those who had betrayed his trust.

His remedy, although effective, did not fully satisfy the host of outraged phantoms who wandered the halls of his conscience. Those horribly defiled young women still clamored for an earthly justice, one equal to the agony they had endured, a penalty beyond Cody's ability to impose. They wanted the man who made their deaths possible: they wanted *him*.

He shifted in his seat and his gaze followed the gentle slope as it ran toward the Russian River, hoping the view would ease his mind. Perversely, Mirko's voice wheedled its way into his thoughts, words that rose above the cries of the innocent: "God will not forget what you have done to us!"

No, Cody thought, He certainly would not.

Probably deserving of Hell—there were too many lies and too many corpses to warrant complete forgiveness—Cody believed his soul was destined for Purgatory; that mysterious way station between Heaven and Hell, an empty gray nothingness described so well by a young aviator floating alone on a vast, fog-shrouded sea.

"Are we ever going to eat?" Drew asked. "I'm feeling faint."

Cody buried his reverie. "Very soon," he replied. "We're having your favorite. It took a lot of diligent research, but I finally coaxed the recipe from an old Siberian comrade of yours."

"Oh?" Drew asked, his face a mixture of curiosity and wariness. "What favorite might that be?"

"Susuman's famous Mystery Meat Stew. As far as I know, Californians seldom eat dog, so we had to substitute. I believe Anne used domestic goat."

Anne poked her husband on the shoulder. "You're awful!" Then she addressed Phyllis and Drew. "Don't believe a word he says. We're having tenderloin; *beef* tenderloin."

"Thank God," Drew muttered, obviously relieved.

Anne rose. "I think we're just about ready for dinner."

"Let me offer a helping hand," Phyllis said. The women rose and disappeared into the house.

After both men re-seated themselves Cody said, "Now that you've had time to settle into your new life, do you have any lingering regrets?"

"None whatsoever. I am happier now than I ever dreamed possible. And I owe it all to you."

"Not really. You didn't have a choice, remember?"

"Ah, the MVD. Yes, perhaps so. But without your help, I might be somewhere else; perhaps confined in a location much less pleasant than this." Drew extended his arm and made a sweeping arc, encompassing the vista spread below, his face creased by a contented smile.

"Maybe so," Cody said.

As far as Cody knew, no other soul was privy to the hoax he had planned and executed—a charade designed to force Drew Thompson from his bleak, memory-soaked apartment in Ussurijsk. Cody intended to keep it that way.

The Trushin-KGB sham—along with many of his other misdeeds—would remain secret. After all, what good or pleasant end would full disclosure serve? Truth could heal, harm, free, confine, or confound, all with equal disinterest. Like some cosmic alchemist, it could also concoct subtle variations; selecting whatever feelings it chose from the limitless range of human emotions. Sometimes, truth served little purpose other than being itself.

Yet, despite all the deceit, here he sat, enjoying a happiness he did not merit and the love of a woman he did not deserve. If this were some sort of second chance, then he would make the most of it. Given enough time and opportunity, maybe he could tilt the unbalanced scales of his life a little more towards the good side. Perhaps he could yet earn what he already had.

He was determined to spare no effort in that regard.

Anne and Phyllis emerged from the house, chatting amiably. Instinctively Cody rose to his feet, as did Drew.

"Dinner is ready," Anne declared.

Cody slipped his arm around Anne's slim waist.

"Not a moment too soon," he said.

CPSIA information can be obtained
at www.ICGtesting.com
Printed in the USA
LVHW09s1332041018
592402LV00001B/43/P